LETHAL LEGACY

Linda Fairstein

WINDSOR
PARAGON

First published 2009
by Little, Brown
This Large Print edition published 2009
by BBC Audiobooks Ltd
by arrangement with
Little, Brown Book Group

Hardcover ISBN: 978 1 408 42789 7
Softcover   ISBN: 978 1 408 42790 3

British Library Cataloguing in Publication Data available

Printed and bound in Great Britain by
CPI Antony Rowe, Chippenham, Wiltshire

For librarians—Guardian angels of the mind and soul

And for my favourite librarian, David Ferriero, Andrew W. Mellon Director of the New York Public Libraries.

CHAPTER ONE

'I want you to open the door for me.'

Only silence.

'Look through the peephole,' I said. 'I'm not a cop. I'm an assistant district attorney.'

I stepped back and squared off so the woman inside the basement apartment could check me out. The hallway and staircase had been cleared of men in uniform, including the detail from Emergency Services poised to knock down her door with a battering ram, which was there when I arrived at the scene a short while ago at one o'clock in the morning.

I didn't hear any sound from within. No sense of her movement.

'My name is Alexandra Cooper. You're Tina, aren't you? Tina Barr.' I didn't say what my specialty was, that I was in charge of the DA's Office Sex Crimes Prosecution Unit. The police weren't certain she had been assaulted by the man who had earlier invaded her home, but several of them thought she might reveal those details to me if I could gain her confidence.

I moved in against the metal-clad door and pressed my ear to it, but heard nothing.

'Don't lose your touch now, Coop.' Mike Chapman walked down the steps and handed a lightbulb to the rookie who was holding a flashlight over my shoulder. 'The money on the street's against you, but I'm counting on your golden tongue to talk the lady out so those guys can go home and catch some sleep.'

1

The young cop passed the bulb to Mercer Wallace, the six-foot-six-inch-tall detective from the Special Victims Unit who had called me to the brownstone on the quiet block between Lexington and Third avenues in the East Nineties.

Mercer reached overhead and screwed it in, illuminating the drab, cracked paint on the ceiling and walls of the hallway. 'Somebody—most likely the perp—shattered the other one. There are slivers of glass everywhere.'

'Thanks, kid,' Mike said, dismissing the rookie. 'No progress here, Detective Wallace?'

'We haven't got a homicide,' I whispered to Mercer. 'And they sell lightbulbs at the bodega on Lex. I don't know why you think we needed Mike, but please get him off my back.'

'Damn, I've listened to Blondie charm full-on perverts into boarding the bus for a twenty-five-to-life time-share at Sing Sing. I've seen her coax confessions from the lying lips of the deranged and demented. I've watched as weak-willed men—'

Mercer put his finger to his lips and pointed at the staircase.

'Tina, these two detectives are my friends. I've worked with them for more than ten years.' I paused to cough and clear my throat. There was still a bit of smoke wafting through the hallway. 'Can you tell me why you don't want to open up? Why it is you won't trust us? We're worried about your safety, Tina. About your physical condition.'

Mercer pulled at my elbow. 'Let's go up for a break. Get some fresh air.'

I stayed at the door for another few minutes and then followed Mike and Mercer to the small vestibule of the building and out onto the stoop. It was a mild October night, and neighbors returning to their homes, walking dogs, or hanging around the hood were checking on the police activity and trying to figure out what was wrong.

The uniformed sergeant from the Twenty-third Precinct, whose team had been the first responders, was on the sidewalk in front of the building, talking to Billy Schultz, the man who had called 911 an hour earlier.

'What's the situation behind the house?' Mike asked Mercer as I caught up with them on their way down the front steps.

'Two cops stationed there. Small common garden for the tenants. Back doors from both the first floor and Barr's basement apartment, but no one has moved since they've been on-site.'

'What do you know about the girl?'

'Not much. Nobody seems to,' Mercer said. He turned to the man standing with the sergeant, whom I guessed to be about forty, several years older than Mike and I. 'This is Mike Chapman, Billy. He's assigned to Night Watch.'

Mike worked in Manhattan North Homicide, which helped staff the Night Watch unit, an elite squad of detectives on call between midnight and eight a.m., when precinct squads were most understaffed, to respond all over Manhattan to murders and situations, like this one, that the department referred to—with gross under-statement—as 'unusuals.'

'Billy lives on the first floor,' Mercer said. 'He's the guy who called 911.'

'Good to meet you,' Mike said. He turned to me. 'What's her name?'

'Tina Barr.'

3

'She your friend?' he said to Billy.

'We chat at the mailboxes occasionally. She's a quiet girl. Keeps to herself. Spent a lot of time gardening on weekends in the summer, so I ran into her out back every now and then, but I haven't seen her much since.'

'Lived here long?'

'Me? Eighteen years?'

'Her.'

'Tina sublets. A year, maybe more.'

Mike ran his fingers through his thick black hair, looking from Billy to me. 'You sure she's in there?'

'I could hear a woman crying when I first got here,' I said. *Whimpering* was a more accurate word.

'Tina was sobbing when I knocked on her door,' Billy said.

'But she wouldn't open up for you?'

Billy Schultz adjusted his glasses on the bridge of his nose while Mike scrutinized him. 'No, sir.'

'Why were you knocking? What made you call 911?'

'Mercer gave us all this, Mike. Let me get back inside.'

He held his arm out at me, palm perpendicular like a stop sign. 'Don't you want the chronology from the horse's mouth? Primary source. Catch me up, Billy.'

I had one hand on the wrought-iron railing but stopped to listen.

'I'm a graphic designer, Detective. Worked late, stopped off for a burger and a couple of beers on my way home,' Billy said. He was dressed in jeans and a sweatshirt. There were smudges of ink or paint on his jeans, too dark in color to be blood, I

4

thought. 'It was about twelve-thirty when I got near the building. That's when I saw this guy come tearing out the front door, down the steps.'

'What guy? Someone you know?'

Billy Schultz shook his head. 'Nope. The fireman.'

Mike looked to Mercer. 'Nobody told me about that. The fire department got here first?'

'Not for real,' Mercer said.

'I mean, I assumed he was a fireman. He was dressed in all the gear—coat, boots, hat, even had a protective mask of some kind on. That's why I couldn't see his face.'

'Did you stop him? Did he talk to you?'

'He flew by me, like there was a forest fire on Lexington Avenue he had to get to. Almost took me out. Even that didn't seem odd until I looked up the street for his truck but there wasn't one around. Just weird.'

'What did you do then?'

'I unlocked the door to the vestibule, and as soon as I got inside, I could smell smoke. I could see little waves of it sort of spiraling upward from the basement,' Billy said. 'We don't have a super who lives in the building, so there was no one for me to call. I figured whatever happened had been resolved. By the guy I thought was a fireman. But I wanted to check it out, make sure there was nothing still burning.'

'Sarge, you want to get me that mask?' Mercer said.

The older man walked to the nearest squad car and reached in for a paper bag while Billy Schultz talked.

'I went downstairs first. It was pretty dark, but I

5

could make out a small pile of rubble in the corner of the hallway, a couple of feet from Tina's door. Nothing was burning—no flames—but it was still smoldering. Kicking off a lot of smoke. That's when I knocked on her door.'

'Did she answer?' Mike asked.

'No. Not then. I didn't hear anything. I figured maybe she wasn't home. I ran up to my apartment, filled a pitcher with water, and came back down to douse whatever was still smoking. Figured the other firemen must have gone off to a bigger job and that the last one—the guy who almost plowed me down—was trying to catch up with them.'

The sergeant passed the bag to Mercer, who put on a pair of latex gloves from his pocket before opening it.

'It's when I went downstairs the second time that I heard Tina.'

'What did you hear, exactly?' I asked.

Billy cocked his head and answered. 'I knocked again, just because I was worried that the firemen might have left her there even though there was still something smoldering in the hallway. She was weeping loudly, then pausing, like to inhale.'

'Words,' Mike said. 'Did she speak any words?'

'No, but I did. I told Tina it was me, asked her if she was all right. I was coughing myself from the smoke. I told her she could come up to my apartment.'

'Did she answer you?'

'No. She just cried.'

'How do you know it's Tina Barr you were talking to?' Mike asked.

Billy hesitated. 'Well, at that point—I, uh—I just assumed it, Detective. She lives there alone.'

6

'What next?'

'I went home to get a bucket and broom. Swept some of the trash into the bucket to throw out on the street—'

Mike glanced at the sergeant. 'Yeah, we got it, Chapman. Looks like amateur smoke bombs.'

'The sobbing was so bad by then, I called 911, from my cell. Maybe she was sick, overcome by the smoke. I waited out here on the stoop till the officers came. Three minutes. Not much longer. That's when Tina went berserk. That's when I knew it was her, for sure. I recognized her voice, when she was yelling at the cops.'

Mercer removed a large black object from the bag and dangled it in front of us.

'Yeah,' Billy said. 'That's what the fireman had on his face.'

'Found it halfway up the block,' the sergeant said. 'Right in the perp's flight path.'

'That's not department gear,' Mike said. 'It's a gas mask. Military style.'

It was a black rubber helmet, with two holes for the eyes, and a broad snoutlike respirator that would fit over the mouth, with a long hose attached.

'Couldn't see a damn thing,' Billy said. 'It covered his entire face.'

'What did the cops do?' Mike asked.

'I led them down to the basement. They knocked on Tina's door and one of them identified himself, said they were police. That's when she started yelling at them to leave her alone. I mean screaming at them. Freaked out. Sounded like she collapsed—maybe fell onto the floor—crying the whole time.'

7

'What makes you think she's alone in there?'

'We're guessing,' Mercer said. 'She's the only one to make a sound—no scuffling, no struggling, no other voices. But that's another reason ESU won't leave.'

Mike prodded my side with his fingers as we started up the front steps. I went back in the vestibule toward the basement staircase.

'One of the cops told Tina he just wanted to make sure that the fire hadn't affected her,' Billy said, drawing a handkerchief from his pocket to wipe his smoke-fogged glasses. 'Asked her if she could stand up and look through the peephole at his badge, for identification. She went wild.'

'What do you mean?' Mike asked.

'Tina screamed at the cop. Told him that's how the guy got in. The fireman. That he showed her his badge and she opened the door.'

'It was the fireman who was inside her apartment? You knew, Coop?'

'That's why Mercer called me. We don't know who the man was, why he was using such an elaborate disguise, why he went inside, and what he did to this woman. Okay? Don't come any closer, Mike. Let me talk to her.'

I walked the short corridor to the rear of the hallway, glass crunching under the soles of my shoes.

'Tina? It's Alex Cooper. We're all still here. The police officers won't leave until I convince them that you're unharmed. I'll keep them outside the building if you'll let me in for just a few minutes.'

'I'd rank that a toss-up,' Mike said. 'Ten minutes with you or the quick punch of a battering ram? Tough call.'

'You think this helps? You think she can't hear you?' I threw up my arms in frustration as I turned to Mike. 'Mercer, please take him upstairs.'

The men marched back to the first floor as I made another attempt to persuade Tina Barr to let me in.

'I'm the only one in the basement now, Tina. The men are all outside. I don't want them to break down your door any more than you do. But they're worried that you've been injured. There was a lot of smoke down here. Can you just tell me if you're hurt?'

There was no answer for more than a minute. Then a soft voice spoke a word or two, which sounded as though the woman was still sitting or lying on the floor inside. I couldn't understand her, so I crouched beside the door and put my ear against it.

'Sorry. What did you say?'

'Not hurt. I'll be okay.'

She spoke haltingly, her words caught in her throat.

'Tina, are you having trouble breathing?'

No answer.

'We can give you oxygen, Tina. Is it the smoke? Is there still smoke in your apartment?'

'No.'

'The man who was dressed like a fireman, did you let him come into your apartment?'

She was crying again as she tried to speak. 'No, no, I didn't let him in.'

'But you told the police officer that—'

'I only opened the door because he showed me a gold badge and told me there was a fire. I could smell the smoke and then saw it. I believed him.'

9

Tina Barr's words came out phrase by phrase, embedded in sobs. 'He forced his way inside. I didn't *let* him in.'

'You can trust us, Tina. Now you know that man wasn't actually a fireman. His badge wasn't real.' Mercer had already checked that with the department and had been telling that to Barr before I got there. 'The cops think the man started the fire himself in order to break in to your apartment.'

She was taking deep breaths on the other side of the door.

I took one, too, and tried to get at what had so far been unspoken. 'I work with victims of sex crimes, Tina. That's all I do. It's why the police thought I might be able to help. I deal with the most sensitive cases you can imagine,' I said, closing my eyes, which burned from the lingering smoke. 'Did this man assault you tonight?'

She coughed again.

I didn't know how long he'd been within the apartment before Billy Schultz saw him running from the building at twelve-thirty in the morning.

'Did he awaken you when he knocked, Tina?'

'No.'

'Do you know what time it was when you first went to the door?'

'Five,' she said.

'Five o'clock in the afternoon?' She must have been confused. 'Look, I'm going to have to let the police work on your door, or the back window in your kitchen, Tina. You may be a little woozy. He couldn't have been inside there that long.'

There was a noise before Tina Barr spoke next, as though she shifted her position. She had gotten

10

to her feet, perhaps angered by my comment. I stood up, too, as she pounded on the door. 'I know exactly what time it was when the man knocked, do you understand? It wasn't the middle of the night, Ms. Cooper. It was five o'clock.'

All the cops and I had assumed the events had occurred within minutes of Schultz's arrival home. Fast, like most break-ins, and while the smoke bombs were steaming. We were wrong.

'I apologize, Tina. That's even more reason for me to know what he did to you.' I didn't want to suggest the word *rape* to her. I needed *her* to reveal to me what had occurred.

'I don't want to talk to any cops, Ms. Cooper. I'll tell you what happened if that will make them go away.'

'I'm alone down here now. The men won't come in.' I paused before I spoke again. 'I give you my word.'

Tina Barr sniffled, then was quiet. I heard the dead bolt turn.

The door opened a few inches and I could see the young woman peering out from behind it, clutching the lapels of her white chenille robe with one hand. Her dark brown hair was disheveled, her eyes reddened from at least an hour of crying, and what looked to be remains of adhesive tape forming a rectangle on the skin around her mouth, where she had probably been gagged.

I reached out a hand to her, hoping to comfort her with a touch, but she recoiled at the movement in her direction.

'You're mistaken if you think this was about a sex crime, Ms. Cooper. He wanted to kill me,' Tina Barr said. 'That man left me for dead.'

11

CHAPTER TWO

'I don't want to press charges.'

Tina Barr was seated in an armchair in the cramped living room of her apartment, and I was opposite her on a small loveseat that was sorely in need of reupholstering.

'That's not even an issue right now, Tina. I'd like to know what happened to you. We don't have a suspect, so there's no one to prosecute.'

'You told me you wanted to make sure I was all right. You see I'm not hurt, so now you can leave.'

She was unnaturally pale and rested her forehead in her hand, as though she needed that support to keep it upright.

'A couple of minutes ago you told me a man tried to kill you. You told me he was with you in here for more than six hours. How can I walk away from this? You don't look well, Tina. You must be terribly frightened.'

'I'm nauseous. I just want to lie down.'

I tried to make eye contact with her, but she was staring at the floor.

'Who did this to you, Tina? Do you know that?'

Her entire body trembled. 'No idea. There was some horrible black mask covering his face.'

I didn't want to press her, to cross-examine her, but it seemed unlikely that her attacker had had the mask on for so many hours. 'The whole time he was here? Didn't he ever take it off?'

'I don't know what he did. I don't remember.'

I expected her to be a difficult interview after the experience the cops had when they got to the building. But I hadn't thought she would stonewall me once she opened the door.

'You don't remember?'

'I was unconscious the entire time that man was here, Ms. Cooper.' Tina lifted her head and looked at me. 'He pushed his way in and threw me down. He put a cloth over my mouth and I couldn't breathe any longer. I just felt dizzy and watched the room turn upside down. I thought I was going to die. I don't have any idea what he did after that.'

Now I had even more reason to be concerned, and greater need not to express it.

'How are you feeling?'

'I've told you already. I'd like to go to sleep.'

'Do you know what he drugged you with?'

Tina rested her head on the back of the chair and snapped at me. 'Now how could I possibly tell you that?'

'I didn't think you'd be able to. That's my point. All the more reason to let the doctors examine you, have them test your blood. You've undoubtedly still got something in your system.'

'I don't want anyone else coming in here—can you understand that?'

'I'd like to take you to the emergency room. There's an excellent hospital less than ten blocks away.'

Tina Barr started to cry again. There was a box of tissues on a desk behind her chair. I crossed the room to get a handful of them, glancing around for any obvious signs of a disturbance. Bookcases lined the walls. End tables, like the desk, were cluttered with a messy array of papers and journals.

'Why don't you take a minute to compose yourself?'

13

I handed her the tissues and reached out to stand the wastebasket upright. There was a large rag in it, and as I leaned over, it smelled sickeningly sweet. I used a tissue to remove the cloth from the basket and put it in the pocket of my jeans.

'Would you like some water, Tina?'

'I'm too nauseous to drink. I'm very thirsty, but I doubt I can hold anything down.'

I retraced my steps to the loveseat. I could get more facts later. I wanted to talk to her about medical treatment. 'I just have a couple more questions, okay? When you regained consciousness, were you still here, on the floor?'

She searched out another spot in the dark pattern of the cheap Oriental rug and stared at it. 'I was on my bed, Ms. Cooper. I was naked. Completely naked. There was some kind of tape over my mouth, and my hands were tied to the headboard with a pair of my stockings. Loose knots, they were. I was able to work them off easily.'

'While the man was still here?'

'No,' she said, breathing deeply. 'I came around just a few minutes before he left. I could hear him in this room, so I just played dead and didn't move till the door shut.'

'Tina, you've got to see a doctor.' I was on the edge of the seat cushion, pleading with her to let me take her to Mount Sinai Hospital. 'They've got a wonderful advocacy program for victims of violence. I just have to call ahead and someone knowledgeable about the process will be with you through the entire exam.'

'I told you before I wasn't raped.' Tina got to

14

her feet and steadied herself before she started walking toward the back of the apartment. 'I'm going to be sick.'

I stood up to follow her. 'Let me—'

'Please don't come inside. I'd like some privacy.'

A door slammed and I couldn't hear anything until the toilet flushed and water ran in the sink. The dozens of questions I had would be answered, I knew, when she was made comfortable and felt safe. I needed to get her to the ER as fast as possible. Once crime scene investigators had access to her bedroom, the trace evidence on the linens and clothing might tell us more about what occurred than Tina Barr could.

About ten minutes later, Tina emerged from what must have been her bedroom and bath area. She was dressed in khaki slacks and a cable-knit sweater.

'If I go with you to the hospital, does it mean I'm pressing charges?'

'Not at all. You have weeks to make that decision, if we catch the guy. This is all about your health, about trying to figure out what he did to you. If you aren't examined now, the tests will never yield the same results in two or three days, when you might have second thoughts about all this.' I knew that if she had been penetrated by her assailant, the natural forces of gravity would eliminate any fluids that could be tested for DNA. Whatever she had been drugged with would be gone from her bloodstream, too. 'It's your own best protection.'

'I'd prefer to take a cab, Ms. Cooper. I can do this myself.'

'There's an ambulance waiting near the

15

building. We were all so worried about you. I can cut through a lot of administrative red tape if I'm along.'

She hesitated again, then went back inside and returned with a small tote. 'I'll go with you. Just don't ask me any more questions, okay?'

'Let me call the detectives, so the ambulance is right in front.' I pressed Mercer's speed dial on my cell.

'You need me?'

'Ms. Barr and I are coming out. I'm going to ride to Sinai with her in the bus. Maybe you can meet us at the ER. And get rid of the guys with the heavy equipment.'

'Done, Alex. Will she let crime scene in to process the apartment?'

I turned to ask her. I wanted the bed linens and bathrobe, the tape and the pantyhose, as soon as possible. I wanted to know if there were any more rags inside, whether he had applied the substance to her face more than once. 'Tina, would you mind if the detectives got to work on looking for evidence in your bedroom? Fingerprints, possible DNA sources—'

'Nobody comes in here while I'm gone,' she said. 'I don't want any other strangers inside my home tonight. Do you understand?'

'Of course I do.' I knew Mercer had heard it, too. I shut off the phone.

Tina walked behind me on the staircase, bracing her hands against the wall. When we reached the stoop, I was relieved to see the police cars and trucks were all gone, and that two EMTs were standing at the rear door of the ambulance, with the gurney between them.

16

I offered her my arm and she accepted it for the short walk. I introduced us to the EMTs, and they asked Tina to sit down so they could lift her inside after I climbed up and wedged myself into a jump seat.

'How you doin'?' the medic asked Tina as his partner got into the driver's seat. 'You okay?'

'I'm sick to my stomach, actually.'

'Take it slow, Howie. Don't bounce in any potholes,' he called out to the driver. 'My name is Jorge Vasquez. I'm just gonna get your vitals, miss. Gotta do that.'

Tina reclined on the gurney and pushed up her sleeve for the blood pressure cuff.

'How old are you, Ms. Barr?'

'Thirty-three.'

'Date of birth?'

She gave the year first, then told him March 14.

'Your height and weight?'

'Five-four.' She was six inches shorter than I, and weighed almost the same. 'One thirty-five.'

'What kind of insurance you got?'

Tina covered her mouth with her hand, as though she was going to be sick again.

'You got insurance?'

'No.'

The EMT looked over her head at me and I nodded. The hospital would get its money from the crime victims compensation board if Barr didn't pay. This wasn't the time or place to dicker about who'd foot the bill for the expensive sexual assault examination.

'How about your occupation?'

'I'm—uh—I'm a librarian.'

'Nice. You like books. Me, I don't have time to

read.' Vasquez was filling in the blank spaces on his form. 'Who's your employer? Would that be the city?'

'I'm not working at the moment. I quit my last job just a week ago.'

'City's got good benefits. You should think about it. Which branch, Ms. Barr? It's regulations. I gotta put something in this box.'

'No, it wasn't the city. It was private. It's over.'

The driver made the turn onto Madison Avenue and we headed north. Vasquez put his clipboard on his lap, took Tina's pressure, and recorded the numbers.

'You mind if I check your eyes?'

The young woman shook her head from side to side and Vasquez leaned in, studying her pupils and making a note, I guessed, about how dilated they were.

'You want to start with what happened to you, miss?'

'I'm not really sure. I know I was drugged, but that's all I can tell you,' Tina said. 'And I've got a terrible headache now.'

'Any idea what kind of drug?'

'Like I told Ms. Cooper, I don't know. But I'm really thirsty,' she said, licking her lips.

'Sorry. You're dehydrated, but the triage nurse will see you in a few minutes. No point giving you anything before that. She may want to start an IV.'

We were at the hospital in less than five minutes. It was background information about Tina Barr that I wanted—something to lead me to why she was victimized this way—but Jorge Vasquez had as much pedigree as he needed.

When he opened the rear doors of the

18

ambulance at the hospital receiving bay, Mercer was waiting for me. I stepped around the gurney and jumped down, holding on to his hand.

'I think we're better off keeping Ms. Barr right here till she's called in for triage. It's kind of zooey in there,' Mercer said.

'We can hold,' Vasquez said. 'I could use the break.'

'They got a gunshot wound in the chest. Fifteen-year-old kid caught in the crossfire of two dealers. A bad car crash on the FDR Drive—three passengers with head trauma—and the typical assortment of fractures and bellyaches. You know a possible rape won't be seen till daybreak unless you can pull some strings, Alexandra.'

Most victims of sexual assault presented to treating physicians without any external physical injury. To an emergency specialist, the trauma had occurred when the crime was committed. The survivor who presented at the hospital was not in need of life-saving treatment like the other medical patients, but rather was there for evidence collection and psychological counseling. Without advocates or forensic examiners on call, these women were often the most neglected emergency room visitors, waiting hours to be evaluated.

'We'll try to get you in as quickly as we can,' I said to Tina, leaving her in the care of Vasquez and his partner as I turned to follow Mercer into the ER.

The security guard stood back as Mercer flashed his gold shield and the automatic double doors swung open to admit us. A dozen curtained cubicles—all seemingly occupied—formed a semicircle around the nurses' station, where Mike had settled in with his feet on the counter, eating chocolates from a box on the desk.

'Have you spoken to the head nurse?'

'Yeah, we're somewhere between the heart attack in that corner and the domestic dispute racheted up till the missus settled it by hurling a meat cleaver at the bum's neck,' Mike said.

One of the nurses emerged from behind the thin curtains of the first treatment area, and Mike waved him over. 'This is Ms. Cooper, Joe. You any good at splinter removal? She's had a stick up her ass for the last couple of months, and I was hoping—'

'We're waiting for one of the SAVI volunteers, Ms. Cooper,' Joe said, stripping his bloodied gloves off and dropping them in the hazardous-waste bin along with the syringe in his hand. He was the size of a fullback, a black man with skin as dark as Mercer's, and not in the mood for Mike's humor. 'Get you in here as soon as we can. I've got one going up to X-ray and another for admission, just waiting on a room.'

'This may not have seemed urgent when the detectives first called,' I said, knowing that it might take half an hour for a sexual assault violence intervention program advocate to reach the ER, 'but Tina's in worse shape than we thought.'

I pulled the rag from my pocket, pinching it on a corner to hold it up. 'The perp soaked this in something and knocked her out by putting it over her nose and mouth.'

'Nice save, Coop.' Mike stood and bent over the counter, sniffing at the rag. 'What's your guess, Joe? Ether of some kind? Not so noxious as that. Maybe chloroform?'

Joe didn't want to come closer. 'If that's what it was, it's enough to cause a fatal cardiac arrhythmia.'

'That baby's going straight to the lab, Coop.'

'Tell the EMTs to bring her right in,' Joe said. 'Let's get your girl worked up.'

The three of us headed for the exit, past the waiting area filled with anxious family members and friends, down the driveway and onto the street. The driver had backed out of the bay to leave room for the next arrival and double-parked on Madison Avenue.

Jorge Vasquez was leaning against the side of the red-and-white ambulance. Mercer waved at him as we approached, telling him to move it in and unload the patient.

Vasquez shrugged his shoulders.

'Don't give me that "not my job" crap,' Mike said. 'Roll it.'

'I'm empty, man,' Vasquez said, brushing his hands against each other like he was dusting off crumbs. 'The broad took off.'

'Took off where?' I asked.

'RMA, Ms. Cooper. I can't be holding nobody against her will.'

Tina Barr had refused medical attention, despite the ordeal she'd survived.

'Which way'd she go?'

'*No sé,*' Vasquez said. 'She told me she never wanted the cops called in the first place. Jumped out the bus and said to tell you to leave her alone.'

CHAPTER THREE

'I still think we could have beat Tina to her apartment,' Mike said, several hours later, as he sat across the desk from me.

'To what end? For some reason, she never wanted any of us involved in the first place. It was the neighbor—not Tina—who called 911.'

'I don't know. Should have scooped her up and made her a material witness till we figured out what happened.'

'No such thing as getting a material witness order unless there's a pending prosecution,' I said, continuing to make notes on a legal pad, charting the chronology of a murder investigation we'd been working on for several months. 'You know that.'

'Are you going to follow up with her now?'

'I'm giving Tina a day to settle down. By then she'll realize the flashbacks and night sweats won't go away by themselves. She might even welcome the chance to talk about it.'

We were in my office in the Sex Crimes Prosecution Unit on the eighth floor of Manhattan's Criminal Courthouse at nine-thirty on Wednesday morning. Mike had brought me a third cup of coffee and took the lid off after he set out his bagel on top of a file cabinet, using a manila folder as a place mat.

'How come Judge Moffett scheduled a hearing on the Griggs case? You don't even have an arrest yet.'

We had been working on the rape-homicide of a

nineteen-year-old-girl named Kayesha Avon that had taken place almost eight years earlier. The case had gone cold long ago, but the recent submission to the databank of the DNA profile of a man named Jamal Griggs and the near match that resulted had given Mike a reason to revive the investigation.

'Jamal Griggs doesn't like the idea that we're so interested in his family tree,' I said.

Jamal and his brother Wesley, known to us as the Weasel, had floated in and out of the criminal justice system for most of their adult lives. Despite Jamal's homicide conviction as a teenager—or maybe because of it—he and Wesley had become part of the entourage that surrounded and sold drugs to the crews of late thug rappers such as Biggie Smalls and Tupac Shakur.

'I applied for a search warrant to get into the California database to see what it tells us about Wesley's DNA, and must have struck a nerve. Jamal's new counsel requested a chance to oppose my motion. I need you and Mattie Prinzer,' I said, referring to the forensic biologist who headed the lab at OCME, the Office of the Chief Medical Examiner, 'to make my case.'

'Jamal get himself a new suit? Last I knew he was a poster boy for the Legal Aid Society. How's he paying for a lawyer?'

'I have the feeling we're going to meet the new suit in the courtroom. He's been dispatched from the City of Angels by the Weasel.'

'Amazing that Wesley made it out the 'hood,' Mike said. The thirty-two-year-old wannabe gangsta had moved from pushing crack cocaine on East Harlem street corners to producing records in

Hollywood, while his baby brother was behind bars again for an armed robbery of a gas station in Queens. 'I think a proper homecoming would be a sweet thing, Coop.'

'I'm a long way from blowing up balloons and mailing out save-the-date cards for the Weasel's return to New York,' I said. 'Would you give these lab reports to Laura, please, and ask her to make copies? I'll have to turn them over to defense counsel if Moffett makes you two testify.'

Mike walked to the door and handed the case file to my secretary. He was wearing his trademark navy blazer with a pale blue button-down shirt and crisply pressed khakis. His dark good looks and irrepressible grin were an appealing combination, and his intelligence and experience made him a trusted partner—like Mercer—in the most difficult cases we'd handled together.

'You think maybe she knew him?'

'Did Kayesha Avon know Wesley Griggs?' I asked.

'No, no, no. I'm thinking about Tina Barr. Maybe she didn't want to cooperate with us because she made the man beneath the mask. Or he actually took it off once he got inside the apartment. If she recognized the guy, could be she knows how dangerous it is for her and that's why she fled the scene.'

I was studying Jamal Griggs's pre-sentence report, trying to get a sense of whether he had a favorite modus operandi. 'Could be.'

'Don't you think that puts her at greater risk now? Don't you need to do something to safeguard her?'

'And what would that be, since she's expressed

herself so clearly? I can't take her hostage if she's so dead set against reporting this.'

'Did you ask for a detail to sit in front of Tina's house?'

'The CO turned me down flat.'

'Use your juice, Coop. There's a couple of dudes at headquarters who think you walk on bottled water. Call in a chit.'

'Yeah, and maybe you can forward my nomination to the Supreme Court in case there's a vacancy. That would be an easier task than getting Commissioner Scully to sign off on a spare RMP for a victim who tied up enormous resources in the middle of the night and then took a hike with no explanation at all.'

There was a shortage of both manpower and radio motor patrol cars because of the spike in violent crimes charted since the summer.

'I didn't know you could qualify for the Supremes if you were living in France. There must be some kind of jurisdictional requirement.'

I looked up from my notes and bit on the tip of my fountain pen, but I was unable to suppress a smile. 'Michael Patrick Chapman. Is that what's bugging you? Have you been working overtime on my love life? All you had to do was ask.'

One of the city's most experienced homicide detectives turned scarlet from his brow to the point where his neck disappeared into his shirt collar.

'No need to pry into that, blondie. You're wearing it all over your puss. Be a shame to waste the latest Parisian fashions under long black judicial robes, if you ask me,' Mike said. 'And that skirt you're wearing is way too short for Judge Moffett. His defibrillator might zap into overtime.'

25

I looked down at the navy blue suit I'd bought on the Avenue Montaigne when I had last visited Luc Rouget, the Frenchman I'd been dating since early summer. Anything not to make eye contact with Mike.

'Make you a deal,' I said. 'Let's get through this Griggs motion today and we can catch up over dinner. I never meant to hold back anything from you or Mercer. Luc turned up in the middle of a killing spree and my personal life deservedly took a back seat.'

'You don't owe me any explanation,' he said, shifting away from me. 'Skip the talk tonight and just feed me, Coop. But you'll have to take yourself out of that chic getup before cocktails. Too rich for my blood.'

'I'll call Mercer. The three of us haven't been out in more than a month. I'm buying.'

'What if it's about kinky sex?' Mike asked, balling up his napkin and tossing it over my head into the garbage.

My turn to blush. 'Kinky what?'

'Not you and the French guy, kid. Tina Barr. Maybe she was tied up 'cause she wanted to be. Could explain why she wouldn't talk.'

We had seen it all, working sex crimes and homicide. Just when one of us thought there was nothing left to shock, along came a new way for two people to amuse themselves in the privacy of their homes.

'A long shot,' I said. 'But always a possibility.'

'Think about it. Broad's tied up and gagged—there's evidence to support that—but tells you she wasn't raped. Wouldn't be anything to call the cops about if she consented.'

26

I slipped my heels off under the desk before Mike could comment on their style, and replaced them with a sturdier work shoe for our court appearance. 'Maybe.'

'What do you know about chloroform?' Mike asked. 'Pick up anything medically useful from your old man while you were growing up?'

'Wasn't it the first anesthetic used for women in childbirth in the nineteenth century? Till the docs found out it was too toxic.'

'Well, it's still around, and it caused three deaths, just in the north, in the last eighteen months,' Mike said.

New York County—the island of Manhattan—was split in half by the NYPD for the management of unnatural-death investigations. Mike's office, the Manhattan North Homicide Squad, responded to everything from Fifty-ninth Street to the tip of Spuyten Duyvil, while its southern counterpart took the territory from midtown down to the Battery.

'You're not talking serial killer again?'

'Nope,' Mike said, topping off his bagel with a handful of red licorice sticks. 'It's a phenomenon called SSD. Sudden sniffers' death. Lieutenant Peterson's been all over these cases lately, he told me yesterday. Easy to buy the ingredients on the Web. Chloroform's a central nervous system depressant. If it doesn't kill you, inhaling it for the high will at least leave you dizzy and tired, with a crushing headache.'

'So you think Tina OD'd accidentally, trying to get tuned up for some kind of sexual encounter?' I asked. 'I don't know, Mike. She claimed the guy tried to kill her.'

'So maybe he did, if you can believe her at this point.'

'It's the "tried to" that stops me short. He was in there for hours. He certainly had the opportunity.'

'She said she played dead, Coop. If her breathing was shallow enough, maybe the perp thought he *had* killed her. Could be why he ran out of the place the way he did.'

'It still doesn't explain his disguise,' I said.

'I'm just saying you should call her. You're the hand holder. You're the one who's supposed to be so good at bonding with your victims.'

Mercer and I liked working with survivors of sexual assault, helping them recover from the trauma they had experienced, in addition to bringing the criminal to justice. Mike was used to the cold finality of death investigations. No victims with ambivalence about their attackers, no quirky personalities to soothe and stroke. Dead bodies and crime scenes might hold puzzles for pathologists and detectives, but unlike their living counterparts, they never lied.

Laura stood in the doorway with the documents. 'Mattie just called. She's going to jump in a cab as soon as possible. Shall I tell her to go right to the courtroom?'

'Good idea, Laura. Thanks.'

The buzzer on my telephone console rang as its red light flashed insistently. Paul Battaglia, the district attorney of New York County for more than twenty years, had a hotline to each of his bureau chiefs. He didn't like to wait for answers to questions handed him by reporters, politicians, rivals, and concerned citizens.

'Yes, Paul?'

'I need ten minutes of your time,' Battaglia said. 'The mayor's looking for where I stand on that legislative proposal we discussed.'

'I'll be over as soon as I finish an argument I've got in front of Judge Moffett.'

'I need you right now, Alexandra. I'm already late for City Hall. I don't expect you to keep the mayor waiting.'

CHAPTER FOUR

Rose Malone, Battaglia's executive assistant and my trusted friend, waved me into his suite without buzzing the intercom. Her lack of a cheerful greeting let me know that the district attorney hadn't started the day in a good mood.

'Do I have a position on this Halloween business, Alexandra?' Battaglia had called me in to discuss a legislative proposal about sex offenders that had become a controversial piece of the city council's agenda. He started walking from his desk to the large conference table at the rear end of his office as soon as he saw me cross the threshold. 'Did I make up my mind about what we're going to say?'

'Not as of the last time we discussed it.'

'Sit down,' he said, his teeth gripping the long unlit cigar in the middle of his mouth. 'What is it, just a few weeks until Halloween?'

'Yes.'

'I guess the mayor is trying to grandstand here. Show that his balls are bigger than mine. What's he up to?'

'I read the proposal. Half a dozen states and a lot of local authorities have been trying to place restrictions on registered sex offenders for just that one night a year,' I said. 'Some communities are requiring them to attend four- or five-hour educational programs on Halloween. In Virginia, they've all got to report to their parole officers between four and eight p.m., so they're not at home to answer the door when kids come trick-or-treating. That's the model the mayor wants to adopt in the city.'

'What do I think of it?' Battaglia asked. He was the consummate politician and had enough confidence in his senior staff to let us participate in important decisions, even though he had a long memory for mistakes.

'Pretty useless.'

He lifted his glasses off his nose and rested them on top of his forehead. 'Sexual predators are one of the major concerns in law enforcement. You've got a holiday here that offers a tantalizing chance for these perverts to have unsupervised contact with kids. The youngsters knock on the door, ask for some candy, and God knows what can happen to them.'

'It's one night a year, boss. If the legislature puts some teeth in the laws we've already got, then maybe the police could actually monitor the offenders they're supposed to be tracking.'

Battaglia rarely removed the cigar when he spoke, just stretching the corners of his mouth around it without slurring any of his words. 'And the advocate groups? Where do they come down on this?'

'Not impressed. Most children are victimized by

30

people they know and trust, not by strangers. This draft doesn't even distinguish between pedophiles and perps who committed crimes against adults. You won't get any heat from victims' groups if you don't support the proposal. Press for enough money to track the registered offenders 24/7. That's where the real problem is.'

Battaglia got up and removed his suit jacket from the back of the chair. That would serve as a dismissal. I stood up to leave the room.

'How about the flip side?' he asked.

'What would that be?'

'Well, that Halloween presents another danger for kids. Offenders could be dressed in costumes, too. Abducting teens or children from the street, or knocking on doors in some kind of disguise.'

'I'll tell you, Paul, we haven't seen any problems on Halloween over the years. Late October hasn't been high season for sex crimes.'

'You're not hanging me out to dry in front of the press, Alex, are you?'

I assumed Battaglia was joking, and I laughed as I started for the door. 'I wouldn't think of doing that until my pension vests, Paul.'

'I'm not kidding. I smell a setup over at City Hall.'

I turned to face him, and he removed the cigar from his mouth. 'This brouhaha last night, Alex. Some guy broke into a girl's apartment dressed up like a fireman, right?' he said. 'How come you didn't call me about it?'

'Well, there isn't actually a case, Paul,' I said. His displeasure was visible in his scowl. I had irked him by neglecting to inform him about a matter that I'd miscalculated in importance, but which must have a link to a player in his political world.

'Somebody at City Hall seems to think otherwise. It's all to do with disguises and assaults, isn't it?'

'I wish I could tell you what happened, but the victim hasn't been cooperative with us.'

'Get on it, Alex. Bring her in. Find out what this is about.'

It hadn't occurred to me while I pleaded with her in the drab hallway outside her basement sublet the night before that Tina Barr had any high-powered clout. I wanted to know who had gotten to Battaglia on her behalf—or on the part of her mysterious assailant, which worried me more.

'You know something about Ms. Barr that I should be aware of?' I asked.

He put his glasses back on and started to read a memo that was on the table. It was an easy way to ignore my question. Either Battaglia had been leaked a tidbit and was looking for me to give him more information, or something so sensitive was involved that he wasn't willing to disclose it.

I tried again. 'Is it the victim you're interested in, Paul, or is it the perp?'

'As long as I'm the district attorney, Alexandra, I'll ask the questions,' Battaglia said. 'You get me the girl.'

CHAPTER FIVE

Mike and I zigzagged our way through the hapless gaggle of criminals—some arguing with their public defenders, others waiting with family members or friends—who filled the fifteenth-floor corridor of the criminal courthouse.

'Somebody's got Battaglia wound up about Barr, or knows something about her attacker,' I said.

'So when we finish here, I'll drive you to her apartment.'

'I just called Mercer. He'll meet us there, too.'

He pulled on the large brass handle of the door in the middle of the hallway, holding it back so that we both could enter Part 53 of the Supreme Court of New York County, Criminal Term.

Harlan Moffett was on the bench, his back to the courtroom, seemingly engrossed in the *New York Law Journal*. Mattie Prinzer, the first woman to head the OCME crime lab, was seated alone in the front row. Only the staff was present—no spectators—and a well-dressed man who appeared to be younger than I, sitting at the defense table, the one farther from the empty jury box.

The court clerk saw us enter and signaled to the reporter, then got the judge's attention. 'We have the prosecutor, Your Honor. Shall we bring the prisoner in?'

Moffett spun in his chair and folded the newspaper. 'Good to see you, Ms. Cooper. Detective, thanks for making yourself available on such short notice. Say hello to your adversary, here. What's your name again, son?'

'Eli Fine.' He got to his feet and extended his hand to shake mine after I entered the well and dropped my files on the table.

'You have a chance to meet your client yet?' Moffett was in his seventies, close to mandatory retirement. His once-thick white hair had thinned and faded to a dull gray, but the garnet pinky ring he sported still sparkled as he twisted it while he talked.

'I spent a couple of hours with him at Rikers yesterday, after I flew in.'

'Let's have Jamal Griggs,' the judge said, motioning to the court officer in charge. 'How long you been out of school, Eli?'

'Six years, sir.'

'I've been a judge for more than thirty.' Moffett had been around long enough to know most of the New York bar that practiced in this forum. The courthouse regulars were used to his schmoozing and put up with his clumsy attempts at humor in hopes he would rule in their favor. The judge didn't bother to clean up his act for strangers.

Fine was biting his lip. 'Judge, would you mind if we—?'

The court reporter had worked with Moffett often enough to know to keep her fingers away from the keyboard until the judge signaled that he wanted to go on the record.

'Take off your sunglasses, Mr. Fine. That's what I mind. We're not in Malibu. You admitted in New York?'

'Yes, sir. I graduated from New York Law School. Took the bar both here and California.'

'Long as we're legal, son.'

The door to the holding pen opened and an officer led Jamal Griggs into the room. He smiled when he saw his lawyer, and waited for his hands to be uncuffed before taking the seat beside him.

Fine was whispering something to Griggs when Moffett interrupted him. 'What brings you to town today?'

'Ms. Cooper and her team have been conducting an investigation, and—'

'We've got a habit here, son. We stand up when we address the court,' Moffett said, turning the motion papers over to read the name of Fine's law firm. 'Stein, Schlurman, and Fine. Ever try a murder case, son?'

Eli Fine slowly rose to his feet. 'Entertainment law, sir. It's our specialty.'

'Entertainment lawyers? That's an oxymoron,' Moffett said, resting his elbows on the bench and tapping his fingertips together. 'Ms. Cooper's had—what is it, dear? Six, seven trials to verdict in front of me. You're not careful, she could take you to the cleaners. What's your motion?'

The young lawyer looked at the reporter. 'Are we on the record?'

Moffett rapped the gavel to regain Fine's attention. 'When *I* tell you we are. Give me a sense of what you want.'

'As you know, Judge, my client is incarcerated for an armed robbery. Despite Ms. Cooper's best efforts to connect Jamal to the unsolved homicide of Kayesha Avon, his genetic profile did *not* match the evidence in the case,' Fine said, reading from notes that I expected had been prepared for him by a defense attorney familiar with the language of a criminal law practitioner. 'Now she's come before this court on an absurd fishing expedition, having applied for an out-of-state search warrant to get into the California database. I'm here to oppose that application.'

'Come all this way to try to stop Ms. Cooper? I'm impressed, son.' Moffett rubbed the hem of his sleeve over the garnet stone in his ring, admiring the polishing job when he finished. 'Now, what's in that databank that's so damn important to the People of the State of New York?'

'Nothing worth invading the privacy of any citizens of California, sir. The attorney general has taken a strict position on protecting the integrity of the state's database.'

'What are you after, Alexandra?'

I was on my feet, ready with my arguments. 'We'd like to do a familial search, Your Honor.'

Moffett cupped his hand to his ear. 'A what?'

'A familial search, Judge. It's a new forensic technique, and we'd like to use it in this matter. The warrant requests the DNA profile of Jamal's brother, Wesley Griggs, which we believe is in the crime scene evidence database of California.'

'Wesley's a convicted felon out there?'

'No,' I said. That would make our task simpler. His profile would probably be in the FBI's CODIS files if that were the case. 'We understand he was present at a drug-related shooting, and that genetic material of his was recovered and processed. He's not in the convicted offender files, but we have reason to believe he's in the evidence databank.'

'Why go through all this red tape?' Moffett said. 'You asked the AG nicely for it?'

'Yes, Your Honor. But Mr. Fine is right. California is among the toughest jurisdictions on kinship searches. They simply don't allow them at this point, although there is precedent in several other states. There haven't been many cases on point. I've submitted documents to you and have a copy for counsel,' I said, passing a memo and stack of scientific treatises to the court officer to give to

36

Eli Fine.

'So you want to make some law here, hon, is that it?' Moffett said, shuffling papers around on his blotter. 'Eli, did you brief this for me?'

'No, sir. I figured you'd take oral argument.'

'From the land of the hip-shooters, young man,' Moffett said, swiveling in his chair and pointing to the elaborate portrait of Lady Justice, standing beneath the flag, with the words *E Pluribus Unum* at her feet. 'You know how that translates, Mr. Griggs?'

Jamal leaned forward and squinted at the Latin inscription, then shook his head.

Harlan Moffett stood and adjusted the belt on his trousers before wagging a finger at the defendant. *'E Pluribus Unum.* Always hire local counsel, Mr. Griggs.'

'Judge, I really object to that kind of comment in front of my client,' Fine said.

'Move for a change of venue if it suits you. You got some nice racetracks in California. I'd like to hold these proceedings somewhere near Santa Anita myself,' Moffett said, taking his seat. He liked the ponies more than he enjoyed writing decisions, since he had an unusually high percentage of reversals by the Court of Appeals. 'Maybe I'd better take some testimony.'

He pointed at the reporter and made a few comments about the nature of the hearing, then asked me to call my witness. I signaled for Mattie to go out to the witness room to wait for her turn to testify, and I called Mike's name into the record.

Mike Chapman walked to the stand and placed his hand on the Bible that the court officer held out to him. I walked him through his education at

Fordham College, where he majored in military history, through his years on the job and early successes that vaulted him to the prestigious homicide squad, and brought him to the current re-investigation of Kayesha Avon's death.

'Did you respond to the scene of the crime, Detective?'

'Yes, ma'am, I did.'

'At what location?'

Mike stated the address. 'On the rooftop of her apartment building, in the projects at Taft Houses in East Harlem.'

I let him describe the heartbreaking sight of the college student's body, after she was abducted from the elevator in her own building on her way home from class.

'Were you present the following day, eight years ago, at Ms. Avon's autopsy?'

'Yes, I was.'

'What findings were made by the pathologist?'

'There were six stab wounds in Kayesha's neck and chest, one of which pierced her heart.'

'Was there any blood evidence found at the scene?'

'No. No, there was not.'

'Any fingerprints?'

'None.'

'Any seminal fluid?' I continued.

'Yes. There was semen in her vaginal vault, and also on her right thigh. She appeared to have been sexually assaulted before she was killed.'

'Was a genetic profile developed by a forensic biologist at the Office of the Chief Medical Examiner?'

'Yes, ma'am.'

'Can you tell us what efforts were made at that time to find a match to that DNA sample?'

'As Your Honor knows,' Mike said, 'back then, we were in the infancy of databanking. We ran the crime scene samples against the entries—many thousand fewer than there are today—and had the lab make comparisons to specific suspects we developed through the tip hotline.'

'Was a match ever declared?' I asked.

'Nope. Not even close.'

'What else did you do?'

'Every six months, I asked Dr. Prinzer at OCME to run the evidence against the convicted offender databank, which has been growing steadily, Judge. Kept going back, hoping to get lucky.'

Mike had been haunted by the brutality of Kayesha Avon's death. He had refused to give up the investigation to the more recently formed cold-case squad, determined to find the young girl's killer himself, with the help of this revolutionary scientific technique.

'Was Jamal Griggs's DNA profile among the samples submitted during the last seven and a half years, Detective?' I asked.

'No, ma'am.'

'Is it correct that Jamal Griggs had a homicide conviction?'

'Yes, he did. But because he had been a juvenile offender at the time of the murder, his DNA was not included in the databank.'

'Do you know the facts of that case?'

'Yeah. I do.' Mike paused and stared directly at Griggs. 'Jamal was fourteen years old. He had dropped out of school to sell drugs with his big brother, Wesley.'

Eli Fine pushed his chair back but seemed uncertain about whether he should be objecting to this line of questioning.

'The girl he killed was sixteen,' Mike went on. 'Jamal stabbed her in the back when she made the mistake of accidentally busting up a drug sale by knocking on the wrong door.'

'Did there come a time when you asked Dr. Prinzer for a comparison to be made to Mr. Griggs's DNA?'

Mike shifted in his seat and ran his fingers through his hair. 'Yeah, about three months ago, just after his robbery conviction.'

'Would you tell the court what result you were given?'

'Objection, Your Honor.'

'On your feet, Mr. Fine,' Moffett said. 'That's the only way I can overrule you. What grounds?'

'Hearsay.'

'You're not offering this for the truth of it, are you, Alex? Dr. Prinzer's going to testify, too, isn't she?' Moffett asked, without waiting for my answers. 'Overruled. It's just a hearing, young man. You got no jury. Save your energy for cross-examination.'

Fine sat down and scribbled furiously on his legal pad while Mike answered the question. 'There was no hit, Ms. Cooper, but Dr. Prinzer told me she had a partial match.'

I finished questioning Mike, establishing that every other means of identifying the perpetrator in Kayesha's homicide had been unsuccessful. Moffett needed to understand that a kinship search was our only alternative. Fine went nowhere with his brief cross-examination, and

Mike stepped down from the stand.

'The People call Dr. Mathilde Prinzer,' I said. She would take the scientific piece of the testimony forward.

It took more than fifteen minutes to list her credentials and establish her unique expertise in this still-evolving field of forensic science. If this case of first impression was to stand up to appellate scrutiny, I wanted the full effect of this brilliant scientist's body of work.

In addition to her daily routine with the five city prosecutors' offices and the NYPD, Mattie had been among the OCME heroes of 9/11, working doggedly with her colleagues to identify victims from thousands of tiny fragments of human tissue.

I ran her through a primer of DNA testing, more familiar to Moffett than to Fine, who had a puzzled look on his face throughout the entire direct.

'When you compare a suspect's DNA profile to a crime scene evidence sample, Doctor, what are the possible outcomes?'

'Traditionally, Ms. Cooper, we have had three results. A match can be declared if you have thirteen loci in common—that is, thirteen places on the chromosome at which the gene for a particular trait resides,' Prinzer said, speaking slowly and looking at Fine as she spoke. 'A suspect can also definitively be excluded if genetic differences are observed. The third option has been a finding of "inconclusive" if we don't have enough information to make a positive determination.'

'Has the scientific community recently accepted a fourth category?'

'Yes. We have begun to develop indirect genetic kinship analyses, using the DNA of biological relatives, in humanitarian mass disasters and for missing person identifications, situations in which we have only small samples of genetic material. We try to compare those to DNA from surviving relatives. In those instances, we're usually working with partial matches.'

'Can you explain to the court the meaning of the term "partial match"?'

Moffett moved his chair closer to Prinzer.

'Certainly. When we look at the thirteen loci needed to declare a match, there are two physical traits charted at every one of them. You see them as peaks on the Avon case lab report Ms. Cooper provided to you,' she said, as Moffett and Fine tried to find the corresponding page. 'These peaks—or alleles, as we call them—come in pairs, one from the mother and one from the father.'

Moffett nodded as he listened.

'In a partial match, at each of the thirteen critical loci, the profiles being compared have at least one allele in common.'

'You could see that on this paper?' the judge asked, bending over the bench and holding out his report to Mattie.

'Oh, yes, Your Honor.' She held the report and pointed to a pair of peaks. 'Look right there. In our business, those graphics really stand out.'

'And what do they tell you?' I asked.

'In the case of Kayesha Avon, we've got high-stringency matches to Jamal Griggs at eleven of the thirteen loci on his sample. So I know I'm *not* looking at the DNA of the person who contributed the crime scene sample, but in all likelihood I'm staring at the genetic profile of someone closely related to him. Probably Jamal's full sibling.'

Probably Wesley the Weasel.

'Has the partial-match technique been used to solve any crimes, to your knowledge?'

'Familial searches have been used with great success in the United Kingdom and Wales,' Prinzer said, citing the cases of child predator Jeffrey Gafoor, serial murderer Joseph Kappen, and James Lloyd, the notorious shoe fetish rapist of Rotherham. 'In this country, in 2005, the process exonerated a North Carolina man who'd been incarcerated for eighteen years and identified the killer who'd left his DNA on cigarette butts at the crime scene.'

'Does the FBI provide information on partial matches, Dr. Prinzer?'

'Not as of this time, Ms. Cooper. My colleagues and I are required to submit a request for the release of the information sought, along with the statistical analysis used to conclude that there may be a potential familial relationship between the suspected perpetrator and the offender.'

'Have you prepared the statistical analysis in the matter of Kayesha Avon?'

'Yes, I have. To begin with, Justice Department figures confirm that fifty-one percent of prison inmates in this country have at least one close relative who has also been incarcerated,' she said. 'And in this case, the donor of the crime scene semen shares twenty of the twenty-six alleles with Jamal Griggs.'

'Can you tell us what that means, Dr. Prinzer, with a reasonable degree of scientific certainty?'

'Yes, I can. It means that we're looking for

43

Jamal's biological brother. For his full sibling—same mother, same father. I believe that's whose semen was in Kayesha Avon's vaginal vault.'

I concluded my questioning and watched as Eli Fine wrangled with Mattie Prinzer. Prosecutors and members of the criminal defense bar took courses in DNA advances every six months to keep current with the technology. The Weasel must have thought his high-priced mouthpiece could bluff his way through opposing the search warrant application, but Fine was in over his head.

Moffett watched Fine struggle for half an hour. Finally the judge stood up and twisted his ring as he began to talk. 'Let me help you out here, son.'

'Judge, I'm perfectly capable of—'

'Sit down, Mr. Fine. I've got some questions of my own.'

Moffett waited until the young man took his seat next to Griggs. 'So, Doc, the FBI releases only perfect matches, am I right?'

'Yes, you are.'

'But in New York—you're satisfied these partial matches are useful?'

'We're one of the few states that generates them, along with Virginia and Florida. Many more allow law enforcement agencies from other jurisdictions to go into their databases if probable cause is established. We believe kinship searches have an enormous potential to solve crimes, to increase database hits by more than twenty percent all over the country.'

'Let me ask you this, Doctor. You know how many brothers Jamal Griggs has?'

I tried to keep a poker face. Moffett was a sleeper, sometimes coming alive mid-trial to hit on

44

the one question that either the assistant DA or defense counsel had overlooked. He'd just handed Fine a gift.

Mattie Prinzer turned her head to the judge. 'I have absolutely no idea.'

'Step down, Doctor. You know the answer to that, Alexandra?'

'No, sir.'

'This Wesley character, is he the only one?'

'I don't believe so, Your Honor.'

Moffett snapped his fingers at the court officer nearest the side door of the courtroom. 'Get me Chapman.'

In less than a minute, Mike walked back into the room.

'You're still under oath, Detective. Have you ever met Mama and Papa Griggs, Chapman?'

'Mrs. Griggs is dead, Your Honor. I have spent some time with Jamal's father, Tyrone.'

'And how many little Griggses did they produce?'

'Six children, sir. They have six grown sons.'

Eli Fine had one of the biggest shit-eating grins I had ever seen spread across his face.

'Where are they, Chapman, the other four?' Moffett was waving his arm in large circles, swinging the sleeve of his robe as he did.

'Tyrone Junior lives right here in Manhattan. The other three don't check in at home very often.'

'How many of the Griggses' sons have rap sheets?'

'Two that I know of, sir,' Mike said. 'Just Jamal, and then Wesley took a few misdemeanor collars for drugs, before he moved his operation to the coast. None of those were designated for databank

45

entry.'

'Let me make it clear, Your Honor,' I said. 'We'd be more than pleased to take a swab from each one of Jamal's brothers. We happen to know where Wesley is, and we know he has a history of criminal behavior.'

Harlan Moffett snapped his fingers again and pointed at the court reporter. 'Take a break, Shirley.'

The portly middle-aged woman clasped her hands over her stomach.

'You believe in this stuff, Chapman?' Moffett asked. 'These familial searches?'

Mike smiled at the judge. 'I do.'

'You understand what she's talking about, with these peaks and alleles and locusts?' Moffett said, aiming his pinky ring at Mattie Prinzer.

'*Loci*, Your Honor. Soft *c*. Couldn't be easier,' Mike said, grinning at Jamal Griggs. 'It all comes down to a simple rule of law: Don't do the crime if your brother's doing time.'

'Hear that, Jamal?' the judge asked before turning to Eli Fine. 'And your objection to Ms. Cooper's request?'

'Ms. Cooper's plan is a violation of the Fourth Amendment rights of every single citizen whose DNA is in the California database. It's an impermissible invasion of privacy, an unreasonable search and seizure.'

Someone in Fine's office had prepped him to regurgitate the key legal buzzwords for his argument.

'Convicted felons give up lots of rights. Who's your client, here? Jamal Griggs or Wesley?'

'Ms. Cooper's made her application in the

46

matter of Kayesha Avon. I'm opposing it on behalf of Jamal Griggs, who has been exonerated in this investigation. People who just happen to be related to criminals haven't given up their own privacy rights. It's genetic surveillance, Your Honor. It violates the Constitution.'

'So you're protecting all the nuts and fruits in California, are you? And you, Alexandra?'

'Suppose Detective Chapman and I were working on a vehicular homicide case, a hit-and-run accident with an eyewitness who saw the whole thing. She tells us the make and model of the car and remembers the first three numbers of a six-digit tag. She gives us a partial plate.'

'Yeah?'

'Would you expect Chapman to just shrug his shoulders and back off from the investigation, or would you expect him to go to the DMV and search it for all the plates—every single one in existence—that include the numbers he was given?'

'We're not talking about license plates, Your Honor,' Fine said. 'We're talking about human DNA. African Americans and Latinos make up a disproportionate amount of the database entries in every state, because of their representation in the criminal justice system. This—this wild-goose chase targets minorities and indigents.'

'You're not disputing that the science works, then, are you?'

'I'm not conceding a thing. It's an outrage that Ms. Cooper thinks she can go through every name in the database.'

'There are no names in there, Judge,' I said. 'The forensic biologists can't see any individual's name in a database—every entry has a numerical designation. If there is in fact a match between the samples, then the techs have to call the state's CODIS administrator to get the person's name. The identity protections are all in place.'

Harlan Moffett stroked his chin again. 'You got any plans to invite Wesley home for Thanksgiving, Jamal? Make it easy for me?'

Jamal Griggs stared Moffett down.

'Tell you what, Mr. Fine. I'll take the matter under consideration. I'll have a decision on this by early next week.'

'I assumed you'd rule on this from the bench, Your Honor. I've got to go back to California in the morning.'

'The State's waited eight years to figure this out. So they'll wait a few more days. You will, too. Tell Wesley to behave himself this weekend.'

Jamal Griggs cocked his head at his lawyer and slammed his open hand on the table.

'I told you, Mr. Griggs, *E Pluribus Unum.* Mr. Fine can't be here, I'll appoint one of the Baxter Street boys to represent you,' Moffett said, referring to the court-appointed lawyers who hung out in street-front offices across from the Tombs. 'Suit yourself, Mr. Fine. It's in your client's best interest—well, it might be—if you show up for him.'

The Weasel was paying good money to keep our noses out of the California database, and Jamal was clearly not interested in disappointing him.

CHAPTER SIX

I left the courtroom with my two witnesses and went back to the office to drop off my papers, eat the sandwich that Laura had ordered in, and explain to her that Mike and I were going to pay a visit to Tina Barr.

There was no traffic on the northbound FDR Drive, so Mike had us on the Upper East Side in twenty minutes, shortly before two o'clock in the afternoon.

Mercer was waiting in an unmarked car almost directly across the street from Barr's brownstone, and Mike continued on until he found a place to park closer to the corner of Lexington Avenue.

'How long have you been here?' I asked when Mercer came up to talk.

'A little over an hour. Have you tried calling her today?'

'Couldn't get a number. She hasn't got a phone—listed or unlisted—and it's a sublet, so if there's a hard line in there, we need to know who the landlord is to get it.'

'Reverse directory?'

'Nothing.' More and more young people were using their cell phones and BlackBerries in place of a traditional phone.

'Knock on the door, Coop,' Mike said. 'It worked for you last night.'

Mercer walked me down the block to Barr's building. The vestibule door was locked, so I rang the buzzer next to her name several times, getting no response. Then I started pressing other doorbells until the man in 4E responded on the intercom by asking who was there.

'Police,' Mercer said. 'I'm trying to get in to speak with Tina Barr.'

'Who?'

'The woman who lives in the basement.'

The man didn't seem to care much about our visit. He buzzed us in and I followed Mercer down to the basement. I knocked but heard nothing from within.

'Ms. Barr? It's Alexandra Cooper. If you're there, I'd like to talk to you.'

We waited a couple of minutes and then I asked Mercer for a scrap of paper from his memo pad. I wrote a note on it, with my cell phone number, and slipped it under the apartment door.

'Let's get comfortable, Alex. We have some time to kill.'

The three of us went up to the corner together to buy coffee. 'I'll sit at this end of the street,' Mike said. 'Better chance she'd be coming from Lex than Third, either by bus or subway. You and Mercer should be right in front of the building, so you can run interference before she gets inside.'

It was a beautiful fall afternoon, crisp and clear, and we leaned against the hood of Mercer's car, talking about the events of the last month, catching up on Vickee and their young son, Logan.

'Now you see why stakeouts are so tedious,' Mercer said, stretching his arms and straightening his back. 'Give it another hour and then go on home. I'll call you when we see Tina.'

'I can't take the chance she'll batten down the hatches again. Battaglia's ripped.'

We took turns walking up and down the street

just to stay alert. I checked with Laura for my messages and made calls on several of my cases. The air chilled a bit as the sun slipped behind the tall apartments that lined Central Park West, and I bought another round of coffee before settling in to the front seat of Mercer's car.

'What have you got?' Mercer said, flipping open his cell phone. He listened and then answered. 'I see him coming.'

It was after six o'clock when Tina Barr's neighbor, Billy Schultz, approached the building from Lexington Avenue. He jogged up the front steps, unlocked the door, and went in. Within the hour, an older couple got out of a taxicab and made their way inside, too. A minute later, a light went on in the third-floor window facing the street.

I heard the sirens before I saw the flashing strobes of the patrol cars that raced into the narrow one-way block from each direction, coming to a stop nose to nose with each other in front of Barr's building.

The passenger in each RMP dashed out of his car and bolted up the steps. Someone—it looked like Schultz's head framed in the narrow space—opened the door, and they disappeared inside.

Mercer was running across the street as I opened my car door, shouting at me. 'Stay put!'

Mike raced downhill from the corner, then took the steps two at a time and pushed through the door that had been propped open by one of the cops. I could see the glimmer of the gold detective shield he had palmed.

A crowd began to collect around the front of the building—people on their way home, going out for dinner, heading for a run in the park, or walking

51

dogs.

I tried to get past the driver of the patrol car who had stationed himself at the building's entrance, but he didn't know me and refused to let me in. I showed him my ID, but he wasn't interested in admitting me without orders from a higher-ranking officer.

'You trolling for bodies, Alex?' I turned at the sound of Ray Peterson's voice.

The lieutenant in charge of the homicide squad had pulled in behind one of the RMPs. He had been at too many crime scenes in his career to feel the need to rush, taking his time for a last drag on his cigarette before nodding at the uniformed cop.

'What do you know, Loo?' I was already feeling guilty about not having pushed Tina to talk to me, and now I was panicked at the thought that her attacker had returned. 'Is it Tina Barr?'

'That your vic from last night?' Peterson said, patting my back. 'We got a corpse, but she doesn't fit that 'scrip. Mike's in there now.'

'Yes, we were waiting together for Barr to get home.'

'What's he doing leaving you outside with the riffraff? C'mon in. I'm sure you've seen worse.'

The officer stepped aside as Peterson guided me up the steps. The commotion was downstairs, and the door to Barr's apartment was open. Peterson led me in, through the little room where I had talked with the distraught woman. Tables and bookcases were overturned, as though the apartment had been ransacked.

Peterson continued down the narrow hallway. I glanced into the bedroom as we passed it, noting the disarray, including empty dresser drawers

52

dumped on the floor.

'Chapman?' Peterson called out as he approached the kitchen.

'Come ahead. I'm out back, in the garden,' Mike said. He must have seen me when he looked up to answer the lieutenant. 'For Chrissakes, Loo, what'd you bring Coop in for? It looks like a slaughterhouse.'

Mercer tried to intercept us before I saw the body, but he was too late. The dead woman was lying facedown, spread-eagled on the wide wooden planks of the kitchen floor, her head split open like a ripe melon. Blood spatter streaked the refrigerator and dotted the ceiling, and what hadn't spurted upward was pooled around her head.

I closed my eyes as Mercer pressed me against his chest. 'The lady's too tall to be Barr.'

'Who is she?' I asked.

'Don't know yet. Mike's talking to Billy Schultz.'

No matter how many crime scenes, autopsies, or morgue visits came up in the course of my work, the individual horror of each circumstance never lost its impact. Peterson liked to tell his men it was time to hang up the job the moment that happened.

I looked again, taking deep breaths to calm myself. There would be a wait for the medical examiner on call, and for CSU to process the apartment and photograph the body. All necessary, but it seemed so cruel to leave her in that position, as a deadly exhibit for the trail of investigators who would be summoned to ferret out clues.

'When do you figure she died, Mercer?'

53

'It's not what you're thinking, Alex. It didn't happen on your watch. There's rigor, and she's been cooling down. Maybe late morning.'

It didn't help to know the body had been there while we had been sitting outside, across the street, for close to five hours.

'Do you remember seeing anyone leave the building?'

'Not a soul,' Mercer said. 'You okay, Alex? Let's go. C'mon, now—you can't help the lady.'

I wondered who the woman was and what connected her to Tina Barr. She looked seven or eight years older than I—in her midforties, perhaps—and almost as tall as my five foot ten. She was dressed in a well-tailored black wool suit, an expensive one, if I was not mistaken. While one shoe was still in place, the other appeared to have come off as the blow to the back of the head knocked her to the floor.

'I'm coming,' I said softly, putting my hands in my pants pocket so that Mike and Mercer, always trying to protect me from the atrocities of our chosen jobs, couldn't see them shaking.

Mike and the lieutenant were huddled in the small backyard behind Barr's apartment, talking with Billy Schultz. He was explaining to Peterson what he must have told Mike minutes ago.

'No, it's not usual for me, if that's where you're going. I'm not a peeper,' Schultz said, sort of bobbing in place while he responded to questions. 'I poured myself a drink when I got home, came to sit here for a while—won't be many more nights so mild I can do that.'

There was a wooden staircase leading down from his first-floor apartment, and two folding beach chairs with a table between them. There was an empty tumbler and an iPod resting beside it.

'Ms. Barr's rear door was open?' Peterson asked.

'Not wide open. It was ajar, which was strange, considering there were no lights on in the kitchen. After what happened here the other night, I didn't want to take any chances.'

I was standing behind Mike as he asked the questions. 'Tell the lieutenant exactly what you did.'

Schultz took a handkerchief out and blew his nose. 'Sorry. I've never seen anything like this before. I—uh—I called out Tina's name. Two, maybe three times. When she didn't answer, I pushed the door in a bit more and said her name again. There was no answer, so I turned on the light—and, well, that's when I saw the body.'

'Then?'

'I took a few steps in. I was—um—you guys do this every day, but I was pretty overwhelmed.'

'Is that blood on your pant leg?' Peterson asked.

'I guess it is. I kneeled down. I wanted to be sure there was nothing I could do for her before I got on the phone.'

I had seen that expression on the lieutenant's face before. *Like what the hell did you think you could do for the broad?* is what he wanted to say. But I understood how Schultz felt. I had wanted to touch her, too. I had wanted to cradle her broken head and body and get her off the kitchen floor to a more dignified resting place.

'Did you touch her?'

'Yeah. I tried to find a pulse.'

'Make sure you swab him, Mike,' Peterson said.

55

'Get his clothes, too.'

Schultz's eyes opened wide.

'It's routine, Billy,' Mike said. 'We need your DNA for elimination purposes. You put yourself in the crime scene. It was the right thing to do, but we just got to account for it, in case you left any trace of yourself there.'

'Do you know who she is, Mike?' I asked.

'If you don't mind, try being the silent partner tonight, Coop. You're here by the grace of God and your good friend Mercer Wallace.' He was probably rolling his eyes, too. 'How long were you in the kitchen, Billy?'

'Less than three minutes,' he said, taking his razor-thin cell phone out of his pocket. 'I couldn't stay in there. I came back out and called 911. I mean right away.'

Peterson lit another cigarette and inhaled, pocketing his lighter, then bent down to examine a large garden ornament that had toppled over on its side, resting next to Barr's back door. Light from within the kitchen reflected on the decorative brass object and its thick wrought-iron base.

That must have been the murder weapon. There was a dark stain covering a dented portion of the brass design, clumped with hair and probably brain tissue, too.

'But you knew who she was,' Mike said.

'Minerva Hunt.'

'You've met her before?'

'I've seen her in the building occasionally. She's Tina's landlady, if I'm not mistaken. Her name was on the buzzer before Tina moved in. I mean, I've never been introduced to her.'

'Did you touch the handbag, Billy?'

'No way.'

'How about the tote?'

Schultz hesitated a second too long before answering. 'Maybe.'

'Whaddaya mean, "maybe"?' Peterson asked.

'Well, I saw the initials on it. M.H. I just turned it around—it was upside down—to make sure I was reading them right.'

'You tell the 911 operator—?'

'That I thought it was Minerva Hunt? Yes, I did.'

I took a few steps backward to the door and glanced toward the body. The shoulder strap of the python-skin bag still hung on the woman's shoulder, but the contents had been strewn on the floor. Next to her was a large vinyl tote, the maker's logo—now drenched in blood—garishly stamped all over it. The gold monogrammed initials of its owner—M.H.—were hard to miss.

'Just a minute, Billy,' Mike said, brushing past me to walk into the kitchen. His cell phone was ringing, and he answered it out of the presence of his witness. 'Hello?'

The caller spoke to him and he held up a finger to me. 'DCPI.'

The deputy commissioner of public information had gotten word of a murder on Manhattan's Upper East Side. Mike would have to keep that office up to speed on every development, no matter how minor, because newshounds would be on the scene in minutes.

'Only a tentative so far. We haven't even started to look for next of kin,' Mike said. 'No driver's license. Nothing confirmed. Peterson's got a couple of guys back at the office trying to run it down.'

I heard the front door of the apartment slam shut and footsteps—it sounded like a woman in spike heels—coming down the hallway. I was hoping to see Tina Barr, thinking she might shed some light on this.

'Give me a break, Guido, we just got here. We're waiting for the ME now,' Mike said. 'The broad was DOA, yeah. Don't go with it yet, but it could be Hunt. Minerva Hunt, okay?'

The Chandleresque brunette—tall, lean, and tough looking—struck a pose in the doorway of the kitchen, dressed also in a well-tailored and probably expensive black suit. She looked through me as though I were invisible, tossed back her hair, and smiled at Mike.

'Now what kind of detective work is that?' she asked him. 'Do I look dead to you?'

CHAPTER SEVEN

Minerva Hunt was perched on the corner of Mike Chapman's desk in the offices of the Manhattan North Homicide Squad.

Mike seemed to be as interested in her affect as he was in her appearance. I watched him look her over again as she glanced around the room. She was casually coiffed and carefully made up to accent her dark eyes and full lips.

'Doesn't exactly have the makings of a physical plant for a think tank, does it?' Hunt said, scanning the room.

The desks that were positioned back to back

with each other had been cheap when they were purchased twenty years earlier. Computer equipment was usually outdated by the time it was installed. The drunken arrestee groaning on the bench in the holding pen behind us, who had beaten his mother-in-law to death just hours ago, was a harsh reminder of the business at hand.

'Most of the time we get it done,' Mike said. 'You feeling better?'

Two hours earlier, when Minerva Hunt first saw the corpse on the kitchen floor, she had lost her composure. But the emotional outburst was short-lived, and a frosty veneer had settled over her like a thin sheet of ice.

'Karla Vastasi?' Mike asked, making notes on the steno pad he carried in his jacket pocket.

'Karla with a *K*, Detective. Could I trouble you to ask the lieutenant for one of his cigarettes, Mr. Wallace? And don't tell me about the no smoking rules. I really need it.'

'There's a chair for you here, Ms. Hunt,' Mike said.

'I'm perfectly comfortable,' she said, recrossing her shapely legs, which had caught the attention of the two older detectives working on the far side of the room.

'How long ago did you hire her?'

'She came to me during the winter. I'd say it's been eight or nine months.'

'What did she do for you, exactly?'

'I told you, Mr. Chapman. Karla was my housekeeper. That's what we call them now, isn't it? I mean we don't say things like "maid."'

'Did she live with you?'

'No. She slept at my apartment occasionally

when I traveled. Took care of the dog if I was called away.'

'And where is your home?'

'Thanks, Detective,' Hunt said to Mercer. She stood up and let him light her cigarette for her, holding her perfectly manicured hands around his. 'I've got a town house on Seventy-fifth Street. Between Madison and Park.'

'Where did Karla live?'

'Queens. Somewhere in Queens,' Hunt said, sticking the edge of a brightly painted red fingernail between her two front teeth while she thought. 'The agency will have an exact address for her. Matter of fact, I probably have some receipts from the car service I use. Sometimes I sent her home that way if it was late or she wasn't feeling well.'

'Family? Do you know anything about Karla's relatives?'

'There's a sister here in the States. Connecticut, I think. The rest are back home.'

'Where's home?' Mike asked.

'Which is the country where the women all have such perfect skin? You know . . . they all come here to be facialists?' Minerva asked, looking at me. 'Romania, isn't it? Yes, she's Romanian. The employment agency has all that information.'

'How old was she, do you know?'

'She told me she was forty-five.'

I guessed Hunt to be a few years older than that.

'Did she have a husband, a boyfriend, a social life?'

'The ex is back in the old country. And no, no social life on my time.'

'She's a good-looking woman,' Mike said.

60

'Never a guy hanging around?'

Hunt inhaled and flicked her ashes on the floor. 'She asked to sleep at the house once or twice because the man she was dating got a bit too possessive, maybe a little rough. But I never went into that with her, and I think they broke up during the summer.'

'Let me ask you, Ms. Hunt, did anyone ever get the two of you confused?'

She looked at Mike as though he had just punched her in the face. 'Confused? The girl could barely form a proper sentence in English. She cleans house, makes the beds, washes the dishes.'

'Physically, Ms. Hunt. Karla was about your height, had a nice figure, hair about the color of yours—'

'And she was the help, detective. I'm not sure who would have had trouble getting that clear. My friends? The dry cleaner? The butcher? I don't know if you meant that as a compliment to her or an insult to me.'

'We've got to figure out if whoever killed Ms. Vastasi was looking for her,' Mercer said, 'or consider the possibility that she was mistaken for you. You own that apartment, don't you?'

'Yes, but I didn't spend any time there.'

'You went tonight.'

'Obviously. I think that's the second or third time I've set foot in it. And I sent Karla there this morning.'

'Why?' Mercer asked.

The detectives were playing Hunt off against each other, Mercer distracting her from Mike's comment that she found so offensive.

'Because I got word that the tenant had moved

out. It was rather abrupt, and I wanted to know what shape the apartment was in. I wanted it cleaned out.'

Mike flashed me his best I-told-you-so look, then shook his head. Tina Barr was gone. I'd been puzzled by her connection to this tragic event from the moment I saw Karla's body, and now the urgency of Battaglia's directive to find Tina made sense.

'You lived there at one time, didn't you?' Mercer asked. Billy Schultz had told us Hunt's name used to be on the buzzer.

'Never.'

'Someone using your name, before Tina Barr moved in?'

'Ridiculous. What reason would anyone have to do that?'

No point pushing her on that tonight. There would be neighbors and witnesses to confirm or deny what Schultz said.

'Ms. Hunt, Karla seemed a bit overdressed to be cleaning an apartment,' I said.

She gave me a glance. 'Remind me, young lady. Who are you?'

'Alex Cooper. From the district attorney's office.'

'Well, then, you're working overtime. I'm so glad I voted for Paul Battaglia, darling. Four times already, or has it been five? "Don't play politics with people's lives"—that's a good mantra for a prosecutor.'

I was tempted to ask her whether she had spoken to Battaglia early this morning, but I knew better than to give her that advantage. I would call him as soon as we took a break.

'The clothes Karla was wearing—'

'They're mine, Ms. Cooper. Old clothes, of course. It's either the staff or the thrift shop. I hate to say I wouldn't have been caught—well, dead—in that outfit again this fall.'

From Park to Fifth avenues, it was often hard to tell the matrons from the nannies, au pairs, and housekeepers strolling the sidewalks. The latter often sported last year's fashions, handed down at the end of the season. They carried home leftover food and goody-bag giveaways in the instantly recognizable shopping bags tossed out by their employers: the robin's-egg blue of Tiffany, the bright orange of Hermès, the pale lavender of Bergdorf Goodman, and the shiny black and white of Chanel.

'The tote with your initials on it?'

Hunt stood and crushed the cigarette with the ball of her black patent pump.

'I hate those logo bags, Ms. Cooper. One sees oneself coming and going. It was a gift, and I passed it on to Karla.'

'It's a bit odd that she went to clean an apartment without taking some work clothes to change into,' I said.

'How do you know she didn't?' Hunt snapped at me. 'Maybe she put them down on her way in, somewhere else in the apartment. Maybe the thief took them.'

'The police didn't find any clothes.'

'We'll give the pad another look,' Mike said. He wanted to be the good cop again. He would like the challenge that this arrogant woman presented, perhaps as much as he liked her looks. 'The ME was wrapping up when we left to come back here.

63

Taking Karla's body to the morgue. We'll go over the place more carefully in the morning.'

'Listen, Detective Chapman,' Hunt said, softening as she talked. 'I'll try to get a number for her sister. If there's any issue about funeral expenses, I'll take the bill.'

'Thanks for that. We'll be doing a lot of work with you on this investigation, so you might as well get to know us. First thing is, call me Mike.'

'Okay, Mike. You do the same.'

'Fair enough. Just tell me what you like. Min? Minnie?'

'Minnie's a mouse, Detective. I'm Minerva.'

'Minerva, the warrior goddess.'

'Now that, Mike, is only a myth.' Hunt crossed her arms, and one side of her mouth lifted into a smile. She was practically nose to nose with him. 'Just a myth.'

There was nothing about military history—from Roman mythology to real-life conflict—that Chapman didn't know.

'The warrior part?' he asked, and Hunt laughed.

'We've got to talk about getting you some coverage,' Mercer said. 'The lieutenant has someone standing by to take you home. And if you don't mind, we'd like to give you a guard for tomorrow.'

The commissioner wouldn't allow the same mistake the department had made, refusing my request to provide protection for Tina Barr.

'I've got my own security. Thanks for the offer, but I don't need yours.'

'Security?' Mike asked.

'The gentleman who dropped me off at the apartment tonight and followed us here. Didn't you make the tail, Detective? You've surprised me again.'

Mike chewed on the inside of his cheek.

'What's that about?' Mercer asked. 'Why have you got protection?'

'I'm a Hunt. And if you were thinking tomato sauce and ketchup, you'd be wrong.'

'I was thinking oil, actually,' Mike said. 'Something thicker than tomato sauce.'

'Even better than that, Detective. Real estate. New York city real estate. My great-grandfather was a partner of John Jacob Astor's. Jasper Hunt was his name. We still own more of Manhattan than it's polite to talk about. Be careful where you walk, Detective. I wouldn't want you stepping on me.'

'Well, what makes you Hunts so unpopular you need security 24/7?'

She looked at her watch as she answered. 'We're not unpopular in most circles, Mike. But my father made a point of teaching me early on to protect my assets. All of them.'

Mercer shook his head at me. He didn't like the direction Mike was going any more than I did.

Minerva Hunt's name was familiar to me from society columns and media coverage of philanthropic events. It made no sense that she, an heiress to a great family fortune, was micromanaging a basement apartment in Carnegie Hill.

'Going back a bit, Ms. Hunt. Perhaps I didn't understand what you meant, but you own the apartment in which Tina Barr was living?' I asked.

'Not that dank little apartment,' she said, tsk-tsking at me without missing a beat. 'We own

65

the building, Ms. Cooper. The whole row of brownstones on that street.'

Then why didn't Billy Schultz recognize her name when he saw it on the buzzer, as he claimed he had before Tina Barr moved in?

'And the tenants pay rent to—?' I asked.

'Not to me, Ms. Cooper. I don't go around collecting with a tin cup on the first of the month. There's a management company, of course.'

'Of course,' Mike said, taking Minerva's part, as though the questions I was asking made no sense. 'What's that called?'

'Mad Hatter Realty.'

'Alice in Wonderland?' Mike asked, laughing.

'Don't laugh. My grandfather, Jasper the Second, was mad. Eccentric is what the rich like to call it, but mad is what he was. My father named one of the companies for him.'

'So you did have a special relationship with Tina Barr, then?' I asked. 'It's not just a coincidence that she lived in your apartment.'

'Tina worked for my father for a period of time.'

'Doing what?'

'He's a collector, Ms. Cooper. Rare books. It's an inherited trait in the male line of Hunts,' Minerva said, talking directly to me for the first time. I thought she was finally giving up her flippant attitude. But she went on. 'For generations they've all seemed to love the same things—rare books, expensive wine, and cheap women.'

'And Barr?'

'She was cataloging the collection. My father's an old man, Mike. He's close to ninety, and quite incapacitated now. Changed his will more often than I change my shoes. I just made sure she had a

66

place to live while she was working for him.'

'Did he fire her?'

'He's not in a condition to fire anyone. Tina quit—that's what Papa's secretary told me.'

Minerva Hunt removed her BlackBerry from her pocketbook and dialed a number, pressing the digits with her long nails. Someone picked up on the first ring. 'Carmine? Are you in front of the police station? I'll be down in a minute.'

'Where did Barr go?'

'Why don't you check with our management office? Perhaps she left forwarding information.'

Hunt was pulling on her short leather gloves—a fashion statement or a sign that she was through with us for the night, not protection against the mild weather.

'You have all my numbers,' she said. 'I expect we'll talk tomorrow.'

'Were you looking for anything in particular in that basement apartment?' Mercer asked as she readied herself to leave. 'Anything you sent Karla Vastasi to retrieve?'

Minerva Hunt backed up a step or two. 'I thought I told you why she was there.'

'Just cleaning up, I think you said. Nothing of value you might be interested in?' Mercer said, talking as he walked into Peterson's office, mimicking Hunt's motion with a pair of latex gloves that he put on as she talked.

'I assume Ms. Barr took whatever belonged to her. The apartment was sublet to her furnished. We keep a few of our properties available for help who need temporary lodging. I wanted to make certain that none of the belongings was disturbed. You'll allow me to do that later in the week, I'm

67

sure.'

Mercer emerged with an object in the palm of his large hand. It was a small book that appeared to be covered with precious jewels.

Minerva Hunt's eyes widened. Her calfskin-covered fingers reached out toward it.

'You know what this is?' he asked.

'It once belonged to my family,' she said, glaring at him while she kept her arm outstretched, in expectation that he'd turn it over. 'Where did you get it?'

'The ME found it after you and Alex left the kitchen. It was on the floor, under Karla's body, tucked inside the jacket of her suit.'

I could see dark stains on the surface of the gems that must have been Karla Vastasi's blood.

'I want the book, Detective. Do you know how much it's worth?' There was nothing playful about Minerva Hunt's attitude.

'Your hand's going to atrophy hanging out there like that,' Mercer said. 'Right now, it's evidence in a murder case.'

'What is it?' Mike asked.

'The Bay Psalm Book,' Hunt said, looking at all of us with disdain for our obvious ignorance. 'This was the first book printed in North America, in 1640. Open it carefully, Detective. It will have my grandfather's name inside. "*Ex Libris,* Jasper Hunt Jr."'

Mercer didn't move.

'There weren't a dozen copies that have survived over the centuries, gentlemen. Jasper's wife had one bound this way when their first son was born. My grandfather treasured it,' she said. 'Kept it by his bedside every night until shortly

68

before he died. It's part of the Hunt collection at the New York Public Library now.'

Mike crossed his arms and whistled. 'Guess I ought to renew my library card. Never saw anything close in my bookmobile.'

'It hasn't been out of that building in almost forty years. Look at it, will you?'

Mercer placed his pinky on the lower corner of the book and gently lifted the cover.

Minerva Hunt stared at the bookplate and sneered.

EX LIBRIS TALBOT HUNT was written on the cream-colored label, decorated with a heraldic coat-of-arms poised above a globe.

'From the library of Talbot Hunt, my ass,' Minerva said, shaking a finger at Mercer.

'Is Talbot related to you?'

'He's my brother, Mike. He's the kind of man who would kill for a book like this.'

CHAPTER EIGHT

'You believe Carmine Rizzali's got a gig like that?' Mike asked. 'His own PI firm, doing security details for the rich and famous. Driving Miss Minerva, maybe even stopping in for dessert. Twenty years on the job, the guy couldn't find a Jamaican on Jamaica Boulevard.'

Mike, Mercer, and I had walked Minerva Hunt out of the squad building and turned her over to the ex-cop who guarded her. We drove down Second Avenue for a midnight supper at Primola, one of our favorite restaurants in the East Sixties,

69

not far from my home.

Giuliano, the owner of the upscale eatery, bought us a round of drinks as we waited for Adolfo, the maître d', to take our order before the kitchen closed.

'Carmine looks like he's enjoying the ride as much as Ms. Hunt,' Mercer said. 'What did you get out of Battaglia, Alex?'

'Don't you remember, Mercer? I give, Battaglia gets. I called to tell him what happened, so he wants me in his office first thing in the morning.'

'Was he surprised?'

'Seemed to be when I told him about the murder. Asked for all the details.'

'Did he react when he heard Minerva Hunt's name?'

'Didn't skip a beat.' I swirled the ice cubes around in the golden brown scotch before taking a long sip.

'*Signorina,*' Adolfo said, 'the chef will do anything you'd like.'

'Just some soup.'

Murder had never been known to have an impact on Mike Chapman's appetite. 'Let me start with pasta. Rigatoni—then throw whatever's left in the kitchen on top of it. Chicken parmigiana after that. And back up my vodka before Fenton falls asleep,' Mike said, pointing at the bartender. 'Mercer?'

'Soup and a salad. That's it for me.' He tasted his favorite red wine. 'You think it's a coincidence that Karla Vastasi was dressed just like her boss?'

'It's possible,' Mike said, gnawing on a breadstick.

'Minerva Hunt sucked you in completely,' I said.

70

'The way you were playing with her, I felt like a third wheel.'

'Sometimes you are, Coop. I was just trying to keep her loose till we sort out the facts.'

'Any looser and she'd have been on your lap. I'm with you, Mercer. The bit with the clothes is too much of a fluke to be unplanned.'

'Karla was dressed for success,' Mike said. 'Just happened to be Minerva's hand-me-downs.'

'The same exact shoes—flat grosgrain bow and brass hardware on the front. It's a classic style, and the ones Karla was wearing weren't even scuffed,' I said. 'That black suit isn't the least bit outdated. I'll bet it's exactly the same one that Minerva had on.'

'So we need to find out whether she bought that monogrammed tote herself,' Mercer said. 'If it wasn't a gift like she claimed, I'm thinking Karla was the canary in the coal mine, sent there to see if it was safe before Minvera went in herself.'

Mercer and I were on the same page. Maybe Hunt was supposed to meet someone in Tina Barr's apartment earlier in the day. Maybe there was a dangerous purpose to the rendezvous, and she had sent her unwitting servant inside to keep the appointment.

'Very hot plate, Alessandra,' Adolfo said, setting the soup bowl in front of me.

'I suppose we'll find out if that little bejeweled book is very hot, too,' Mike said. 'Maybe it's stolen and someone was trying to scam Minerva, tempt her to buy it back. I think I see a date with a librarian in my future.'

'Battaglia will be our matchmaker for that,' I said. There would be no overture to a major New

71

York institution before he greased the wheels at the very highest levels. No point any of us going in through the back door when he could command the attention of the top dogs.

'Well, whoever committed the murder didn't exactly come to the scene armed. Someone can make a good case that it wasn't premeditated,' Mike said. 'Never seen a garden ornament as a murder weapon before.'

'An armillary sphere.'

'It wasn't a spear, Coop. Didn't you see it? Her head was cratered by that big brass-and-iron thing, weighs a ton.'

'Sphere. I didn't say *spear*. Probably a Hunt antique,' I said. 'They were used centuries ago by astronomers, before telescopes.'

Mike's cell phone vibrated on the table. He looked at the caller ID on the display and answered with a mouthful of pasta. 'Excuse me, Mom. We're just having our supper. No, no, no. I can't talk about it now, 'cause I don't want you to have any bad dreams. I'll call you tomorrow. Yeah, I'll say hello for you. Just tell me the question, okay?'

His widowed mother lived in a small condo in Bay Ridge, next door to one of his three sisters. Mike's father, Brian, had been a legend in the NYPD—honored for his bravery on countless occasions, and enormously proud that his only son had shown such academic promise. He retired from the department while Mike was at Fordham, but died of a massive coronary two days after handing in his gun and shield. No one who knew Brian and how much his son admired him was surprised when Mike enrolled in the academy the day he got his college diploma.

' 'Night, Ma. Talk to you tomorrow,' Mike said, putting down the phone. 'The Final Jeopardy category is "Steel Wheels," got it?'

'Now, when did you have time to set this up?' Mercer said, laughing.

'I called her when we were in front of Barr's house. I figured we might be outside there for hours. Didn't want to miss my chance to make a score off Blondie. Pony up the money.'

Mike's fondness for trivia was the other habit that rarely took a back seat to homicide. He liked to bet on the last *Jeopardy!* question of the night and found a way to be in front of the television whether in the squad room, the morgue, or a neighborhood pub.

'I'm glad you showed a little respect for Karla Vastasi tonight,' I said, smiling at him. 'I was touched by your restraint when we were in the kitchen, even though it was showtime.'

'I like it when I please you, kid, but in all honesty, I didn't see a TV there, did you?'

'Twenty bucks for the winning question,' Mercer said.

'I'm in,' I said.

'Double or nothing.'

'Well, damn, man. Seems to me you've heard the answer. And your enthusiasm suggests you've already got a good guess tucked away. So I'm holding at twenty,' Mercer said.

'Picture your boyfriend Trebek reading the answer, Coop. "Steel Wheels' it is. Fastest speed at which New York City subway trains are designed to run.'

I held up my empty glass to signal to Fenton that

I wanted a refill while I stalled. 'What is . . . ?'

'It helps if you ride underground every now and then, even though you act like you're allergic to public transportation.' Mike hummed the *Jeopardy!* music to time me out. 'Hurry it up.'

'What is forty-five miles an hour?' Mercer asked.

'Not a bad guess, Mr. Wallace, but not the right one. Don't be thinking of that City Hall station, Coop. You got big curves like that and grade, the steel wheels go much slower.'

'Thanks for the reminder. An afternoon with you two on that platform was enough to keep me in taxis for a lifetime. I'm going with thirty-five.'

'And once again, you would be wrong, ma'am. What is fifty-five miles per hour, folks? I'll trust you to pay up after we eat. It's a speed rarely reached because it requires long, uninterrupted acceleration, but that's what they're made to do. My pop used to ride me up front on the trains when I was a kid. Loved all that stuff. No subways in the suburbs, kid. That's one of your problems.'

My privileged upbringing in Westchester County, along with my education at Wellesley College and the University of Virginia School of Law, had been made possible by the loving encouragement of my mother and father, Maude and Benjamin Cooper. In addition to her long legs and green eyes, I'd inherited a fraction of the extraordinary compassion Maude exhibited as a nurse. My father and his partner's great contribution to cardiac surgery—a small plastic invention called the Cooper-Hoffman valve—had endowed me with more tangible assets. Despite the enormous differences in our backgrounds, I

74

had never made better friends than Mike
Chapman and Mercer Wallace.

'Fortunately,' I said, 'it's way too late tonight to
ask what you think my other problems are.'

I pushed the soup bowl away and concentrated
on my scotch. The image of Karla Vastasi's
crushed head would be with me all through the
night.

'There'll be no more picking on you for now,'
Mercer said. 'Soon as Mike finishes his dinner, I'll
drop you at home.'

My feelings about Mike had grown more
complicated over time. His teasing and humor got
me through the worst situations imaginable—some
devastatingly traumatic to witness, like the one this
evening, and others actually life-threatening
moments in which he and I had faced off against
deranged killers. Occasionally I questioned
whether my concern for maintaining our
productive professional relationship stopped me
from exploring the attraction I felt for him.

'I've got the autopsy in the morning,' Mike said.
It was part of his duties to attend the medical
examiner's procedure. 'You'll call me when you
finish up with Battaglia?'

'Will do,' I said, getting up from the table.

'I hope they've got good insurance at the
morgue,' Mike said, taking a last slug of his drink.
'Between that murder weapon and the little psalm
book, there's enough burglary bait there to tempt
the dead.'

CHAPTER NINE

I was surprised to hear voices when I approached the door to Battaglia's suite. I had assumed that I would beat him to his office, even though he told me to be there at eight a.m. Rose Malone wasn't at her desk yet, so I turned the corner to present myself.

The district attorney stopped midsentence, a cigar gripped between the knuckles of two fingers. 'C'mon in, Alexandra. Figure out how to get that damn coffeepot working and then we'll get started. Jill, I'd like you to meet Alex Cooper.'

'Hello, Alex. I'm Jill Gibson.'

I walked behind the conference table at which the pair were seated, measured the coffee, and started the machine, reminded of how much Rose had spoiled Battaglia.

'Good to meet you,' Jill said.

The tabloids were spread out in front of Battaglia. I had picked up copies on my way downtown and seen that the item about Karla Vastasi's murder was buried in a single paragraph near the end of the news section. The difference in status between the housekeeper and the heiress had put this story on the back burner and given us breathing room to work on the case without a media frenzy.

'Jill's an old friend, Alex. Came here two years ago from Yale, where she ran the Beinecke Rare Books Library,' he said. 'She's the deputy chief executive at our NYPL now—the number three job—and the first woman in that position.'

'That's impressive.'

There was a quiet elegance about Jill Gibson. She was probably in her mid-fifties, with frosted hair and an easy smile.

'I want you to describe what happened last night,' Battaglia said, planting the unlit cigar in his mouth. 'It's okay, Alex. I've already told Jill the little I know.'

The DA had caught my momentary hesitation. It was unlike him to debrief me about a pending case in the presence of an outsider. It was clear that Jill Gibson had his confidence and might even be the person who alerted him to the situation earlier in the week about Tina Barr.

I described the events from the time Mercer, Mike, and I had arrived uptown to wait for Barr to get home. Battaglia double-tasked, making notes in the margin of a wiretap application that one of my colleagues from the Frauds Bureau had submitted for his signature. He didn't look up until I mentioned Minerva Hunt's name.

Then he asked Jill, 'Do you know Minerva?'

'No, I don't. I've seen her around from time to time, but we've never been introduced.'

'She's not involved with the library?'

'Not in any major way. Her father's still on the board, and she's called in occasionally on matters that concern him. He was chair at one time, as you probably know. Jasper Hunt the Third. A hugely powerful force there for quite a while, in the 1980s and '90s. And Tally, her brother, is also on the board. From what I understand, Minerva has other interests.'

The super rich have plenty of avenues for charitable giving, whether for causes about which they are passionate or for structuring the tax benefits of their estates. Art, ancient or avant-garde; dance, classical or modern; museums, paintings or extinct animals, cultures or ethnic heritage; and poverty, local or global, are among the competing enterprises that attract major donors.

'I think she's disease,' Battaglia said, pointing at the coffeepot. 'Used to be ballet, but I'm pretty sure Minerva Hunt is running the capital campaign for one of the hospitals.'

Naming opportunities at medical centers for pavilions and wings and research facilities were fast becoming ways for baby boomers to insure a jump to the head of the line when a family member needed a heart transplant or an experimental drug for an aggressive illness.

'Ms. Hunt told me her father was very ill,' I said. 'Do you know what's wrong?'

'He's a recluse,' Gibson said. 'Old and frail. That's what I've been told.'

'I haven't seen Jasper Hunt out and about for the better part of two years now,' Battaglia said, putting down the sheaf of papers. 'Go back to the murder scene. Tell me exactly what went on. How did Minerva react when she arrived?'

I took Battaglia through the details of the entire evening, including the way Karla Vastasi and Minerva Hunt were dressed. I described the conversation at the squad with Mike and Mercer as I got up to pour coffee for the three of us.

There was only one thing I left out of the conversation. I didn't mention the Bay Psalm Book. I didn't know Jill Gibson or the reason the district attorney trusted her enough to include her

78

in this meeting. The little jeweled treasure was a crucial piece of evidence, and I needed to figure out its connection to the institution where Gibson worked before I leaked its existence.

'Does Chapman have a hunch?' Mike had made arrests in some of the most high-profile murder cases in Manhattan, and Battaglia respected his unerring street sense.

'Nothing he was ready to let me in on, Paul. There was some discussion with Minerva about things that might have been in the apartment. I know Mike vouchered some property to be analyzed at the lab. At least one book, I'm pretty sure.'

Jill Gibson seemed more interested in that fact than did Battaglia.

'But no sign of the young woman who lived there?' he asked.

'Nothing. She's a librarian, Jill. Her name is Tina Barr. I thought perhaps you might know her,' I said.

'No, I'm afraid I don't,' she said, seemingly uninterested in the missing girl. 'What kind of books did the detectives find?'

This was a no-win situation for me. If I withheld information that Battaglia wanted Jill Gibson to know, he would be furious with me. But if I disclosed something that was not going to be made public at this point in time, who knew what Gibson would do with the information?

'Is there an actual Hunt collection at the library?' I asked. 'I heard Mike say it had something to do with that.'

Jill Gibson pulled her chair up to the table. 'Their family helped establish the library, Alex,

79

more than a century ago. The collection they've amassed is enormously valuable. We make it a practice not to do anything to disturb the Hunts,' she said, making her point to Battaglia.

'Well, I'm certainly going to have to meet with each of them,' I said.

'We'll talk about that after Jill leaves, Alex. She and I have had a couple of meetings in the last two weeks about some problems they've been experiencing at the library. It may be that this case isn't an isolated event.'

Now Battaglia had my complete attention. 'What kind of problems?'

'Do you know the library?' Jill asked.

'I think it's the most magnificent building in New York City,' I said, refilling our mugs. The Carrère and Hastings Beaux Art masterpiece, with its massive triple-arched portico, dominated Fifth Avenue at the corner of Forty-second Street.

'You've spent time there?'

'I majored in English literature when I was at college. I was fortunate enough to be admitted for a month between semesters to do research for my senior thesis.'

'You might want to know why the Hunts are so important to us, Alex. Why we try to tiptoe around them, keep them out of the headlines,' Jill Gibson said. 'I'd also be happy to give you private access to their collection. It's got some extraordinary pieces.'

'I'd appreciate that.'

'New York City came late to the idea of establishing a great library,' Jill said. 'The French had the Bibliothèque nationale and in London the fabulous domed Reading Room was built at the British Museum.

80

'These institutions were symbols of civilized societies and cultures, founded in ancient seats of national government, with documents and books descended from kings and noblemen over the centuries. Americans, on the other hand, were struggling to emerge from the shadows of colonialism, with no comparable government funding for these purposes. By the 1890s, our domestic rivals for intellectual prestige—Boston and Chicago—had already built central libraries, and in Washington, the Library of Congress moved out of its home in the Capitol to the first of its own buildings.'

'We had no libraries here before that time?' Battaglia asked.

'There are two very different kinds of facilities, Paul. One is what's called a circulating system.'

'Elevate the masses by giving the people books,' I said, recalling my nineteenth-century history. 'Advancement through self-improvement. Weren't they usually the work of well-to-do ladies in their communities, making sure that poor little girls had wholesome stories to read?'

'Exactly. They're what led to the branch libraries, here and all over the country. The other type is the well-endowed reference library. That's how the NYPL developed—as a research facility, in which the books are never allowed to leave the building. We were a gift to the city from some of the richest men in America.'

'Who founded it?' I asked.

'It began with private collections. The largest was put together by the first American millionaire, John Jacob Astor,' Jill said.

'Jasper Hunt's business partner.'

'In some ventures, Alex, that's correct. Astor loved literature and had many literary friends. In fact, Washington Irving was the first president of the Astor Library. By the 1890s, the collection John Jacob had bequeathed to his younger son, William Blackhouse Astor, had more than a quarter of a million books.'

'Where could they possibly have been housed?' Battaglia asked.

'Lafayette Street, Paul. That wonderful redbrick brownstone where the Public Theater is today. That was the Astor Library,' Jill said. 'And the city's other devoted bibliophile was James Lenox, who was also a real estate mogul and a merchant. He built himself a palatial marble library on the Upper East Side—today it's the Frick. From Lenox we got the first Gutenberg Bible brought to America, the original autographed manuscript of George Washington's Farewell Address, and the most complete first editions of Bunyan and Milton.'

Jill Gibson was animated now, her eyes sparkling as she expressed her obvious joy for these treasures.

'What brought the Astors and Lenoxes together?' I asked.

'Samuel Tilden, actually, at the end of his life. A bachelor with an immense fortune that he wanted to leave for the public good.'

'Nothing like a politician,' Battaglia said. 'Tilden lost the presidential election to Rutherford Hayes, but he was one of the finest governors of this state.'

'Tilden was also a leader of the civic movement bemoaning New York's lack of a great free public library and reading room. He formed a trust to establish one as his legacy to the city, consolidating the unique private collections already in existence and infusing them with fresh funding. The Tilden Trust and Astor and Lenox libraries joined in 1895 to form this new cultural entity—the New York Public Library.'

'Public?' Battaglia asked.

Jill Gibson smiled. 'Open to the public, but a private, nonprofit corporation governed by a self-perpetuating board of trustees.'

'Tight-lipped and tough-minded, that group is.'

'Exactly, Paul. The power rests entirely in that board, to this day.'

'And the building itself?' I asked.

'The board asked the city to supply a site and maintain the building and grounds—the beginning of this public-private partnership. The city chose Reservoir Square—the huge, gloomy, and obsolete home of the Croton Reservoir, a central crossroads of Manhattan at the time, between Fifth Avenue and Bryant Park.'

'Of course. The reservoir was demolished in order to create the library,' I said, remembering the process that led to the construction of the vast underground system of tunnels to bring water to the city so long ago.

'You can still see the foundation of the reservoir in our basement,' Gibson said. 'Sixteen years after the trust was set up—in 1911—at the cost of nine million dollars, close to two hundred million in today's terms, the building was hailed as the greatest modern temple of education.'

'What about the Hunts?' I asked. 'Was their collection part of the original gift?'

'Jasper Hunt the Second wasn't so quick to get

on board. He was skeptical about relinquishing his father's precious books—and those he'd continued to acquire. That reluctance kept the original trustees from inviting him to join the board.'

'Who were they?' Battaglia asked.

'Best described, Paul, as twenty-one rich white men past their prime. Social status, gender, and economic standing were intentionally homogeneous, to encourage a harmony of action and purpose,' Gibson said. 'Schuylers and Cadwaladers, Bigelows and Butlers. Jasper Hunt had the money, but not the class.'

'Was it his eccentricity?' I asked.

Jill Gibson laughed. 'The library papers suggest that eccentricity was part of his charm. To this group of trustees the Hunts were practically outlaws.'

'Even with the Astor business connection?'

'Jasper Hunt the First started life shoeing horses for John Jacob Astor. You know the Astor quote about real estate?'

'No, I don't.'

' "If I could live all over again, I would buy every square inch of Manhattan," ' Jill said. 'And Astor came pretty close to doing just that. He took a liking to young Hunt. Brought him into the real estate company before Hunt was twenty years old, funded his first acquisitions, and introduced him to extravagances like the rare books that gave Astor such pleasure. Hunt was smart enough to follow in his master's footsteps.'

'Sounds brilliant for a kid who started by shoeing horses,' I said.

'Then Astor withdrew from the fur trade and most of his other ventures to concentrate on purchasing land in Manhattan, investing all the proceeds in pushing north of the city limits. His genius was in never selling anything he bought, insisting that others could pay rent to use the properties. Jasper Hunt went along with him, but the younger man's greed tempted him to go a bit too far.'

'In what way?' Battaglia asked.

Gibson sat back in her chair. 'John Jacob Astor's fur business took him all over the Pacific Northwest, and then to China, where he and his partners traded skins, as well as teas and exotic woods. Then he began to purchase tons of Turkish opium, shipping the contraband to China to smuggle into this country.'

'I didn't know Astor dealt in opium,' I said.

'Wisely, on his part, he didn't do it for very long. But there was such a fortune to be made that Jasper Hunt couldn't bring himself to cut those ties, as Astor had. Even Junior kept his hand in smuggling for a time.'

'And the book collection?' I asked.

'The New York Public Library was a stunning success from the moment its doors opened. People like the Hunts who'd been uncertain about participating began to change their minds.'

'Want to top off my coffee, Alex? It's cold,' Battaglia said.

I got up and waved a hand at Gibson, who'd raised her eyebrows at the command. 'It's not personal. He'd make any of the guys on the legal staff do the same thing.'

'You're good at this, Jill,' Battaglia said. 'You probably know the first book a reader asked for opening day.'

'A young émigré came in to request a Russian-language study of Tolstoy. Not what anyone expected, but a sign of the changing culture of the community. This library is really the soul of the city,' Gibson said. 'I just love it there.'

'I take it that Jasper Hunt Jr. rose to the occasion,' I said.

'Two things happened. Within a decade, the library had risen to the front ranks of research institutions, here and abroad. The collections grew in size to more than a million volumes.

'Then, in 1917, the steel magnate Andrew Carnegie retired to embark on a massive philanthropic distribution—his "gospel of wealth." He wanted to give his money away in his lifetime, saw libraries as the best gift to any community, and in 1917 promised to build sixty-five branch libraries in New York, provided that the city would maintain them. Can you imagine?' Gibson asked. 'Carnegie's plan established more than twenty-five hundred libraries in the English-speaking world.'

'So then Junior kicked in,' Battaglia said.

'Yes, he did. With his father's rare book collection as well as his own, which he continued to add to for the rest of his life. They've got good genes for longevity, those Hunts,' Jill said. 'Junior died in 1958, well into his eighties. He hoped that his possessions would buy him a place on the board along the way. But that never happened.'

'Jasper the Third finally made it,' Battaglia said. 'The old boy is still kicking around.'

'The family had divested themselves of the smuggling operation, contributed a few million dollars to the library, and become model citizens by the 1920s,' Jill said.

'And Tally?' Battaglia asked. 'Do he and his father get along?'

'In the boardroom,' Jill said, 'everyone's on his best behavior. The real intrigue doesn't happen inside the library walls.'

I couldn't take my eyes off the small color photograph on a document to the right of Battaglia's hand as I refilled his mug. It was a copy of an employee identification tag from the New York Public Library, dated earlier in the year. The woman who'd posed for the camera to get her security clearance was the elusive Tina Barr.

CHAPTER TEN

'I'm going to step out and let you finish your business with Jill,' I said. 'Why don't you call me when she's gone, Paul?'

I was reeling from seeing Barr's face on a library document just moments after Gibson told me she didn't know the girl.

'What's the matter? You see a ghost?' Battaglia asked.

'Yes, I did. The one I've been trying to channel since you told me to find her.'

I was angry about being a pawn in the middle of their deal. Jill Gibson had lied to me, and the district attorney let her do it.

Jill leaned over and tapped her finger on the table. 'You've tipped your hand, Paul. It's the photograph.'

Battaglia wasn't rattled. He had a reason for playing this the way he had chosen, and irking me was of no consequence to him.

'Sit down, Alexandra. Pouting doesn't become you.' He waved at me with the lighter that he held to the tip of the cigar. 'Jill's in the middle of some professional difficulties and I'd just agreed to open an investigation when the Barr girl got herself tied up the other night.'

'*Got herself what?* Not exactly the way I'd describe that attack, Paul. What do you know that I don't? I understand how sensitive the issues are at an institution like the library.'

'We've spent so many decades dealing with the renovation and modernization of the building itself, Alex, that we've dropped the ball on most of the other problems,' Jill said. 'They've festered and grown.'

'Tell her why you were brought in,' Battaglia said, puffing on the cigar that was plugged into the middle of his mouth.

'I spent the first twenty years of my career at the NYPL, so I know the collections—and the characters—quite well. In the century since we opened, there was never any relationship between the research library—this central building—and the branches. I'm heading the long-overdue consolidation of the two divisions. There are now ninety-three branches, so that's a big enough undertaking of its own. But at the same time I've walked into a firestorm.'

'Why?' I took my seat across from Jill Gibson.

'There are personal issues involving some of our trustees that have spilled into the boardroom. Battles over family fortunes have us in and out of court. A century ago, Samuel Tilden's nieces and nephews fought tooth and nail to break his

88

testamentary trust so that the library would never be created, from the first day of probate. Brooke Astor's estate wasn't the first to be dragged through a court of law—by her own son, no less—and it won't be the last.'

'That can't be unusual for museums or any other institutional beneficiaries, can it?'

'Certainly not. But we aren't a museum, Alex. That's one of the things that makes our situation unique.'

'What do you mean?'

'Very often, when trustees or benefactors of the library die, we inherit not only their manuscripts and books. We get other works of art, too. But we're a library and a research institute. We can't care for great art, nor can we curate it. Most of the time, we can't even hang it on our walls. And yet, if we violate the wishes of the dearly departed, we're likely to lose everything else bequeathed to us.'

'So there's been trouble in-house because you've been selling art that the library owns?'

Jill looked to Battaglia before she answered.

'That's part of it. I think it's what Paul refers to as our lack of transparency. One of the committees made the decision to deaccession a major painting a few years ago that had been left to us by one of our most famous donors, and after the full board learned about the transaction, some of the trustees really thought it was grounds for murder.'

'Tell me more about it.'

'Forget it, Alex,' Battaglia said, drawing back his lips around the cigar. 'I've got someone on that.'

'From the U.S. Attorney's Office?' I asked. The feds had jurisdiction over matters involving culturally significant works of art, but it was unusual for Battaglia to want to share a major investigation with them.

'Nobody mentioned the feds, did they?'

'Who did you assign to it, Paul? I'll work with him,' I said. 'We'll make it a joint investigation. Whatever has been going on might have something to do with Barr's assault, or the murder of Karla Vastasi.'

'Someone's been stealing from the library, Alex,' Jill said. 'That's the reason I called Paul for help. Whoever it is—or they are—has got to be stopped. We've got treasures under our roof worth millions of dollars, some of them not even cataloged, and we're starting to bleed from the losses.'

Now I felt guilty for holding back the information about the jeweled book that had been found under Vastasi's body.

'What do you know about the Bay Psalm Book?' I asked.

Battaglia's eyes narrowed as he listened to Jill's answer. 'It's a very rare piece of Americana. Interestingly enough, the Puritans considered Hebrew to be the "mother" of spiritual languages and used it in many of their services. The book is a makeshift translation of David's Psalms from the original Hebrew into English, printed in Massachusetts when the first presses were set up. It's one of the most important items that came to the library with the Lenox collection.'

Now Battaglia shifted his gaze to me. 'I guess your memory's improving, Alex. Is that the book the cops found last night?'

'Can't be the same. The one they vouchered came from the Hunt collection, not from Lenox. Minerva was quite emphatic about its history.'

Jill Gibson's elbows were on the table and she rested her head in her hands. 'The police have it? Is it covered with precious stones?' she asked without looking up.

'Yes.'

'That will be another blow to Leland Porter,' Jill said, referring to the library's president. 'I don't think anyone's aware that the Hunt piece had gone missing.'

'Stolen or deaccessioned?' Battaglia asked. 'We've got to know that before we go looking for bad guys. You'll check on that, Jill. Does it literally have jewels on the binding?'

'Yes, it does. Jasper Hunt took a perfectly interesting piece of history—not important literature—and turned it into a garish little objet d'art, a personal vanity. It's been locked away in a library vault for as long as I can remember,' Jill said. 'The only one we display—the one that scholars work with—is the Lenox version of the Bay Psalm Book. Thank you, Alex, for letting me know about this.'

I couldn't tell whether my revelation would come back to bite me or not.

'Do you know where Tina Barr is?' I asked Gibson.

'No, I don't.'

'But you know her, don't you?'

Jill grimaced as she looked to Battaglia again. 'I'm sorry I lied to you before. I, uh—I wasn't sure Paul wanted me to tell you the story. Yes, she used to work in our library. She trained there as a conservator.'

'What exactly do conservators do?' I asked.

'It's a field that requires great skill. They're

91

responsible for the preservation of all our rare documents and books. They've got to be knowledgeable about the history of the materials, and have enough scientific education to understand the structural stability and characteristics of whatever they're working on. Tina's young, but she's one of the best.'

'When did she stop working at the library?'

'She was full-time with us until a year ago. Then she started working with Jasper Hunt,' Jill said. 'But that isn't unusual. All the private collections of that quality have conservators, and because we have our own lab, many of them—like Tina—do their work right in our facility.'

'So it wasn't a problem that she went to work for Hunt?'

'Of course not. We viewed it as an advantage for Tina to catalog everything in his home. We expect to get the rest of his collection some day. It's been promised to us.'

'Unless one of his children convinces him to change his will,' Battaglia said.

'But Tina's no longer working for Mr. Hunt,' I said. 'That's what Minerva told us.'

'I didn't know anything about her current situation,' Jill said. I thought her voice was beginning to tremble. 'I had no reason to, until she called me this week.'

'When did she call?' I asked, looking at Battaglia out of the corner of my eye.

'It was very early yesterday morning, the day after she was attacked. She awakened me, in fact, on Wednesday.'

No wonder Battaglia had known about Barr's assault when he called me into his office a couple

92

of hours later.

'What did she say? What did she tell you?'

'That she was terrified,' Jill said. 'She told me she was going to take some time off, leave the city for a while. I guess Tina thought of me as an ally, from the old days when she was first hired at the library. She wanted to know if I would help her get her job back when she returned.'

'Did you agree?'

'Certainly. I told her to come in to see me that very day. I wanted to make sure she was all right. I even mentioned that I knew the district attorney and perhaps he could help with her case. I had no idea that you had been called out on the matter during the night.'

'And did she come in?'

'Tina said she'd be there yesterday,' Jill said, lowering her voice, 'but she never showed up. Then Paul called me late last night to tell me about the woman who was murdered in Tina's apartment. To ask if I knew her.'

'Did you?'

'No, no, no. Absolutely not.'

'I'm going to ask you again,' I said, trying to make eye contact. 'Do you know where Tina is now?'

Jill pursed her lips and shook her head.

'Do you know whether she had taken another job? Was she working for someone else?'

This time Jill nodded, just as someone knocked on the door.

'Come in,' Battaglia said.

I turned my head to see Patrick McKinney, the head of the trial division, striding toward the table. He was senior to me, and although I reported

93

directly to Battaglia on sex crimes, McKinney had oversight for all homicides and other felonies. The district attorney respected his investigative abilities, but McKinney was rigid, humorless, and small-minded, and made it his regular business to stab me in the back whenever an opportunity presented itself.

'Morning, boss. Sorry I'm late. Good morning, Jill,' McKinney said, shaking hands with her. Battaglia must have put him in charge of the library issues that Jill had brought to him. 'Alex, I wish you had called me last night. I just spent fifteen minutes getting up to speed with the chief of d's. He had to fill me in on the Vastasi murder himself. You talking about Tina Barr?'

'I was just explaining to Alex that she had recently left Jasper Hunt to start working for another one of our patrons,' Jill said.

'Who is he?' I asked.

'His name is Alger Herrick. She was quite happy,' Jill said. 'It was actually a much better fit for her than Jasper Hunt.'

'Why is that?'

'Herrick is also a collector, with a special interest in cartography.'

Battaglia's lips drew back again. 'Maps.'

'Most conservators have a specialty, Alex. The work has increasingly become so technical that they usually develop an expertise in one area. For Tina, it's been rare maps,' Jill said. 'And Alger is much younger than Jasper Hunt. He's in his mid-fifties—a very vibrant personality.'

'You've talked to him about Tina?' I asked, glancing from Jill Gibson to Pat McKinney.

'He's as puzzled by her disappearance as the rest

of us,' Jill said.

McKinney seated himself next to Battaglia. 'I'm on it, Alex.'

'Did Tina tell you why she was terrified?' I asked.

'Well, given what had happened to her the night before, there wasn't much reason to ask,' Jill said. 'The attack made her even more anxious to get out of the apartment, too. Minerva Hunt was furious with her.'

'Did she tell you why?'

'Minerva hates Alger Herrick. They've crossed swords in some business deals, is all I know,' Jill said. 'Tina couldn't move out fast enough once Minerva knew she was working with Alger.'

'It's crazy to double-team this, boss,' McKinney said to Battaglia. 'Karla Vastasi's death wasn't a sex crime. Alex and I can sort this all out ourselves.'

I could almost feel the point of his elbow digging into my side from across the wide oak table. 'I'd like to find Tina Barr before anyone causes her more distress, Pat. The woman is still my victim.'

'Tina Barr isn't anyone's victim, Alex. She's a thief,' Pat McKinney said. 'Don't wrap your bleeding heart around her. She's a forger—and a common thief.'

CHAPTER ELEVEN

'I disagree with Battaglia,' Mike said.

It was two-thirty on Thursday afternoon, and he was eating his second hot dog, leaning against the

95

blue brick wall of the building that housed the morgue on First Avenue at Thirtieth Street.

'I was hoping you would.'

'Not about taking you off the murder case. About how you look when you pout.'

'Maybe you'll ask the lieutenant to go to bat for me. Keep me on the team.'

'You should get your feelings hurt more often, Coop. Kind of cute. You look almost vulnerable.'

'All these years together and I thought you liked edgy and cool. You want to see vulnerable, watch McKinney try to undermine me.'

'Nah, that's when you go all pit bull on me. Did Battaglia set ground rules?'

'For the time being, I can work with you and Mercer on Tina Barr. I guess setting up this interview with Alger Herrick, the man she's been working for lately, is my consolation prize. Pat's sitting on the larger matter of the library, and the DA may force him to let me in on it.'

'What's McKinney's reason for bumping you off Vastasi's murder?'

'I may be needed as a witness if there's an arrest and trial, so I can't be the prosecutor. What did we see during the surveillance? Did I touch the body or the evidence? What did Billy Schultz and Minerva Hunt say to me? That's why I thought we could get back to work on Barr. The two crimes can't be unrelated.'

'Why did McKinney call Tina Barr a thief?' Mike asked.

'He interviewed Jill Gibson last week, before any of this happened. She was talking about some of the things that have disappeared from the library in the last couple of years. In order to get

96

your hands on the most valuable items you'd really need to have special access to the best collections. That's why the executives think most of the thefts had involved insiders.'

'This Gibson woman fingered Tina Barr?'

'No, she actually likes Barr. But it's clear that the conservators work on materials from different parts of the library. Her name was one of the common denominators that kept coming up as the individual curators were interviewed. It's McKinney who's drawn a bead on her.'

'Stealing these priceless objects for herself,' Mike said, 'and the best she could do was live in a basement in one of the Hunts' buildings?'

'Thefts to order, Mike. That's apparently the big scam. Rich collectors are all scrambling for the same limited goods. They know that thousands of these artifacts are shelved in stacks that nobody ever sees, or warehoused for decades, like the little book Karla Vastasi hid inside her jacket. And Barr was courted by many of these collectors because she's so extraordinarily talented and had such unique access inside the building.'

'You have time to Google this Alger Herrick after Battaglia booted you from the inner sanctum?'

'Yes,' I said. 'McKinney only interviewed him by phone, last week when Herrick was still in England. That was about the problems at the library, so Barr's name came up in the conversation, but I thought we should go deeper.'

'He was here in New York when Barr was attacked?'

'Yes, and for Vastasi's murder, too,' I said. 'He arrived last weekend.'

'You want a bite?' Mike asked, holding his hot dog out to me.

'Thanks, I had lunch at my desk.' I took a napkin from his hand and wiped the mustard from the corner of his mouth.

Mike grinned at me. 'The guy must be a real gent if you're cleaning me up for him.'

'Very upper-crust, this Mr. Herrick. He's English, he's rich, and he's very proper. I thought it would be refreshing for him to meet you.'

'Four fifty-five Central Park West. If he's so rich, how come he's living in the DMZ?' The area that bordered the park on the Upper West Side, north of Ninety-sixth Street, has seen more than its share of violent crime.

'According to the search I did today, when that landmark building was renovated and apartments went on the market three years ago,' I said, 'Alger Herrick paid eight million dollars for the most coveted space in the joint.'

'And just seven years ago,' Mike said, shaking his head, 'it was like a big old haunted house. The deadbeat hotel next door was a crack den and it was worth your life to walk down the block without being robbed by junkies or hit up by prostitutes.'

'So you know the building?'

'Had a nightmare of a case in four fifty-five back then. Three teenage boys from the 'hood killed up on the third floor, execution style, 'cause they were playing in there and witnessed a buy. The place had such a spooky history, most of the neighbors would cross the street rather than pass by too close to it. Only things inside were stray cats, dead pigeons, and half-dead crackheads.'

'I'd never heard of it until I just read the story

98

about Herrick.'

'It was the New York Cancer Hospital in the 1880s,' Mike said. 'The first one of its kind in the country to devote itself to the care of cancer patients.'

'The photo of it online looks more like a French château. The article said it was built with money from the Astor family. I guess they really did round up a load of real estate.'

'Wait till you see it. It's got turrets on each side, round towers like in a castle,' Mike said. 'The architect actually designed them on the theory that germs and dirt wouldn't collect in corners. I can't exactly say we had a guided tour, but Peterson and I got to know every nook and cranny in the place. It was the predecessor to today's Memorial Hospital on the East Side.'

Mike's late fiancée, Valerie Jacobsen, had been treated at Memorial a couple of years before—successfully—for breast cancer, only to be killed in a skiing accident. During those months, he had applied himself to learning as much about the disease as he knew about military history.

'And now it's been transformed into elegant co-op apartments,' I said. 'Maybe it'll bring the rest of the neighborhood along with it.'

'Everything in New York used to be something else,' Mike said, tossing his trash into a pail on the corner as we waited for the light to change. 'These old buildings have stories, Coop. They're here to tell us who we were, who we used to be.'

'Herrick's home seems to have mostly sad stories.'

'The mother of one of the boys who was killed there became a one-woman campaign to clean it up. Learned everything there was to know about its history. She told me she used to sit in the same desolate room where her kid was offed, just staring out at the park, thinking about how many people had come to the end of their lives in that forsaken place.'

'Back when it was built,' I said, 'cancer was incurable. Treatment was just palliative.'

'Patients went to that hospital to die, eased by morphine and champagne, Sunday carriage rides in the park,' Mike said. 'Story was that the hospital whiskey bill was higher than the one for medical supplies. Even Marie Curie came to visit.'

'She did?' I asked as we crossed the broad street, dodging taxis and buses, to get to Mike's car.

'The Curies discovered radium in 1898, and doctors here pioneered the first techniques to burn cancers away with it. The largest repository of radium in the country was kept in a steel vault right in that building.'

'I don't know that I could live in a place like that,' I said. 'Too many ghosts.'

'Life goes on,' Mike said. 'The Octagon—the old lunatic asylum on Roosevelt Island—has been turned into a housing development, and the building where more than a hundred people died in the Triangle Waist Company fire in 1911 is a biology lab at NYU now. Like a phoenix from the ashes.'

I had just cleared the passenger seat of half a dozen empty soda cans, a tie, a book on the Crimean War, and a gross of Tic-Tac boxes when I heard Mike's beeper go off.

He looked at the display and slammed the car

100

door. 'It's Peterson.'

My cell was in my hand. I speed-dialed Mike's boss and handed him the phone.

'Hey, Loo, what's up?' Mike listened to the answer. 'Got it. Yeah, she just bought me lunch at the medical examiner's outdoor café. We're on it.'

'Detour?' I asked.

'Quick stop on Ninety-third Street,' Mike said.

'Tina's apartment? Why?'

'Because Billy Schultz played hookey from his office today. He's working from home.'

'So?'

Mike was driving up First Avenue, weaving between cars to catch the lights while he talked. 'Precinct guys spent the morning canvassing the buildings that face the garden behind the apartment. Got a rear-window thing going on. Remember Billy told us he hadn't seen much of Tina since the summer? Well, the little old lady who takes the fresh air on her fire escape saw Billy out back with Tina over the weekend. Saturday, right around dusk.'

'Doing what?'

'Digging.'

'You mean gardening?'

'I would have said it if that's what I meant. She says digging. With a great big shovel and mounds of dirt. No pansies, no tulips, no vegetables.'

'Why didn't he tell us?' We were cruising past the United Nations, and Mike put on his whelper to cut a course through the slow-moving traffic. 'Did you see any disturbance in the garden?'

'Actually, Coop, I was distracted by the broad on the floor with the bad headache. I thought there was a messy patch in the yard, and I just figured it

101

was where the perp pulled the armillary out of the ground to whack her. Anyway, Crime Scene will have photos,' Mike said. 'Peterson's got a uniform outside his apartment, rope-a-doping him into answering questions about all the other tenants till we get there. And I buried the lead.'

'What's that?' I held the dashboard as Mike slammed on the brakes to avoid an Asian deliveryman, then accelerated again.

'That gas mask the cops picked up a few doors away from the building the night Barr was attacked?' Mike asked.

'Don't look at me. Look at the road,' I said. 'What about it?'

'Preliminary on the DNA inside the mask. There's a mixture, of course,' Mike said. 'I'd expect that with something like a mask—especially if it isn't brand new. And one of the profiles matches Billy Schultz.'

'Are you serious? I never thought of him that way for a minute. He was wearing the damn thing?'

'Skin cells, sweat. I don't know what else they got.'

Once we passed the turn-off for the Fifty-ninth Street Bridge, we made the left onto Ninety-third Street in less than three minutes.

I could see an officer talking to Schultz on the sidewalk as we pulled up in front of the building. He looked over when he heard the car door shut and started up the steps as Mike approached.

'Yo, Billy,' Mike said. 'I need a couple of minutes of your time.'

Schultz was wearing a plaid flannel shirt, sleeves rolled up, and he frowned as he checked his watch before telling Mike that he had to get back upstairs for a conference call. 'I can't talk to you now.'

'A guy could get a complex. Only person who's ever happy to see me is my mother,' Mike said. 'It's just a little thing.'

'Really, I've got to make a call.'

'This Minerva Hunt thing's got me puzzled.' Mike was doing his best Columbo imitation, a look of complete befuddlement on his face. He seemed too dense to be able to figure out much of anything. 'When you phoned 911, you told the operator you thought the dead woman was Minerva Hunt, right?'

Schultz looked annoyed. 'That's what I said.'

'That you'd seen her in the building on other occasions.'

'Exactly.'

'You were standing with me when the *real* Minerva Hunt walked into the kitchen, weren't you?'

'In the garden, yes.'

'Did you see her?'

'I did.'

'I'm just trying to get straight which of the two women you'd seen around the building before that night. That's all I want to know.'

'The way you came speeding up the street, I thought it was something more urgent,' Schultz said, seemingly relieved that was the reason for our visit. 'I—uh—I was mistaken when I called for help. The outfit, the general physique, the bag with her initials. I couldn't really see her face—it was such a mess—I just jumped to that conclusion. As soon as I saw that other woman talking to you, I knew I'd been wrong.'

'Very helpful, Billy. I didn't mean to hold you

up,' Mike said with a wave of his hand. 'What are you growing this time of year? Pumpkins?'

'Excuse me?'

'In your garden. My lieutenant asked me to find out what's in bloom.'

'It's all put to bed, Detective. Come back next spring and see what we've got,' Schultz said, heading up the stairs.

'The big dig, Billy. Last Saturday. What was that about?'

Schultz continued on his way.

'People saw you with Tina out in the yard. You want to tell me what you were doing together?'

Schultz stopped but didn't answer.

'Don't be going back out there for a while, Billy. Cops are on their way to seal it up now, till we have a chance to check it out. It's off-limits.'

The man turned to look at us, clearly displeased. 'Tina asked to borrow my shovel, okay? I didn't ask her why. I didn't need to know. I took it down to her and talked for a minute or so. That's her little plot. I don't care what she does with it.'

'But you told us you hadn't talked to her—' I said.

'Maybe I just forgot. It was such an insignificant exchange, I simply forgot.'

Mike took a step closer and put his hand on the railing of the staircase. 'Easy to understand, Billy. A lot easier to understand than the fact that you left your droppings in that freaking mask you ran around in the other night.'

'What are you talking about? That's not my mask,' Schultz said, angered. He raised his voice and his face flushed.

'The lab got your DNA sample last night, and

104

they say it looks pretty good that you were the guy who had his mug in that contraption. You forget to tell us that, too? Why don't we take this conversation inside, Billy. Your place or mine?'

'Don't come any closer, Detective. Yeah, did I see the fireman—the guy who ran out of here—throw something on the ground? Sure I did. It was only two, three car lengths up the street. Yeah, I picked it up and looked at it—and maybe I did just hold it up over my face. I couldn't figure how he could see out of it. Then I just dropped it back down. Figured your buddies would pick it up.'

'I think you'd be doing yourself a favor if you came up to the squad and sat down to go over all this a little more carefully, you know?'

'I'll do you a bigger favor,' Schultz said, opening the vestibule door and shouting before he disappeared inside. 'I'll have my lawyer call you.'

CHAPTER TWELVE

A doorman admitted us at the entrance of the elegantly restored Gothic building on Central Park West and directed us to the concierge.

'We're here to see Alger Herrick,' I said, taking in the opulence of the décor in the lobby. The architectural detail of the last century had been carefully preserved, but there were discreet signs pointing to an indoor lap pool and the spa.

'He's expecting you?'

'Yes. I'm Alexandra Cooper.'

The concierge rang the apartment, and when someone answered, he announced me. 'Take that elevator to your left.'

'And what floor do I press?'

'The lift only goes to Mr. Herrick's home.'

I followed Mike into the small elevator and pressed the button that said Up. Seconds later, it came to a stop and the door opened.

'Good afternoon, Ms. Cooper. I'm Alger Herrick,' he said, extending his right hand to help me step off. His left hand was tucked into the pocket of a charcoal gray cashmere sweater, set off against a yellow ascot that framed his long, narrow face.

Mike introduced himself as I moved onto a small balcony that hung above the main room of the apartment. It took my eyes a minute to adjust to the dim light, and then I looked around at the vaulted ceiling and the large stained-glass windows that ringed the cavernous space of the perfectly appointed room.

'I was in here years ago, but I'd never recognize the place,' Mike said, whistling softly as he moved in behind me. 'This used to be the hospital's chapel, wasn't it?'

'Precisely, Detective. Did you know it in the old days—after the hospital closed—when these glorious rooms were filled with decay?' Alger Herrick asked. 'This was indeed the chapel of St. Elizabeth of Hungary. Patron saint of the suffering.'

I felt a chill run down my spine.

'I had a rather long conversation with your colleague, Mr. McKinney, from my home in London late last week,' Herrick said. 'Thursday evening, I believe.'

He led us down the winding staircase of the

duplex and seated us in the living room, waiting for the butler to return with our ice water and his tea.

'Things have happened since then,' Mike said. 'A woman's been killed in the apartment Tina Barr was living in, and Barr herself has disappeared.'

'Yes, I got back to town on Sunday. Jill Gibson called yesterday, asking about Tina. Apparently she seemed to have left without a trace.'

'Were you surprised?'

'I was, Mr. Chapman. She's been working with me for several weeks,' Herrick said, 'and I thought we were getting on very well. I owe her quite a large amount of money, so I assume she'll be in touch with me about that.'

'Do you know anything about her family, her next of kin?' I asked. 'Any idea where she might have gone?'

'Her father died when she was very young. I know that. Tina spoke of her mother. I understand she lives in one of those artists' colonies on the west coast of Mexico.'

'Would you have the mother's name, or an address for her?'

'I'm afraid not. No reason for me to have it.'

Herrick was standing a few yards away from me, but I could barely see his face because of the lack of light in the room.

'You mind turning up the wattage?' Mike asked, also frustrated by not being able to gauge the expressions on Herrick's face.

Herrick walked to a panel near the staircase and pushed the dimmer. The mountings on the wall, all in gilded frames, were maps—oceans and continents, familiar territories and foreign names.

'Sorry, Mr. Chapman. I'm so used to living at

lamp level—that's what we call it when you work with ancient documents—that I forget others aren't accustomed to it. The objects in my collection, whether on parchment or vellum or paper, are better protected by low lighting. That's why it's so dark in here,' Herrick said. The dimness added to the solemnity of the room. 'I'd only got to know Tina a little better about a month ago. We hadn't worked out the details for her fees yet.'

'Hope you figure it out before next April,' Mike said. 'She'll have taxes to pay.'

'Frankly, Detective, Tina wanted to be paid off the books. Cash. I was quite uncomfortable with that. I gave her some money up-front, to get her going, but I hadn't formalized our arrangement.'

The butler returned with our drinks and handed me water in a heavy crystal double-highball glass. While Mike questioned Herrick, I checked out the sumptuous fittings of the old chapel and admired the brilliant colors of the antique hand-drawn maps and charts.

'Where did you meet Tina?' Mike asked.

'At the New York Public Library. I'd seen her there over the years, exchanged pleasantries and such, and I was aware that she'd built up a good reputation for herself,' Herrick said, resting his teacup on the mantel above the fireplace. 'It seemed the perfect opportunity for both of us, with my collection and her skill.'

'Wasn't she already working for someone else?'

'Jasper Hunt. She'd been hired by someone to do some projects for the old man himself.'

'Not hired by him?'

'Jasper? Entirely gaga at this point, Detective. At least, that's what I heard. It was probably one of

108

his children, trying to get their greedy hands on his treasures,' Herrick said, taking a sip of his tea. 'You've met them, have you?'

'Tell me what you know,' Mike said.

'Talbot's a bookman. That's how collectors are known. The father always favored him because Tally's got the same nose for books as Jasper, the same appreciation—had it since he was a child. He's probably close to fifty now, a bit younger than me. Been very involved in running the family property empire, expanding it to pass on to his children.'

'So they get on, father and son?'

Alger Herrick ran his finger along the edge of the mantel. 'There are others closer to Jasper who could tell you more than I.'

'But you've heard rumblings. You must have had something in mind when you hired Tina Barr away.'

'Idle gossip around the library,' Herrick said. 'Tally's getting impatient, hoping to keep some of his father's fortune in the family. Make sure it isn't all given away. That sort of thing.'

'Even to the library?' Mike asked. 'Even though he's on the board?'

'I have the impression that Tally would like to have control of something substantial at this point in his life. Something of his very own. There's a certain feeling of entitlement that comes over a man like that by the time he's reached middle age. His grandfather was such an eccentric that no one's quite sure how much of the fortune is still intact. A lot of the Hunt money has already been given away, and Jasper himself kept threatening to change the provisions of his will. Mind you, that's just the talk.'

'And Minerva?'

Alger Herrick raised his teacup. 'I'll have to switch to something stronger than this, Detective, if we're to talk about that viper. I have a bad taste in my mouth at just the mention of her name.'

'Why so?'

'You seem intrigued by that one, Ms. Cooper,' Herrick said. He caught me staring at a beautifully drawn map of the European coastline, the compass roses highlighted in gold paint. 'By all means have a closer look.'

'Minerva Hunt,' Mike said, drawing Herrick back to the conversation. 'Why do you dislike her?'

'She's a lightweight, Mr. Chapman. A complete cipher. Minerva's a girl who was handed every advantage in life on a silver plate, and she still hasn't worked out what to do with it all. Other than the income she derived from it, the family business never interested her. Books were Tally's thing, so that put her off becoming a bibliophile. But even on a personal level, I know she's been a great disappointment to Jasper,' Herrick said. 'He confided that to me years ago.'

'How long have you known Jasper Hunt?'

'My goodness. Half my life, I suppose. It's a small world we collectors live in. Very few of us with the means to indulge ourselves in this market. Jasper used to keep a flat in London, where I have a house. He was always there for the big sales and auctions. I learned a lot from him, from the time when I was just an eager young man. Jasper Hunt had a brilliant eye.'

'When did you first meet Tally and Minerva?' Mike asked.

'I think they were both still at university. Tally at Oxford, where his father had done a year as well. The old man had his eye on me for Minerva,' Herrick said, shaking his head at the thought. 'He introduced me to her one weekend. She was in her first year at Bryn Mawr then.'

'So you dated?' Mike asked.

'Heavens, no. I was already engaged at the time. You've met her, haven't you?'

'Yes, briefly.'

'Tough as nails, is that what you Americans say? I don't know about you, Detective,' Herrick said, smiling at Mike, 'but I like my women a bit softer.'

'I'll drink to that,' Mike said, winking at me. 'Fragile. Almost vulnerable.'

'Indeed.'

'Did you see Tina this week, after your return?'

'She was here on Monday,' Herrick said. 'She was working upstairs in my study.'

'On what?' Mike asked.

'She finished her first big project for me—I let her audition on a piece of moderate value. And then she's been sorting through some of my recent acquisitions, trying to help me determine which items are candidates for restoration.'

'When did you talk with her next?'

Herrick put his right hand in the deep pocket of his sweater, lowered his head, and started to pace around the perimeter of the room.

'Not again,' he said. 'I haven't spoken to her since.'

'Were you concerned when she didn't show up yesterday?' Mike asked.

'Not at all. No. She wasn't supposed to come in. She was planning to spend the day at the library.

Tina was only working for me part-time. Due back today, actually.'

Herrick paused in front of one of the chapel's stained-glass windows. The tapered conical ceiling rose almost thirty feet over his head, and although he was a tall man, he seemed almost overwhelmed by the space of the once-hallowed room.

'Have you done anything to try to find her?'

'I should think, Mr. Chapman, that responsibility falls on you. I barely know the woman, and if she chooses to take a holiday as a result of the break-in that Jill Gibson described to me, there'll be plenty of work for her when she returns.'

'Mr. Herrick,' I said, standing to approach him, 'what does Tina Barr have to do with Minerva Hunt?'

'I haven't any idea, to be honest with you. Tina told me she'd met Minerva at Jasper's home. The woman frightened her, quite frankly. I told Tina that she frightens lots of people.'

'You've done business with Minerva?'

'I'd hardly describe it as business. Every now and then she goes after something I'm keen on. She's got in my way from time to time. Nothing serious, mind you.'

'But I thought you said she doesn't collect?' I said.

'Not books, Ms. Cooper,' Herrick said, doubling back to the fireplace, crossing in front of it, pausing beside an enormous wooden stand, almost as tall as he, in which an antique globe was mounted. 'Maps. Minerva Hunt likes to dabble in rare maps.'

'Like you.'

'I'm not a dabbler, Detective. With me, it's a passion,' Herrick said. 'I'm trying too hard to point out the differences between us, that's true. There's nothing scholarly about my interests. They're purely visual. Very different from book collecting, I can assure you. I just go after the best-looking things.'

His self-deprecating comment was meant to belittle Minerva Hunt.

'You've got hundreds of books here, too,' Mike said, pointing up to the balcony from which we'd descended on our way in.

'Atlases mostly,' Herrick said. 'You can circumnavigate the globe with those books, Mr. Chapman.'

'Did Jill Gibson tell you about the murder in Tina's apartment last night?' I asked.

'She did. She called me a little while ago. Minerva's maid, was it? Carrying one of Tally's books. Something like that. I'm just glad Tina wasn't at home when the bastard got there. Looking for something valuable, no doubt. How did the woman die?'

'Fractured skull, Mr. Herrick,' Mike said. 'Split her head in half and crushed her brain. No use for the patron saint of the suffering, 'cause she didn't suffer very long.'

Herrick didn't react. 'You think the killer knows Tina Barr?'

'I don't know anything about him at this point, who he knew or what he wanted. Only that he was at least your height, 'cause the woman was tall, and the blow that took her down struck the crown of her head.'

'Heavens, Detective. The world is full of people

as tall as I am. Even Minerva Hunt fits the bill.'

'I'd say you'd need a pair of strong arms to heave that thing,' Mike said. 'I think Minerva would be afraid she'd ruin her manicure.'

Mike was baiting his subject, trying to get a rise out of him.

Alger Herrick took his hands out of his sweater pockets. There was a glint of metal against the dark wooden globe as he reached to spin it. The oceans and continents began to whirl around on the solid wooden stand, and I could see that where his left hand should have been there was only a single hook.

CHAPTER THIRTEEN

'Did I startle you, Mr. Chapman?' Herrick asked. 'I don't want you putting me at the scene of the crime without getting to know me a little better.'

'You called me on that one, sir. I'm sorry if I was rude.'

'Just obvious, Detective. I was born without a hand—a defect the doctors assume was caused by the medication my mother was taking during pregnancy. I'm used to people's stares and gasps. I've got a modern prosthesis I wear when I'm out, in case you're wondering. But this is what I had when I was growing up, and it suits me fine. Now what were we discussing?'

'Mike and I are trying to get to know the world that Tina Barr moved in,' I said. 'It's hard to imagine that books and maps, and the quiet reading rooms of the public library, would expose her to danger, but the two attacks this week took place in her apartment. Perhaps you could tell us about some of the people she worked with. You, Mr. Herrick, tell us about yourself.'

Herrick crossed the center of the long room and seated himself at a desk near my chair. I wanted to understand Tina Barr, and if my appeal to his vanity guided me to learn about things in which she had immersed herself, it would be time well spent.

'I don't like talking about myself, Ms. Cooper, but I can tell you all you want to know about these beautiful things,' he said, sweeping his good arm around in a circle.

'When did you start collecting?'

'My life has been a matter of great good luck, after a very bumpy start,' Herrick said. 'I was deposited on the steps of an orphanage in Oxfordshire, or so I'm told, by a single mother— a teenager herself—who must have been overwhelmed at the prospect of taking care of a child as handicapped as she thought I would be. I don't remember anything about that part of my life, so you needn't imagine all sorts of stories about eating gruel and being forced to pick pockets as a child. Shortly before my fourth birthday, I was adopted by the Herricks, a local family who had lost their only son to polio about five years earlier.

'My adoptive father, Charles, was a wonderfully kind man, a barrister who made a respectable living. They gave me a loving home, and an introduction to material comforts.'

'I wouldn't think many barristers could afford these digs,' Mike said.

'About the time I was a teenager, my father

came into a large inheritance, Mr. Chapman. You know about primogeniture, of course. He was the third son of a third son and so on. But when his uncle died without any heirs—his uncle Algernon, in fact, for whom I was named when they adopted me—the old fellow left most of his estate, including his home and his library, to my father. Hence to me.'

'I like stories with happy endings.'

'So do I, Detective, so do I. And yes, I've tried to make a contribution of my own. If Jill hasn't told you, I've been a member of the Council of the Stock Exchange. Investments and such. Very lucky indeed,' Herrick said. 'Have either of you ever heard of Lord Wardington?'

'No, no, I haven't,' I said.

'He was a mentor of my father's, known to everyone as Bic. His family had built a spectacular library over several centuries, and he himself amassed the greatest collection of atlases in England. I used to spend hours at Wardington Manor as a child. I was painfully shy—because of this,' Herrick said, examining his hook as he spoke. 'So I was more than happy to spend my time in the silence of the great reading room there.'

'That's easy to understand.'

'Bic was incredibly generous to me. He saw that I loved old books—I loved smelling them and touching the rich Moroccan leather. There were early English Bibles and Shakespeare Folios, incredibly fine incunabula—'

'What's that?' Mike asked.

'Books from the infancy of printing, Detective. From before 1500. The books were my friends— my only friends, in fact, for a long time—but it was

116

maps that fascinated me the most. My father had a pair of globes. Not as fine as this one, but they were brightly colored and they towered above me, and I never tired of making them spin.

'And it was at Wardington Manor that I discovered atlases,' he went on. 'Bic continued the tradition of acquiring books for the family library, but he became obsessed, much as I have, with maps.'

'Why is that?' I asked. 'They're quite beautiful, but what makes them so special to collectors?'

Herrick opened the oversize leather-bound book in front of him and turned to look at the pages he had selected. 'Think of how the ancients must have imagined the world, Ms. Cooper, long before most of them were ever able to travel it, to take measure of it in their journeys. There have been maps as long as there have been walls or vellum on which to write and draw. Who was the first man to give us a mathematical picture of the universe? Do you know?'

Both Mike and I shook our heads.

'Ptolemy, of course, in his *Cosmographia,* which was based on voyages and itineraries of early travelers, and on their fantasies as well. About AD 150. His was the first account to locate places in terms of longitude and latitude. For hundreds of years afterward, monks and madmen all over Europe were able to draw maps of what they believed to be the world.'

'Where's Mercer when we need him?' Mike said.

'Excuse me?'

'We've got a friend named Mercer Wallace whose father was a mechanic at LaGuardia

117

Airport,' Mike said. 'Has a thing for maps, too, only not rare ones. His dad used to hang all the airline routes on the walls in Mercer's room when he was a kid, teaching him about faraway places. So he also grew up on maps. Bet he'd love to hear this.'

'Then you must bring him with you next time,' Herrick said, smoothing the page and running his forefinger over the outline of the northern coast of Africa. 'Everything changed with the invention of the printing press, of course. Imagine the amazement of people seeing printed maps for the first time.'

Herrick prodded the book with his hook to swivel it around, allowing us to see the two-page illustration, colored in red and green inks, the seas a pale blue, with odd-looking creatures lurking on the corners.

'This is Ptolemy's Atlas. The very first one ever printed, Ms. Cooper. Presented in Bologna in 1477.'

The images were breathtaking in their complexity and surprising in their accuracy depicting the landmasses bordering the Mediterranean.

'Twenty-six maps in the volume, done with double-page copperplate engravings, and then hand-colored. Taddeo Crivelli's work—he was a genius. There are only thirty-one copies of this atlas in the world, and only two in private hands. Go ahead, touch it. I promise it won't bite.'

Mike reached over me to feel the paper. He lifted the page and studied the image on the underside before sitting back.

'Did that say anything to you, Mr. Chapman?'

'Like what?'

'Like whether what I'm telling you is true? I'm teasing you, Detective, but Tina Barr is skilled enough to call my bluff on that. The real Bologna Ptolemy that I own is in England under lock and key. That one's worth more than a million pounds. I bought it at Sotheby's, when Lord Wardington sold most of his collection a few years ago. This is a much later edition—you'll even find America in here—and it's damaged by those small wormholes and some tears in its margin. Hasn't nearly a fraction of the value of the Bologna printings. The green coloring has seeped through the paper, as sixteenth-century green often does.'

'I'll give you a hundred bucks for it,' Mike said, smiling.

'I'm afraid you'd be fifty thousand pounds short.' Herrick smiled. 'You must understand that with the Age of Discovery, Detective, came an explosion of new information. Sea monsters disappeared from the edges of the ocean and distant places began to take on more precise shapes. California is discovered, as you see in these subsequent volumes. For two hundred years—to the European mind—it was drawn as an island. Brilliant to watch the history of the world unfold through these documents. There was a military purpose to them, too.'

'That must have been critical,' Mike said.

'Usually a hanging offense for a merchant or soldier to share a country's maps with a foreign power. That handsome example on the wall that you were admiring earlier,' Herrick said to me, 'is the *Neptune François*, a collection of sea atlases commissioned by Louis XIV to give the French navy an important advantage over the British. Meticulous engravings they were—all about navigation—so soundings and rhumb lines and the markings for every little coastal port were of major importance.'

'Did it help the French in battle?'

'Well, it would have, Mr. Chapman, if the charts hadn't been copied quite so quickly by the Dutch and distributed abroad. With the advent of printing, scholars of every nation were able to compare and revise, leading to a considerable advance in geographical knowledge.'

'Help me understand,' I asked. 'What's more valuable? The individual maps, like those hung on the walls here, or the bound atlases?'

'Ah, now you've hit on a point of contention. Scratch the surface of this and you'll find real scoundrels, Ms. Cooper.'

I was looking for a stronger word to describe our perp, but I'd settle for some direction instead.

'Unlike rare books,' Herrick said, 'maps were not greatly prized by collectors until thirty or forty years ago. Lord Wardington's a perfect example. The family amassed books for generations, going back over four hundred years. He focused his attention on maps and created what was indisputably the world's best private collection in the last four decades.'

'Why the disparity?'

Herrick pursed his lips and frowned. 'Individual maps—the kind that sailors and traders and explorers used every day—were just utilitarian pieces of paper. Not many were considered works of art, with elaborate decorations and fine calligraphy—the kind that wind up bound in atlases. They were essentially untethered documents to be used in their own time—not carefully maintained, without any record of their provenance—just meant to get the traveler or the sailor from one place to another.

'The better maps wound up in books—printed, then hand-colored, and bound in all of the wonderful ways you see in collections. They were only sold separately when the books were damaged. You want to point a finger at the enemy?' he said, chuckling softly. 'It's the modern dealers.'

'Dealers?' I asked.

'They're the atlas-breakers. They're the ones who manipulate the market, trying to keep up with old-fashioned supply and demand.'

'What's an atlas-breaker?'

'Remember I told you that this was a purely visual passion, not a scholarly one?' Herrick said. 'The desirability of old maps—out of books and on the walls—was strictly a result of the fact that fashionable interior designers discovered how attractive they are, back in the 1970s and '80s. English country style, if you will. The maps became more highly sought after than the books that held them, so dealers started hoarding the atlases and dismembering them. Taking the maps out and selling them separately was far more profitable than finding one buyer for the whole book.'

'Are there many of these dealers around New York?' Mike asked.

'You're both too young to have known Book Row,' Herrick said. 'Fourth Avenue, between Union Square and Astor Place, was a bibliophile's paradise for almost a hundred years. All that's left of it these days is the Strand. So, in fact, there are only a handful of serious dealers at this point, working in the price range we're talking about. I can tell you exactly who they are, if that's what you need.'

'I think what we need is to figure out where Tina Barr fits in this picture,' I said. 'What kind of person is she?'

'I can't help you there. I only know her professionally. She's incredibly well trained and has a great eye for detail. That's one she finished for me just last week.'

I walked to the wall between two tall windows and studied the minuscule calligraphy on another exquisitely rendered old map.

'Saxton's cartographic survey of England and Wales,' Herrick said, 'commissioned by Elizabeth the First.'

'Is Tina capable of reproducing something as beautiful as this?'

'These days, Ms. Cooper, digital processing would make it possible for almost anyone to reproduce documents such as that one.'

'I mean, a copy good enough to fool—well, to fool a dealer or a collector.'

'Are you talking about a forgery? Heavens, no, Ms. Cooper. To begin with, one would have to have the proper vellum, which would be pretty difficult to come by these days. The best quality vellum was made from the skins of unborn animals. In England, you know, we still print our Acts of Parliament on it, but you'll never find something that could be dated and matched to the original. On top of that, she'd have to be a first-rate artist, not just a meticulous restorer. Then I'd

122

say we'd need to give her three or four years to work on it.'

'What is it that Tina did on the map you started her with?'

'Minor repairs, mostly. Decades ago, when maps were mounted for display—like this one was, in Hampton Court—they were first backed with muslin. The glue that held it in place was very destructive. So Tina removed the backing, cleaned up the tears and discoloration, and deacidified it.'

'Where did she do the work?'

'There's a state-of-the-art facility in the public library—the Goldsmith Conservation Laboratory. She did it there.'

'Are you on the board of the library?' Mike asked.

'No, Mr. Chapman, but I make handsome contributions. You'll find I'm quite welcome there.'

'You must have a system for doing background checks on your employees,' I said. 'I assume you don't just meet a conservator and invite him in with free access to possessions as valuable as yours.'

Herrick stood up and leaned against the desk. 'There's a very serious vetting process, and Tina passed with flying colors. I never considered her a security risk.'

'There are people at the library who think she—'

'People at the library should take their heads out of their books and stop pointing fingers at the worker bees. Every time there's been a major problem, it's a trustee or a donor who was responsible.'

'What do you mean?' I asked.

123

'All the new money on the board—hedge fund managers and the like who think that if they splash enough cash around they can buy themselves some instant class—it's created considerable tension at the library. There's a man called Jonah Krauss waiting like a vulture for that last great dame to die—the one before Brooke Astor—so he can sell some of her collection.'

Mike was making notes of the names.

'And I can't think why they'd go after Tina Barr when the real map thief was paroled just a few months ago.'

'The *real* map thief?' I asked.

'Eddy Forbes, Ms. Cooper. The chap Minerva Hunt was in bed with,' Herrick said. 'I don't mean that literally, but I don't doubt for a minute that she subsidized his travels.'

'What travels?'

'Eddy Forbes flooded the market with stolen goods, Detective. Some of the finest maps the world has ever seen, stolen right from under the noses of all the brass at the public library, on Jill Gibson's watch at the Beinecke, from the Boston Library, the British Reading Room, the Hague— shall I go on or do you get my point?'

'How did Forbes get access to all those collections?'

'He was a dealer, of course. A dealer, a scholar—so he liked to think—and a complete fraud. It's always the inner circle, Ms. Cooper. That's where you've got to look, not at the earnest young worker bees.'

'I don't understand,' Mike said, reaching out to touch the four folio-size volumes stacked on Herrick's desk. 'How does the librarian, or the

124

security guard let you get out the door? You walk out of a library and nobody notices you're carrying these great big books in their fancy leather jackets with shiny gold lettering? Maybe once you could fit one in a shopping bag, but most of these are even too large for that.'

Herrick opened the desk drawer again and removed a small object with his right hand. He rested it on the blotter and closed the finely tooled cover of his sixteenth-century copy of *Cosmographia*. Then he reached for an even larger black leather-bound book with gold lettering on its spine.

'No need to wince, Ms. Cooper,' Herrick said, holding up an X-Acto knife—a short, sharp blade mounted on a metal body the size of a pen. 'I'm not going to cut anyone's throat.'

With a single swipe, he ran the blade down the length of the page, separating it from the binding of the book. He rolled it up and slipped it through the cuff of his sweater.

'Don't fret, either. This book was already disemboweled by one of the thieves before I bid on it. Here's the rub, Detective. Steal a single page from a first folio of Shakespeare and you walk away with nothing of value. An interesting sheet of paper, perhaps, but of no value in the marketplace without the entire folio.'

Herrick held up his arms, as if in triumph for making the page disappear. 'But slip just one sheet like this up your sleeve—a single map, say, from John Smith's great atlas of Colonial America—and you walk out of the library with a ready-to-sell, largely untraceable treasure worth hundreds of thousands of dollars.'

125

CHAPTER FOURTEEN

'Much less punishing than my last encounter with the police,' Alger Herrick said as he led us up the staircase to the elevator.

I turned my head to look at Mike. 'And what was that?'

'I was on my way to the country from London a few years ago, after a spectacular score I made at auction. Mercator's atlas—1595. The first book in the history of the world to be called an atlas, in fact,' Herrick said. 'My wife took me out to dinner to celebrate, and I'm afraid I should have known better than to drive.'

'Wind up in the hoosegow?' Mike asked. He dismissed my concern with a smirk.

'No incarceration, Detective. Had my license taken away for a few months, plus a hefty fine, but not as hefty as the purchase I'd just made,' Herrick said, opening the door to the elevator. 'If I can be of help with any introductions, I'd be happy to do that. I'm hoping Tina will calm down and come back to work before too long.'

'We'd like very much to find her,' I said. 'Thanks for your time.'

'Pleasure.'

Mike made small talk on the way down in the elevator, waiting to get away from the building's workers before he asked me about Herrick. 'I don't know about you, but I'd still bet there's enough grit in that guy's upper crust that he could swing our murder weapon or just about anything else.'

'You just don't like him because he doesn't

share your affection for Minerva.'

'We've got to get back on her dance card, don't you think? Fill in some blanks.'

'Tomorrow morning when I get to the office, I'll sit down with McKinney and stroke him. You've got to talk to all the Hunts—Minerva, Tally, Jasper. As long as I make Pat feel like he's in charge, I'm sure he'll let me go along with you. See what you can schedule.'

'Did you open a grand jury investigation on Barr today?'

'Yes,' I said. 'Right before lunch. Laura's typed up subpoenas for her cell phone records, credit card—anything to tell us if Tina's on the move. It's sad that she doesn't really have a network of any kind.'

'All that freelance work—some of it in the library and a lot of it at either Jasper Hunt's home or Herrick's—so it wasn't like she was in a setting where somebody would be concerned during the first day or two if she didn't show up.'

'You think there's any point in talking to the guys at Missing Persons again? Don't you think it would help to get her photo out on the news?'

'Catch-22. Tina Barr's an adult, for one thing. With no signs of foul play after she walked away from the ambulance, you got the forty-eight-hour rule,' Mike said. 'Nobody's complained that she's missing, Coop.'

It was well known in law enforcement that the overwhelming number of adults who vanish without any indication of criminal activity do so voluntarily.

'We're just going on forty-eight hours now. Maybe I can push Battaglia to leak her disappearance to the press. Think that's the way to go?'

'Start making your lists of things to do, kid. We'll find her,' Mike said, unlocking the car. 'I'll drop you off at your place.'

'You don't have an extra ticket for tonight? Can't sneak me in?'

He started the ignition and grinned at me. 'Who squealed?'

'Vickee called. Told me Mercer snagged four seats right behind third base.' The Yankees had won two out of three games in the division playoff series and were back at the stadium tonight, looking to clinch. 'I'm insanely jealous.'

'He's invited Ned and Al,' Mike said, referring to two of my favorite detectives from the Special Victims Unit. 'And I'm his date. Sorry to disappoint you.'

'Then you might as well scoot me home,' I said. 'It's after four-thirty.'

'I'm psyched. Haven't been to a game since July. We make it to the pennant, your pal Joan is going to collect on my promise. Told her last year I'd take her.'

My best girlfriends—in the office and apart from it—all adored Mike and had gotten to know him well over the years. They liked his intelligence and his humor, too, but mostly appreciated the way he covered my back in every conceivable circumstance.

Nina Baum and Joan Stafford were my two closest confidantes, lifelong buddies with whom I'd been through every triumph and tragedy. Nina, my college roommate, lived on the West Coast with her husband and son, while Joan and her husband split their time between New York and Washington, D.C.

'Joanie's in town. I'll be watching at her place tonight,' I said as we went through the underpass in Central Park. 'She'll never let you welsh on that one, so you'd best get on that advance ticket line at the crack of dawn. And count me in on that round.'

'Deal.'

By the time we made a rough plan about our approach to the witnesses we needed to interview, we were less than a block from my apartment.

'I'll jump out here, Mike. I need to stop at the cash machine and pick up some groceries.'

'Call you in the morning,' he said, pulling over to the curb.

'Only if we win. If you don't pull the Yankees through tonight, I may hand you back over to McKinney.'

He whelped at me once as he drove away, and the coven of little old ladies on the corner of the street turned to stare.

I did some errands and walked another block to my apartment, enjoying the opportunity to be at home much earlier than was usual. Neither of the doormen stepped out to greet me as I approached, but one of the porters came running from the mail room when he heard my footsteps. 'Sorry, Ms. Cooper. Need a hand?'

'I'm fine, thanks. Where's Vinny?' I said, walking to the elevator.

'He's on meal and Oscar went home sick. I'm trying to cover, but it's been crazy busy.'

When the elevator reached the lobby, I pressed twenty and rummaged through my tote for my keychain, replaying the information that had unfolded throughout the day.

If Billy Schultz was telling the truth about recognizing Minerva Hunt, why had she been to Tina Barr's apartment on other occasions? Was it weird, or was it just natural curiosity that led him to pick up the mask that the perpetrator had worn—if he had not in fact been the masked intruder?

I turned the key in the lock and went inside, flipping on the foyer light. I left the bag with the orange juice and English muffins next to the credenza and started down the hallway toward the linen closet with the cosmetics I'd bought at the drugstore.

The bedroom door ahead of me was closed. In a split second I reminded myself that it was Thursday and that my housekeeper had not been in today. I was sure I had left the door open, as always, and I slowed my pace.

I heard noise from within—a sound like the closing of a dresser drawer. I began to back up, wondering for how long the building's entrance had been unsecured this afternoon, and whether someone who didn't belong here had gotten inside. My thoughts flashed to members of the Latin Princes gang, whose leader I had successfully prosecuted, and who had stalked me relentlessly during the summer.

I scrambled to retrace my steps to the front door, and as I turned, the long strap of my tote caught on the door handle of the guest bedroom. The contents dumped out as I bent to unhook it, and the drugstore purchases scattered onto the floor.

I let go of everything and dashed to the foyer. I

130

could hear the bedroom door opening and my adrenaline kicked in as I ran faster. In that short sprint, I was breathing as rapidly as if I'd completed a 5K race. I pulled on the doorknob just as I heard the man's voice.

'Alexandra? *C'est toi?'*

I exhaled and steadied myself against the door, throwing my head back, thinking how unnerved I'd been by the thought of an intruder.

'Have I upset you, *mon ange*? This was meant to be such a great surprise,' Luc Rouget said as he stepped over the packages to make his way toward me, wearing only the towel that was draped around his waist. 'Are you all right, Alex?'

I nodded and smiled. He wrapped me in an embrace and I held on to him with all my strength.

CHAPTER FIFTEEN

We were still in bed together nearly an hour later, Luc cradling me in his long, slender arms, laughing about the fact that Joan Stafford's wonderful plan to help him surprise me had almost backfired.

'I'm telling you, we both thought it was foolproof,' Luc said. 'I had to be in Washington last night to meet with some investors, so we took the shuttle up together today and had lunch around the corner at Swifty's. So perfectly American, that place. Then Joan brought me up here to settle me in. *Faites comme chez vous,* she told me, and so I did.'

Joan and I had always had keys to each other's apartments, and the doormen knew her as well as they knew my parents and brothers.

'I'm delighted you made yourself at home,' I said, kissing the tip of his nose.

'We did all the shopping at Grace's Marketplace so that I could fix you a delicious dinner by the time you got here from the office. But Joanie said you never, never get out before seven, eight o'clock. *Jamais, jamais.*'

'I rarely do. But we were working on an investigation uptown, not far from here. I've had a few late nights this week, so it was a treat to be early. I don't know why I was so jumpy.'

Luc brushed back the curls from around my forehead and kissed me on the mouth, long and tenderly. 'Are you feeling better now?'

'Like a different person.'

'I don't want you to be someone else, Alexandra. I made love to you, not to any other woman.'

'I'm not the least bit confused about that,' I said, rolling onto my side to sit up.

'Because if you are, then I'm happy to try to remind you.' Luc reached up and playfully pulled me down beside him. He ran his finger slowly down my spine, then along the back of my leg, kissing the crook of my knee. 'Looks exactly like you, feels exactly like you, and tastes deliciously the same as you did last time.'

'I might taste even better after I clean up.'

'Take one of your luxurious bubble baths, darling. I'm going to start preparing dinner.'

'Will I be the guinea pig for any new tastings?'

Luc's father, Andre Rouget, was a great French restaurateur who'd changed the culinary scene in New York City when he founded Lutèce in a

132

townhouse on the East Side. Luc had followed in his father's footsteps in a French village called Mougins, where his elegant four-star restaurant was a destination for locals and travelers in the south of France. He'd been courted by several backers to reopen Lutèce and restore the reputation of the famous eatery, and was making frequent trips to America to move the plan forward.

'No, no. I've had my nose in so many French menus these last few weeks that I decided to cook Italian tonight. *Ça va?*'

'*Ça va bien.* Anything I can do to help?'

'In the kitchen?' Luc asked. 'Then I would really be concerned I was with an imposter. You just relax, Alexandra. I don't need a sous-chef; I need a hungry woman.'

I went into the bathroom and ran the hot water, sprinkling in bath salts that I'd brought back from Paris.

The relationship with Luc had no emotional complications. He was mature at forty-eight and quite direct. Divorced after fifteen years of marriage to an unfaithful woman, Luc was devoted to the two children whose custody he shared with his ex. I liked that about him, and looked forward to meeting the boys he so adored.

The only issue that nagged at me as I found myself falling in love was what Nina teasingly referred to as his 'GU'—the geographic undesirability of his faraway home. Luc's spending so much time in the States as he explored his new business venture made it easy for me to stay focused between his visits, but the reality was that most of the time we were separated by an ocean

133

and the craggy foothills of the Maritime Alps.

When I finished bathing, I pulled on a pair of leggings and a five-year-old navy blue sweatshirt with Jeter's name and number 2 on the back. If I couldn't be at the Yankee game, at least I could carry the colors. I swept my hair into a ponytail and dabbed Luc's favorite perfume behind my ears and on my throat.

The telephone rang as I was about to leave my bedroom. Luc came toward me from the kitchen. 'You want me to answer?'

'I'm just screening,' I said. 'I'm hoping it's not business.'

It took most of the guys I dated a while to understand that whenever senior prosecutors were working investigations, phones and beepers went beyond the boundaries of eight-hour workdays.

'I'm at the stadium, Coop.' Mike's voice talking to my answering machine jolted me as though he had just stepped into the bedroom between Luc and me. 'Can't find a frigging television anywhere. If you haven't left for Joan's yet, be sure you catch *Jeopardy!* for us. I'll speak to you tomorrow.'

I took Luc's glasses off the bridge of his nose and kissed his forehead.

'Ah, that's one of your detective friends, *non*? You and Joan have talked about him. He calls about this trivia game, too?'

I continued down the hallway toward the kitchen, changing the subject. 'The sauce smells fabulous. What is it?'

'He's the one Joanie told me—how do you say?—has a crush on you.'

'We've been friends since my rookie year in the office. I think he'd laugh out loud at that

134

suggestion.'

'I'd like to meet these guys who get to spend so much time with you,' Luc said, reaching around me, as he kissed the nape of my neck, to put out the wineglasses.

'Next time you're here we can do that,' I said, dreading the thought of my favorite alpha-dog detective going head-to-head with my very confident French lover. 'That way maybe I can get an actual arrival date from you.'

Luc turned me around and pulled me in, kissing me again and again. 'So much for my surprise.'

I wrapped my arms around his slim shoulders and kissed him back. 'I love your surprise. I'm very happy tonight.'

'Then I'll let you in on my schedule. On Saturday I fly to San Francisco. I've got meetings in Napa and Sonoma, with vintners. Then to Los Angeles, Houston, Atlanta—'

'Food tastings everywhere?'

'Poor me, right? And then I'm back here in about ten days. You think you can get away for a weekend on Martha's Vineyard? You tend to the fireplace and I'll keep you well fed.'

Luc didn't want to hear that my answer depended on the progress of the investigation.

'That gives me something to dream about.'

He took me by the hand and led me back to the kitchen. 'I know this isn't your forte, but I'm going to give you this wooden spoon and have you stir for me while I check on the chicken.'

'I didn't think you trusted me enough to let me near one of your creations.'

'I've got a lot riding on this dish, Alexandra. You know puttanesca sauce?' Luc asked. 'Named for the Neapolitan ladies of the night. Legend has it that when these women brought home sailors to entertain, this recipe was used as an aphrodisiac.'

'Then I'll stir more vigorously,' I said.

Over dinner, I told Luc some of the details of the case. He had used his warmth and charm, ever since we met months earlier, to get me to open myself to him.

'You're not drinking,' he said. 'Won't you have some wine?'

'I'm so tired after this crazy week we've had. Just these few sips are enough.'

'How's my sauce working?'

I rubbed my stomach and nodded. 'Those girls in Naples knew exactly what they were doing.'

Luc stood up and blew out the candles. 'I think I know what I'd like for dessert.'

I led the way back to the bedroom and we undressed as though we'd been apart for weeks, making love again before falling asleep in each other's arms.

When the telephone rang, I could see the time on the clock radio next to my bed. It was after one in the morning and I grabbed the receiver before the second ring.

'Sorry to wake you, Coop.'

'That's all right. I fell asleep early.'

'Before we gave up the grand slam in the top of the eighth, I hope.'

'Yeah,' I said, sitting up to get my bearings, knowing that Mike wouldn't be calling at this hour unless there was a break of some kind in the case. 'I was exhausted.'

'I got worse news than the loss, kid,' Mike said. 'Tina Barr is dead.'

136

Luc grabbed my hand and squeezed it when he heard me groan.

'They found her body wrapped up in a tarp, just off Sixth Avenue, inside Bryant Park.' That was less than a city block away from the rear door of the New York Public Library. 'She's been dead for at least twenty-four hours, Coop. Looks like a dump job.'

CHAPTER SIXTEEN

Crowds lined the sidewalk at the intersection of Sixth Avenue and Forty-second Street, even though it was two o'clock in the morning. The uniformed cops who had picked me up at my apartment muscled through the onlookers and lifted the yellow police tape that kept them out of the park so we could duck under it.

Huge bright floodlights were mounted on a metal catwalk that framed an enormous JumboTron screen. Below the massive structure, dozens of NYPD men and women were still scrambling to secure the perimeter of the crime scene and push back the cameramen who were trying to climb the low wall to photograph the activity.

'Over here, Alex,' Mercer called out. 'Watch your step.'

The old cobblestone-and-gravel path was littered with debris, and on both sides of it there were tall stacks of folding chairs and wheeled pallets loaded with objects covered with canvas and strapped in place. Fall plantings had been trampled and expensive landscaping would have to be restored.

'Tina?'

'Body's there,' Mercer said, pointing to the far side of the plaza beyond the metal superstructure that framed the screen. 'The ME got here fifteen minutes ago. She'll finish up soon.'

'What's all this?' I asked, looking around at the equipment that cluttered the twin promenades of the beautifully landscaped park that ran the length of a football field.

'There was an event here last evening. One of the mayor's goodwill gestures,' Mercer said. 'Had the JumboTron put up yesterday, and bused in Scout troops—a few thousand kids—from all over the city to see the game. Free. Everybody was pretty orderly when it broke up at the end, and then the workmen started to take the place apart.'

I followed him to the edge of the walkway, staring off at the group of cops who were standing shoulder to shoulder, holding up sheets around what was obviously the body of Tina Barr.

'That's when someone found her?'

'Yeah. Her body was wrapped in one of these tarps, just like all the other gear they were about to load up and move out of here.'

'Do you think she was—?'

'Fully clothed. Doesn't look like a sexual assault, Alex.'

I could see the medical examiner, a short, plump woman with dark skin, emerge from behind the sheeting that had given her some privacy to examine the body. Mercer led me in her direction.

'Detective Wallace, Ms. Cooper,' the doctor greeted us as she pulled off her gloves and handed

138

them to her assistant. 'Not exactly the best conditions for what I've had to do, but if you'd like to step into my temporary office, you can see what the young lady looks like for yourselves.'

Mike was kneeling beside the body of Tina Barr, studying her face. He didn't move when Mercer and I came inside the makeshift morgue.

'As you can see, Ms. Cooper, the killer slit her throat.'

Dr. Assif delivered her preliminary clinical findings in a flat monotone. The detective standing behind Tina's head shone his flashlight on the corpse as she spoke.

'Butchered her,' Mike said, without picking up his head. 'Mercer, would you tell Hal Sherman I want some more photos?'

It was almost impossible to recognize the face of the woman I had talked with after the attack in her home a few nights ago. There was a long incision across her neck, and a deep wound that exposed layers of muscle beneath the skin. Her vacant eyes were open toward the night sky, and her mouth was agape.

'He's working on the tarp now. Crime Scene's trying to figure a way to move it downtown without losing anything,' Mercer said. 'He'll be right back.'

Barr's body was resting on a clean sheet that the ME's crew had brought with them. The tarp in which she'd been wrapped would be processed for clues.

'She must have bled buckets,' I said. There were dark stains all over the front of her short-sleeved V-neck sweater.

'Clothes are a mess,' Mike said. 'But there's nothing on the tarp.'

139

'Probably because she was killed a day or so before she was placed inside it,' Dr. Assif offered.

'Any other signs of a struggle?' I asked.

'I'll know more, of course, when we get her clothes off,' the doctor said. 'But it doesn't appear to be the case now. No other bruising on her arms or chest. No defensive injuries. I want you guys to bag her hands before she's moved, but I don't see any broken fingernails either.'

'How is that possible?'

'Let me examine the wound margins and pattern on the neck, Ms. Cooper. I'll have a better sense of whether I think she was attacked from behind, and what kind of weapon you're looking for.'

'Let me know if it's a small sharp blade, like an X-Acto knife,' Mike said.

I thought of Alger Herrick as he slit through the long page of the old book.

'Wouldn't you expect her to have time to fight her attacker, or at least to scream?' I couldn't think of a place in Manhattan so remote that no one would hear such a commotion.

'You're thinking of exsanguination,' Assif said. 'You're assuming that your victim bled to death— slowly. But a postmortem X-ray will tell me if the injury caused a fatal air embolism.'

Mike stood up. 'That would figure, Doc.'

'When one of the larger neck veins is penetrated,' the pathologist explained to me, 'air is sucked into the vessels because of the negative pressure in the veins. That air mixes with blood and instantly forms a foam, causing a valve lock in the ventricular chamber of the heart.'

'Then Tina may have gotten off a gasp or two, but the embolism brings on an extremely rapid collapse,' Mike said.

I listened to them talk about the sudden death that might have resulted from this slice across the victim's neck, but I couldn't take my eyes off the gruesome sight of her discolored, distorted face.

'The body's very well preserved,' Assif said. 'She must have been in a cool place, not exposed to the elements. No small animals or even insects.'

Hal Sherman, a longtime crime scene investigator, pulled back one of the sheets and stuck his head in. 'I thought I gave you everything you need, Chapman. Hey, Alex—that's a pretty mean cut, isn't it?'

'Take a few straight over her head, will you?' Mike asked. 'I want to check her pockets, so stand by.'

Hal was ready with his camera and flash. He moved in over Tina Barr's body and focused his lens on her face and neck while Dr. Assif backed out of the way.

'Did the guys in the office check the weather service for you, Mercer?' Mike asked. 'What time is sunrise?'

'Six-thirteen.'

'Then tell the lieutenant we need sixty, maybe eighty uniformed guys here at six-eleven this morning to walk a grid,' Mike said. 'I don't care where the commissioner pulls them from. They're going to have to eyeball every piece of equipment that moves out of here, talk to every single stagehand who set up this gig. Maybe looking in the grass for a knife or blade—anything sharp that could have done the job. Probably a complete waste of time, but it's got to be done.'

'You think Tina was dumped here before the

141

game?' I asked.

'Hard to know. The outside of the tarp was a mess. Footprints all over it. Could have been dumped here—wheeled over on one of these dollies—while the crew was busy unloading everything. The park must have looked like an anthill on fire, getting stuff in place for the game.'

Mike lifted the edge of Tina Barr's sweater and reached into her right pants pocket. There was nothing in his gloved hand when he removed it.

I kneeled down beside him.

'Jeez, Coop. What the hell did you do? Put a clove of garlic in your Chanel bottle?'

I covered my mouth with my hand. 'Sorry.'

'Something I don't know? You're being stalked by a vampire? At least you and Joanie had time for a good dinner,' Mike said, reaching across Tina's body into her other pocket. 'Here's something.'

He sat back on his heels and held up a small laminated tag on a long chain. 'It's her library ID—the original one,' Mike said. 'She must have been dying to get back in there to get a book.'

I stood up and turned away from the body. There was no point in trying to change Mike's ways, to discourage the black humor that got him through the relentlessly dark territory of his work.

'Maybe she was dying to get out,' I said.

He turned to look at me for the first time since I had arrived at the scene. 'Not a bad thought. Wouldn't have been a long haul to get her here, but where the hell could she have been inside that place that was so isolated? It's for scholars and students, for Chrissakes. Me, I think there's just some kind of symbolism in this. Somebody making a statement by dumping her right at the back door

142

of the library.'

Hal snapped close-ups of the tag, front and back, and Mike placed it in a paper bag to send to the lab. He went back into the woman's pocket, withdrew a folded slip of paper, and opened it to read.

'Hey, Coop. Isn't this a call slip?'

He lifted the small rectangular piece so that I could see it. 'Yes,' I said. 'It's got Tina's name on it and Tuesday's date.'

Mike lifted the corner and below it was a pink slip, then a yellow one, both attached at the end to the top paper. 'It's still in triplicate. Looks like she didn't submit it.'

'What book was she asking for?'

'*Alice's Adventures in Wonderland,* an 1866 edition. Mercer, you got a bag for this?' Mike asked. 'Maybe she realized her landlady, Minerva Hunt, really is a Mad Hatter.'

'Just a minute, Mike,' Hal Sherman said. 'There's some writing on the back.'

He took a photograph of the front of the slip, then Mike turned it over.

'What does it say?' I asked.

Hal bent over and started to read. ' "The evil that men do . . ." '

'That's all?' Mike said.

'Why? There should be more?'

' "The evil that men do lives after them," ' Mike said, picking up the paper after Hal took a picture of it, and getting to his feet. 'Finish it off, Coop.'

' "The good are oft interred with their bones." '

Mike winked at Hal. '*Julius Caesar,* Detective Sherman.'

'Quite the poet, Mikey,' Hal said, backing away

from Tina Barr. 'I'm impressed.'

'Coop knows her Shakespeare. I know my Roman generals.'

One of the cops holding up the sheets lowered a corner to tell Mike that the men were ready to put Tina Barr in a body bag and get her into the ambulance.

We all stood still, silent for a moment, saying our own goodbyes to the slain woman. Then Mike nodded at one of the officers, signaling for the morgue attendants to take her away.

As I moved to make room for the men, the quiet within our space was broken by the shrill ring of a cell phone. A second ring, and I realized the sound was coming from somewhere on Tina's body.

Mike kneeled again and slid his hand beneath her, pulling something from her rear pants pocket. 'You answer it, Coop. It's a woman they're expecting to hear,' he said, passing me the razor-thin phone eerily buzzing for its dead owner.

I flipped it open and muffled my voice with my hand, saying, 'Hello.'

The caller waited a few seconds, then disconnected. I could have sworn I heard him laugh before he did.

CHAPTER SEVENTEEN

I was waiting in the lobby of my building when Mike and Mercer pulled in the driveway just after seven a.m. that morning.

'Did you two get any sleep?' I asked, climbing into the back seat.

'Catnap on cots up at the squad,' Mercer said. 'How about you?'

'I rested.' No matter how many murder victims I had seen, it never got easier to find a peaceful zone that wasn't already inhabited by killers and cops.

'No whining, then, Coop,' Mike said. 'We got a long day ahead of us.'

'You never heard that girl whine, Mr. Chapman. Mind your mouth.'

I had been comforted to have Luc beside me when I got home several hours ago, holding me and not asking any questions once I told him the bare outline of what had happened. At six, I had gotten out of bed again to call Battaglia with the news, knowing that he would prefer to be awakened with information from me rather than learning it from a newspaper headline on his doorstep.

'What's first?' I asked.

'How about the New York Pubic Library?' Mike said. 'Thanks for giving me Jill Gibson's number. I phoned her after you left, to tell her about Tina. She agreed to be here early to have security let us in. Said we'd meet her at seven-thirty.'

Mercer opened the lid on a cardboard cup of black coffee and passed it to me as Mike pulled out of the driveway.

'Still no contact for Tina's mother?'

'The lieutenant is sending someone to the Mexican consulate first thing. See if they can smoke her out that way.'

'My paper hasn't been delivered yet. Is there a story?'

Mercer held up the *Times* and tabloids. 'Lucky for us, the body was found too late for the morning news. May give us a few hours' jump on talking to people.'

'I've got to get through to legal at the phone company. Let them know that subpoena I sent out covers the call that came in this morning,' I said. Tina Barr was dead, but her cell phone account was still live.

'Freaked me out when that sucker started to ring,' Mike said.

Mike got onto the drive in Central Park, looping around to the West Side and exiting on Central Park South. He cruised down Seventh Avenue, turning east onto Forty-second Street—the Deuce, in police parlance—and parked beside the corner entrance to Bryant Park.

The mild weather was a break for the cops. Plainclothes detectives were lined up along the balustrade on the western border of the park, doing one-on-one interviews with men who appeared to be from the JumboTron construction crew. Huge trucks bordered the avenue, waiting to be loaded with equipment that should have been taken off-site in the early hours of the morning, before Tina Barr's body was found.

We walked over and Mike listened in on ten minutes of an interview. 'This'll take all day. They're checking each guy's ID so they can run record checks. Getting them to re-create every minute of the setup and breakdown, whether there were any strangers lurking around,' he said, shaking his head. 'And the bus lanes will be tied up till midnight with these trucks stuck on the street.'

Commuters emerged from the corner subway station, confused to find the cheerful breakfast and sandwich kiosks within the park still shuttered and closed, cordoned off by police tape.

We started down the path toward the library building. The phalanx of uniformed cops that Mike had demanded were already in place, clustered in groups to search for anything that might provide a clue.

'Look at all the litter,' I said. Ice-cream wrappers and soda cans had been discarded by kids who had watched the ball game. 'I can't imagine any items of evidentiary value would survive the presence of the Scout troops.'

'Yeah, I wouldn't get my hopes up, Coop. Hair bags and hotheads,' Mike said. 'Looks like all the commish came up with on short notice to do the search are old-timers who never made it out of uniform and kids fresh from the academy. Cross your fingers.'

'They've found needles in bigger haystacks,' Mercer said.

'It's kind of ironic that whoever killed Barr left her here,' Mike said, stopping to stomp his foot on the ground. 'You know what's underneath this park?'

'No,' I said.

'Dead people. Nothing but dead people.'

'What do you mean?'

Bryant Park was a green oasis in the middle of one of the city's busiest commercial districts. Thousands of office workers in nearby skyscrapers escaped their buildings every day—until the middle of winter, when it was turned into a skating rink—to eat lunch, read books, meet friends, enjoy the carousel, and relax in the atmosphere of a French formal garden.

Mike turned and walked backward, sweeping his

hand around the park. 'During the Revolutionary War, this site was a killing field for Washington's troops when they fled the British after the Battle of Long Island.'

'Well, they're surely not below the park now,' I said.

'Listen to me, Coop. The whole feng shui of this place is death. After the war, the city made this ground a potter's field. Final resting place for the indigent and unbefriended. Dead folk down there, one on top of the other, I'm telling you.'

'I thought this place used to be the site of the reservoir,' Mercer said.

'No, no, no. The reservoir was right over where the library stands,' Mike said, pointing at the back of the elegant structure. 'This spot was the burial ground. I know there's dead people under here, Coop. It's a fact. The city decommissioned the potter's field in the 1850s to build a crystal palace for the first World's Fair. When that burnt down, they turned it into a park.

'When my old man came on the job—the 1970s—Bryant Park was one of the most treacherous places in Manhattan. Dope dealers ran the place, he used to tell me. All crime all the time.'

'Over here, Sarge,' a voice called out, and a hand went up in the air. The three of us stopped in our tracks.

'Whaddaya got?'

The young cop was wading through a bed of pachysandra. 'Used condoms. Do I pick 'em up?'

The sergeant's answer was drowned out by three other officers yelling that they had also found condoms. 'Everything goes to the lab.'

148

Mike continued walking east. 'Be prepared. Isn't that the Scouts' motto? Glad they came to the game with condoms. Maybe they were cross-pollinating with the Brownies while the Yankee bullpen was falling apart. Those techs are going to have their hands full, testing all the crap that turns up.'

At the end of the pathway, we found an exit onto Forty-second Street and left the park to elbow our way to the front of the library, which stretched down two long blocks. The midtown crossroads at the corner of Fifth Avenue was a hub of pedestrian and vehicular traffic.

'Is that Gibson?' Mike said.

I looked ahead and could see Jill, talking on her cell, as she paced below the statue of one of the two spectacular marble lions—iconic New York City landmarks—that stood on guard at the foot of the terraced steps of the great building.

I introduced her to Mike and Mercer, reminding her that Mike was the detective who had called her early that morning.

'I'm heartbroken about this, Alex. It's just unthinkable that someone could have done this to Tina. We were all so willing to help her, but I couldn't get her to come in,' Jill said, turning to lead us up the first tier of steps. 'I've called security. They're sending someone to the front door to open up.'

'You ought to put some mourning ribbons around the lions' necks,' Mike said, patting the large paw of the one to his right as he passed by it.

'You know their names, Mike?' Jill asked.

'I didn't know they had names.'

'During the Great Depression, Mayor

LaGuardia called them Patience and Fortitude. He felt those were the qualities New Yorkers needed to endure the hardships of the times.'

'The same traits will serve us well this week,' Mercer said.

Mercer was as quiet and steady as ever, knowing that we were moving deeper into a tangled thicket of characters and motives, that we had a series of crimes that would not be solved as quickly as Mike might like. Mike, on the other hand, was long on fortitude and short, as always, on patience.

We continued our climb, and I admired the stunning array of sculptures and reliefs—sphinxes, winged horses, allegorical figures, and literary inscriptions—that decorated the massive portico of the library. At the very top, we passed under one of the arches and waited at the front door for a worker to admit us.

Mike reached into his jacket pocket and removed some folded papers. 'This is a Xerox of the call slip that Tina had in her pocket when she was killed,' Mike said. 'The one I mentioned to you on the phone.'

Jill Gibson read the notations on the first piece of paper—Tina's name, the date, and the book she must have been about to request. On the second page was the partial quote that had been scrawled on the back of that slip.

Jill looked at them both again, just as the man inside opened the series of locks and pulled back the huge wood-and-glass door.

'Tina didn't write this,' Jill said. 'Someone made this call slip out in her name.'

'You mean one of the librarians?'

'Well, you saw the original, Mike. Was it made

150

out in pencil or in ink?'

'The front side, with her name and the book title, was done in ink. The notation on the back—see how faint it is here on the copy? That was written in pencil.'

'The librarians in the reading room don't allow ink in there. Most research libraries are like that. You can only use pencil,' Jill said. Her hand was trembling as she folded the slip in half. 'I know Tina's handwriting well, Detective. It's quite distinctive, whether in print or script. She didn't write that information on the call slip. And it's unlikely any of the librarians did, either. Certainly not in ink.'

Mike took the papers back and compared the two writing styles. I knew what he was thinking. We'd have to bring in another expert—someone familiar with the very unscientific field of handwriting analysis. One clue that seemed promising at two o'clock in the morning now created a new level of obfuscation.

'The second page—that quote on the back of the slip—that's Tina's writing,' Jill said. 'But she didn't fill out this form. We have several early editions of the Lewis Carroll work, all of them quite rare. Maybe another person asked her to make the request to see one of these books.'

Maybe someone who didn't want to be associated with the request filled out the call slip, counting on the fact that he—or she—could persuade Tina to deliver it and retrieve the book. Maybe it was the person who killed her.

151

CHAPTER EIGHTEEN

'Where are the books?' Mike asked. 'I don't see a frigging book in here.'

Mike, Mercer, and I were standing in the middle of Astor Hall, one of the most magnificent interior spaces in New York. Jill had gone off to find the chief security officer to ask him to guide us through the enormous building.

'It's not a lending library, Mike. It's a home for scholars to use, for research,' I said. 'Books have to be accessed through a formal system. They're not out on open shelves, and they never leave.'

'Unless they're stolen. So where the hell are they?'

'Upstairs, in carefully maintained private collections,' I said. 'And under your feet, in the stacks. You'll see.'

Mercer was walking around the great vaulted space. 'Looks like we've time-traveled back to inside a medieval castle.'

The great hall, dressed entirely in white marble, had a self-supporting vaulted ceiling that covered the space between the two broad staircases leading up to the second floor. Four giant torchères—also marble—stood sentry around the large, empty room.

'Did you see her hand shake?' I said, whispering so that my voice didn't echo throughout the hall.

'Jill's?' Mercer asked. 'I missed that.'

'When Battaglia and I were talking to her yesterday and McKinney jumped in, he referred to Tina Barr as a thief and a forger.'

'And you said Jill didn't seem to buy in to that.'

'Yes. But someone working in here must think so.'

'What's your point?' Mike asked, standing under one of the arches across the room.

I walked toward him so that I didn't have to shout. 'How can Jill say for sure that the writing on the call slip wasn't done by Tina?'

'You mean, if Tina was capable of forgery, maybe she intentionally wanted it to look like someone else wrote it out?'

'That's possible. Once she turned in the original slip, it would become the permanent record that the library would have for the request. That's who they'd look to if the book went missing.'

Mercer came up behind me. 'It's also possible Jill got the shakes 'cause she recognized the penmanship on the slip, Alex. Maybe it's given her an idea about who wrote it but she chose not to tell you just yet.'

We heard her approach on the marble staircase and stopped talking.

'Why don't you come this way?' Jill said, pausing halfway down.

We crossed the room, our footsteps echoing throughout the hall, and followed Jill as she turned and walked up to the second floor. At the top, a man about my height with a thick build was standing cross-armed, dressed in a drab green uniform.

'This is Yuri,' Jill said, introducing him to each of us. 'None of the security supervisors is here yet. He's one of our engineers, so just tell us what you'd like to see and we can get started.'

'Top to bottom,' Mike said. 'Entrances, exits,

153

any way in or out of this place.'

'Obviously,' Jill said, 'we've just come in the front door.'

'Is that how the public enters?'

'Most of the time, Detective. There's also a smaller entrance on the Forty-second Street side. Yuri,' she said, 'why don't we start upstairs and work our way down?'

'What's your security like?'

'Since September 11 it's been a lot tighter. Our doors open at ten most weekdays. Guards check bags on the way in and on the way out.'

'I saw two metal detectors at the door,' Mike said. 'They good enough to catch a thief with a razor blade or knife coming through?'

'So you know how the bad guys used to cut out the desirable pages?' Jill was a few steps ahead of us, with Yuri. 'A thing of the past, Mike. Between metal detectors and the arrest of a few major map thieves, those particular tools have become obsolete.'

Yuri was leading us up another flight of stairs.

'You mean people don't steal old prints or maps out of books anymore?'

'Sadly, the thefts go on. It's just that the methods change. The bad guys have moved on to dental floss.'

'Floss?'

'Try it, Detective. Wet some floss. Soak it for a while to stiffen it up. Keep it moist by balling it up inside your cheek when you get to the library. The thieves have found it just as effective for ripping out pages with exactly the same result. Takes about ten minutes to soften up the old paper by applying the floss to it, so it's a bit more nerve-racking than

154

the old-fashioned technique. But it works just fine.'

'Not even against the penal law. Armed with a dangerous instrument—wet dental floss,' Mike said, trying to catch up with Jill. 'You sure got a lot of steps.'

'All part of the master plan. The first floor has that grand open space, and a periodical room that the public was allowed to use from our earliest days. Then up to the second floor—you'll see our offices later—where the private collections are housed, and then up to the third level, to the great reading room. The nineteenth-century design idea was to lift the scholars away from the noise and pollution of the street so they could get their work done in the lightest, airiest part of the library. Still a good idea. Is this where you did your college research, Alex?'

'The reading room? Yes, it is.'

'It's been completely restored to its original condition. You'll hardly recognize it,' Jill said, pausing at the top of the steps.

Yuri took a key from among the many on the ring that dangled from his belt. While he unlocked the massive wooden doors, I looked up to the barrel vault on the ceiling, at the brilliant painting of Prometheus bringing the gift of fire to man, which soared in the rotunda overhead.

He stood back to let us into the room. Mike and Mercer entered before me, and both seemed stunned by the beauty—and size—of the Rose Reading Room.

'Go ahead,' Jill said. 'There's a quarter of an acre of space in here, meant to accommodate seven hundred scholars. It's one of the largest uninterrupted rooms in the city—almost the full length of two blocks. For me, it's the heart of the place.'

Library table after library table with aisles on either side lined up in rows from end to end. Atop each were lamps and ports to service laptops at each station.

'It practically glows in here now,' I said.

The large multipaned windows that flanked the room flooded it with morning light. 'Can you imagine?' Jill asked. 'That glass was all painted black during World War Two, and stayed dark until only a few years ago, with this recent renovation.'

I walked along the parquet floors in search of the table at which I'd situated myself day after day to work on my senior thesis more than fifteen years ago. I looked up at the ceiling—perhaps the most beautiful in the city—for a marker among the hanging chandeliers, a gilded cherub whose once-tarnished wings now gleamed again. She was still surrounded, as I remembered her, by coffers ornamented with angels and satyrs, and luminous paintings of blue skies and puffy white clouds in the style of the old masters.

I sat in one of the chairs and leaned back to take in the murals and all the detail that seemed to have been refurbished to its original brilliance.

'Don't get too comfortable, Coop,' Mike said. 'What's the process, Jill? Say Tina wanted to get this book, this particular edition of *Alice in Wonderland*. What would she have had to do?'

Jill walked to the center of the long room, which was divided by the catalog area.

'She would have come here, as she'd done many times before,' Jill said, placing her hand on the top of the counter. 'Tina—or any researcher—hands in the call slip to the clerk and is given a delivery number. The clerk figures out where the book is, whether in a collection upstairs or below us in the stacks, and sends for it using a pneumatic tube system.'

'Pneumatic tubes?' Mike asked. 'I thought they went out with covered wagons.'

'Old systems die hard in the library business. We're trying to convert to something a little more current—electronic—but that will still take years to effect.'

'Did she need a letter of introduction?'

'Tina's credentials are well established here, Detective. As newcomers, each of you would have to start out with references, but not someone with whom we're familiar. The letters in support of her application would still be on file.'

'Makes an inside job even easier to pull off,' Mike said. 'Your staff develops a comfort level with the researcher when they see her here regularly.'

'Quite true.'

Mike took the papers out of his pocket again and smoothed them on the countertop.

'So how does the clerk know which copy of *Alice in Wonderland* to fetch?'

Jill had her back against the wooden partition and was talking to all of us. 'She would have asked Tina to specify that. They'd have looked in the card catalog to see where the different volumes are.'

'Let's do that,' Mike said. 'Where's the catalog?'

'Not in little wooden boxes anymore, Detective, if that's what you're thinking. Those books against the wall—eight hundred of them—reproduce the original catalogs. Everything else is online now. It's a program called CATNYP—Catalog of the New York Public Library. One can access it here, of course, but also from anywhere in the world.'

'So Tina, or anyone she was working with for that matter, might have looked for the existence of a book from a computer in her own apartment?'

'Quite easily.'

'Why don't you show us how?' Mike said.

Jill didn't seem eager to comply. She looked at her watch, but it was still too early to be expecting anyone on staff to appear.

'C'mon. I'd like to see the way it works.'

Jill walked behind the counter and logged on to one of the computers. We watched as she typed in the request. Mike stepped in to look over her shoulder.

'We've got several early copies in the Central Children's Room, but that collection isn't housed in this building anymore. Tina knew that, so she wouldn't have been looking for any of those by putting a slip in here,' Jill said, moving her finger down the screen. 'Okay, in the Special Collections section, we have one in Arents. An 1866 edition.'

'What's Arents?'

'George Arents was an executive at P. Lorillard in the early part of the last century. You know, one of the big tobacco companies. He bequeathed us his library in 1944—it's called the Tobacco Collection, because every book and artifact in it is related to that subject.'

'So why would *Alice in Wonderland* be shelved there?' Mike asked.

'The caterpillar with the hookah,' I said. 'Smoking opium on his mushroom.'

158

'Exactly. Then I see another 1866 edition in the Berg Collection,' Jill said. 'Quite the rare piece. Very valuable. It's the author's presentation copy to Alice Liddell, inscribed by Carroll to her. The first approved edition, bound in blue morocco. You can certainly have a look at that one.'

'Alice Liddell's father was the dean of Christ Church in Oxford,' I explained to Mike and Mercer. 'Charles Dodgson—he used the pen name Lewis Carroll—was a math tutor at the college, and friendly with the Liddells. He first told his stories of a girl's adventures after falling in a rabbit hole to Alice, who was believed to be his inspiration for them, and later published the book.'

Jill Gibson was scanning the catalog. 'That's all I find for 1866.'

'How about in the Hunt Collection?' Mercer asked, leaning his elbows on the counter.

'Let me see,' she said, scrolling down to that field. 'There's an 1865 edition, but that one was never approved. The author and illustrator didn't like the quality of the drawings. And there are letters of Carroll's, some of his correspondence. There are also originals of some of the pictures he took of Alice. You may not know, but Carroll's hobby was photography.'

'I've seen some of the images—ten-year-old Alice posed half naked,' I said. 'Guess that's what started the speculation that Lewis Carroll was a pedophile.'

'We'll never know, will we?' Jill said.

'Coop would have gotten to the bottom of it. Load the old boy's hookah with something to suppress the urge and pack him off to prison,' Mike said, pushing the copy of the call slip in front

159

of the keyboard. 'You know, Jill, I kind of got the feeling you've seen this handwriting before.'

She kept her eyes on the screen in front of her. 'I never said that. Maybe I spoke too quickly. It's quite possible Tina printed the words herself. I shouldn't have jumped to another conclusion. Here's the original of Lewis Carroll's diary covering the period he wrote the book. That's in the Hunt Collection.'

'Pat McKinney thinks Tina was a forger, Jill. Do you?'

'She was an artist, Detective. Very skilled at her work.'

'I'd like you to look at this slip of paper again, Jill. Why won't you do that?'

She clasped her hands and rested them on the countertop, looking down at the copy.

'You were so emphatic a short time ago that the words on here weren't written by Tina Barr. Isn't that because you recognized the penmanship as someone else's?' Mike asked. He was standing so close to her that he seemed to have her pinned in place, pressuring her to answer. 'You shook like a leaf when I handed you this paper outside the library. Why, Jill?'

She pushed Mike's arm away from her and turned to face him. 'There are people in the library—employees as well as board members— who didn't trust Tina. Alex knows that. Mr. McKinney was talking to many of them for his investigation, and all the while I've been defending the girl. Then you show me this,' Jill said, picking up the paper from the countertop. 'I'd hoped never to see this writing in one of my libraries again.'

'Who do you think it is?'

160

'A man named Eddy Forbes. I don't suppose you know about him.'

'A map thief,' Mike said. Alger Herrick had talked about Forbes yesterday. Herrick said he'd been released from jail and was involved in some kind of deal with Minerva Hunt.

'The most prolific map thief we've ever come up against. And a lot of what he stole was from the Beinecke Library in New Haven, during my tenure there,' Jill said, bowing her head.

'You were blamed for the lax security?' Mercer asked.

'By some. There were others who thought worse.'

'That you partnered with him on proceeds of what he stole from your library?'

'Yes, Alex. I fought that battle once and won. I was lucky I had friends among the trustees here who believed in me. They let me come back to work. That won't be the case a second time, if it turns out Eddy Forbes had a plan to use Tina—and perhaps someone else on the inside.'

'I thought his specialty was maps,' I said. 'That doesn't seem at all connected to Alice and her adventures underground.'

'If Forbes is involved, count on the fact that there's a map in the mix.'

'Was Tina capable of imitating someone's signature?'

'Probably so. In this digital age, the ability to copy or even to forge has been made so much easier by all the technology available. Almost anyone could do it, let alone someone as artistically gifted as Tina.'

'Why did Pat McKinney tell me—tell the district

161

attorney—that Tina Barr was a forger and a thief?'
I asked.

'I haven't known Minerva Hunt and her brother,
Talbot, to be aligned on very many issues for as
long as I've been around. But both of them have
accused her, to the president, of stealing from the
family collection in the past few months.' Jill
Gibson started to lead us out of the catalog area,
back to the hallway. 'Quite frankly, until I looked
at this call slip and made the link between Tina
and Eddy Forbes, I didn't believe it for a minute.'

Mercer was walking the length of the room,
bending down to check beneath the desktops,
examining the volumes along the wall.

Yuri followed behind him like a shorter, stubby
shadow, protecting his turf.

At the far corner of the room there was a
narrow opening.

'Where does that lead to?' Mercer asked.

'Goes nowhere. Is attic. Is only air handlers for
the building,' Yuri said.

'Is there an exit up there?'

'Is nothing, I told you.'

Jill Gibson waved them off. 'Nothing there. No
one except engineering's allowed in the attic. The
public doesn't have access.'

'But is there an exit from the library?' Mercer
asked.

Yuri was beginning to stutter. He had a burly
build, and he lurched forward, swinging his thick
arms as he walked. 'You—you want see? Is just
roof.'

Mercer stepped aside as Yuri turned the corner,
and the three of us followed. A small caged
elevator was the only thing in the small dark space

behind the reading room.

We all fit in it, tightly crunched together.

It was a quick ride—maybe fifteen seconds—up to the attic, literally, to the rafters below the library roof.

'Careful, miss,' Yuri said, pointing to the catwalk. 'No slip.'

The space was remarkably clean and open, with giant metal pipes that circulated fresh air throughout the building.

I held on to the wooden railing as Yuri led us along the open walkway to a narrow ladder, and above it, a small hatch. Mercer climbed up behind him and stepped outside for a few seconds before rejoining us.

'Where does it go?' Mike asked.

'No egress to the street. Kind of a dead end,' Jill said. 'It's an interior courtyard, and it's covered.'

'What if the guy was a jumper?'

'I'm afraid he'd go right through the glass roof directly below. You didn't want to take my word for it, but that hatch is above the Bartos Forum. That's the part of the library covered entirely in glass, to replicate the old Crystal Palace. Have you had enough, gentlemen?'

Jill seemed anxious to move us out of this space. She started along the catwalk, leading us back to the elevator.

'What are those things?' Mike asked, pointing at two huge cylindrical tanks.

I knew he was as surprised as I that the attic was so exposed, not likely to have been used to conceal a body.

'Water tanks, Mike. More than a century old. Cork-insulated barrels that sit right on top of the world's largest plaster ceiling, with the library's entire water supply running through them,' Jill said, pausing to look over at the giant casks. 'Fire and water, Detective, are the two things a librarian has most to fear.'

Mike steadied himself on the beam and crouched down, looking under the barrels to make certain nothing was behind them.

'Hold on, folks,' he said, shimmying himself forward till his head and shoulders disappeared beneath one of the water tanks. 'You more afraid of fire and water than dead bodies in your belfry?'

We all stopped in a line behind Jill Gibson. 'What?' she asked in a shrill voice.

'You're moving too fast for me, lady,' Mike said. 'I just wanted to get your attention. There's no body in here, but it looks like a nice pile of overdue library books. Might get yourself a healthy fine paid, if you come across the thief.'

Mike worked himself back out from underneath the tank, and Yuri scrambled to help him up on his feet.

'Ms. Gibson, I swear,' Yuri said. 'Was here yesterday, eleven o'clock in the morning. Once every twenty-four hours, check under tank for leaks. No leaks. Was nothing there. Myself did it. Myself.'

'We'll discuss that later, Yuri. Be still.' Jill wasn't interested in his protestations. She stepped off the catwalk and I followed her over to where Mike had moved the small pile of books. 'May I have them, please?'

'I think they're ours for the time being,' Mike said, removing gloves from his pants pocket before he lifted the cover of the first slim volume.

'*Tamerlane,* 1827. Edgar Allan Poe.'

'One of thirteen existing copies in the world, Detective. Fifty printed—his first published poem. A treasure, to say the least.'

'From . . . ?'

'It was kept in a vault in the Berg Collection. That's on the second floor, Mike. I'll show you where.'

'Walt Whitman's *Leaves of Grass,* 1860,' Mike said. 'You caught a break here. It's only a third edition.'

'That particular copy has actually got greater value than the firsts,' Jill said, nervously poised over Mike's shoulder. 'It's called the Blue Book. Whitman kept it at his desk while he worked as a clerk at the Department of the Interior, constantly making edits in it. The secretary found it and thought it so obscene that Whitman was fired on the spot.'

The four books beneath that were larger. Three were brilliantly colored illuminated manuscripts of Petrarch's poems, Horace's works, and Aesop's fables, all with spectacular calligraphy done on ancient vellum. Mike read the titles aloud to us, including the fourth one, which was an archive of the paintings of Asher Durand.

Jill Gibson exhaled. 'That will raise some board eyebrows.'

'Why's that?' Mercer asked.

'Durand was a nineteenth-century artist,' she said. 'His work helped define the Hudson River School. And it's his great painting—*Kindred Spirits*—which was bequeathed to us and which we sold for a fortune in 2005.'

'Over the heated objection of many of your

trustees,' I said.

'That's putting it mildly.'

'Can you give us a breakdown later of who was for and against it?' Mercer said.

'Certainly.'

Mike lifted the oversize folio that had been at the bottom of the pile. 'John James Audubon, *Birds of America,* volume one.'

'Heads will roll,' Jill said. 'That's from the Hunt Collection—one of its jewels—and worth a king's ransom today. If Jasper gets word that we haven't had the ability to protect the best things he's given us, we stand to lose all the rest.'

Mike gently lifted the cover. 'Talk about the emperor's new clothes. These birds either flew the coop, Coop, or somebody beat us to them.'

He held the book up for us to see inside, and it was clear that pages had been sliced out of it. Only blank parchment was left between the ends of the fine leather bindings.

As Mike stood up with the heavy tome in his arms, he flipped through the few remaining sheets in it. He turned the last page, and a two-foot-long fragment of a larger antique map—not bound into the old book—slipped out and fluttered to the floor.

Jill reached down for it as Mike yelled out, 'Don't touch it.'

I kneeled beside her and looked at the detailed engraving: a piece of the Asian continent, and the figure of a man standing beside a map of the world. The cartouche over his head proclaimed him to be Amerigo Vespucci.

'What's he got to do with birds?' Mike asked.

'Nothing at all,' Jill said, steadying herself with

166

one hand on the floor, the other clasped to her chest. 'What you may be looking at is a piece of the most valuable map ever made, in a little village in France, in 1507.'

'How valuable is it? Worth enough to kill for?' he said, trying to make out the detail in the woodcut engraving.

'If all twelve sections of this puzzle actually do exist, there's only one other map like it in the world. The price tag on it would be close to twenty million dollars.'

'That's a staggering number,' I said. 'Maybe enough to turn Tina Barr into a thief.'

'I don't know why she wouldn't have been tempted by it,' Jill Gibson said. 'Half the members of my board would sell their souls to own this map.'

CHAPTER NINETEEN

'If you're looking for the Holy Grail of rare maps,' the petite librarian said to us, grinning as she gazed at the woodcut that Mike had placed on the table in front of her, 'this is as good as it gets.'

Bea Dutton was in charge of the map division of the library, home to more than half a million of them and more than twenty thousand atlases and books about cartography. Jill had called her to come in to the office early, moments after Mike made his find, and she appeared within the hour.

'Did you know this map was missing?' Mike asked.

'What do you mean?' Bea said. Her white cotton

gloves—a tool of her trade—looked more civilized than Mike's plastic ones. She was short and slight, and leaned her elbows on the long trestle table to get a good look at her subject.

'I'm sure you must know exactly when something as precious as this disappeared from your collection.'

'You've made a bad assumption, Detective. We've never had a map like this under our roof. I can't even imagine what this portion of it was doing here. I've been waiting a professional lifetime to see if another one of these treasures came to market. The only known original in the world is in the Library of Congress. Didn't Jill tell you?'

'This is your bailiwick, Bea,' Jill said. 'I've seen it on your wish list but really didn't know whether or not we owned any of the individual panels.'

'Let me explain what you've found here,' Bea said, inviting Mercer, Mike, and me to sit around the table. We were on the first floor of the library, in an elegant room with dark wood paneling, three long tables, and copies of antiquarian maps of all varieties mounted in gilded frames along its walls. Only the coat of arms of the City of New York on each pedestal of the tables betrayed that we weren't being entertained in a fancy British manor home. 'That is, if I can take my eyes off it. You're looking at one of the pieces of what many people call America's birth certificate.'

Mercer looked closely at the ancient drawing. 'How so?'

'This panel is part of a map that was the very first document in the world on which the word "America" appears as the name for a body of land

168

in the Western Hemisphere.'

Mike bent forward to look for the notation.

'Not on this particular fragment, Mike. Remember, there are twelve pieces of this beauty, each the same size as this. Once joined together, the map is four feet tall by eight feet wide. It's quite an unusual masterpiece.'

'Who created it?' I asked. 'What made it so special?'

'The primary author was Martin Waldseemüller, a German cleric and cartographer who spent his life in Saint-Dié, France, part of a small intellectual circle there. Until this was published in 1507, the European body of knowledge about the world's geography was entirely based on the second-century work of Ptolemy. This map,' Bea said, tapping her gloved finger on the table, 'radically changed the worldview.'

'In what way?' Mike asked.

'Think of it, Detective. The Spanish and Portuguese kept returning to Europe at the end of the fifteenth century with dramatic news of explorations down the African coast and across the Atlantic, where no Europeans had ever been before. To us, this map looks incredibly accurate, but to his contemporaries, Martin's map ignited a great deal of debate. It presented a revolutionary vision of the world.'

'Why?'

'This was the first document ever created that depicted a Western Hemisphere, standing alone between two oceans, the first to represent the Pacific as a separate body of water, and the first to give the new world its own name: "America." In those times, they were completely radical ideas.'

Mercer's huge frame was bent over the table as he examined the fine print in the woodcut. 'Used to be, according to Ptolemy, the Atlantic stretched from Europe and Asia right over to Japan, Cathay, and India, with a little bit of terra incognita along the way.'

'Exactly,' Bea said.

'What about Columbus?' Mike asked. 'He was over here before Vespucci. How come he didn't get the whole caboodle named for Christoforo instead of Amerigo?'

'Well, that's another reason this map was so controversial. Both men made several voyages across the Atlantic. Vespucci enjoyed more popularity throughout Europe because he wrote many publications that were read widely by intellectuals and explorers—he was a best seller in his day—and he actually went farther down the coastline of South America, convinced there was another ocean, entirely separate, on the western side of that landmass,' Bea said. 'Columbus, on the other hand, died in disgrace. Do you remember your history?'

'Yeah, I guess he did the first Terra Nova perp walk, didn't he?' Mike said. 'He was the governor of Hispaniola, and the king had him arrested for mismanagement.'

'Right. He also maintained, till his dying day, that he had reached Asia on one of his voyages. It was Vespucci who realized that both he and Columbus had come upon another continent—not Asia, not the Indies—that most Europeans didn't know existed. So he got the credit,' Bea said. 'It's kind of remarkable when you think that this single obscure mapmaker—as great as he was—chose the name for the entire Western Hemisphere.'

'And that he named it for a man who was still alive at the time, Amerigo Vespucci. No waiting for the verdict of history or going the traditional route of naming it for a mythological figure,' Mercer said, straightening up.

'Then he feminized it,' Bea said. 'Don't forget that, Alex. Asia and Europa got their names from mythical women—so that tradition of the feminine ending of a continent remained intact.'

'But it's this little group of clerics and geographers who were so taken by Vespucci's writings that they placed his name on this map?' I asked.

'No longer Terra Incognita or Terra Nova, as the new world was called by the ancients. Martin and his team just went ahead and christened these lands America—their very own idea,' Bea said, 'and as soon as this work was published, cartographers everywhere adopted that name for the Western Hemisphere.'

'How many of these maps were printed at the time?' Mercer asked.

'A very sizable run for those days, actually. One thousand copies.'

'What became of them all, do you think?'

Bea smoothed her curly red hair with the back of her glove. 'Like many objects of intellectual interest in the sixteenth century, part of the plan was to distribute them as widely as possible across Europe, to spread the new knowledge that the explorers were acquiring with each trip they made. That broad dissemination accounts for the loss of many things, and makes the ones that made it through time, warfare, pillaging, and the usual historical turmoil so very rare.'

'And its size?' I asked.

'Another problem indeed. The larger an old map, the rarer it has usually become. The huge size and very inconvenience of form of this one certainly quickened its destruction. It was so much greater than many of the charts of the day, folded once—never bound—inside an elephant folio. So the mere difficulty of keeping twelve large panels like this one in pristine condition, and not allowing the dozen sections of it to be separated, was an enormous obstacle to its survival.'

'What's an elephant folio?' Mike asked.

'It's the term for a very large book, Detective. Usually greater than two feet tall. That Audubon in which you found the map is actually a double elephant folio—easy to conceal your map in because it's so large. Let me show you something.'

Bea got up from the table and disappeared behind the reference desk, returning minutes later with a volume of elephant-folio size.

'This one is a book of reproductions of famous maps,' she said, placing it beside the piece that Mike found inside the Audubon. 'It will give you an idea of how startling the real thing is when you see all the panels joined together, as originally planned.'

She unfolded the enormous pages and spread them before us. The dozen individual engravings came together as a gigantic rectangular map of the world, separated by the seams of the individual pieces. The portion that Mike had discovered in the library's attic, stashed under a water tank, was one from the top panel, in the third of four columns.

'It's not only beautifully drawn,' I said, scanning the continents and islands, oceans and seas, and their relationships to one another. 'But you're right. It's incredibly accurate for its time.'

'Men who'd never left their villages in Europe combined their own dreams of the greater world with this outpouring of information from the explorers,' Bea said. 'Today, there is no more terra incognita. From your handheld GPS you can pull up a satellite image of your own backyard, or an atoll in the Pacific. These early maps charted the unknown, and they're remarkably exciting for that reason.'

'You say there's a complete original of this one at the Library of Congress?' Mike asked. 'When was that found?'

'Don't get too excited, Detective. More than a century ago. This sheet you stumbled over this morning is the first fresh sighting in a hundred years.'

'Tell us about the last one.'

Bea Dutton was as enthusiastic as she was knowledgeable about her cartographic history. 'Have you ever heard of a German Jesuit priest named Josef Fischer?'

None of us had.

'A brilliant scholar and perhaps a bit of a rogue. There's a very rare piece at Yale called the Vinland Map, purchased for the library there by the great philanthropist Paul Mellon. Had it been proved to be authentic, it would have shown that the Vikings predated Columbus's voyages to this continent by fifty years.'

'Sounds like you don't think it's real,' Mike said.

'Carbon-fourteen analysis dates the parchment

to the 1430s, Mike, but a chemical study of the ink puts us in the 1920s. It's on old paper—the kind you can slice right out of an ancient book, sad to say—but the ink gave it away.'

'So Father Fischer's a fraud?'

'Well, most of us in the field think the only person he was trying to defraud—and embarrass—with his doctored map was the führer.'

'Then I'm all for the old boy already,' Mike said. 'How's that?'

'Hitler was using Norse history as Nazi propaganda. He likened the Norse to Aryans by claiming that their territorial ambitions were similar to his own empire-lust,' Bea said.

'So Fischer put the Roman Catholic Church in the mix,' Mike said. 'Didn't want the Nazis to get away with their propaganda without a little bit of religion thrown in.'

'There's lot of Catholic imagery in the Vinland Map,' Bea said, pointing out notations with her white glove in the same book of reproductions. 'Father Fischer was so outraged by the Nazi persecution of the Jesuits that he just teased Hitler by creating this fake document. If the führer wanted to believe the Vikings led the way to the new world, Fischer wouldn't let him have that victory unless he accepted that the Catholic Church was also along for the ride.'

'So what did Father Fischer have to do with finding my map?' Mike asked.

'See, you've got the fever already,' Bea said. '*Your* map, is it?'

Mike smiled at her. 'I've got a lot of empty wall space in my crib. You tell me what I'm looking for and let's go for the whole dozen panels. I'll let you come visit any time you'd like.'

'That's a deal, Mike,' Bea said, continuing her story. 'Fischer was doing research in 1901, in a private library in a German castle. As happens with so many important discoveries in history, Fischer simply lucked upon something he'd never set out to find—in this case, a dusty portfolio in an obscure corner of a nobleman's home. Cartographers had been searching for remnants of this particular lost map for so long that they had begun to believe the great Vespuccian model never really existed as such.'

'A complete accident, then?'

'Exactly. Prince Waldburg's ancestors had collected maps for generations. While Fischer was studying papers of the early Norsemen in Greenland—his own personal area of interest—he came across a large manuscript that had been in the family for generations. It was a prize collection of the famous sixteenth-century globe maker named Johannes Schöner that had been acquired centuries earlier. Schöner, we figure, had purchased the Waldseemüller map of 1507 in order to incorporate its new worldview in his work so that he could use it to make his own globes more up-to-date.'

'What a find,' Mercer said.

'And especially because the twelve panels had never been assembled. Each one was carefully concealed inside the pages of this enormous folio, untouched for four centuries,' Bea said, shifting her attention back to the segment that Mike had found just a couple of hours earlier. 'I'd say this looks just about faultless, too.'

'What became of the one that Father Fischer

found?' Mike asked.

'It stayed in private hands—at the castle—for another hundred years. In 2003, one century and ten million dollars later, this map became the crown jewel of the Library of Congress. The *universalis cosmographia.*'

'What?' I asked.

'The world map of 1507 is how we know it as librarians. *Universalis cosmographia secundum Ptholomaei traditionem et Americi Vespucii aliorumque lustrationes.* That's its formal name.'

'A map of the world according to the tradition of Ptolemy and the voyages of Amerigo Vespucci,' Mike said, smiling at Bea, who looked surprised by his translation ability. 'You don't think those nuns at parochial school liked me for my good behavior, do you? My Latin wasn't half bad.'

She flipped back to the copy in her book of reproductions and again unfolded it before us.

'What are the chances that Mike's find is a forgery?' Mercer asked.

Bea Dutton frowned. 'Because of what I told you about Father Fischer?'

More likely Mercer had asked that question because of rumors about Tina Barr.

'Yeah.'

'The Vinland Map presented an entirely different issue. The Vikings were the greatest explorers of the Middle Ages—nobody disputes that. They just never made maps. Not a single one,' Bea said. 'They didn't have a concept of the world that encouraged any of them to draw diagrams, so lots of scholars were skeptical about its authenticity from the get-go. Then there's the ink. You know how ink is made?'

176

I'd never given it a thought. 'Actually, I have no idea.'

'It's the reaction between iron in ferrous sulfate and tannin from oak trees. Together they oxidize on a page and literally burn the letters or drawings into the paper. Over centuries, the blackened mark starts to turn brown.'

'And the Vinland Map ink?' Mercer asked.

'Document examiners subjected it to microprobe spectroscopy, which yielded a synthetic substance—something called anatase—that was in the ink. And that wasn't manufactured until World War One. Heave-ho to the Vikings.'

'And this?'

'Look closely at it, Mercer.' Bea pushed the tip of the antique panel closer to us and started to explain it to us. 'This is exquisitely elaborate, do you see?'

There was a masterfully drawn portrait of Vespucci, holding his navigational instruments, at the top of the large panel. Below him was the upper portion of the map, representing an area that was bordered by the Arctic Ocean, and below it a landmass with tiny writing that described interior regions and portrayed the topography of the area. Behind Vespucci was a chubby-cheeked figure—the northeast wind—blowing across the frigid waters.

'The detail is astonishing,' I said.

'See the inset?' Bea asked. On the upper-left quadrant of the panel was a small world map. 'It's actually different than the larger image, if you were to see them all assembled. As Vespucci completed more voyages, the latest descriptions were added to these smaller insets.'

177

'Too detailed to forge?' I asked.

'Not only that, Alex. The Vinland Map is just ink on parchment. This one is a woodcut. It's truly a work of art, and I'd say impossible to re-create today. After all, we do have one original in Washington against which any discoveries like the one you made this morning can be compared.'

Mike was poring over the reproduction that Bea had unfolded. 'Every section of this map tells its own story, doesn't it?'

'That's one of the things that's so magical about it,' she said.

The margins of the twelve panels were festooned with figures of the wind and sea, and cartouches that chronicled the most important features of these newly charted territories.

'Could be the reason that this piece of the map was stored in that particular book might point us to whatever Tina Barr—or her killer—was looking for,' Mike said, nodding to Mercer. 'Maybe something in one of these images, or a link to the part of the world that's portrayed in the fragment we found, you know?'

'The section of the map featuring Amerigo himself is stuck inside a book about American birds. Not a bad idea,' Mercer said. 'Bea, is there any way to get a copy of the full map that's reproduced here in your book?'

'You want the four-by-eight-foot version, I guess.'

Mike was right. If the stack of books deposited under the water tanks in the last twenty-four hours was connected to Tina Barr's death, then this high-priced piece of a jigsaw puzzle might prove to be a clue.

'We've got a photocopy machine behind the reference desk that duplicates folio-size pages,' Bea said. 'Just give me a minute and you'll each have one to go.'

She disappeared around the corner just as there was a loud banging on the door.

'Ignore it,' Jill said. 'We don't open to the public until ten.'

'There'll be no public today,' Mike said, checking his watch. 'Crime scene techs will be swarming all over the library within the hour. Nobody's getting in till the whole place is worked over.'

The banging didn't stop. 'May I check?' Jill asked.

Mike stood up as she walked to the door.

'Goddammit!' a voice thundered at her. 'Get your foot out of the way and let me in.'

'I've got some police officers with me,' I heard her whisper to the man in the hallway. 'Why don't you wait in my office and I'll meet you there shortly.'

'The hell with the police,' he said, pushing open the door so that Jill tripped over herself getting out of his way. 'I'm here to get what belongs to me.'

There was no mistaking Talbot Hunt. The physical resemblance to his sister, Minerva, was striking, and the air of Hunt arrogance as he approached Mike Chapman was equally identifiable. He was tall and whippet thin, with straight dark hair and dark eyes.

'Talbot, I'd like you to meet Detectives Chapman and Wallace,' Jill said, trying to catch up with Hunt. 'And Assistant District Attorney Alexandra Cooper.'

179

'I've already wasted two hours of my time yesterday with your colleagues,' Hunt said. 'That business about my sister's housekeeper—'

' "Business"? Oh, you mean the fact that she was murdered in an apartment your sister owns, dressed exactly like her,' Mike said. 'And the idea that she might have been killed because she was carrying a book that belongs to you, or that *you* say belongs to you.'

'Who says differently? Is it Minerva?' Hunt asked, talking to Mike but repeatedly glancing over at the map on the table.

'I don't remember anyone inviting you here this morning,' Mike said.

'Some members of Ms. Gibson's staff seem to place more value than she does on the library's relationship with my family. Now I'd like to see the Audubon volume that you found,' Hunt said. 'And my map.'

'*Your* book of psalms, *your* birds, *your* map,' Mike said, shaking his head. 'I just can't imagine the commissioner is looking to turn these things back over to you until he's damn sure nothing that has gone on involves *your* indictment, Mr. Hunt.'

Hunt took a few steps toward the trestle table and Mercer stood to block his approach. Bea came back into the room with her arms full of copies of the map, and stopped short when she saw Talbot Hunt.

'It's a panel from the world map, isn't it?' Hunt asked. 'Am I right, Ms. Dutton?'

'You are, Mr. Hunt.'

'That is mine, Detective,' he said, each word separated by a dramatic pause, as though a nail had been driven between them as he spoke. 'My

180

father's lawyers will want to speak to you as soon as I reach them.'

'You're telling me you knew about the existence of this particular map?' Mike asked. 'That you knew it was here, at the library?'

Hunt didn't seem to want to answer that question.

'Bea, I thought you said you've never seen one of these panels,' Mike said. 'That the library never owned one.'

'That's true,' the petite woman said, holding her ground. 'I haven't, and we don't.'

'The world map of 1507,' Hunt said. 'Martin Waldseemüller. The only known original is in the Library of Congress.'

'Tell me something I don't already know, Mr. Hunt.' Mike peeled back the wrapper on a pack of Life Savers and popped one into his mouth.

'I can do that, Detective. I can tell you something almost nobody in the world knows,' Hunt said. 'There's another original of that 1507 map that survived. My grandfather bought it from the Grimaldis—the royal family of Monaco—more than a century ago.'

Bea Dutton's head practically snapped as she turned it to look at Talbot Hunt. 'You have the other pieces to complete this map?'

'We can race against each other to find the missing panels, Mr. Chapman, if you won't agree to return this one to me,' Hunt said, choosing to ignore the earnest librarian. 'I can leave you to your own devices.'

'That's how come they gave me a gold shield,' Mike said, crunching the mint between his teeth.

181

'I can assure you that if you fail, someone else is bound to die.'

CHAPTER TWENTY

Talbot Hunt was seated at the head of the table, one leg crossed over the other and his hands touching at the fingertips. 'For the moment, Detective, wouldn't you say that I'm in the driver's seat?'

Mike was pacing, his back to Hunt as he walked away from us. 'Coop?'

'I'm not bargaining with possessions—no matter how valuable—in exchange for information connected to two murders, Mr. Hunt. Either you talk to us, or you tell it to the grand jury,' I said. 'The decision about who owns these things will be made in a courtroom, not because you're here to bully us. I assume the library can establish what belongs in this building and what doesn't. Things that have been donated to the Hunt Collection—'

'And all those other things they are desperately hoping will be left to them,' he said, glaring at Jill Gibson. 'Fortunately, while my father is still breathing, everyone here is likely to be on his best behavior. It takes so little time to change a codicil these days.'

'How did your grandfather get the map?' Mike asked. 'And how come nobody knows he had it?'

'There are a few people aware of the fact— some more dangerous, more desperate to find it than others.'

'Your sister, Minerva? Is she one of them?'

'Did you ever see a pig looking for truffles, Detective? My sister would have her carefully sculpted snout deep in the dirt if it would help her find the rest of the panels.'

'Why would any of this cause someone to be desperate?' Mercer asked.

'Because the more time that passes before the pieces of the map are reunited, the greater the likelihood they will never be found,' Hunt said.

'And there's much less value to the individual pieces than to the work as a whole,' Mike said. 'But if your grandfather bought it intact, how did it get broken up?'

'Because Jasper Hunt Jr. was mad.'

'Your sister mentioned that.'

'First honest thing I've heard out of her mouth in ages,' Hunt said. 'We hardly knew him—he died when we were very young—but the stories about him are legion. He was all about games and pranks and tricks, Mr. Chapman. The older he got, the more difficult. Like many rich men, he wanted to take it all with him. Very torn about whether he should create a legacy that would outlive him or go out like a pharaoh, with all his worldly goods surrounding him for the long ride.'

'How did he come to buy the map?' I asked.

'According to my father, Grandpapa was thirty years old when the discovery of this map was made by Josef Fischer. The news spread worldwide, of course, and even though Jasper's interest was primarily in books, like most collectors he was fascinated with the idea that one could still uncover such treasures, untouched over time, in a personal library. And so he made a plan.'

'And what was that?' Mike asked.

'Jasper asked his curator to study the small royal families of Europe, like the Waldburgs of Wolfegg Castle, where the map was found. Kingdoms, principalities, and duchies that had libraries in 1507, when the great map was printed, and had perhaps managed to hang on to those residences throughout the four intervening centuries. It was well known that royals were among the first to buy these documents at the time they were printed.'

'Sounds reasonable,' Mercer said.

'By the time they finished a careful survey of European history three years later, Jasper was surprised to see how few of the existing properties had not been pillaged or changed hands numerous times. So he and his curator—and his personal banker—decided to embark on a grand tour of the continent.'

'Just to search for that map?' I asked.

'The ostensible purpose was that the great American book collector Jasper Hunt Jr. was making a pilgrimage to Europe's oldest royal libraries in order to add to his own. But Grandpapa was also counting on the fact that while many of these princes had retained their titles, they had lost most of their riches and their long-gone feudal lifestyles. Some of them might be ready to offer to sell him valuable works—maybe even the great world map.'

'But wouldn't there already have been a feeding frenzy, after the announcement of the discovery of the one map?'

'Actually not, Mr. Wallace,' Hunt said. 'You see, Prince Waldburg had no intention of selling his. The great excitement at the time was that it existed at all, and in such perfect condition. Cartographers

184

everywhere wanted to see and study it, but the prince made it clear that there was never to be a price tag placed on the map, so it was never assigned a commercial value in the marketplace. A century later—just a few years ago—we all learned that the Library of Congress had made known its interest in acquiring the map.'

'So your grandfather never knew that it was worth millions of dollars?' I asked.

'Grandpapa had a great eye for the rare and beautiful, but not even he could have guessed the price this would have ultimately been worth. No one could have.'

'How did he find it?'

'In 1905, they were traveling through Belgium and the Netherlands, actually making some magnificent purchases of incunabula and very old illustrated manuscripts, when Jasper was summoned by Prince Albert of Monaco—Albert the First,' Hunt said. 'The two had known each other for quite some time because Albert had married a rich American girl from New Orleans whose family was well acquainted with the Hunts. It seems that Albert got word of Jasper's search, and from Jasper's perspective, the Grimaldi family was high on his list of prospects. They had ruled Monaco since the thirteenth century, and being in such an important strategic position on the Mediterranean seaport, would likely have been interested in a map of the New World at the time it first appeared.'

'Yeah, but the Grimaldis had been chased out of town at least once,' Mike said. 'They didn't retain possession of their palace for that whole passage of time.'

185

Talbot Hunt's furrowed brow suggested his puzzlement at Mike's display of knowledge, which was doubtless some factoid of military history. 'You're right, Detective. That, too, was part of Prince Albert's story.

'Don't forget that Monaco is built on top of a rock, Detective—literally, a fortress atop a great cliff above a strategic harbor, with ramparts constructed all around to reinforce it. Before the Grimaldis fled the palace during the French Revolution, they were able to stash many of their treasures—crown jewels, the art collection amassed by Prince Honoré, and a good portion of the royal library—inside a series of catacombs built into the rock in medieval times. Everything still high and dry when the next generation was restored to the palace thirty years later.'

'Why did Albert contact your grandfather?'

'Word had spread throughout these European principalities about the questions Jasper was asking during his travels. And Albert was an unusual prince for his time, far more interested in intellectual pursuits than most others. In fact, he is best remembered as an explorer—a very serious oceanographer—which explains his attachment to maps.'

'There's a great oceanographic museum in Monaco, isn't there?' I asked.

'Indeed. And it was founded by Albert—in 1906.'

'One year after your grandfather met with him.'

'And thanks to Grandpapa's largesse,' Talbot Hunt said. 'You see, Princess Alice—the rich American wife—left Albert a few years earlier, after he slapped her in the face during an evening

186

at the opera, when he learned she was having an affair with a famous composer.'

'Like you say, Coop'—Mike pointed at me—'nothing new about domestic violence.'

'And when Alice walked out, she took her sizable dowry with her. By selling the 1507 world map to my grandfather, Prince Albert pocketed a small fortune for himself and was able to establish the oceanographic museum and library, which is still thriving today.'

'Nobody in the principality complained that he was deaccessioning such a rare document?'

'Ms. Cooper, I daresay not many people knew of its existence. My father claims that Albert told Grandpapa that the panels of the great map had been protected because they were inside a series of books—books that had intrigued Albert from the time he was a young child.'

'Do you know which books?' I asked.

'Certainly. Some time after the Grimaldis returned to power in 1814, the royal library acquired the entire collection of the *Description de l'Égypte.* All twenty-four volumes. Where the pieces of the map had been stored for safekeeping during the revolution, I don't suppose we'll ever know. But whoever found them thereafter decided that the double elephant folios of the Napoleonic expedition would be just the right size to protect the panels.'

'What are they?' Mike asked.

'The Description of Egypt was the largest publication in the world at that time—in its physical size, not in the number of copies—and a very prized possession, too,' Jill Gibson explained. 'Napoleon led a failed invasion of Egypt in 1798.'

'I know that. The British defeated him in the Mediterranean and his troops were cut off from France,' Mike said. 'He abandoned his army and went home.'

'But a horde of civilians accompanied the military, and stayed on in Egypt to create an exhaustive and meticulously drawn catalog of everything from the obelisks and large statues along the Nile, to the great tombs, to the flora and fauna,' Jill said.

'And the very last volume of the first edition of the Description of Egypt is an atlas—the book that captured the imagination of the young Prince Albert, and the one in which he found the even older map,' Talbot Hunt said. 'The map he sold to Jasper.'

'Do you know where your grandfather kept his panels?'

'I wouldn't be searching for them today if I knew where they were.' Hunt stood up and frowned at Mike.

'I mean, did he display them, or did he hide them inside other volumes?'

'He was a bookman, Mr. Chapman. Ten, twenty, thirty years after he bought the world map, there had never been another peep about the original one. Nothing about its existence or its value since the first news accounts of its discovery. My father told me that Grandpapa lost interest in it, just like everyone else.'

'So Jasper Hunt bought this map a hundred years ago,' Mike asked, 'let me guess—for sport?'

'Why do very rich men collect rare objects, Mr. Chapman? Paintings, coins, motor yachts, Arabian stallions, Ming vases?'

'Got me on that one. I gave up on collecting when my mother threw out nine shoe boxes full of my baseball cards after I moved out of the house.'

'So other very rich men can't claim the ultimate prize,' Hunt said. 'If there were two of these maps in the world, and a reclusive prince owned one of them, then Jasper Hunt Jr. wanted the other. It sat in his library, in a specially made leather box, for thirty years after the idea of owning it had captured his fancy, and by then no one in the world seemed to give a damn about it. He was long onto other, more talked-about treasures. He didn't live long enough to see the revived interest in his forgotten map.'

'Does anyone—perhaps your father—understand why the twelve panels of your grandfather's map became separated?' I asked.

Talbot Hunt cleared his throat. 'You can't make sense of an eccentric. If my father knows why, he's never told me.'

Either that was true or Hunt wasn't letting go of any other family secrets in front of Bea Dutton and Jill Gibson.

'Did your grandfather own a first edition set of this Napoleonic expedition?'

'Yes, he did, Mr. Chapman,' Hunt said. 'But my father gave that to the library—oh, I'd say twenty years ago or more. Our curator—and the accountants—will have a record of that gift.'

'Bea,' Mike said, standing up and rapping on the trestle table with his fisted hand. 'So where's the atlas? Let's have a look.'

'We can locate it for you, certainly. And pull it,' Jill said. 'Why do you ask?'

'That's the volume in which Prince Albert found

189

his copy of the map. Maybe Jasper was playing on that fact, if he was such a prankster. This panel we just found,' Mike said, sweeping his arm over the trestle table, 'was nested inside the Audobon folio, which used to belong to Grandpa Hunt. Maybe the killer was looking for places the map might have been concealed by the old man as one of his tricks, in another one of his books. Was that his brand of eccentricity?'

Talbot Hunt nodded. 'Grandpapa wanted to keep my father on a leash, never assuming he would inherit everything without working at it.'

'Wouldn't an atlas be part of the collection in this very room?' Mike asked.

'You want to know how things disappear, Mr. Chapman?' Hunt said, almost bellowing. 'Certainly there are maps and atlases in here. But there are more maps in the general stacks, and yet again others in the various rare-book rooms. We've got one collection in the building—the Spencer— that's just about rare bindings. The curator there doesn't give a damn if he's got roadways or rodents between the covers—it's all about the leather and decoration on the outside of the books. If there's even a drawing of a tobacco leaf—say, in a depiction of the Virginia colony—in one of the cartouches, then that map might be housed in the Arents Collection. The maps are spread out everywhere throughout the library.'

'Why isn't the Hunt Collection all in one room, like most of the others?' I asked.

'Because the library didn't have enough space to maintain it that way by the time his gift was made,' Hunt went on. 'The Audubons, for example, and the Egyptian expedition volumes—well, he agreed to the library's plan to let them reside where its curators deemed they were most appropriate.'

'So where are these particular books?' Mike asked.

Jill Gibson spoke more calmly. 'At the time of Napoleon's travels, Egypt was considered part of the Orient. So they're in our Orientalia section— Asian and Middle Eastern.'

'You see what I mean, Chapman? They run these great libraries like a shell game,' Hunt said, walking to the far side of the room. 'I can't tell you how many millions we've given to these people over the years. I've got every damn right to pull the plug and demand an accounting immediately.'

'Surely the card catalogs have—' I started to say.

'They tell us nothing, Ms. Cooper,' Hunt said. 'Maps are rarely mentioned in library catalogs, and those within the atlases aren't ever individually described. Take a razor to a page and it's hard to prove what was ever there. They're unmoored, maps. Unmoored and generally ignored. Not like books at all.'

Jill looked at her watch. 'Perhaps some of the curators have arrived. I can call and have someone bring us the Egyptian atlas.'

'I don't think you understand the plan,' Mike said. 'There are cops at every door of this place by now. No one is touching any of these books unless we're along for the ride. And no one's entering the building until the crime scene detectives have been over every inch of this place.'

'That could take days. You can't close the public library.'

'Faster than you can say Dewey decimal system, lady,' Mike said, tapping me on the shoulder.

191

'Coop, call Battaglia. Tell him to get on the horn with the commissioner. The pair of them can shut this mother down in a minute.'

'I'll wait in Jill's office, then,' Talbot Hunt said.

'Mercer, why don't you escort Mr. Hunt to the nearest exit?'

'These are *my* books, Chapman.'

'That's not so,' Jill said. 'You've got no personal claim to any of the things your grandfather gave to us.'

'Don't embarrass yourself, Mr. Hunt,' Mike said, pointing at the neatly embroidered letters— TH—on Hunt's shirt, just visible below the sleeve of his jacket. 'I don't have monogrammed handcuffs. You wouldn't want to be photographed when I eject you wearing metal bracelets.'

'I'll hold you personally responsible, Detective,' Hunt said, turning his back to us.

'For what?'

Hunt's freshly polished loafers snapped like gunshots on the bare floor as he stomped toward the exit of the map room. He was furious, but couldn't express a reason that made any sense. 'For the loss of . . . of . . . of any valuable property that should have been rightfully restored to me.'

'Shoulda, woulda, coulda. You didn't even know the frigging map existed for most of your life,' Mike said as Mercer followed after Hunt. 'Tell me the real story about it, why don't you? Or sue me. Maybe you actually need all the savings I got in my piggy bank.'

'Would you mind telling us where you spent the evening last night?' I asked as Hunt pulled open the door.

'I wasn't in Bryant Park, Ms. Cooper. I'm not a

192

baseball aficionado.'

'Strikes me as a much more sporting type, Blondie, doesn't he?' Mike said, sneering at Hunt. 'Cold-blooded and calculating. Fox hunting, deer shooting, and all those genteel upper-class pastimes where you kill things for the fun of it.'

'Tina Barr isn't worth anything to me dead, Mr. Chapman,' Talbot Hunt said, glancing back over his shoulder. 'You ought to talk to my sister, Minerva. There's a girl who knows how to hold a grudge.'

CHAPTER TWENTY-ONE

Bea Dutton and Jill Gibson sat together at the farthest table from the reference desk, staring off in different directions, like two schoolkids in detention. I had used the landline to call Paul Battaglia, to tell him the latest developments and get his help with Commissioner Scully.

Mercer returned within minutes. 'You're growing quite a crowd outside, Mike.'

'Front steps?'

'The employees come in through the service entrance on Fortieth Street. Seems like most of them hadn't heard any news reports about the body in the park.'

'Is the detail in place?'

'Yeah. Chief of d's has everything covered. A fresh Crime Scene crew is unloading now. They should be in the lobby in five.'

Mike walked to where Bea and Jill were sitting. 'Bea, I'm going to have a uniformed cop sitting here with you for the day. Just to make sure no one gets past the door and tries to come in.'

She smiled at him wanly. 'You mean just so I don't start doing my own treasure hunt, don't you?'

'A little of both.'

'I've got an appointment—some engineers from the city due at eleven.'

'Why?'

'There's a problem under the old Penn Station railroad tunnels. They need a footprint—a vertical search—before there's any structural damage. It sounds pretty urgent.'

'What can you do for them?'

Bea Dutton explained. 'I can search the particular property or plot of land back before the time of the Civil War, when maps of the city were created for insurance companies. You can see exactly what structures existed at any location over time, and what the topographical conditions are. There was flooding in the sub-basement of the Empire State Building last spring—'

'Flooding from what?' Mike asked.

'There's a stream that cuts through the southwest quadrant of the building, way underground. It shows on the old maps, before midtown was built up. Because of all the snow last winter, the stream swelled with the spring melt and dumped six inches of water into that sub-basement. The engineers need to get into the train tunnels before the snowstorms start, to make sure they can prevent any potential for collapse.'

'And you can help them with that, Bea?'

'Like I said, the old maps give you a historical footprint of every inch of the city.'

'They'll have to wait another day,' Mike said,

rolling his eyes at her request as he walked back to the desk. 'Give the guy a call and cancel your date. We may need you as we go along.'

'What did the DA say?' Mercer asked.

'Expect this place to be swarming with cops within the hour,' I said. 'Between Scully and the mayor, we'll have everything we need.'

'Let's get moving,' Mike said to me. 'Mercer, you mind going back out to get one of the rookies to babysit Bea?'

'Done.'

'Keep yourself busy, Bea, baby. Do me a historical footprint of Bryant Park. Where the murder was,' Mike said, trying to make her smile again, while he summoned Jill to the desk. 'So where exactly was Tina Barr working when she was here?'

'Well, most recently she spent time upstairs in the reading room. And of course she had access to some of the special collections.'

'We've been upstairs, Jill. Which collections?' Mike was tapping his fingers on the countertop.

'I can't be certain. We'll have to talk with the curators.'

'How about the conservation laboratory?' I asked.

'Well, yes. Tina used to have access there, when she worked here.'

'Do all your employees?'

'Oh, no. It's kept quite secure. Very few people have clearance to get in there.'

'Why?' Mike asked, heading for the door and waving at Jill and me to follow.

'It's where the most fragile items in the library are taken for repair. They're often left out on worktables overnight, with strict environmental controls. We've got only four conservators working in there, and a lot of expensive equipment.'

'Take us in,' Mike said, holding open the door.

'I—I can't. If none of the conservators is inside, I'd have to have the code in my library identification tag to be swiped at the entrance. I've no reason to have one.'

'I've got Tina's.' Mike reached into his jacket pocket and removed Barr's ID—the one he had found with her body the night before. 'Just lead the way.'

'That won't work,' Jill said, clutching at her own plastic card dangling from the chain around her neck. 'She was supposed to have surrendered it when she quit. It should have been deactivated.'

'Let's give it a try.' Mike took out his cell and called Mercer. 'We're going down to the conservation lab. Before you come back in, check at the employees' entrance, where all the staff is waiting. See if you can scoop up a conservator to give us a guided tour.'

Jill moved into the dark hallway and started a reluctant march to the far end of the building. Uniformed cops had taken up positions inside the front door and at the bottom of each of the grand staircases. We continued to the end of the corridor, and through an exit that led to steep steps down to the basement.

As we descended, I could see where the white marble and granite of the library foundation rested upon the actual rough red brick of the old reservoir walls, built almost two centuries ago.

If there were lights in the corridor, Jill didn't know where the controls were, so we made our way

196

slowly through this windowless subterranean maze. Metal trolleys and dollies were everywhere, parked on angles against the wall like dozens of abandoned cars. They were obviously used to transport books of every size, and could easily accommodate something larger.

Jill stopped in front of the double doors marked with the conservation lab sign. Mike raised Tina's pass to the small electronic pad below the bell. As he moved it back and forth, the buzzer sounded, and Mike turned the knob to open the door.

Jill hesitated before stepping over the threshold and flipping on the light switch.

I followed her in and looked around. The grace and elegance of the library rooms above bore no resemblance to this workhorse in the underbelly of the building. Large tables, most covered with tools of all shapes and sizes, filled the center, and along the sides were smaller cubicles that appeared to be stations for the staff.

'Why does it smell so bad?'

'Chemicals, Mike. There are a lot of toxic materials used in this work. Solvents of all kinds, ammonium hydroxide—things that draw acids out of old paper. The students actually have to study organic chemistry before they're accepted into a conservators' program.'

Mike was snooping around all the machinery in the room.

'This was the library's original bindery,' Jill said, pointing to an enormous wooden table straight ahead of us, 'so when they have to repair the spine of an eighteenth-century rare book, they've still got to dissolve a block of animal glue. Hot animal glue, layers of it, from cattle, rabbits, tigers—more than

197

a century's worth—adds to the foul odor in here.'

The doorbell rang and Mike turned back to admit Mercer, who was accompanied by a young woman. She was slightly built, with auburn hair, and a long fringed scarf doubled around her neck.

'Good morning, Lucy,' Jill said. 'You've met Mr. Wallace. This is Alex Cooper, from the DA's Office, and Mike Chapman, another detective.'

'It's true about Tina?'

'I'm afraid so,' she said, completing our introductions to Lucy Tannis.

'Why did you want to see me?'

'The detectives need to understand what goes on down here, and whatever you know about what Tina was working on.'

'Or who she was working with,' Mike said.

'I don't know very much. It's not like she confided in any of us.'

'Had you known her very long?'

Lucy shrugged. 'A few years. There aren't many of us trained in this field, Detective. The four of us who work here full-time, we're a pretty tight-knit group. Spend most of our days together in this little hole below ground, which seems odd to most outsiders. But we get to touch some of the most exquisite works on paper ever created.'

'And Tina?' Mike asked.

'She just didn't fit. Good at what she did, no question about that. But she was cold as ice and never really seemed to enjoy her work the way the rest of us do. At least not lately.'

'Did you see her this week?'

Lucy thought for a moment and then nodded. 'Twice. Tina was here twice. She was in for a little while on Monday morning. I remember that because I was sort of surprised to see her. She was working for some rich guy—from England, I think—and she needed to pick up some supplies.'

That would have been a day before she was attacked in her apartment.

'And Wednesday. I'm sure it was Wednesday. She got here right as I was cleaning up to leave. But you'd know that, Jill?'

'Sorry? Why would I know?' Jill said, looking surprised.

'Tina told me she was here to see you that evening. That you had asked her to come in for a meeting. She seemed pretty nervous about it.'

'I told you, Alex. I—I wanted her to come in, but she never showed up,' Jill said, turning to me to protest Lucy's suggestion that she had actually seen Tina on Wednesday. 'But that was to make sure she was okay after—well, after Tuesday's break-in.'

'Well, she was still here when the three of us left, shortly after five,' Lucy said.

I couldn't get a fix on Jill Gibson. I wanted to trust her, but as fragments of information developed, I wasn't sure that I could.

'Can you give me a sense of what you've been working on recently?' Mike asked Lucy, trying to make her more comfortable before he went back to the details of her last encounter with Tina.

Lucy waited for Jill to nod at her and started to explain. 'Sure. You can see on this table over here, I've been doing some restoration on a copy of the Declaration of Independence.'

Mike was on top of it in a second, leaning over to study the document. 'In Jefferson's hand?'

'Yes, one of two that survived. And repairing a

tear in the last letter that Keats wrote to Fanny Brawne.'

I tried to make out words in the script that the dying poet had penned to the lover he left behind in London when he ran off to Rome.

'Most of the time we're working on a dozen things at once. There are tidemarks on this manuscript of *Native Son* that I've got to get started on today.'

'Tidemarks?' I asked.

'Water stains. I've got to try to remove them. And foxing is the probably the most common thing we see. That's mildew to you. It occurs when ferrous oxide—F Ox in chemistry—is attracted to the paper and activated by humidity.'

'I can see why you love this,' I said. 'I realize it's very hard work, but I envy the opportunity you have to enjoy these riches every day. And the other conservators?'

'One is rehousing some sixteenth-century prints on the far side of the room, and another is working on new bindings for books in which the bindings have failed. See this?' Lucy asked. 'Post-it notes are the bane of my existence.'

'How so? I couldn't live without them,' I said. 'I wouldn't remember half the things I have to do.'

'What holds them in place are little globules of adhesive that explode when you stick them to a page. The adhesive is stronger than the paper, so it eats away and makes the paper translucent if left there too long. That's a constant problem for us. We go from the excitement of saving documents of great historical importance to the tedium of repairing everyday damage caused by a reader's carelessness.'

'What was Tina doing?' Mike asked.

'Same stuff as us, when she worked for the library,' Lucy said. 'Right now, I'm not sure. She was given permission to use the lab—as long as someone else from staff was in here—'cause she was doing private consulting with some of the big donors.'

'Did you see her with any maps? Atlases?'

'From time to time, Detective. She liked working on maps. She had a great talent for that.'

'And recently? In the last few weeks?'

'No. I'm sure of that.'

'Why?'

' 'Cause I would have noticed. Old maps are so beautiful, so visual—none of us would have missed seeing them in these close quarters.'

'Where did she work?'

'Whatever table was free. Sort of depended on what she was handling.'

Mercer was more interested in the tools that were mounted on the walls and grouped in coffee mugs on shelves above each cubicle. 'Tell us about these.'

Lucy loosened her scarf and unbuttoned the top button of her blouse. I looked at the clear skin on her neck and flashed back to the sight of the deep wounds that brought Tina Barr's life to an end. No wonder Mercer was examining the array of knives displayed above the workstations.

'About what? My tools?'

'Yeah.'

'Each of us has a set, Mr. Wallace,' Lucy said, walking to her desk in the next alcove. 'Part of the conservation process is that we each create our own tools, to fit our styles, the size of our hands,

201

the kind of work we do. Mine are over here.'

She picked up an ivory-colored piece about the size of a ruler with a sharp, pointed end. 'This is a bone folder. It's made from the bones of a cow's leg.'

So much for the refined life of a library conservator—animal glue and spare body parts.

'I bought it at an art supply store, then ground and burned it until it fit exactly the shape I like to work with.'

'What do you use it for?' I asked.

'It's got thousands of functions here. Leather bruises very easily when it's wet, so if I'm working on an old binding, I'll smooth it carefully with this. Or turn damp pages of a book that's got water damage.' Lucy began to point out her equipment with the tapered end of the bone folder.

Above her head were mason jars and coffee mugs filled with a mix of household objects and art tools. Pens, pencils, and brushes were clustered in some, while others held tweezers and an assortment of dental picks.

Then there were knives, several dozen of them in all sizes in a large plastic tub on her shelf. 'Why so many knives?' I asked.

'They look like weapons, not tools,' Mike said. 'Sharp?'

'Razor sharp,' Lucy said, reaching for one to hand to Mike. 'We have to keep them that way. We're cutting all the time—from fine paper to edging the leather on bindings.'

'Mercer, check those shapes,' Mike said.

Lucy described their importance. 'These are lifting knives, and these are scalpels I use to carve fine lines. These are skifes, and the blades that go

202

with them.'

'Skifes?'

Lucy slowed down and smiled at me. 'Taxidermists' tools. They're used to skin dead animals. Gets the top layer off without puncturing the flesh. Serves the same purpose on book bindings. And these are paring knives.'

'May I see one?' Mike asked.

'Sure,' Lucy said, standing on tiptoe to remove one from the mug in which it was standing.

The knife was about seven inches long, with an angled steel blade and wooden handle. Mike held it in his left hand and with his right thumb tested the cutting edge. 'Wicked.'

He passed it to Mercer, who studied the beveled edge. 'We ought to take a few of these to the morgue. They'd make a pretty distinctive cut.'

'Was Tina . . .?' Lucy couldn't finish the sentence.

'We're not sure what happened to her yet,' Mike said. 'We're just trying to help the medical examiner out. Did Tina keep her tools here?'

'Some of them,' Lucy said. 'They're in this next cubicle.'

The three of us followed her to the desktop at which Tina had been working. Her station had been left in perfect order. It was a smaller space than Lucy's, and there were fewer tools displayed, but Tina had been spending only part of her time at the library.

'Would you know if any of her knives or scalpels was missing?' Mike asked.

'I haven't any idea. These things are our security blankets. I can look at my shelves in the morning and be able to tell you exactly where everything is.

But that's unique to each conservator, and we never touch each other's tools.'

'Visitors,' Mercer said. 'Did anyone visit Tina while she was here?'

Lucy thought for a few seconds. 'When she was on staff, of course people from other departments dropped in to talk about their needs, or just take a break. Lately? The usual people coming by to queue up their projects, beg us to jump the line. Some of them know Tina, so they chatted.'

'Any outsiders?'

'Just one that I can think of, several weeks ago.'

'Do you know who he was?' Mike asked.

'She, actually. It was a woman. And I didn't know her.'

'Can you describe her?'

Lucy closed her eyes and pulled up an image. 'An attractive woman, about fifty years old. Tall and really thin, a little overdressed and jeweled for eleven in the morning.'

A good shot Tina's visitor was Minerva Hunt. 'Did they arrive together?'

'No. She rang the bell and one of my colleagues let her in. She asked to see Tina, so I assumed it was someone she was working with.'

'Do you know any of the Hunts?' Mike asked.

Lucy looked over her shoulder to see whether Jill was in earshot, and when it seemed she was far enough away, Lucy leaned back against one of the worktables.

'Not personally,' she said. 'Sometimes we joke about the collectors. We know some of their books so well, we feel like we've lived with them. In my imagination, I've been talking to Jasper Hunt the Third for years, even though we've never been introduced. His father had exquisite taste, that's for sure.'

'Have you met either of his children?' Mike asked. 'Talbot or Minerva?'

'Just his leather-bound babies, Detective.'

'The woman who came to see Tina,' I said. 'Do you remember how long she stayed?'

'I don't think she was there more than ten or fifteen minutes.'

'What did she want?'

Lucy looked away from me. 'None of my business. I don't know.'

'But your desks are so close to each other. They're back to back.'

'They argued, okay? That's all I know. The woman seemed to have a bad temper. I didn't hear words, but she was displeased about something Tina had done. She sort of chewed Tina out, and then she left.'

'Did Tina talk about it at all?'

'Not to me. Not to any of us, I'd guess,' Lucy said. 'But as soon as the woman left, Tina broke down and started crying. I asked if she was okay, and she said she was just upset and needed to go outside for some fresh air. That's all I know.'

'What day that was?' Mercer asked.

Lucy was beginning to understand there was some importance to what she had observed. I wondered if that would jog her memory.

'Two, maybe three weeks ago. You can ask my colleagues if they can place it. The only other person who engaged Tina in any kind of—well, *personal* conversation was Mr. Krauss. But he actually came to see me. Sort of surprised him that she was here, and I guess he asked her what she was doing.'

'Krauss?' Mike asked, looking at me for help in placing the name.

'Would that be Jonah Krauss?' I asked Lucy. I remembered that Alger Herrick had mentioned his name to us.

'Exactly. He's on our board. Drops in every now and then—a lot of the trustees do—to see what we're working on and what we might need.'

'Did Krauss know Tina?'

Lucy pushed a lock of hair behind her ear. 'He certainly seemed to. I can't imagine he has a clue who I am, but once he caught sight of her, he made a beeline right for her and called her by name.'

'Did you—?'

'I didn't hear a word, Detective, and it all seemed very cordial. I just thought it was strange that they knew each other.'

There was an index card tacked to the wall on the side of Tina's desk. 'What's that?' I asked.

'Might be the list of things she had in the works. I track mine on my laptop, but everyone does it differently.'

I pulled the thumbtack and the card came off with it.

'Is this Tina's handwriting?' I asked.

Lucy glanced at the card. 'Yes. She always printed.'

I thought of the call slip that had been in Tina's pocket. This was not written in the same style. I read the list to Mike as Mercer walked off, making his way around the far end of the large room.

' "The Nijinksy Diaries—Performing Arts Collection. The Grunwald Correspondence—Rare Books. The Whistler Sketches—drypoint—Art and

Architecture." '

Lucy Tannis interrupted me. 'That can't be current, Ms. Cooper. Those are all items from collections in this library. Tina had finished those projects. I saw the papers down here when they were assigned to her. She's only doing private work now.'

I skipped to the bottom of the list. 'What does this mean, Lucy? "The Hunt Legacy." What's that?'

She squinted to look at the words, then shook her head. 'I'm pretty familiar with the Hunt Collection. I've never seen that expression before.'

I passed the card to Mike, who pocketed it as Mercer called his name.

'Wassup?'

'In here, in the back room. You and Alex come quick. Leave the girl.'

Mercer's voice had an urgency to it that I rarely heard. I broke into a trot and made my way around the old wooden tables that filled the room.

There was an archway into the adjacent space, a darkened work area that had large mechanical equipment—paper cutters and a standing book press—and along one side of the room, where Mercer was waiting, three huge stainless steel chests were lined up end to end.

'These are freezers,' he said, lifting the lid of the first one to show us the books—four of them—inside. 'Remember how cool Tina's body was?'

'Yes, but this doesn't look like it's been disturbed at all,' I said.

Mercer lifted the closure of the second one and revealed a single volume, folio size, resting in its icy storage container.

When he shifted to the third freezer and hoisted its heavy lid, I gasped. The book inside was small and slim, its gold calf binding elaborately decorated with gilt designs and lettering: *The Poems of Elizabeth Barrett Browning.*

The cold blast of air from within the chest couldn't hide the dark red stain, most likely blood, that had seeped into the pale calfskin—and three strands of brown hair that had frozen onto the cover of the old book.

CHAPTER TWENTY-TWO

'What's with the freezers?' Mike asked Lucy.

'Why? Do you think . . . ?'

Jill had gone over to Lucy when she heard us run to the back. She was standing with her arm around the girl, who seemed to be trying to absorb the fact that Tina's body may have been concealed right under her nose.

'How often do you open them?'

'Not—not often. Not for months at a time,' Lucy said.

'What are they for?'

'Disaster recovery. Freezing the books stops mold from doing more destruction. It kills insects that have infested them. You want to do some damage control to a hurt volume, you put it in the freezer, record that in the log in the back room, and nobody opens it again for six months.'

'And everybody working down here knows that?' Mike asked.

'Yes. But not just us. All the curators upstairs

208

know it, too. So do most of the collectors we deal with,' Lucy said, wide-eyed with concern, as though Mike were accusing her of Tina's murder.

'Frozen coffins,' Mike said to none of us in particular. He was trying to get a signal on his phone. 'How frigging convenient. Plenty of room for a short broad. Odor proof—and it already stinks in here. An unwelcoming basement room with no windows for anyone to peek inside. Whoever killed her could have kept her on ice for weeks, if the mayor hadn't made the evening so convenient for a nearby disposal.'

'The thermostat's right on top,' Mercer said. 'I imagine he turned up the temperature till he took the body out.'

'Same effect. Cool but not so stiff he couldn't move her after the rigor passed,' Mike said. 'By the time somebody discovered a body, there'd be so much contamination in this room that no forensics would be of any value.'

'Cell phones don't work down here,' Lucy Tannis said. 'You can use the landline near the door.'

'Why don't you wait here with Lucy while I grab the Crime Scene crew?' Mike said to Mercer. His impatience was palpable. 'She can explain this place to the guys. You show them what you found. I'll take Coop and Jill with me. We'll make that map room the command post.'

Mike took the stairs three at a time, yelling back at us to wait for him in Bea Dutton's office.

There was no reason for me to separate Jill and Bea at this point. I walked to a corner of the room, away from them, to call Pat McKinney and give him an update. I was unlikely to get any goodwill out of letting him be the one to tell Battaglia about the developments, but it was worth a try.

By the time I finished answering McKinney's questions, Mike had returned.

'Did you catch up with the guys?'

'Yeah,' he said. 'They're going to process the conservation lab first. You going downtown to your office?'

'That makes the most sense. If you need a warrant drafted or any subpoenas, I'll be at my desk.'

'Excuse me, Mike,' Bea said as she approached us. 'Are you going to keep me locked up all day? I don't want to be a nuisance, but if your plan is just to make me sit here, I'll go stir-crazy.'

I could tell that he liked her manner—feisty and direct.

'Now how about that assignment I gave you? That should keep you busy.'

She laughed at him. 'A historical footprint of Bryant Park? Who do you think prepared the one that was actually used when the place was restored twenty years ago?'

Mike walked me to the door, and I turned to thank Jill for her cooperation.

'Dead bodies, right? Like I told Alex, nothing but dead bodies down there.'

'Dead wrong, Detective,' Bea said, wagging a finger at him.

'What do you mean?'

'Books. Eighty-eight miles of books.'

'What happened to the bodies?' Mike asked.

I stopped in the doorway, thinking about the spot near Sixth Avenue where Tina Barr's body was found. It was a long city block away from the conservation lab just below us on the Fifth Avenue side of the library. 'What do you mean, there are books under the park?'

'The entire piece of land below Bryant Park was turned into an underground extension of the library a while back.'

I let go of the door and it closed behind me. Mike rubbed his hands together and then scratched his head. 'Connected to this building?'

'By a one-hundred-and-twenty-foot-long tunnel,' Bea said, coming alive again as she explained the setup to us. 'They couldn't build an extension that would change the appearance of the main library, because that's landmarked. So when the park was closed for restoration, the old Revolutionary War battleground and the potter's field were dug up. Originally, the stacks were right beneath us in this section, but we outgrew that space ages ago. The Bryant Park extension has greater capacity than this entire library.'

'How do we get there?' he asked, ready to dash off to the nearest stairwell.

It had never occurred to any of us when Barr's body was found the night before that below the park was a cavernous structure that coupled with this one.

'May I show them, Jill?' Bea turned to ask.

'Yes, of course. Whatever they need.'

'Does anyone work in there?'

'There are two levels underground. That's where the conveyor system that takes books up to the call desk winds up, so there are always a few staffers on the first floor throughout the day to pull the requested volumes and ship them back upstairs. The lower floor is usually deserted.'

211

'And books?'

'Just a few million of them,' Bea said as I held open the door.

'Valuable ones?'

'Everything here is valuable to somebody.'

Her short legs couldn't move fast enough for Mike. This time, she led us down the other direction of the long corridor to a service elevator, trying to keep up with Mike's pace. She had to catch her breath as we waited for the doors to open, and then waited again for the old lift as it creaked and groaned to deliver us down to the north end of the basement.

When we got out, she told Mike that the entrance to the stacks was only accessible from the stairwell straight ahead. This time, he started off and I ran with him, leaving a slightly bewildered Bea Dutton alone in the quiet hallway, with an order for her to ask one of the cops in the main lobby to send some men to help us.

The two of us pounding down the steps made as much noise as a small herd of ponies, the sound reverberating through the great empty space. The granite and marble so prominent throughout the rest of the library building ended abruptly at this point. There was a long, sloping steel ramp that started at the bottom tread, and I grabbed on to the red metal handrail along the wall to keep my balance as we rounded corners, racing farther below ground.

The path flattened and the narrow entryway opened onto a cluttered workspace that looked like a scene from a Victorian novel—industrial, impersonal, damp, and cold.

Mike stopped to scope the area—a handful of

unoccupied desks, piles of books ready to be restacked and shelved, and ahead of us and on the floor below, several acres of volumes, row after row of shelves, that formed this enormous hidden book vault beneath the formal gardens of Bryant Park.

'It's like a catacomb of forgotten books,' Mike said, his hands on his waist.

I ventured past the desks to the beginning of the tightly packed shelves that stretched out in the distance farther than either of us could see. The space was musty and airless. It was impossible to think that anyone really knew what was among the pages relegated to this dank reserve.

'What are we looking for exactly?' I asked.

'A way out.'

'We just got here. Bea said it's the only entrance.'

'What she said is that it's the only entrance from within the library. I'll never look at the park the same way again,' Mike said. 'I want to see if there's an exit near the Sixth Avenue side.'

'Why don't we wait for someone to guide us through it?' I asked.

'You and your damn claustrophobia again. Let's go over it fast, kid, before we've got the whole department tied up here,' Mike said, brushing past me. 'You're looking for blood, a weapon, clothing. Any sign this was part of the killer's escape route. And another staircase.'

Mike headed off down the first row to our right. I watched him as he loped along, ignoring the books shelved from floor to ceiling on both sides of him, looking instead at the floor, pausing to pick up a scrap of paper, which he eyeballed and then

213

slipped into his pocket.

I took the left half, setting off on a slow jog to look for anything out of place. By the time I reached the end of the third row, I was coughing so badly from the dust that I had to stop and clear my throat.

'You okay?' Mike shouted.

'I'll be fine. Why do you sound so far away?'

'I got smart, Coop. I'm going down to the other end, closer to Sixth Avenue. I'll work my way back from there. Meet you in the middle. You just keep going.'

Every now and then I bent over to pick up a blank call slip that had fallen out of book, but none had any writing on it.

I trolled through the Slavic and Baltic sections and was in the middle of an archive of Islamic manuscripts from the Asian and Middle Eastern collection when I saw something shiny on the floor, between two of the tall racks of books. From a distance, it appeared to be shaped like one of the scalpels I had seen at Lucy Tannis's desk.

I stepped out of the aisle between the already overcrowded mechanically operated shelves to get closer to the object so that I could better tell if it was something for the Crime Scene cops to pick up. But as I knelt down, I could see that it was a silver-colored ballpoint pen, its body matted with enough dust for me to know that it had been on the floor there for some time.

Another two rows farther on and something else caught my eye. Also metallic, but this was shorter in length and much flatter than the pen.

It was a few yards in from the long aisle, and I got right on top of it, kneeling again to inspect it. It was a small key, and it wasn't covered with dust. I had no idea if it had any significance to our search.

I held on to the edge of a divider to steady myself, making a mental note of what row I was in—between large folios of the designs for the Royal Pavilion at Brighton and watercolor plates illustrating dress during America's colonial period—when the entire bookshelf behind me began to move, quickly and quietly, pinning me against the one that I had grasped.

Someone was trying to crush me between the heavy compact movable shelves, and I screamed for Mike as my wrist twisted and I fell onto my side.

CHAPTER TWENTY-THREE

Yuri—the engineer who had taken us up to the attic this morning—was the first person to reach me. 'Was accident, miss. Was my accident.'

'What are you doing down here, Yuri?' Mike asked. 'What hurts, Coop?'

I was sitting up, massaging the fingers of my left hand. 'My tailbone, my wrist, and mostly my pride. You think everybody on Forty-second Street heard me scream?'

'Miss Jill send me. Miss Jill make me come.'

'You moved the shelves? Why'd you do that?' Mike shouted at Yuri.

The man was flustered and struggling to express himself. 'I don't see nobody in aisle. Shelves not on line.'

'On line?'

Jill Gibson walked up behind Mike in the company of two uniformed cops. 'He means aligned. I'm sure he means aligned.'

'Let him tell me what he means,' Mike said. 'Why'd you touch the controls?'

'Is my job, Mr. Mike. In morning, I check things and make even again.'

At the end of each long row was a round handle, like the steering wheel of a car. I had passed scores of them in the last few minutes, and knew when cranked they compacted the shelves to allow more inventory. But I never gave a thought to anyone's activating them while one of us was between the densely packed bookcases.

'Alex couldn't have gotten trapped in there,' Jill said. 'I'm sure the movement just frightened her. There are motion sensors that won't let the shelves close completely if something—someone—is in between them.'

'Is there a way to override that?' Mike asked.

'Well, I guess any system can be meddled with,' Jill said. 'There's probably an override. Yuri, you didn't happen to do anything—?'

'Everybody's got a dose of Columbo in him,' Mike said. 'Just jump in with your questions, Jill. Then you can lift the fingerprints and pick up the evidence and find the little double helixes. You've seen it all on television and it looks so easy, doesn't it? Well, you know what? My buddies in blue here will take Yuri upstairs and he'll have a chance to explain exactly what happened. How's that for law and order?'

Mike stooped beside me and lifted my chin to look me in the eye. 'You ready to dance yet, kid?' he said. Then he reached out to take my right hand to pull me up.

'Just about. I need your handkerchief for a minute.'

I didn't want Jill or Yuri to see the key I had stopped to pick up, but I didn't want to touch it either. I dabbed at my nose and then reached under my calf to adjust my shoe, palming the key inside the white cotton square Mike had given me.

'Alley-oop, Blondie.'

I stood up and brushed myself off.

'I came down here because I thought I could save you some trouble,' Jill said. 'I didn't know quite what you were looking for, but I can certainly tell you about the emergency exit.'

'Maybe Bea should have thought of that,' Mike said, annoyed with Jill Gibson.

'She doesn't know about it. Most people who work here have no reason to know. The space was designed and built with a single entrance—the way you came in—to better protect the books against both theft and the elements,' Jill said. 'But we failed all the fire department codes on the first inspection.'

'So what did you do?'

'Yuri can show you, if you'll allow him. Down at the far end—'

'Near Sixth Avenue?' Mike asked.

'Yes. There are two emergency hatches, small steel plates, just about two foot square, that were dug into the ceiling.'

'Are they kept locked?'

'Just latched on the inside. That's the whole point. No one can get them open from above, but theoretically, whoever was down here could be evacuated. If someone was working and, say, a fire

217

broke out—worst-case scenario—he'd have to be able to push the hatch up. There's a short folding ladder that drops down.'

'And bingo—you're in Bryant Park. Watching the Yankees give up a five-run lead,' Mike said. 'And from up top?'

'The plates are camouflaged with dirt and shrubbery this time of year. No one can get close enough to walk on them because of the little railing around the plants, and yet the bushes are light enough to let you lift the lid beneath them.'

I remembered arriving at the park last night and noting the disarray of the greenery in the area where all the heavy equipment was standing.

Mike took me aside while he talked to the two young officers who were waiting for an assignment. 'We're killing the Crime Scene Unit with this case. They're working another part of the library now, so one of you needs to stay put till they arrive. Keep this guy Yuri with you. Let him show you these hatches Ms. Gibson is talking about, so they can check them over, inside and out, okay?'

They both nodded.

Mike handed one of them a card with his phone number on it and told them to call with any questions or developments.

Jill asked me what we wanted her to do.

'Let's go up to your office,' I said. 'I'd like to get a list of your trustees—names and addresses.'

'The president of the library and the board chair are in China, on a major acquisition trip,' she said, looking glum. 'I'm hesitant to do anything involving our trustees until I can reach them.'

'Look, Jill, these are names I can get off your website or in your annual report. We need to talk with some of these people today. Now. Before facts and misinformation start to appear in the news. All I'm asking for is to speed this up by giving us a way to get to the folks we need. We'll get it done with or without you.'

She pursed her lips. 'Which ones do you want?'

'I'm not playing that game, Jill. We want them all.'

She started walking briskly up the long ramp that led to the elevator. Mike and I were several paces behind her.

'Stay on her ass, Coop. I'll be back to get you. Let me slip outside and see if I can spot the hatch while the crime scene's still taped off. See if it was disturbed recently.'

Mike separated from us in the lobby of the building, and Jill and I continued on to her office, past another uniformed cop who'd been posted at the door. She encouraged me to take a seat in the anteroom, but I insisted on following her to her desk.

Reluctantly, she opened a file drawer and removed a list of the current board members and handed it to me.

I scanned it and could see that the addresses of the names that interested me most—Jasper Hunt and Jonah Krauss—were nearby, on the East Side of Manhattan.

I asked Jill about other members whose names had not come up so far in the case, in part to educate myself and in part to let her think we'd be moving too fast, with too many trustees, for her to try to run interference.

When we finished talking, I used her phone to call Laura and let her know I'd been sidetracked by the discovery of Barr's body.

'Don't worry about it. It's Friday and very quiet down here.'

'Any calls?'

'McKinney's secretary. Says he wants you to check in with him by the hour if you're not coming in today. Battaglia's orders. I'm only the messenger.'

'Not to worry. I'm behaving like Pat's new best friend.'

'And Moffett's law secretary called about that familial search issue in the Griggs case,' Laura said. 'Is Mr. Fine the defendant's lawyer?'

'Yes.'

'Moffett let him go back to California 'cause he hadn't finished writing his decision, so he won't announce it until Wednesday, when Fine can be back in town. I've got you calendared to be up in court at ten a.m.'

'Thanks, Laura. We've waited eight years for a good lead in Kayesha's case. One more week won't be a deal breaker.'

'I'll call you if anything else comes up. Tell Mike not to work you too hard.'

Ten minutes later, Mike came through the door of Jill's office. He had been running, I guessed, from the way he was panting.

'You mind stepping out, Jill? I need a minute with Alex.'

She was almost bristling now, put out in every way possible and cut off from her staff. She left the room without answering.

'First of all, it's like a mob scene on the street. We'll have to try to duck out with some cover on the Fortieth Street side, unless you want your puss

220

all over the news. The staff comes and goes by the old carriage entrance—shipping and receiving now—so maybe an RMP can pull in and take us to my car.'

'Employees?'

'Nah. Lieutenant Peterson's playing hardball out there. He's let a few of the curators in, in case CSU needs them as they work their way around. Everybody else has been told to take the day off and come back on Monday.'

'What then?'

'I haven't seen so many guys in uniform since the Paddy's Day parade. Only this time they're sober,' Mike said. 'And if you think that good-looking army of cops—and the shitload of yellow tape that's wrapped around the entire circumference of Bryant Park—hasn't attracted every crime reporter in town, you'd be mistaken.'

'And the hatch?'

'Couldn't have made it easier unless somebody shot the body out of a rocket launcher.'

'How?'

'Look, Coop. Yesterday afternoon, that end of the park was teeming with workmen. Say our boy was anywhere in the 'hood and saw the staging area setting up for the ball game. Here's his golden opportunity.'

'Well, you're assuming he's familiar with the library.'

'Damn right I am. This scheme wasn't launched by some junkie looking to get high. Five o'clock last night, the whole place goes dark. Everybody scatters for home.'

'Tina's dead?'

'Killed in the lab. What did Dr. Assif say?

Maybe the evening before. No struggle. She knew the guy, I'm thinking. Trusted him. Maybe they were hanging out together for a reason. Hoist on her own petard.'

'What?'

'The weapon. I'll bet the weapon came right off the top of her desk,' Mike said. 'Now back to last night.'

'Yeah, but if the killer doesn't work in the lab, how did he get back in to get her body?'

'He had her ID tag. Swiped it and came back. Covered her little body with a tarp, took it out of the freezer, and dollied it down the hall, down the ramp, down to the stacks.'

'It must be so sinister there at night.'

'Nobody around to get in his way. Push up the hatch and roll one more tarp among all the others,' Mike said. 'Count on the fact that he's a Red Sox fan to even think of screwing up a Yankee game like that.'

'It's incredibly risky,' I said. 'Smarter just to leave the body in the freezer. Who knows when it would have been found?'

'You're not thinking, Blondie. My guy didn't go there for the body. That was just pure carpe diem. Carpe corpse. My killer went back for the books.'

'What books?' I asked.

'The ones I found under the water tank. The one that had the map inside,' Mike said, doodling on a paper on Jill's blotter. 'I'm figuring he might have had them stashed in the freezer with Barr's body, then moved them upstairs last night after he disposed of her.'

'So when did he leave the library?'

'Who says he left?'

222

'That's a chilling thought.'

'You know how enormous this place is—above and below ground? That's why nobody's getting in until it's swept by Scully's finest.'

'What if he just walked *out* the door this morning?'

'Who?'

'Your killer. I mean, security wasn't letting people in, but nobody said anything about letting anyone out. Especially with all the commotion outside, and the staff gathering at the entrance. What if he passed for a detective and just walked into the crowd?'

Mike's eyebrows raised. 'You think too much. That's one of your problems.'

'So why am I wasting time with this list of trustees, Mike? Your scenario doesn't quite fit what I'd assume would be the modus operandi of all the deep-pocketed Seconds and Thirds, the Juniors and Seniors who sit on this board. Or Minerva Hunt.'

'Partners in crime. Some grunt getting paid to do the dirty work. What did Jill Gibson tell you the other day? That map thieves steal to order. We ought to talk to that master thief, Eddy Forbes. See if his parole officer can lean on him to squeal. If he's got anything to give, maybe you can cut him a deal. Forbes can't be the only library rat ever running around loose in the stacks. He might know some of the other players.'

'I'm yours for the day,' I said.

'Start making your wish list. Your afternoon itinerary,' Mike said, opening Jill's office door. 'I just need to call the morgue and see when they're going to autopsy Barr, grab Mercer, and then we're

223

off.'

Jill was sitting in the alcove of the executive suite. She stood up as we came toward her, and Mike asked if he could use the phone on the desk.

I was staring at a portrait that hung on the end wall of the narrow room as Mike dialed.

'Jasper Hunt,' Jill said to me. 'The First. Done by the great Thomas Eakins, while he was teaching in New York at the Art Students League in the 1880s.'

It wasn't the striking figure of Hunt that had caught my attention.

'Look at that, Mike,' I said. 'Look at his hand.'

'I'll be damned. It's Hunt and his armadillo.'

'Armillary, not armadillo,' Jill said, in a humorless effort to correct Mike. 'The brass rings represent the principal circles of the heavens.'

I walked closer to look at the detail. Jasper Hunt's hand was resting on the brass skeleton of the sphere.

'It's the one.' There was no question from the markings and detail portrayed that it was the weapon that had killed Karla Vastasi.

'You know the painting?' Jill asked. 'We're so fortunate that Mr. Hunt gave this to us. You don't see many Eakinses outside of Philadelphia.'

I couldn't think of anything else except connecting the lethal antique to Jasper Hunt himself. But Jill continued explaining the significance of the art to us.

'Important men often had their portraits done with their armillaries. It was such a complex device that it was used to represent the height of wisdom.'

'Sit tight for a few hours, Jill. We'll call you later.' Mike hung up the phone. 'Saddle up, Coop.'

He broke into a run and I trailed behind him, out of the executive suite, down the great staircase to the lobby. 'I'm all turned around,' he said. 'Which way is the map division?'

I pointed to the north end of the hall and tried to stay with him as he picked up speed. He threw open the door and startled Bea, who was sitting at her computer.

'How long will it take you to work up a historical footprint?'

'Depends on the location. You picked a good day, Detective,' she said, winking at him. 'I seem to have some time on my hands. What's the address?'

Mike gave her the number of the brownstone on East Ninety-third Street in which Tina Barr had last lived, the building in which Karla Vastasi had been murdered.

'There's a whole row of houses there that have been in the Hunt family for more than a hundred years. Tell me anything about those properties you can learn from your maps, Bea. Dig me up some footprints as fast as you can.'

CHAPTER TWENTY-FOUR

It was only eleven-thirty in the morning, but I felt as though a week had passed since Mike called me about Tina Barr's body.

A patrol car had backed in to the receiving bay of the library and the three of us were able to get through, without incident, the crowd of photographers, reporters, and local ghouls feasting on rumors of the dead girl in the park.

225

Mike examined the key wrapped in his handkerchief. It was old-fashioned—a long, cylindrical shaft with a notched tip, and an ornate bow to grasp and turn.

'You got an evidence bag?' he asked the driver of the patrol car.

'Yeah.'

Mike dropped the key in the manila envelope and made a note of the cop's name and shield number. 'Get this down to the lab right now and voucher it. Ask for Ralph Salvietti. He's been assigned to the case. Tell him Chapman needs this yesterday, okay?'

It was a short drive up Park past the corner of Fifty-ninth Street, where a new luxury tower had opened a couple of years ago amid the stately old buildings that lined the avenue for the next thirty-five blocks.

We were throwing out ideas as we walked to the building, adding to the ever-growing list of chores.

'Who's going to check with the shipping companies and post office to see whether Tina mailed some of her belongings off, like to her mother?' I asked. 'She must have done something with her possessions when she cleaned out of the apartment.'

'I got Al Vandomir doing postal, UPS, FedEx, and all the storage locations near the apartment and the library,' Mercer said.

Every item one of us thought to add to the list led to three or four more. The squad working on each murder—Karla Vastasi and now Tina Barr—would be expanded to a task force and the media would pump up the fear factor across the city. Any witnesses we couldn't reach today would be on notice of the scope of the investigation by the time the morning news dropped on their doorsteps.

I asked the concierge for Jonah Krauss's office, and we were directed to the forty-third floor. The elevator interior was sleek and high-tech, with two small-screen televisions—one that ran the local all-news station and the other, a stock ticker.

When we got off, an attractive young receptionist greeted us with a polished plastic smile. 'How may I help you?'

Over her head was a sign with the company name and logo: MONTAUK WHELK MANAGEMENT.

'We're here to see Mr. Krauss.'

She looked at a schedule on her desk and frowned. 'Is he expecting you?'

'It's a condolence call,' Mike said. 'One of those sudden-death things.'

'Oh, my,' she said, startled by the news. 'Jonah is in the gym. He should be finished there in a few minutes. Is it somebody close to him? May I tell him about it?'

'Thanks, but we've got to do it ourselves,' Mike said. 'What block is the gym on? We can pick him up.'

She pointed at a frosted-glass door twenty feet away. 'It's right there. But he's wheels-up from the Thirty-fourth Street heliport in an hour and I've got to get him there. Are you guys the police or something?'

'Something. And I'm wheels-up from the morgue at four o'clock, so we should be fine.'

The girl swallowed hard and told us to take a seat.

'What's a hedge fund, anyway?' Mike asked me.

I sunk into a leather sofa and took my lip gloss

out of my pocket. 'They're private investment funds, usually only open to a limited range of investors. Hedge funds are exempt from direct regulation by the SEC, the way brokerage firms or mutual funds are managed. So they're considered riskier than a lot of traditional investments.'

'Riskier how?'

'They often invest in distressed securities—like companies going into bankruptcy. Many of them aren't very transparent, since they don't have to disclose their activities to regulators. Sort of secretive.'

'Like you, Coop,' Mike said. 'Krauss runs one?'

'The thumbnail sketch on the library contact sheet said Krauss manages hedge funds. Forty-six years old, graduate of Dartmouth, with homes in Manhattan, Montauk, and Lyford Cay. Still on his first wife—Anita.'

'That's refreshing,' Mercer said.

'And still wanting to use his new money to elbow out the good ole boys on the board to be the chair, according to Alger Herrick.'

'Don't you think it's supposed to be *wealth* management?' Mike asked me, looking at the firm's name on the wall sign.

'I get that all the time,' the girl said, looking up at Mike. I hadn't realized she could hear us talking. 'Don't you know what a channeled whelk is?'

Mike reached for one of the candies in a silver bowl on her desk. 'I'm drawing a blank.'

'They're these clams that are in the ocean all over the eastern tip of Long Island, and the white part of the whelk is the most valuable. That's what wampum comes from—you know, Native

228

American money. And Jonah is from Montauk, so it's his play on words.'

'Must have a great sense of humor, your boss.'

'Excuse me. Jonah, these guys—and her,' she said, waving in my direction. 'They're here to see you.'

Teeth whiteners must have come with the firm's annual bonus. Jonah Krauss picked up his head and flashed a broad smile at us as he crossed between the reception desk and our seating area. 'Whatever you're selling, come back next week,' he said. 'I told you time was tight today, Britney. I'm out of here.'

The girl couldn't have been anything but a Britney.

'They're cops, Jonah,' she said, standing up to grab his arm before he disappeared between the sliding glass doors that opened automatically as he neared them.

Krauss turned to look at the three of us. Still smiling—more cheesily than did most people on whom we dropped in—he introduced himself and offered a handshake to each of us. His curly brown hair was still wet from the shower I assumed he had taken after his workout. He was dressed in a warm-up suit and sneakers, ready for his weekend getaway.

'What's this about, folks?'

'A homicide investigation,' Mercer said.

'Really? Murder?' Krauss said, some of the sparkle gone. 'Who died?'

'Tina Barr.'

'Tina? From the library? She does conservation work. Let's take this inside my office, shall we? Brit—hold all my calls and tell the pilots to expect a delay.'

The doors parted again and we followed Krauss a few steps to another set of doors that slid apart on our approach.

I stood at the threshold, surprised by the sight. Most corporate executives who pay forty-third-floor midtown rents want forty-third-floor Manhattan views, river to river.

Instead, Krauss had created a thoroughly modern, high-tech, translucent glass-and-steel library—carefully lighted and hermetically sealed—within the core of this new business tower. The only clue that we were anywhere near a corporate office was the four television screens— one in a bookcase on each wall, so that they could be viewed from every angle in the room—on which the Bloomberg channels ran continuously.

'No windows?' Mike asked as Jonah glanced at the numbers as they glided by.

'Can't do. The books have to be protected from the sun, from any dampness or dust that seeps in,' Krauss said. 'But it suits me fine. I'd rather be surrounded by them all day than staring out at the city. The kids who work for me have their offices on the perimeter. Big views, so they can dream bigger. Keeps them hungry. Want to tell me about Tina?'

'Somebody killed her,' Mike said.

'How did it happen? Why?'

In the fifteen-second intervals when Krauss wasn't distracted by the ticker, he seemed genuinely surprised by the news.

'We're still trying to figure that out. Nobody from the library called you?'

'What does her murder have to do with the
230

library?'

'Everything, apparently. How well did you know Tina Barr?'

'Not much better than I know you, Detective. I met her when she worked at the library. I guess you got to me because I'm on the board. She was handling some important restoration projects, the kind of thing it interests me to learn about. I looked over her shoulder a few times, but that's as close as it got.'

Mercer was making his way around the room, tilting his head to study the titles of the books. 'Did she do any work for you directly?'

'No. No, she didn't. I have someone in England who handles all my books. I just hadn't any need for Tina's services, although I admired her talent. Look, guys, what happened to her?'

'Somebody killed her,' Mike said.

'Where? I wasn't sure Tina was still in town.'

'I expect it happened in the basement of the public library.'

'*What?*' Krauss seemed truly shocked. He sat at his desk, gesturing to us to take seats as well, giving Mike his complete attention. 'That's impossible. Right under our roof? That's got to be the safest place in town.'

'Once upon a time, maybe.'

'And who do you think is responsible? A workman? A trespasser? I know our security isn't foolproof, Detectives, but the idea of a murder inside the building is preposterous.'

'More likely it's going to be someone who knew Tina,' Mercer said. He was standing behind me, his large body framed by shelves of books with gilt and silver-tooled decorations and lettering on their

231

spines.

'Such a quiet girl. I can't imagine she made many enemies. How can I help?'

'When's the last time you spoke with her?' Mercer asked.

'A month ago, maybe two. I hosted a cocktail party for the opening of our Dickens exhibit. We've got an extensive collection that hadn't been seen all together in a dog's age. I know Tina was there. Everyone in the conservation lab had done some work on that over the last couple of years, and I thanked her for that. I don't think—wait a minute,' Krauss said. 'I did see her again.'

'When?' Mike asked.

'Within the last couple of weeks. I had stopped in at the lab because one of the girls had been working on an illuminated manuscript of Petrarch's poems. Stunning little book—brilliant pigments and elaborate detail. I was surprised to see Tina there. I didn't think she worked at the library any longer.'

'And so you went over to talk to her?' Mike said.

'Actually, no. She said hello to me, and then—then she asked me a question, something to do with an investment idea I'd had earlier. Something I'd abandoned a while back. She was at her desk, and I guess we chatted for three or four minutes.'

'Had Tina ever talked with you about investments?' I asked.

His expression suggested my question was ridiculous. 'Never.'

'Then why?'

Krauss put his hands in the pockets of his warm-up jacket and swiveled his chair back and forth. 'I had a crazy idea a few years ago. Tried to put

232

together a consortium of investors to acquire something for the library. Some bull—excuse me, Ms. Cooper—some cockamamie plan that started with board gossip. I was surprised Tina even knew anything about it.'

'But she did,' Mike said.

'Well, Detective, she wanted to.' Krauss took his left hand out of his pocket and looked at his watch. 'I had nothing to tell her.'

'What was your plan?'

'I was approached by a guy who goosed me to do a joint venture. Wanted me to put up most of the money to try to buy a valuable property that would fetch a fortune, if the damn thing even existed. I figured I could find some buddies in the business to ride it with me, but the whole thing turned out to be a hoax.'

'Who told you about it?' Mike asked.

Krauss threw back his head. 'You don't want to know.'

'Try me.'

'His name's Eddy Forbes.'

'The map thief?'

Krauss gave Mike a thumbs-up. 'What's this? Know your library felons? At the time Forbes sniffed me out, he was a scholar and a private dealer, helping some of my fellow trustees elevate their tastes and shape their collections. He fooled a lot of people in the library world.'

'What is it that Forbes wanted you to buy?'

'An old map, Mr. Chapman.'

It was the answer I expected from the lead-in Krauss gave us. What he didn't expect was Mike's comeback.

'The 1507 Waldseemüller world map?'

233

Krauss turned on the dental brights again. 'Anytime you get tired of working for the department, I might have a job for you, Detective. Now, how'd you know about that?'

'Some guys are good at missing persons. I got a sixth sense about missing things,' Mike said. 'Seems like everybody on your board wants a piece of it.'

'Yeah, but they're just spinning their wheels. 'cause if Eddy Forbes couldn't find it or steal it, then that map is just one more piece of the legend of Jasper Hunt Jr., made up to get the rest of the rich boys buzzing.'

'You gave up on the project?' Mike asked.

'I shouldn't have gotten involved in the first place. I'm not into maps,' Krauss said. 'There was a well-known bibliophile named Holbrook Jackson, famous for saying, "Your library is your portrait." Look around this room. There's not a single map on display.'

'So why did you entertain Forbes's folly to begin with?'

'The deal, Detective. The deal always grabs me. Could have been searching for a rare map or Captain Kidd's sunken treasure or King Solomon's mines. It would have been spectacular if the damn thing even existed,' Krauss said, picking up a model helicopter from his desk and twirling the rotors as he talked. 'People would have been throwing money at me left and right if I'd come up a winner. Instead I got hosed. Probably all went to Forbes's defense attorney anyway.'

'And you haven't heard from Forbes since?'

'That's one of the conditions of his probation,' Krauss said. 'He can't be anywhere near a library

234

and he can't communicate with any staff or trustees.'

'Why'd he pick you in the first place if he knew you didn't care about maps?' I asked.

'Money.'

'Everybody on your board has money.'

'Hard to get those tough old guys to part with their dough. Most of their money is older than they are.' Krauss smiled again. 'I figure there's always more to be made where the last pot of gold came from.'

I was certain that Alger Herrick had told us that Minerva Hunt was involved in a deal with Eddy Forbes.

'Didn't you try to discuss this consortium idea with Jasper Hunt the Third? Doesn't he still sit on the board with you?' I asked.

'What was that saying about Boston Brahmins? The Lowells talk only to Cabots, and the Cabots talk only to God?' Krauss asked of no one in particular, reciting the singsong doggerel. 'The Hunts talk only to Astors . . . and maybe to God, as long as he isn't a Jew or a black man. Or even worse, a woman. Jasper hasn't been on the scene much the last four or five years. And he's not exactly a fan of mine.'

'Why's that?'

Krauss wound the screw on the side of the helicopter and launched it, watching it crash to the carpet beside him. 'I guess he doesn't like my style.'

'How about Talbot Hunt?' I asked. 'How well do you know him?'

'Only in the boardroom.'

'Get along?'

235

'I wouldn't turn my back on Tally for very long,' Krauss said. 'We have different ideas about the direction the library should be going. Nothing deadly, I wouldn't think.'

'Didn't he have any interest in Forbes's idea? After all, the map was supposed to have been his grandfather's purchase.'

'I don't think Eddy Forbes and Talbot Hunt are on the same page either. Would have surprised me if they were even before all of Forbes's legal troubles. Besides, Talbot's sister, Minerva, wanted a piece of the action. I'm sure once she was in, her brother wouldn't have been a likely partner. There's bad blood between those two.'

'But you know Minerva?'

'We've met a handful of times. Eddy introduced us. She was willing to put up some of the seed money. She'd done that for Forbes before. I guess she was the one who told him the story of the missing map. He had access to most of the inner circle then. Minerva got all psyched up when the Library of Congress bought the only original that was thought to exist, because she remembered hearing stories about the second one—her grandfather's—when she was a kid.'

'So what was in this for you?' Mike asked.

Krauss leaned over and picked up his little toy. 'Like I said. I put up a couple of million dollars. A few partners kicked in. We find this sucker? Forbes told me it would sell for maybe twenty million today.'

'Sell . . . to the library, you mean?' I asked.

'Not likely. We'd get a much bigger bang from a private collector. That's what Eddy Forbes did. He helped these map nuts build their collections. The

236

whole time, he was probably stealing from one of them to feed the others.'

'Maybe it's naïve of me,' I said, 'but I just assumed that as a member of the board, your loyalty would be to the library.'

Krauss launched the whirlybird again and this time it circled his desk and came to a gentle landing on the table beside me. 'You know why I get in trouble at the library? 'Cause I happen to think the place should be all about books. Screw the maps, screw the art. That's why so many of those guys have no use for me.'

'But the maps—' I started to say, thinking of Alger Herrick's description of their beauty and importance.

'So your cousin Sally marries a dentist from St. Louis and moves out there, Ms. Cooper. You stroll up Madison Avenue to some overpriced gallery looking for a wedding present and you buy a map of the city as it looked in 1898, framed and all. Three hundred bucks. Probably sliced out of an atlas in a library—maybe even by the master thief himself, Mr. Forbes,' Krauss said, standing up and walking to a bookshelf behind his desk. 'Or your buddy builds himself a ranch in Montana—Jewish investment banker cowboys—we're resettling Montana and Wyoming like they were the promised land. Some shyster will sell you a hand-colored print of whatever prairie town you want, at whatever your price point. It's not great art, it's not even a book you can hold and read and reread. What's the point?'

'Did you inherit your collection?' Mercer asked.

'I didn't inherit squat, Detective. My father sold used cars in Merrick, Long Island.'

237

'How did you get into this . . . this . . .'

'Addiction. That's what it is. The first time I ever bought a book—I mean an old book, something I didn't have to read for school or to get me through a long plane ride—I was in Paris, walking around those little shops on the Left Bank after dinner one night. It was my first time there, I was flush with my first Wall Street bonus and some serious Bordeaux, and I stopped to look at the titles. I needed something for the flight home. I saw *Gatsby* and picked it up. I'd always loved the story when I was in college, figuring out how I could get me a piece of the American dream. You should have heard the proprietor scream when I pulled that copy off the shelf.'

'Why?' Mike asked.

'F. Scott Fitzgerald. *The Great Gatsby.* I'm not talking about the paperback you read in high school,' Krauss said, moving his hand along the bookshelf and lifting out a small volume, running his hand lovingly over the dust jacket, protected in its mylar sleeve. 'This is the first edition. Modern firsts, that's how I started. Have you ever seen a more perfect image? It's totally iconic.'

Jonah Krauss handed me the book. The jacket was cobalt blue, and the features of a woman's face looked down on an amusement park version of New York City at night.

I turned it over and noted the faint spots on the rear cover and the slightly faded lettering on the spine.

'Open it.'

'That's okay?'

'Open it,' he said again.

I lifted the cover and read. *Ernest—I think this*

238

*book is about the best American novel ever written.
Scott Fitz. 1925.*

'See what I mean?' Krauss took the book back and turned the pages. 'Fitzgerald handled this himself. You touch these things, you imagine who held them before you did, you smell them and breathe in the print, the history, the romance. Guess what I paid?'

I had a few modern firsts, but nothing like this. 'I can't.'

'Fifteen years ago, thirty-five thousand bucks. My entire bonus and then some, gone in a flash,' Krauss said, snapping his fingers.

'I'll be lucky if my pension's that good,' Mike said under his breath.

'Stopped the Frenchman in his tracks when I told him to wrap it up for me. At auction today, it would draw double. After that I had to have everything Fitzgerald I could find. Hemingway next. Dos Passos. Wolfe. It's totally addictive.'

'You obviously moved on to older collectibles, too,' I said, scoping the room.

'I had to teach myself about them. See, the great private libraries have been amassing rare books for centuries.' Krauss crossed the room, pausing in front of the Bloomberg, then continued on to shelves stocked with leather-bound books of all sizes. 'I didn't know Keats from Yeats, Samuel Johnson from Samuel Pepys. But I'm a quick study.'

He stopped in front of a shelf on which an open book rested in a cradle, two matching volumes standing beside it. He picked them up and offered them to Mike and me to admire. Each was bound in black leather, inlaid with mother-of-pearl.

'Beautiful, huh?'

The silver writing, embellished with an intricate floral design, announced that we were looking at Charlotte Brontë's *Jane Eyre*. 'Three volumes, 1847. The library has a set of its own, without the inlay. It's even got the writing desk Brontë used when she traveled.'

His excitement seemed quite genuine, and he clearly wanted us to appreciate the collection.

'Do you have any atlases?' Mike asked. I figured he was testing Krauss about his interest in maps.

'Not my thing,' Jonah Krauss said, as he saw Mercer reach for a book that was displayed on a shelf at the far end of the room. 'Whoa, you don't want to pick that one up, Detective. Some of the pages are loose.'

'Sorry,' Mercer said, replacing the large book on its stand and repeating the title on the spine. 'It looks like the court record of an old English trial. The 1828 proceedings against the murderer Aaron Keyes.'

Krauss looked nervous. He stepped in front of Mercer and rested his fingers on the open page. 'It's, uh . . . different.'

'Different how?' Mercer asked.

'It's . . . it's an anthropodermic binding, Mr. Wallace. Extremely rare. Most unusual to find.'

'Anthropodermic?' Mike asked. 'Help me out, Coop. Means what?'

'Don't know.'

'The binding is made from human skin,' Jonah Krauss said, folding his arms and speaking quietly. 'That inquest record is bound in the skin of the murderer, Detective.'

Mike lowered his head. 'It doesn't get much

240

creepier than that.'

'Aaron Keyes raped and killed a young girl in the English countryside. He was sentenced to be hung, and after that his skin was tanned and used to make this binding.'

'Human skin?' Mike asked. 'You're not joking?'

'Not at all, Detective. Most libraries don't want books like these, of course—although Harvard has a few—but many private collectors do. It's a very specialized market, human skin. Not for everyone's taste.'

Krauss turned away from the book and went back to his desk. His lips parted and the whitener on his teeth reappeared. 'Lighten up, guys. It's from the murderer, not the dead girl.'

Mike Chapman wasn't amused. 'Like you said, Mr. Krauss. Your library is your portrait.'

CHAPTER TWENTY-FIVE

'That's frigging sick,' Mike said, when Krauss stepped out of the room to give Britney a new ETA for his pilots.

'Doesn't make him a killer,' Mercer said.

'Sorry,' Krauss said when he returned. 'What else can I do to be useful?'

'Let's go back to your last conversation with Tina Barr, when she asked you about the consortium looking for the map,' Mike said.

'I didn't have anything more to say,' Krauss said, packing some folders into a soft leather briefcase. 'I told her it was a bust, okay? I thought maybe she was getting mixed up with the wrong people. I

241

cautioned her to be careful.'

'Careful of the wrong people? Alger Herrick? Minerva Hunt, or her father? That's who Tina was working for most recently.'

'When she asked me the question, I was actually worried that Eddy Forbes had gotten to her. He's a very seductive guy.'

'You think he went after Tina as a romantic interest?' I asked.

Jonah dismissed me with the back of his hand. 'Not that kind of seductive. He was a genius at scamming the best collectors. Had his own gallery and a handful of rich clients who trusted his judgment implicitly. Forbes had the cunning to steer some of these serious collectors to donate important works to the library, and once the transaction was complete, he stole from those very treasures.'

'Don't people bother to ask what the source of a rare sixteenth-century map is when they go to buy it?'

'A guy like me might *hondel* a bit, Ms. Cooper. Bargain hard, ask questions, get tough in a negotiation. That's my nature. Eddy just has to whisper in the ears of those old buzzards that some fourth-generation blowhard had gone through the family fortune and had to break up the jewels. All hush-hush, 'cause every one of these dynasties has had deadbeat offspring who might come to the same end. Circle the wagons. Building, inheriting, and disposing of these library pieces has a tremendous element of secrecy involved.'

'Secrecy?' I asked.

'In the antiquarian business, knowing where the books are—the atlases, the maps—whose hands

242

they're in, that knowledge is power. It's money. And a great many of these things that have been in families for generations aren't even insured. They couldn't possibly be, at today's prices. There are things inventoried in the great private collections of the world that haven't been seen for decades, so it's impossible to know what's become of them,' Krauss said, holding his forefinger to his lips. 'That's why I told Tina Barr to be careful.'

I didn't like Jonah Krauss, and he could smell that.

'You want to tell us about yesterday afternoon? About where you were last night?' Mike asked.

'You guys are serious, right? I don't believe this. I ran a meeting in our conference room till six-thirty. Britney can give you the names of all the attendees. Then my driver picked me up and took me to the Bronx. Is that a crime?' Krauss reached into his warm-up jacket and pulled out the thinnest phone I'd ever seen. He pressed an icon and then hit zoom. 'Have a look, Detective. Yankee Stadium with my boys. Right up until the bitter end.'

'Great seats,' Mike said, passing me the phone. Krauss had taken snapshots of his two young sons from his box, right over the dugout.

I handed him back the phone and he put both hands up in the air. 'Who sent you here, really? Some of those trustees just hate my guts, don't they? Try to mix me up in a murder case.'

'Who hates you?' Mercer asked. 'And why?'

'Now, that's something I really don't have time to answer today.'

'Put your bag down, Jonah, and take a seat,' Mike said. 'Give it a try.'

'If you had any idea of the turmoil inside the

public library—inside most libraries—you'd be able to understand the depth of the animosity, Detective. It all looks so scholarly and benign from the outside, but there are real battles being fought,' Krauss said, refusing to sit.

'Over what?'

'Start with the future of the library. What do you think the biggest problem is?'

'Funding,' I guessed. 'Money to keep a facility like this—'

'We're pouring money into it, Ms. Cooper. The problem is that ten years from now, who's going to need a library?' Krauss was snarling at me. 'Our attendance has been plunging for years, not just in New York but all over the world. Research libraries like ours in particular. The computer and the Internet are killing us, making us obsolete. We've been given a conservative estimate that at least ninety-five percent of all scholarly inquiries begin on Google.'

'But these rare books in research libraries are so unique,' I said.

'And sooner or later, every one of these beauties will be digitized. We've got fifty-three million items in this library, and already, the images from hundreds of thousands of them are available on the Web. How do we stay relevant? What if we just become a damned book museum? Those are some of the things we fight about.'

'Where are you in these battles?'

'I'm trying to move the dinosaurs forward. That's part of their animosity. Within the next decade, Google will have digitized fifteen million of our works. I'm all for scanning the great libraries of the world. Sit at home in Dubuque with your laptop and look at everything we've got. Why not?'

'Because there's something so different to holding the physical book,' I said, remembering my own research in the great reading room. 'Coleridge and Keats—each of them annotated the margins of their books with their thoughts, their ideas. You can see what mattered to them when you read their own work, and how that affected their creative process.'

'Paper disintegrates, Ms. Cooper. Books crumble, unless you can provide the environment in which to protect them, as I can.'

'There are things a computer will never be able to tell us. I remember doing my thesis research at my regular seat in the reading room, next to the same quiet guy every day. He was a medical historian, trying to track down the history of disease outbreaks in eighteenth-century England,' I said, talking more to Mercer and Mike than to Jonah Krauss, who finished packing up his briefcase. 'I couldn't understand why he kept sniffing the papers he was studying. It seemed so odd.'

'You cross-examine him?' Mike asked.

'Gently. He told me he was reading letters from an archive that came from the Cotswolds. At the time, people took to sprinkling vinegar on the correspondence, in hopes that it would disinfect them and stop the spread of cholera. He could still trace the scent on some of the old paper.'

'A very romantic notion, Ms. Cooper, but it's not the future. Any chance I can be released for the weekend?'

'What's the source of your disagreements with

245

the Hunts?' Mercer asked.

'Look, Detective, we've buried the sword. It's been almost five years. I assume Jasper's gotten over it. You might want to keep an eye on Tally. I think he'd pull out the rug from everything to get his father's bequests.'

I thought of the bejeweled book that had been found with Karla Vastasi's body. Minerva Hunt said it had been given to the library years earlier, when her grandfather died, but the 'Ex Libris' plate bore Talbot Hunt's name.

'Why do you say that?'

'Five years ago, Ms. Cooper, when I led the charge to deaccession an Asher Durand painting, Jasper Hunt literally threatened my life,' Jonah Krauss said, spreading his palms as he leaned on the desk. 'Check with your commissioner. I had police protection 24/7.'

'All because of a painting?' Mike asked. 'This library's got more action than any crack den in Bed Stuy.'

'A very famous work of art, detective. *Kindred Spirits,* it's called.'

'What's so deadly about that?'

'It was one of the library's sacred cows, Mr. Chapman. My committee made a decision to sell it, and quite frankly I thought the board would just rubber-stamp us. Turned out I was wrong.'

'What's the story?'

'Durand is one of the best-known artists of the Hudson River School founded by Thomas Cole. Landscape paintings. Cole's best friend was the poet William Cullen Bryant,' Krauss said.

'Bryant Park?' Mike asked.

'Exactly. Together, Cole and Bryant became

246

leaders of New York City's civic and cultural life.'

'Why was the painting in the library in the first place, and not an art museum?' I asked.

'You're catching on, Ms. Cooper. Bryant's daughter gave the painting to the Lenox Library in 1904. So when this building opened, and the park was created in her father's name, it seemed like a fitting home. But it just moved around from one end of a dark hallway to another. In my view, it didn't belong here at all.'

'So your committee decided to sell it. Was there an auction?'

'That was another one of my problems,' Krauss said. 'We didn't hold a public auction. You know that like most other major cultural institutions, our endowment dropped precipitously after September eleventh. We figured a healthy sale of a few pieces of our art would rally some investment income to buy important books that we wanted. We are, after all, a library.'

'So there was a silent auction instead?'

'Yes. Sotheby's acted as our agent, and interested parties were invited to submit sealed bids.'

'How much did it bring?' Mike asked.

'Thirty-five million dollars. Highest price ever paid for an American painting,' Krauss said, the side of his mouth pulling up, as though he couldn't suppress a smile. 'Me, I'm not the sentimental type. I thought it was a great deal.'

Mike whistled. 'What museum had that kind of money?'

'The Met was outbid, Detective. The Wal-Mart heiress Alice Walton bought the Durand for a small museum her family plans to open soon in

Arkansas.'

'Attention all Wal-Mart shoppers! At that price, it went to a discount store? What were you smoking, Jonah?'

'The art critics wanted to stone me, the *Times* said the sale was the crime of the century—that *Kindred Spirits* is a national treasure that belongs in New York—and the rest of the board caved in to the public outcry.'

'What spooked Jasper Hunt to go after you personally?' Mike asked.

'He said that we'd never be able to attract future donors. They'd be put off by the fact that their own bequests might eventually be disposed of in some secret way. But I think it was all about Hunt himself.'

'What do you mean?' I asked.

'When my committee was figuring out what to deaccession, we stumbled on a few things that had come in to the library through Jasper the Second— Hunt's father,' Krauss said. 'Things the library doesn't really need. We've had a Gutenberg Bible from the time this library was built, right? Printed in 1455—a simply amazing accomplishment, for the man to invent a movable press that re-created the finest Gothic scripts of his age. Maybe one hundred and eighty of them printed, and close to fifty survive. Ours is usually on display on the third floor. James Lenox donated it when the library was built—the first Gutenberg that was ever brought to America. You've seen it, haven't you?'

'Yes.' It was one of the centerpieces of the library's collection.

'Well, Jasper Hunt gave us another one, not in such good shape as the Lenox gift. Questionable provenance. Why do we need it locked up in a vault somewhere underground when we could sell it for a healthy price?'

'Still sounds like it would be a pretty desirable thing to have, from a curator's standpoint,' I said.

'J. P. Morgan set the standard for Jasper Hunt, and that's not a compliment. Neither one was a very picky shopper. They both bought up English and European estates by the boatload. Morgan's library has three Gutenbergs. I say one is enough. His advisors had the good sense to make him get rid of the objects that didn't enhance his collection—medieval tapestries, Egyptian sculpture, second-class art. We could sell the excess and get things our curators really want and need.'

'Was that what you wanted to deaccession?' Mike asked. 'His Gutenberg Bible?'

'It wasn't at the top of my list, but it was there. I would have preferred to start with a gaudy little prayer book that came from his father's collection. Extremely rare volume when Jasper Hunt the First bought it, but then he had it covered in jewels—to commemorate his son's birth.'

Mike cocked his head. He was obviously thinking of the object that had been found with Karla Vastasi's body.

'Rumor has it that the president of Cartier offered the Hunts a king's ransom to buy it. Seems the jewels were chosen and set by Louis Cartier himself, and the current managers of the business are peeved that it's collecting dust in storage.'

It appeared that everyone had lost the significance of the prayer book's original purpose.

'What became of Jasper's death threat?' I asked.

'Sort of withered and lost its energy, just like he did,' Jonah Krauss said, snapping the lock on his case. 'Three or four months of aggravation, then he was on to his next enemy. Now, I'd like to get a start on my weekend, Ms. Cooper. Any objections?'

Krauss had the briefcase in his right hand, and with his left he reached down to pick up a gym bag.

'That looks like it weighs a ton,' Mike said. 'Let me help you out with it.'

'Part of the reason I lift weights, Detective. I've got twenty-five pounds of catalogs for the winter auctions, in addition to my own paperwork.'

'One last thing, Mr. Krauss. You got any idea where Jasper Hunt's little jeweled book is now? I mean, like where in the library is it, if I wanted to see it today?'

Krauss held open the door for us, then stopped and turned to answer Mike. 'I haven't a clue. Last I heard, Tally was taking lessons from the ne'er-do-well son of Brooke Astor. I made such noise about selling off the things that didn't belong in our collection that he started to try all kinds of tricks to break his father's will, transfer some of the bequests made to the library ages ago out from under our roof.'

'But how could he do that?' Mike asked.

Krauss pressed a button at the side of the glass door and it seemed to zap every system in his room, dimming lights, turning off electronics, and sealing the exit.

'I assume his lawyer explained the legal liability to him, Mr. Chapman. I guess that's why he probably resorted to theft.'

CHAPTER TWENTY-SIX

'You see his pecs?' Mike asked Mercer as he held open the car door and ushered me into the back seat. 'Bet Krauss could lift that armillary sphere with two fingers. Smash the daylights out of Karla Vastasi. Good we got there in time so nobody skinned her to decorate his library.'

'There's no middle ground with you,' I said. 'It's easy to dislike the guy, but what's a motive for him to be snooping around Tina's apartment? Killing Vastasi?'

'They're all so greedy, Coop. The Hunts spend generations coveting and buying and preserving all these things, and this clown's ready to discard them all.'

'Krauss is new to the 'hood, but he has surely learned fast,' Mercer said. 'Those Hunts, though, I think it's in their genes. I can't figure how Tina Barr got caught up in this.'

'It wouldn't be the first time I got fooled by someone who wasn't what she appeared to be,' I said.

'Did you hear back from Minerva Hunt?' Mike asked.

I checked my cell for messages. 'Nothing new.'

'You called her?'

'Twice since you told me to this morning. Why don't you try your magic? She seemed to like you.'

Mike didn't answer.

'I get it,' I said, ruffling the hair at the nape of his neck. 'She hasn't returned your calls either. That's why you're hounding me.'

He flipped open his cell and dialed information. 'Yeah, operator. In Manhattan, Rizzali Investigations. Connect me.'

Someone answered the phone.

'Mike Chapman here. Homicide. Looking for my buddy Carmine. You got his cell for me?'

Apparently, whoever was in charge didn't want to give that out.

'Okay, patch me through,' Mike said, waiting for the receptionist to make the connection. 'Yo, Carmine. How's things? Someday I'm going to have my own secretary, too. You're living the good life, man. You working with Ms. Hunt today?'

I could hear the gruff voice barking back at Mike.

'Where at? No, no. I don't want to see *her*. I want to make you a hero, Carmine. Ms. Hunt dropped an earring in the office the other night. I'll hand it off to you, you give it back to her,' Mike said. 'Why would I kid you? One high-maintenance broad on my hands is enough. Where are you? Yeah, right now.'

Mike gassed the car and we were off.

'Where to?' I asked.

'He's parked at the corner of Fifth Avenue and Eighty-third Street. I tell you, Minerva may pay him a lot more than the City of New York did, but Carmine is still one dumb schmuck. Take off one of your earrings, kid.'

I instinctively clasped my hands to my ears and covered the small gold hoops. 'I like this pair. Way too simple for Minerva Hunt. Can't have it.'

'Once she tells him he's crazy, Carmine'll give it back to me. I'm just trying to get to the broad.'

I unhooked one earring and passed it to Mike.

'What did you find out about that tote that Karla Vastasi was carrying?' he asked.

'Oops, I dropped the ball on that. Didn't think it would be important until we saw her again.'

'You're about to get your wish, if I know Carmine.'

I dug my cell out of my handbag and it was my turn to call information. 'Bergdorf Goodman,' I said, and accepted the operator's request to dial the number of the department store that carried the distinctive bag.

'I'm wondering if you can help me,' I told the saleswoman when the switchboard connected me. 'I was with a friend of mine last week. She had one of those open totes with the geometrical pattern— that French line that you've carried for the last couple of years.'

She mentioned the designer's name, reminded me that Bergdorf's had the exclusive, told me the exorbitant price, and asked if I wanted to purchase one.

'Yes, but before I make the trip over, I want to be sure I can get exactly the same color, same monogram style. I'm not sure if she got if from you, or while she was traveling.'

The woman groaned at my insistence. 'Who's your friend?'

'Minerva Hunt.'

'Ms. Hunt?' I could envision the saleswoman standing at attention at the sound of the name. 'Yes, of course. She has that bag in three colors. Would you like the black or the navy? We can stamp the monogram on overnight. I don't think we have the burgundy in stock.'

'Too bad. That's the one I wanted.'

'Would you like me to special-order it for you?'

I had already disconnected the phone as I announced to the guys, 'Minerva lied. Remember when she said that tote was a gift to her and that she didn't like it? Well, she bought three of them herself.'

'You think people go to their doctor and say they've got a bellyache when their ears hurt? Or a sore throat when it's hemorrhoids?' Mike asked. 'But they've got no problem lying to the prosecutor. See how smart she is and whether she can figure out the truth.'

Mike squared the block in front of the Metropolitan Museum of Art and pulled in on Fifth Avenue, behind Carmine's Mercedes S500. I looked through the list of library trustees and found Jasper Hunt III. 'I think Minerva may have dropped in on her father. He lives on this block.'

'Twofers, kid. May be our first break.'

Carmine was wiping the side of the car with a chamois until he looked up and saw Mike. He dropped the polishing cloth on the hood and headed toward us.

'Coming at my bait,' Mike said, 'faster and dumber than a guppy swimming up for food. Maybe he thinks Minerva'll give him a reward.'

'Carmine's looking pretty buff himself,' Mercer said. 'He could hoist a garden ornament over my head, don't you think?'

'No question about it.'

'Got the earring, Chapman?' Carmine said, his thick hand gripping Mike's door.

'In my pocket. Let me get out,' Mike said, stepping onto the sidewalk as he fumbled with his jacket. 'You waiting to get in to see the Monets?'

'Nah, she stops by to check on her father every couple of days,' Carmine said, pointing his thumb over his shoulder. 'Lemme see.'

'Minerva have you working last night? We could have taken you to the Yankees game with us, isn't that right, Mercer?' Mike was checking Carmine's whereabouts—maybe Minerva Hunt's, too. 'Here it is.'

'Had a breather last night. She didn't want no company, and me and my goomada had a quiet night at home. No charity balls, no Thursday-night shopping spree. Like doing a day tour, back when I was in your shoes.'

Mercer got out of the car and opened my door.

'Whoa. You told me you weren't looking for Minerva. Where you all going?' Carmine asked. 'Hey, these ain't hers. She don't have anything without sparkles. Someone else dropped this. Check the projects, you jerk.'

'Could have fooled me,' Mike said. 'I was sure it was Minerva's. What number, Coop?'

'Right here—the one with the green awning.'

Mike straightened his blazer and adjusted his tie as he approached the doorman.

'Jasper Hunt,' Mike said, displaying his gold shield. 'And no, he isn't expecting us, but his daughter will be by the time her hired goon gets off the phone.'

Carmine's face was red and his eyes bulging as he stood on the sidewalk with his phone in hand.

The doorman spoke to someone on the intercom and gestured to the elevator. 'You want the penthouse.'

The three of us got in, and Mercer pressed the button while Mike sat on the red velvet bench behind. The mahogany paneling and brass trim were complemented by the small oil painting over Mike's head. 'This is decorated nicer than my apartment,' he said. 'And I think it's bigger.'

'You've refused all my offers to help you put your place together,' I said.

'I didn't say I wanted it to look like a brothel, with all your fancy tassels and pillows and stuff.'

I remembered how his fiancée, Val, had transformed the small space of the dark walk-up he referred to as the coffin,' and I bit my tongue rather than remind him of her.

There was only one apartment on the floor, and as the elevator door opened, we were greeted by a woman in a white uniform. Before she could say a word, Minerva Hunt stepped in front of her.

'Why don't you go out for a walk, Martha. Father won't need you while I'm here.'

'Yes, mum. I'll just be getting my jacket.'

'So, Detective, Carmine tells me you're a bit desperate to see me.'

'Actually, I stumbled into him while we were on our way to meet your father.'

'Oh, he can't be talking to you, sir,' the woman, whom I assumed to be a nurse, said to Mike as she reached for a jacket in the hall closet.

'I'm dealing with this, Martha,' Minerva said, her long arm stretched across the door frame. 'We've just finished lunch and he's resting, Mr. Chapman.'

'I'm famished. Must be some leftovers. What do you feel like, Mercer?'

Minerva let down her arm so that the nurse could exit, and Mike stepped into the foyer of the apartment. 'Cook has plenty of roast beef left,

Miss Minerva.'

'So you're in, Detective,' Minerva said, turning her back to us and following Mike into the living room. 'Exactly what is it you want?'

Mike had crossed through to the living room, an enormous space flooded with early-afternoon light from the tall windows that provided a view over the top of the museum and the fall foliage of Central Park. The antique furniture and old masters paintings were extraordinary.

'I'm about to leave,' Minerva said, looking over her shoulder at Mercer and me. 'You've got no business being here. If your issues are with me and about my housekeeper, then let's go somewhere to talk.'

'We need to speak to your father. This is bigger than Karla Vastasi. It's about the library now,' I said. She didn't give any hint that she knew about the murder of Tina Barr. 'I'd like you to stay until we've finished with him.'

Her navy turtleneck sweater and pencil skirt showed Minerva Hunt's slim frame to advantage. She tugged at her collar and pulled it up against her chin. 'He's too weak to do this so unexpectedly. I'll get you the number for his lawyer—Justin Feldman. Let him set the appointment for you.'

I smiled at Minerva. 'I've got Mr. Feldman's number on my phone,' I said. 'He's a great litigator and a powerful adversary, Ms. Hunt. I've worked with him often. I didn't realize he did estate work, too.'

She practically slapped the phone out of my hand. 'No, that's right. He's not—um—not handling those matters. You tell me right now what anything has to do with my father's estate. The

257

man isn't dead yet.'

'Temper, temper, Minerva,' Mike said. 'We'll explain that to him ourselves.'

Sliding pocket doors opened and a butler appeared, summoning Ms. Hunt. 'I'll be right in. Why don't you show my friends out?'

'We'll take a couple of roast beefs on rye before we go, and I'll stay with Minerva, if you don't mind.'

The butler looked more perplexed than the nurse had been. Minerva pushed the doors wider apart and led us down a hallway, past the grand dining room and a parlor to a cheerful sunroom that caught the southern exposure.

Seated in a leather armchair was an elderly man dressed in a black jacquard smoking jacket, and perfectly groomed. A large yellow cat sat on his lap, stroked by the man's trembling, liver-spotted hand. A second one, identical in color, was curled against his slipper.

'This is my father, Jasper Hunt. Father, these gentlemen are from the police department. Ms. Cropper—is that your name, dear?—works for Paul Battaglia. You remember Paul, don't you?'

Jasper Hunt lifted his head and met us with a vacant stare.

'We're having a family chat,' Minerva said. 'I know you've met my brother, Tally. Perhaps you'd like to meet father's favorite children.'

'Siblings?' Mike asked.

'Of course. They're in the will—doesn't that make it so?' she said, approaching her father. 'That's Patience, on his lap, and Fortitude, on the floor. Golden Maine coons. Longhairs. Have I got them right, Papa?'

The old man smiled and kept stroking.

'Little library lions, Detective. When Leona Helmsley kicked the bucket a few years ago,' Minerva said, referring to the hotel magnate known as the Queen of Mean, 'she left twelve million dollars to her dog. Gave Father all kinds of bad ideas. I've done everything reasonable to change his mind, but for now I'm sweet as I can be to those pussies. I may have to adopt them one day.'

'Good afternoon, Mr. Hunt,' Mike said, getting on one knee to try to make eye contact with the patriarch of this unusual family. 'Pleased to meet you.'

Hunt's eyes followed the sound of Mike's voice, but he made no response.

I turned at the sound of footsteps behind me as Talbot Hunt came into the room.

'I forgot to tell you we've got visitors, Tally,' Minerva said as her brother stopped in his tracks. 'I think you've met them before.'

'And I forgot to tell you when I arrived that Tina Barr is dead,' Talbot Hunt said. 'Murdered, of all things. In the library.'

CHAPTER TWENTY-SEVEN

It was obvious that Talbot Hunt had come to his father's home after leaving us at the library this morning. I wondered whether it was a coincidence that he and Minerva met here.

'I thought maybe you were organizing a memorial service for Tina,' Mike said. 'Seems like

259

she had something to do with all of you.'

'Why don't we move into the office?' Talbot said.

'Because my first order of business is to talk with your father.'

'I think you're smart enough to see he's not having a good day,' Minerva said.

Mike stood up, took her arm, and walked with her to the door of the room, out of Jasper Hunt's earshot. 'What's his condition?'

'He's old, Mr. Chapman. In case you hadn't noticed. He's infirm.'

'Any dementia?'

Minerva looked at her brother, and neither answered quickly. 'He's clear most of the time,' Tally said.

'I guess he has to be if you're trying to change the will. Isn't that so?' Mike asked. 'We got a little bit of Brooke Astor going on here?'

The great Mrs. Astor, who spent half a century distributing her husband's fortune—more than one hundred million dollars—wound up with her estate in the middle of an ugly battle. The will she had signed years earlier—leaving much of the Astor trust to New York institutions she loved, such as the library—had a subsequent codicil bequeathing most of those same assets to her only son.

'I don't get it, Detective,' Tally said.

'The issue was Mrs. Astor's competence—her mental competence—at the time the codicil was signed,' I said.

'Mrs. Astor was a dear friend of my father's,' Minerva said. 'I'm familiar with the case. I just don't see what it has to do with us.'

'Hello, Minerva.' I heard a weak voice from

260

across the room. 'Who's here with you?'

'Your turn, Coop. You're good with the old guys.'

'Father, I think it's time for you to take a nap.'

I started toward Jasper Hunt and kneeled beside Fortitude, who raised up and started to rub herself against my leg, her bushy tail tickling my face and her big tufted feet padding the carpet like a miniature lion's.

'Don't marginalize me, Minerva. Who's this nice young lady here? Have we met?'

He reached out to touch my cheek and I held my hand over his. 'I'm Alexandra Cooper, Mr. Hunt. I'm a lawyer. A prosecutor, actually.'

'Bully, Ms. Cooper. Doing justice, are you?'

'We're trying, Mr. Hunt.'

Mercer was attempting to steer Tally out of the room, but he stood firm.

'Have you met my babies?'

'Patience and Fortitude,' I said. 'They're beautiful.'

'They're smart, young lady. Better than beautiful. Never caused me a moment's trouble. The only price for their loyalty is a small bit of food.'

'Are you too tired to talk to me for a few minutes, Mr. Hunt?'

He was staring at Patience, and I turned to look at the foursome behind me. Minerva and her brother seemed frozen, fearful that Jasper would betray whatever secrets this dysfunctional family held close.

'I'm always tired. But I like to talk to young girls.'

'We've just come from the public library. We

know how generous you've been to them over the years.'

'I used to have a wonderful library of my own. Right here. It's all gone, plundered by thieves.' Hunt lifted his bent forefinger in the air.

'That's not true, Father. I'll be happy to show Ms. Cooper your library,' Tally said. 'It's an extraordinary collection, as you might imagine.'

Hunt grasped at my hand. 'Yesterday I took a long walk in the park—Central Park. Do you know it? I couldn't find my way home. It was frightening, actually. I walked for miles and miles and still couldn't get out of the park.'

'Don't get agitated, Father,' Minerva said, coming up beside up. 'That was just a dream you had. You haven't walked in the park for years.'

'Did you say your name was Alice?'

'Almost, sir. It's Alex. Alexandra.'

'Did you ever meet Alice?'

'Sorry?' I looked to Minerva for help.

'Alice Liddell. The girl for whom *Alice in Wonderland* was written. My grandfather had an obsession with that child—or maybe with the book. I think this is Papa's long-term memory at work.'

'Would you like me to come back with *Alice*?' I asked the old man. 'With that book? Perhaps read to you?'

Why did that children's story play such a recurring role in these events?

Jasper Hunt looked up at me and smiled. 'Of course I'd like that.'

'Do you remember a young woman named Tina? Tina Barr?'

His eyes closed and he repeated the name several times, as though trying to locate it in a

262

crumbling memory bank.

'Do we know her, Minerva?' he asked.

'Yes, Father. That nice girl who was helping you with your books. Cataloging the collection, restoring some of your Melvilles.'

'Then I know her, if my daughter says I do. Was that your question?' He looked at me again.

'Do you remember talking with her?'

He closed his eyes and shook his head from side to side two or three times.

'Did you know that she left you to go to work for Alger Herrick?'

'Herrick? There's a lucky man,' Hunt said. 'I once thought he'd be a fine match for my Minerva. She didn't agree—did you, dear?'

Minerva Hunt cackled like a witch. 'I'm glad you remembered that.'

'What became of Alger? Have I seen him about?'

'He's got a wonderful apartment here in New York, Mr. Hunt,' I said. 'Full of the most magnificent maps.'

'You can't read maps, young lady,' he said, almost scolding me. 'You can't hold them, fondle the smooth bindings, finger the parchment and vellum, and caress them, as you can books. I don't care for maps. Herrick's folly, not mine.'

'Tally told me that your father had a map,' I said, checking with Talbot Hunt as I tried to get to the subject. The son looked grim, avoiding my eyes. 'One of the rarest in the world. It had a dozen separate pieces, twelve panels.'

'Did you know my father was mad, young lady? Absolutely mad.'

'She wants to know about the Waldseemüller

263

map, Father,' Tally said, his arms folded and his words sharp.

'They all want the map, boy. I wouldn't have any visitors if it weren't for that damn map, you know. How long has it been since you've been by to see me?'

'Don't take it personally, Father. Tally's afraid he might run into me if he came to call,' Minerva said, smoothing the front of her skirt. 'Two hours together and it already seems like a month.'

The old man mumbled something under his breath. I thought I heard him say, 'Even the Jew.'

I leaned closer to him. Had Jonah Krauss been to see him, too?

Minerva queried him. 'Even a few what, Papa?'

Jasper Hunt's chin rested on his chest and his eyes closed again. His short defense of bookmen—his ancestors and himself—and the troublesome questioning about the map had seemed to devour all his energy.

'My father's a doctor, Mr. Hunt. He's a brilliant man, and an especially kind one, too.'

Hunt's glassy eyes fixed on me while I talked.

'It's a remarkable legacy he's set in place,' I said, looking back at Minerva and Tally to see if either of them reacted to the sound of that word. 'Your father, sir—and your grandfather—their philanthropic giving has been a stunning gift to so many great institutions. What do you think the Hunt legacy is?'

'Still searching for that, are you? My father would find it amusing, I'm sure. Tried to take it all with him, in case there was no one left to care. He'd be so pleased that we're sitting here today, trying to figure what he was all about, talking

264

about him. That keeps him alive in a strange way, doesn't it?'

'Searching for what, exactly?' I wanted to go back to that.

' "The evil that men do lives after them," ' Jasper Hunt said. 'That's usually the case, isn't it?'

I froze at the sound of the Shakespearean words that had been scrawled on the paper found with Tina Barr's corpse.

'But what evil?' I asked. 'Your father was good and generous to so many people.'

'He quoted that phrase all the time. Probably figured no one would long remember his good deeds. Just his madness,' Hunt said, his eyelids fluttering closed. 'Is it time for a cocktail, Tally?'

Minerva answered. 'Not yet, Father. You need your medications.'

I could see that the conversation was a strain, and I stood up, patting the hand that held the golden cat.

Minerva picked up a small silver bell and rang it until the butler appeared in the doorway. 'Will you help me settle Father inside?'

'Certainly, madam.'

'Mind if we ask you a few more questions?' Mike said to Tally Hunt as he led us toward the living room.

'I should think you'd have your fill of answers by now.'

Mike showed that he wasn't leaving by settling in to the deep pillows of a sofa covered in a silk damask print with birds and butterflies. 'So, it looks like you shot up here for a surprise visit as soon as you saw the panel of the map that we found this morning.'

265

'Hardly seems to be illegal, Detective.'

'Who tipped you off to it?'

'It wasn't Jill, if that's where you're going. The library is a closed world, a tight one. Word travels fast.'

'Your father's trust and estate lawyer?' Mike asked. 'Your sister doesn't seem to know.'

Talbot stood by one of the windows that overlooked the museum. 'It was that fellow Garrison. Francis X. Garrison.'

'The lawyer Brooke Astor's son used to try to defraud his mother,' I said. 'Battaglia indicted him.'

'I've been interviewing for a new lawyer, actually. Haven't hired one yet. I've been my father's business advisor for years. I've taken good care of his affairs.'

'I'd think you'd have a hard time convincing a surrogate's court judge about any changes to the will that have been made in your favor lately, considering the condition of his health,' Mercer said.

'My father is not the least bit delusional, Mr. Wallace. He has occasional problems with his short-term memory, but he's quite sound. He's demonstrates solid comprehension of things he needs to know—just dangle a dollar sign in front of him. Mrs. Astor lived to be one hundred and five, you will recall, and made frequent amendments to her will in the last five years of her life.'

'That's what tied her estate up in court for so long, isn't it?' I asked. 'Deciding whether her son had taken advantage of her deterioration to divert millions of dollars intended for the New York Public Library to his own pockets.'

'Despite her fortune, Ms. Cooper, she was living in squalor. Her apartment was looted and most of her servants were let go,' Talbot Hunt said. 'Don't lecture me about my father's condition. There are enough millions to go around. Even for the damn cats.'

'Tell us about the Bay Psalm Book,' Mercer said, moving closer to Talbot Hunt. 'We know its significance to your great-grandfather. But how did it come to be in your possession?'

He didn't like answering our questions, but it was clear that he wanted to stake his claim to the valuable little book.

'Understand, Detective, that the moment my sister comes into the room, this conversation will cease,' Hunt said, fuming as he glanced at the hallway. 'This is between my father and myself. It has nothing to do with Minerva.'

'All right.'

Talbot Hunt talked to Mercer. 'My father's instincts were good enough, just several years ago, for him to see the writing on the wall. Our fellow trustees had the gall to start deaccessioning several important objects—paintings, manuscripts, archives of writers who had fallen into obscurity— that kind of thing.'

'The *Kindred Spirits* sale.'

'Exactly.' Once again, Hunt raised his eyebrows, seemingly surprised that the NYPD was up to speed on art and literature.

'My grandfather kept that prayer book, which celebrated his birth, next to his bed—at home or abroad—for all of his life. He wanted the library to have it, to treasure it as he had. He never expected it would be warehoused or he wouldn't have willed it to them. When Jonah and his allies wanted to put the book up for sale, my father wouldn't stand for it.'

'Was that the person your father was referring to?' I asked. 'Does he call Jonah "the Jew"?'

Talbot Hunt studied me as if to divine my genetic fingerprint.

'Yes, I'm Jewish. I can deal with it, Mr. Hunt. Jonah Krauss came here to discuss the lost map with your father?'

'Apparently so, Ms. Cooper. I wasn't aware of that. I know he despised Jonah from the time he set foot in the boardroom. No class, new money— that sort of thing. You know what I mean.'

Jewish. That was mostly what Talbot Hunt meant. 'So your father made a deal?'

'Yes.'

'With whom?'

'Leland Porter, the president of the library.'

'How convenient that Porter is somewhere in Outer Mongolia this weekend,' Mike said.

'Well, I assume that's the way Father got the psalm book back. Leland is the only person in a position to negotiate something at that level.'

'Are you telling me you don't *know*?'

'The key word is supposed to be "transparency," Mr. Chapman. But behind the scenes, where many of these transactions occur, it's thick as mud.'

'Thick as thieves, we say in my business.'

'My father wanted me to have the Bay Psalm Book. In exchange, he told me he was giving the library something they wanted even more.'

'What's that?' Mike asked, looking to me to vet the credibility of Talbot Hunt's answer.

'A book of illustrations—twenty rather macabre

268

watercolors—that were done by William Blake in 1805. *Designs for Blair's Grave,* it's called. The poet kept a set of the paintings for himself. Had them bound into book form. Simple, but quite striking— a meditation on mortality and redemption.'

'That must be the only complete set,' I said. There had been a major controversy just a few years earlier, when Sotheby's had broken up a recently discovered group of nineteen plates from the same work—unbound—for sale at auction.

'That's correct, Ms. Cooper. If you know that, then you're aware that it's worth many more millions than our prayer book.'

'And the library owns that volume of watercolors now?'

'The library's Berg Collection is strong on Blake. They've coveted this for a very long time. Pleaded with my father to pass it on to them. The book is in their hands, not to be displayed until after Father's death—at his own direction—to avoid controversy about the transaction.'

Footsteps in the hallway announced Minerva's return.

Her gait was firm and fast. She walked past me and directly to her brother, stopping only to slap him across the face before she turned away.

'If you paid any attention to your father you'd know there was an intercom in every room, so the nurses can hear him if he calls for anything,' she said. 'What else have you swindled me out of, you selfish bastard? What else, besides that precious little book?'

CHAPTER TWENTY-EIGHT

Mike stood up and stepped between the spoiled siblings.

'No secrets anymore, Mr. Hunt. Looks like your sister trumped you on this one. When did the psalm book disappear from your home?'

'Check with his wife, Detective. She probably took it to the consignment shop for resale, along with those dreadful things she calls clothes. She'd have dug those jewels out with her teeth, were it possible.'

'About three weeks ago, Mr. Chapman,' Talbot Hunt said. 'And leave Josie out of it, Minerva.'

'She is out of it, Tally. Always has been. Father despises her. Imagine, Detective, leaving her church-mouse-of-a-husband minister for Talbot Hunt. True love, I'm sure.'

'Why didn't you report the theft to the police?'

'Not very complicated, is it? I knew it had to be an inside job—someone who understood the personal value of its worth to me. Nothing else was disturbed in the entire apartment. I figured it was about blackmail, and that at the right moment, I'd be contacted. One can't very well call the police about a theft of an object for which one doesn't even have proper title. The Bay Psalm Book still belongs to the New York Public Library, in theory.'

'Where were you when the theft occurred?' Mercer asked.

'I was—I mean, we were,' Talbot said, correcting himself immediately to protect his wife from Minerva's sharp tongue, 'we were in

Millbrook.'

'The family estate, Mr. Wallace. My great-grandfather bought land in Dutchess County before he died. My grandfather loved it there, too. A big horse farm,' Minerva said. 'Just not big enough for all of us at any one time.'

'Who else besides you and your wife lives in the apartment?'

'The children are away at college. It's just the two of us. And a housekeeper, but she traveled with us to the country.'

'Do you mind if we get some guys in to go over the place with you?'

Talbot Hunt *pfumphed* for a few seconds. 'I told you, it's been weeks. There's no harm in it, certainly, but what do you expect to find?'

'You never know. We might catch a break,' Mike said. 'Where exactly did you keep the psalm book?'

Hunt stared at his sister but didn't speak.

'Do you have a library in your home?'

'Yes. Yes, I do. But that isn't where I had it.'

'Like I give a damn, Tally. Tell the man, will you? I'm not after your books.'

'Then how come your maid was clutching it when she died?' he shouted at her. 'Who were you expecting to meet there? Your low-life buddy Eddy Forbes?'

'Imagine one family with this much dirty laundry, Mr. Chapman. It's lifesaving that my brother married a washerwoman,' Minerva said. 'You see, Tally couldn't keep the book in his safe—the one in the bedroom closet—because that's where the cow keeps her jewelry. Don't be shocked, Ms. Cooper. Father always called Josie the cow. Suits her dead on.'

'How do you know about the safe in your brother's bedroom closet?' Mike asked.

'Because Tally's first wife—his *late* first wife—was a very dear friend of mine. I went there often when she was alive to borrow some of the pieces my mother had left to her. And yes, she died of natural causes—don't think I wasn't on his case about that.'

'There's a bureau in my dressing room, Detective. I kept the book in a false drawer. Actually locked in that drawer, at the base of the bureau.'

'Locked . . . with a key?'

'Yes.'

'Do you still have the key?' I asked, thinking of the one I found on the floor in the stacks.

'I do. It's at home. You can have it if you like.'

'Was the lock broken?'

'Not at all. Picked, I'd say.'

'Who knew about the drawer?'

'Well, obviously, my wife.'

Minerva crossed her arms and let out a long, low 'moo.'

'I'm not sure anyone else would know.'

'The housekeeper?'

'Certainly, she cleans in there, but I can't imagine she'd be involved. She's been with me for twenty years, Mr. Chapman.'

'Anyone else?' Mike asked. 'Workmen, guys doing construction or repairs, people in the building?'

'It's a Park Avenue building. Quite secure. And no one was doing any work for us inside the apartment.'

'Who was helping you in the library?' Minerva

272

asked, rearranging the French tulips in a vase near the sofa. 'You've always had someone to watch out for the books. Who now, Tally?'

'The same curator I've had for years. He'll be happy to talk with you. He's only there one day a week.'

Minerva Hunt snapped the stem off one of the flowers and focused her attention on her brother. 'That's not what I mean, Tally. Who's your book doctor these days, hmmm? Who's been doing your preservation assessments? Mending your tears? Checking your clamshell boxes?'

Talbot Hunt was trying to ignore Minerva, but she was like a steam engine picking up speed.

'Now I see it,' she said. 'Tell the nice detectives what they ought to know.'

'It has nothing to do with this.'

'Tina Barr was working for my father, Mr. Chapman. She was treated well here, as you might guess. Then all of a sudden she quit. Quite abruptly.'

'And started working for Alger Herrick,' Talbot said.

'Only part-time,' I said. That's what Herrick had told us.

'You hired her away from Father, didn't you? You knew Tina had all the information about his collection that you weren't able to get from him yourself. How far in did you let her, Tally?'

His face was red and he looked like he was ready to spit at his sister.

'She wanted the extra work. She didn't enjoy it here. This is more like a mausoleum than a library. I was doing her a favor, Minerva. Can you understand that?'

'How far did you go, Tally? That's all I asked.'

'It's not what you think,' he said, gritting his teeth.

'You were sleeping with her, weren't you?'

'Stop it!' he shouted at Minerva. 'Don't be such a fool.'

'A fool to figure it out, or to say it in front of the detectives?'

I'd only seen Tina Barr in the immediate aftermath of her first victimization. It was hard to think of the distraught young woman as anyone's paramour.

Talbot Hunt started toward the foyer.

'Didn't figure she was your type, Mr. Hunt,' Mike said, following him. 'So what kind of favor did you do for her? How long did your affair go on?'

Hunt stopped long enough to say, 'Hardly an affair, Detective. Tina came on to me, that's all it was. She was lonely—and, well . . . things happened.'

'I get lonely myself, Mr. Hunt. Doesn't mean I crawl into bed with the first weasel that comes along,' Mike said. 'What kind of things? Did you and she have a sexual relationship?'

He looked past Mike at Minerva, his teeth clenched.

'I won't tell Josie,' Minerva said. 'You must understand, Mr. Chapman, he's terrified of his wife. He's already given her far too much stake in Hunt properties, and she dangles that over his head like a sword.'

'Did you sleep with Tina Barr in the bedroom of your apartment?' Mercer asked. 'Where you kept the book?'

274

Hunt took too long to think. The answer must have been yes.

'But where was your wife?' Mike asked.

'One of the cats must have his tongue, Detective. Josie spends most of her weekends in Millbrook. Tally's to the manor born, of course. And she's to the barn born—but to the manor well-adjusted. Loves living the grand country life there.'

Mercer stepped closer to Talbot Hunt, pressing Mike's arm to encourage him to move away. 'We need to have this information, sir. Did Tina Barr know about the psalm book?'

'Of course she did. She's a—she was a very accomplished conservator. It interested her as much as anyone else in our world.'

'Were you intimate with her?'

They were face-to-face, ten steps away from Minerva and me, in the darkened foyer.

'Yes, Mr. Wallace, I was.'

'We're going to need to know when that relationship started and when it ended.'

'I told you that it wasn't a relationship. I'll try to give you any specifics I remember.'

'Did she spend time in the bedroom of your apartment?'

'Yes, Mr. Wallace. Are you through humiliating me? Yes, she did.'

'Did she have a key to your apartment?'

'Of course. She was doing work there for me. I trusted her with my entire collection. Why wouldn't I give her a key?'

Mercer's voice seemed to get lower with every question he asked. 'Did she know where the drawer was, the one in which you locked the book when you left town?'

Talbot Hunt paused for several seconds. 'I—I guess she might have. It's possible she saw me fetch it from the bureau after a weekend away.'

Minerva turned away, reached for a small silver bell on one of the tables, and rang it. 'I think I need a drink.'

'My sister, the virgin queen. Hard to take criticism on this subject from you.'

Mercer tried to keep Talbot focused on Tina Barr. 'After you realized the book was missing, did you talk about it with Tina?'

No wonder he hadn't called the police. He'd first have to explain the probable suspect to his wife.

'I'm really not sure. I must have mentioned it to her.'

Minerva was more incredulous than I was. She didn't let the appearance of the butler interfere with her response. He stood silently and waited for her order. 'How could you not have known, Tally? I don't even spend time at the library, but I know that she'd lost their trust, too.'

At my first meeting in Battaglia's office with Jill Gibson, Pat McKinney had called Tina Barr a forger—and a thief.

'A vodka gimlet,' Minerva said.

'Now, madam? At this hour?'

'Now, Bailey. Right now,' Minerva said. 'If you didn't know it, Tally, then you're the last one in town. The girl shared a bed with the master thief, too, before he got caught. Tina Barr used to run with Eddy Forbes.'

CHAPTER TWENTY-NINE

'If you don't feed me,' Mike said, 'I'm going to put some mustard on my shoe and eat it. Then I might start on your toes.'

It was midafternoon, and the list of things we had to do and people we had to find and interview continued to grow.

'That's about as dysfunctional a family unit as I can imagine,' Mercer said, shaking his head. 'All the money in the world and the two cats are probably the only living things Hunt can trust.'

'Coop's starving me. I can't even think, man.'

'Let's not waste time on a meal. Pull up in front of P. J. Bernstein's,' I said, referring to my favorite Upper East Side deli. 'I'll hop out and get sandwiches while you call the feds and get an address on Eddy Forbes.'

'Make it two turkey clubs for me, a bag of chips, a cream soda, and you got a deal. Mercer?'

'Ham and provolone on rye toast.'

We were less than five minutes away from the Third Avenue classic deli. Mike double-parked while I ran in and placed my order with the counterman.

'What do you know?' I asked as I climbed into the back seat.

'The lieutenant just called. They had to let Billy Schultz go. His alibi for last night held up just fine. Three other guys working late with him. That's the bad news.'

'What's the good?'

'His office is less than ten blocks away from the

library. Think they need to work those alibi witnesses a little harder.'

'I still don't like his DNA in the mask from the first break-in at Barr's apartment,' I said. 'His explanation strikes me as weird.'

'I told you the lab said it's a mixture, Coop. Enough saliva there to get another profile—it just doesn't match anyone in the databank.' Mike had spread a napkin across his lap, holding half a sandwich in his right hand as he navigated uptown again with his left.

'Tell her what Peterson said about the phone call,' Mercer said.

'Traces back to a booth on the corner of Sixth Avenue and the Deuce.'

'So this creep lurked around the library and watched until Tina's body was found—and about to be bagged—and then dialed up her cell?'

'We're dealing with a freaky-deaky guy, in case you hadn't figured that,' Mike said, looking at me in the rearview mirror. 'C'mon, girl, you still gotta eat.'

'The whole damn crew is freaky,' Mercer said. 'You got a sister-brother act that's as ugly as anything in Greek mythology, a too-nosy neighbor whose DNA winds up in an important piece of crime scene evidence, a one-armed guy who lives in the chapel of an old cancer hospital, a library executive who lied to Alex the first time they met, the most successful map thief in recent times now on parole, and a young turk with books bound in human skin who was so anxious to be wheels-up that—'

'I'll be wheels-up his ass if he neglected to tell us about his visit to Jasper Hunt,' Mike said. 'And this

278

dead girl—may she rest in peace—gets more complicated by the hour. What was she doing in bed with Talbot Hunt? And Eddy Forbes?'

'What did you learn about Forbes?'

'Sentenced to only three years, over the objection of just about every library director in the galaxy. Got out seven months ago, with some time off for good behavior. Reports to his parole officer in Maine every week.'

'Didn't he ever live in the city?'

'Yeah, in Chelsea, but he lost his lease when he went to jail. The feds seized all his books, maps, papers. They're still in the process of trying to match up the stolen things with libraries that haven't even missed them yet.'

'Any family here?' I asked.

'A younger brother on the West Side. Chow down and I'll have you there in no time.'

I nibbled at the corner of my sandwich. 'Who's his brother?'

'Name is Travis Forbes. That's all I know at the moment. Don't get pushy.'

'Well, where?'

'First floor in a brownstone on West One Hundred and Fourth Street, off the park.'

We had visited Alger Herrick in his opulent apartment only one block away. 'That's close to where Herrick lives.'

'A universe apart, actually. This area's still a run-down bunch of tenements.' Mike had devoured the first sandwich before we entered the transverse drive. He washed it down with a swig of soda and a handful of chips before starting on the second one.

When we reached 104th Street, Mike turned in to the block. School had let out for the day, and

279

kids, most of them black and Hispanic, had clustered on the sidewalk. The department Crown Vic—an obvious intrusion in the 'hood—caught the attention of most of them, who watched with interest as we got out of the unmarked car.

I climbed the steps and opened the vestibule door. The name T. Forbes was next to a buzzer, and I pressed it. Several seconds later, I heard a voice through the intercom.

Mike nudged me out of the way. 'Travis Forbes?'

A man answered. 'Yes.'

'Mike Chapman. NYPD. I'd like to talk with you.'

There was no response.

'You there, Forbes?'

A dark-skinned kid who appeared to be about twelve years old had followed Mercer up the steps.

'He don't let nobody in, dude. He real shy or something.'

'You know him?' Mercer asked.

'I seed him around. Yo, you know his brother real famous. Got locked up. Got took away in handcuffs. His picture was in the paper and they even looks alike,' the kid said, totally animated. 'You the man?'

Mike pressed the intercom again. 'I am. But I guess Mr. Forbes doesn't think so.'

'You give me ten dollars if I get you inside?'

'Not by breaking in,' Mercer said. 'You live here?'

'Down the street.' The kid smiled and tsked at the suggestion he might do something illegal. 'Naw. Hit four-C. Ms. Jenkins.'

I pressed the buzzer.

It must have taken almost a minute for her to get to the intercom. 'Hello?'

'Give me the ten,' the kid said to Mercer, who took a bill out of his pocket.

'Yo, Ms. Jenkins? It's Shalik. You need anything from the store?'

'Milk. I need milk and a loaf of bread, dear.'

'Let me in so's I can get the money.'

The buzzer sounded and Shalik opened the door for us. He pointed to a door behind the stairwell. 'That his,' he said, starting the climb to the fourth floor.

Mike went ahead of me and pounded on Travis Forbes's door. The three of us waited in the hallway, and Shalik stopped in place.

'Police,' Mike said, banging again.

'Do you have a warrant?' the voice inside responded.

'You watch too much television, Travis. Open up. I just need some information about Eddy.'

'He's not here.'

'That's a good start. Now open the door.'

'You can't come in. I've just got a robe on. I'm dressing to go out.'

'As long as you're not gonna expose yourself to me, crack the door.'

I heard the lock disengage and the door opened several inches, coming to a sharp stop as it strained against the small chain that secured it. I could see a shock of brown hair, but the man's face was shadowed.

'We want to talk to you, and I'm not gonna do it in the hallway,' Mike said.

'How many of you are there?'

'Three of us.'

281

Travis Forbes paused. 'There isn't room for you. It's a very small apartment.'

'I'll send in my thinnest partner. She'd fit in a closet,' Mike said. 'Put some clothes on. I'm not moving till you do.'

'Give me a few minutes then,' Forbes said. He closed the door and walked away from it.

Mercer backed up and turned around. 'Let me check out the building. Wouldn't want to spook him out the window. There a fire escape?' he asked Shalik.

'Yeah. Go through the back alley. You could climb up it, see all the crazy shit he got piled in there.'

Mercer left as the kid came down the steps and approached Forbes's door, squeezing his wiry frame between Mike and me.

'Whoa, Shalik. Where're you going?' Mike asked.

The kid turned the knob and gently pushed on the door till it caught against the chain. He slipped his skinny arm through the space—just several inches wide—twisting his body as he slid the metal catch out of place.

'Future perps of America,' Mike said. 'You can't do that, Shalik.'

'I be done,' he said, standing back from the door, which swung open. 'You look, Mr. Detective.'

From the floor to the ceiling of the entryway, with only enough room for a single individual to pass through, were stacks upon stacks of books, magazines, and yellowed newspapers, piled on top of one another and towering over my head. They were so densely packed together that although they gave the illusion of being about to tumble over, there wasn't anywhere for them to fall.

'Get on your way, Shalik. Scram,' Mike said. He had one foot in the hallway and one over the threshold. 'You call the lieutenant, Coop. Tell him to stand by. Tell him we've got a Collyer situation.'

CHAPTER THIRTY

I knew Mike well enough to do as he directed before I asked why. He was on his cell to Mercer, asking if he'd seen any sign of Travis Forbes from the alley behind the building.

'Well, he hasn't come back out yet. Call if you spot him.'

'What's a Collyer?' I asked as we waited in the quiet hallway, the door still ajar.

'Cops, firemen—all 911 responders—that's the designated expression for a house so full of junk it's treacherous to get inside, or back out,' Mike said, reaching up to pull newspapers off the top of the nearest pile. 'Look at this. Dated three years ago. You never heard of the Collyer brothers?'

'No.'

'Two very rich guys who lived in Harlem in the 1930s. Well educated, from a prominent family, but really eccentric. They saved every piece of junk they could find on the street. Hoarders, they were. Hermit hoarders,' he said, reaching up to the second pile. 'Here you go, catalogs from rare book auctions in London.'

Still no sign of Travis. Mike handed two of the catalogs to me. '2002,' I said. 'A little late to put a

283

bid in.'

'Homer Collyer, the older brother, went blind. So the younger one began to save newspapers,' Mike said, sweeping his arm across the piles of Forbes's out-of-date dailies.

'Why?'

'In case Homer ever regained his sight, Coop. Then he'd have all the news that he'd missed to read. They even booby-trapped the whole place against thieves. So the younger one got stuck in one of his own traps and buried in the rubble, while Homer starved to death. Rats took care of the rest of him.'

'I get the point.'

'You get a call to a Collyer, you don't know what to expect to find under the debris. Junk? Stolen books? Maybe a body or two?'

Mike's phone rang. He listened and then repeated to me what Mercer told him. 'Travis just peeped out the back. Made eye contact with Mercer. Maybe now he'll move our way.'

'Hey!' Forbes called out from the far end of the hallway. 'You can't come in here. You can't just break the lock.'

'I swear I didn't,' Mike said. 'I guess it just—just fell. What have you got here, Travis? You know how dangerous it is to keep paper jammed in here like this? A regular fire hazard.'

Travis Forbes was either embarrassed by Mike's discovery or simply didn't like to make eye contact. I guessed him to be in his late twenties, about my height, with a sad expression lingering within the intense gaze of his dark, bespectacled eyes.

'I understand,' he said.

'What's with yesterday's news?' Mike asked.

284

'I started saving things for Eddy. Things I didn't think he could get in prison. It's—it's just a habit.'

'Somewhere along the way, I guess Eddy told you the federal can is like summer camp, no? The *Times*, the *Journal*—that's all those swindlers and crooks read.'

'I told you, it's a habit. It's what I do.'

'You into rare books, too?' Mike asked, taking the catalog from my hand.

'No. No, I'm not. I—I was keeping that for Eddy.'

'This auction took place years before your brother's arrest, years before he went to prison,' I said.

'Then he must have given it to me to hold for him,' Travis said, shrugging. 'I've got lots of Eddy's stuff.'

'The feds ever been here?' Mike asked.

'These things were released to me after Eddy got in trouble. He had to give up his apartment and had nowhere to store them. The FBI went through everything he owns. They know all about it.'

It was as obvious to Travis Forbes as it was to me that Mike wanted to get inside and ferret through every piece of paper, looking for stolen books and maps, or anything else of value. It was also obvious he didn't have a leg to stand on, other than the one that was planted inside the door.

'Who lives here with you?' Mike asked.

There was a wooden board on a slice of the wall beside the door, with several jackets hanging on pegs.

'Nobody.'

'You collect clothes, too?' There were windbreakers in different colors and weights on top of one another, and a workman's denim jacket with the label of a Maine utility company on the sleeve, covering the upper part of a white lab coat.

Forbes didn't answer.

'When was the last time Eddy was in town?'

'He hasn't been here since before he was sent away. I haven't seen him.'

'Pets. You got pets?'

'Tropical fish. I have an aquarium.'

I imagined Forbes sitting alone in his fortress of useless papers and old books, staring at brightly colored fish in a tank. He seemed far too aloof and cold to be a companion to any warm-blooded animal.

'What do you do, Travis?'

'I wait tables.'

'Where?'

'Near the Columbia campus, on Broadway. Place called the Lion's Pub.'

'How long have you been doing that?' I asked.

'Since I ran out of money to finish graduate school, a year and a half ago. I'm a neurobiologist. At least, I will be when I complete the program.'

'What are your hours there?'

'Eight p.m. till we close. Four in the morning.'

'And last night?' I asked.

'Same,' Travis said, while I tried to penetrate his blank stare. 'What does this have to do with my brother?'

My exhaustion had me seeing suspects at every turn. If Travis Forbes had the same access to the library that his brother once enjoyed, he could have found his way to Tina on Wednesday evening, in the conservators' office, and back again to move the body last night. But if his alibi held tight, he

286

wouldn't have been standing on a nearby street corner—with us in his sights—at the time the body was found and the ghoulish, laughing caller rang on Tina's cell.

'Do you know a girl named Tina Barr?' Mike asked, refocusing the conversation.

'Who?'

'A friend of your brother's.'

'Eddy's a lot older than I am. We never really socialized together.'

'This is someone he worked with,' Mike said. 'A conservator. Restores rare books and old maps.'

'I know what a conservator does, Detective,' Travis said, growing more churlish by the question. 'Ask Eddy. You must have his number.'

'Why don't you give it to me, just in case?' The ex-con was likely to have two phones—one that his probation officer used and one for his friends and family.

'I'll have to ask him if he wants me to do that.'

'I'll wait.'

'Not in here, you won't,' Travis said, taking his hands out of his pockets to try to close his front door, dislodging Mike's foot.

Mike tried to keep his balance by grabbing at the jamb with his left hand while his right one settled on Travis Forbes's wrist. 'Sorry. I get it. We're out.'

Travis shook loose of Mike's accidental grasp. At the same moment, we both saw the cuts on the back of Travis Forbes's left hand. Long narrow strips of red-lined flesh protruded from both ends of a bandage strip.

'What's with the scratches, pal?' Mike asked. 'Your fish got fangs?'

287

The soft-spoken young man covered his bad hand with the good one. 'Leave me alone.'

'You ought to have that looked at,' Mike said. 'Could get yourself a nasty infection. I got a doc who'll check it out for you.'

Mike wanted to see the injury, just as I did. He wanted to compare the size and shape of the wound to the marks on Tina Barr's neck. Maybe she had tried to defend herself with one of the sharp tools from her own desk.

'I've already been treated,' he said, putting both hands back in his pants pocket.

'By whom?'

Footsteps charging down the staircase overhead signaled the reappearance of Shalik, on his way from Ms. Jenkins's apartment to run her errands.

'How'd you get those cuts?' Mike asked. 'You drop a steak knife on the job? I'm trying to help you out here.'

Now only Mike's fingers on the door jamb prevented it from closing. 'Who cut you?'

Shalik stopped to listen to the conversation, squatting on one of the steps, his nose between railings of the banister. But Travis Forbes didn't speak.

Shalik let out a low hissing sound, and Forbes's head snapped up to look at him.

'Quiet, kid,' Mike said. 'I'm asking you once more, Travis, before I tell Ms. Cooper here to get me a subpoena to photograph your hand. Who cut you?'

'Hisself.'

Shalik repeated the word he had said the first time, when I had misheard him.

'Look in his pocket, man. He do it at night

sometimes in the summer, sitting on the stoop. He crazy, Detective.'

'A subpoena for what?' Travis Forbes said, withdrawing his right hand from his pocket again. He spread it open and in it was a razor blade. 'Talk to my shrink. I didn't think my problem was illegal.'

Travis Forbes unbuttoned the cuff of his shirt and started to roll up his sleeve. Scars lined his inner arm, and marks that looked like they'd been left by lighted cigarette butts dotted the skin on the outer side.

Mike's hand dropped to his side.

'Take care of yourself, Travis,' he said, backing away. 'Here's my card if I can do anything to help.'

CHAPTER THIRTY-ONE

'I gotta tell you, Mercer, I took one look at the guy's messed-up paw and I was ready to throw the cuffs on and collar him,' Mike said, turning off Central Park West for the ride through the park to my apartment. 'We gotta slow this down before I make a mistake.'

'I never saw Mike turn on a dime so fast,' I said from the back seat, patting him on the shoulder. 'He went from executioner to social worker in a heartbeat.'

'Yeah, well, what makes you such an expert on self-mutilation, kid? I don't think I've ever had one of these.'

'Alex and I have seen more than our share of it because the highest incidence is among teenage girls.'

'Does it mean that Travis Forbes is suicidal?' Mike asked.

'Not necessarily,' Mercer said. 'It's a form of intentional self-harm without actually having the wish to die.'

'So why do they do it? I mean, not the psychobabble, but what do you know about it?'

'The docs tell me that self-mutilation is some sort of outlet for strong negative emotions,' I said. 'Usually anger or shame. Anger at someone else that's then directed against the self.'

'So maybe he's embarrassed about Eddy,' Mike said. 'Mad at him for ruining the family name, being such a jerk to get caught. Is it always done by cutting?'

'Knives and razors,' Mercer said. 'They're the most popular. Biting or bruising yourself, pulling out hair, putting out cigarettes on your skin.'

'That fourteen-year-old we had last year,' I said to Mercer. 'Remember? The one whose mother blamed her when the baby brother died?'

'Yeah. The shrink said she was dissociating. That her mind just split off that memory, which was too painful to keep in her conscious awareness. Whenever she hurt herself, she felt alive again.'

'Well, I should have given Shalik a bigger reward. He saved me from making a fool of myself with Forbes.'

'And it doesn't seem that Travis has his brother's book interests. I mean, you wouldn't keep rare books in a junk heap like that,' Mercer said.

'We've still got to get to Eddy. His name just comes up in this too many times to ignore,' Mike said. 'I'm dropping you at home, Coop?'

'Please.'

'I'll hang with you for the autopsy,' Mercer said to Mike.

It was almost four when I got out of the car and walked into my lobby. I stopped for the mail and went upstairs, as anxious to know whether Luc was waiting for me there as I was to step into the shower and clear my head of the day's confusion.

I unlocked the door and went inside. 'Luc?'

He didn't answer, and I was almost relieved to have a brief respite to myself.

There was a bouquet of white lilies on the table in the foyer, and a piece of notepaper next to the vase.

Darling—Must be you had a very busy day. I missed hearing your voice, even to tell me you had no time to talk. Joan reserved for the four of us at 7:30 at Patroon. Très Americain, *which suits me fine. Dreaming of a great steak, a serious Burgundy, and a night with you. Am off to some appointments and will see you there.* à toute a l'heure, ma princesse.

I didn't want to leave the comfortable cocoon of my home. I wanted to give Luc all my attention before he left for the West Coast in the morning.

His professional world—completely luxe and extravagant—was so diametrically opposed to the trauma that surrounded my colleagues and me that sometimes it was hard for me to imagine how we communicated at times like this. An overdone salmon, not enough mustard in the vinaigrette, or a table that couldn't turn over on time seemed to me, an outsider, to be the kind of urgencies restaurateurs confronted. I knew there was more to Luc's business than that, but on days like this

291

one, it all seemed so frivolous.

I went into the bedroom and stripped off my clothes. I tried to sneak into the bathroom to turn on the water for a steaming hot shower without glancing at myself in the mirror, but there was no escaping how tired I looked, and how overwrought I felt.

I dried off and wrapped the towel around me as I slipped under the comforter to take a short nap, setting the alarm to make sure I didn't oversleep.

At six-thirty, I awakened and put myself together for the evening. My wardrobe palette was heavy on pale blues and greens, even for fall and winter, but I didn't feel like color tonight. I dressed in black—a clingy sweater and a short pleated skirt.

The makeup helped, and a crystal barrette to hold back my hair added some sparkle around my face.

I was ready to go downstairs to find a taxi when my phone rang. Caller ID displayed the telephone exchange of the morgue.

'Hey, Coop. Just thought you'd like a heads-up, give Battaglia a shout about the autopsy results,' Mike said. 'Dr. Assif called it. Fatal incised wound associated with an air embolism in the jugular vein. The cut is longer than it is deep. Killer just hit the right place. Tina would have collapsed immediately. No struggle. No defensive wounds.'

'And the weapon?'

'It's not any of the ones we submitted for comparison, but Assif likes the angles on those conservators' paring knives. She'll be testing a slew of them.'

'So sad,' I said. 'And still no news of Tina's

mother?'

'Commissioner Scully has the State Department on it now. I'll let you know what we hear,' Mike said. He hesitated before speaking again, and for some reason I couldn't explain, I stayed on the line. 'Coop? Everything okay?'

'Just thinking about the week, the two women. Tina Barr and Karla Vastasi.'

'You sound down.'

'I just took a nap. I'll shake it off.'

'Want company? Me and Mercer—'

'No—'

'Sorry. Forgot I was dealing with the grammar police. Mercer and I can come over for a while.'

'Thanks, Mike. You need to chill as much as I do.'

'Call you tomorrow, then. Double or nothing on *Jeopardy!*'

I left a message on Battaglia's home machine. In another effort to put the day behind me, I dabbed perfume behind my ears and down the length of my throat.

I wrapped a long cashmere stole around my shoulders, applied a new layer of lipstick, and headed for the lobby.

Oscar held the door open for me and I waved good-bye, grateful for the crisp autumn weather.

I walked to the end of the driveway on Seventy-first Street, knowing the odds were better that I'd find a yellow cab from there. The Marymount College auditorium was just down the block, and weekend nights there was a steady flow of drop-offs for theatrical events at the school.

I stepped off the sidewalk and raised my arm in the air. Three or four cabs were lined up on the far

293

side of the one-way street, queuing to discharge their fares. Another that was already empty flashed his headlights and lurched in my direction.

When I got into the cab, I leaned toward the opening in the Plexiglas partition and spoke to the driver. 'Good evening. I'd like to go to Forty-sixth Street, between Lex and Third.'

'You got it.' He started the meter running and I sat back, my head against the window.

After the second light, he made the turn onto Lexington Avenue on our way downtown. The reggae music coming from the speaker behind my head was too loud, but there was no point getting into a squabble during the short ride.

'You got a team, miss?'

'Excuse me?'

'I aksed you if you got a team. Baseball.'

The driver was looking at me in the mirror. I could see only the outlines of his black face highlighted by white teeth.

I returned the smile. 'Yankees. I'm a Yankee fan.'

'Dodgers. I like the Dodgers.'

'You're lucky—you got Joe Torre.'

'That's not why they my team. It's Los Angeles. I got family in Los Angeles.'

'Nice,' I said, looking at the designer windows at Bloomingdale's as we drove by.

'You got family, miss?'

There was no winning. Tell the guy I wasn't interested in his chatter and I'd be lucky if all he did was call me rude.

'You hear me?'

'I do.'

'Where? Where they be?'

294

I smiled wanly this time. 'All spread out.'

'Sisters and brothers?'

'Two brothers.'

'Here in New York?'

'No.'

We were speeding past the nondescript buildings on Lexington till we were stopped by a red light at the rear entrance to the Waldorf, mercifully close to my stop.

'I aksed you where they be?'

His voice had an edge to it now. I put my hand on the door handle, grabbing a ten-dollar bill from my purse. Then I did what I told every nervous tourist to do in a yellow cab, and looked below the partition for the driver's permit and photo. The plastic sleeve that was supposed to hold his identification was empty.

'Texas,' I lied. 'Texas and Minnesota. You want to release the lock, please?' I was pulling at it, but the driver clearly had the controls.

The light changed and he floored the gas pedal, throwing me back against the seat.

'Good to know, miss. Case I want to do my own family search,' he said, laughing at my growing panic. 'And you ought to leave Wesley right where he's at in Los Angeles. Be real good for your health to do that.'

How many days and nights had this cabbie been waiting for me to come out of my building alone?

'It's Griggs, Miss Prosecutor. Anton Griggs.'

'Open the door,' I screamed at him, trying to grab my phone.

He braked to a halt on the corner of Forty-seventh Street and I heard the click of the lock. I practically fell onto the pavement as I pushed at the door and jumped out of the cab, scraping my arm against the rough edge of the door. The shawl caught on the exposed metal as I slammed it shut.

'You let Wesley be, girl,' he called out to me. '' 'Cause I got more brothers than you got brains.'

My chest was heaving as Anton Griggs sped away, the cashmere stole hanging from the side of the cab like a limp body being dragged through the city streets.

CHAPTER THIRTY-TWO

'You sound like you can't breathe,' Mercer said. 'Slow down, Alex.'

I had practically run the block and a half to the restaurant before calling Mercer.

'I'll be all right. Are you with Mike?'

'He's on the phone in Dr. Assif's office. Why?'

'I want you to know what happened,' I said, describing the nightmare cab ride and how I had played right into the patient hands of Anton Griggs. 'Obviously, you have to tell the lieutenant, and I'll call Battaglia, but hold off on Mike for tonight. He's likely to go ballistic and head off after Anton and Tyrone Griggs. We don't need any more trouble.'

'And the judge?'

'I'll tell him in chambers on Monday. It's smarter to have one of the guys from the DA's squad handle this. I need Mike as a witness in the underlying murder case.'

'I'll run Anton Griggs. You get a plate number?'

'Not even a partial. I wasn't thinking. I just

wanted out.'

'Understood. You want me to stay at your place tonight?'

'No, thanks. I've got—well, um, Luc is in town. We're having dinner with Joan and Jim. I'll be fine.'

'Sounds like Anton had his moment if he was going to do anything more than scare the pants off you.'

'A total success at that.'

'You're on the street? I heard a car honking.'

'Just going into the restaurant, I promise.'

'I'll check in with you in the morning. You got your Saturday ballet class?'

'I've just done my best leap. I'll play hooky tomorrow.'

'You know Battaglia will put someone on you the minute you call him,' Mercer said. 'I'd just as soon have it be me.'

'So would I. But I want to wait till Luc goes to the airport in the morning. I'd like a semblance of a normal social life for the evening.'

'You're entitled to that. We'll talk.'

Ken Aretsky welcomed me to Patroon with his usual warmth and charm. We embraced and exchanged kisses. 'Good to see you, Alex. I hope you're not coming down with something.'

'No, Ken. Why?'

'Well, you're all flushed and perspiring a bit.'

That was a polite way of telling me I was sweating and shaking. 'The traffic was wild. I had to sprint the last couple of blocks.'

'Better for me. That's bound to make you even hungrier,' he said, leading me into the dining room, where New York's power brokers gathered

297

to make deals over the superb food for which Aretsky was known. 'Joan's at the table. Jim took Luc upstairs to show him the private dining rooms and the rooftop bar. Happy to know I'm getting you into my business.'

'That's entirely Luc's doing, I'm afraid.'

Ken led me to the banquette in the front corner of the room and left me to bask in Joan Stafford's effusive greeting.

I slipped onto the seat beside Joan, and after we hugged she asked to be brought up to the minute on everything I'd been doing.

'Sweetheart, did you even have time to see the news tonight? Your case is all over it. What did that poor girl do to deserve to die like that?'

'Isn't it tragic?'

'I know you can't tell me anything, but it's so dreadful. We like to think of libraries as uplifting sanctuaries, but there have been murders and thefts associated with the best of them. Someone walked out of Cambridge University with a million dollars' worth of rare books a couple of years ago when my play was in rehearsal in London.'

'I didn't know about that one. It's mind-boggling, isn't it?'

'Mark Antony plundered the entire library of Pergamon so he could give it to Cleopatra as a wedding present. Nothing new under the sun.'

A novelist and playwright, Joan knew more about literature than anyone I had ever encountered. Brilliant, funny, and incredibly chic, she was happily married to an expert in foreign affairs who wrote a nationally syndicated column. Joan and my college roommate, Nina Baum, were the most loyal of friends, and I leaned on their

298

shoulders during my more serious investigations.

'So I'm learning. And the characters who people this world—'

'Tell me about it. I go to those library benefits, and let me remind you that it isn't all classy trustees like Louise Grunwald and Gordon Davis. The NBC reporter said the Hunts might be involved in this brouhaha,' Joan said as Stefan, the maître d', came over to fill my flute with champagne. 'You don't want to find yourself between Minerva Hunt and a rattlesnake. She'll take your eyes out in a flash.'

'How about Jonah Krauss?' I asked. Joan had one of the grandest homes in East Hampton, where she'd been summering all of her life. There were few people of substance there that she didn't know.

'You're talking very north of the highway now, Alex,' she said, referring to the less fancy neighborhoods on the far side of Route 25, which split the Hamptons in half, where many of the newly rich had built their McMansions.

'We met with him this afternoon. He's actually got a book bound in human skin.'

'Check his wife's plastic surgeon. She's had so much work done, they probably had enough left over to bind an encyclopedia,' Joan said, clinking her glass against mine. 'Listen, sweetheart, when the reporters come after you on this one, promise me you'll trowel on some foundation. You came in here all flushed and now you're so white, you look as though you've seen a ghost.'

'I thought I had, Joanie.'

'You must just be exhausted. Let's give you some delicious comfort food and send you home to

299

bed. Here come the guys,' she said, pointing at Jim and Luc, who had stopped in the bar to talk with Ken. 'Things going okay with Luc?'

'He's wonderful to me and it's been very exciting. There can't be a worse week for him to be here, though. I've been so unavailable on every level—physically and emotionally.'

'If I see your head fall into the bisque during dinner, I'll kick you under the table,' she said, reaching out and squeezing my hand.

'I'll stay awake,' I said, as Joan's usual good humor restored my calm.

'Not to worry.'

Luc came directly to my side, bending over to kiss me on each cheek before he and Jim took seats opposite us. 'I was so worried that Mr. Battaglia wouldn't give you the night off, darling. How do you feel?'

'Better, for the three of you.'

Luc lifted his glass for a toast to Joan and Jim, then turned his attention back to me.

'I'm going to miss you terribly, Alexandra. You look stunning tonight.'

'Please don't—'

'She's right to stop you, Monsieur Rouget. Or I'll never believe anything you tell me,' Joan said, wagging a finger at Luc. 'She looks drawn and tired and thin. Awful is how she looks. Stunned, not stunning.'

'My English doesn't need correction, *chère madame.* After all, Alex was called out by the police in the middle of the night. She's had absolutely no rest, and she's got me to deal with, too.'

'You were there?' Joan said, turning to me. 'You

had to go out to the scene? You didn't tell me that.'

'Let's talk about somebody else's week, okay?'

'I just sit in a room and make up stories all day. This was one of the mornings the muse decided not to visit. Can't I ever come out to a crime scene with you?' Joan asked. 'Mike would let me, wouldn't he?'

'He adores you. Of course he would,' I said. 'Did you accomplish anything today, Luc?'

'For me, it was very exciting. I was just telling Ken that I think I've found a property, a townhouse very much like the original Lutèce, also on the East Side, in the Fifties. As soon as I talk with my advisors, I'm going to make a bid on the building.'

'You must be so happy,' I said, pleased to disengage from my own worries and participate in Luc's enthusiasm.

'How divine,' Joan said, lifting her glass again. 'I'll give the opening party.'

'*Pas si vite*, Joan. It won't happen that fast,' Luc said, talking to Joan but looking at me. We both knew she enjoyed the role of matchmaker and was trying to push us together at a speed greater than we could deal with.

Jim's diplomatic skills saved the moment, and he arranged for Stefan to take our order. He had just interviewed the British prime minister earlier in the day and had marvelous insights into the economic conference about to start at the United Nations.

By the time Joan and I shared a profiterole that made up for all the calories I had missed during the week, I was ready to fold. Jim's car was parked in front of the restaurant, and they offered to drop us off on the way home.

I took Luc's arm for the short walk to the car, searching the dark street to make sure Anton Griggs hadn't circled back to wait for me again.

'So who's the killer?' Joan asked as she buckled her seat belt.

'You're worse than Battaglia. Give me a week or so, will you?' I said, as Luc gently hugged me closer.

'How's your Flaubert?' Joan asked.

'*Madame Bovary.* That's it.'

'Luc,' she said, completely focused on the homicide case again. 'You know *Bibliomanie?*'

'*Bien sûr.*'

'It was the first story Flaubert published, Alex. And it was based on an historical event, wasn't it, Luc?'

'*Oui. C'est vrai,*' he said. 'Fra Vincente was a monk in Barcelona in the Middle Ages. A bibliomaniac.'

'He became so obsessed with owning a particular rare book about the mystery of St. Michael that he killed to get his hands on it. A monk, Alex. Just think what some of your characters might do. I'll get you a copy so you can read it.'

'That's the last thing I want to do, Joanie.'

'You see? I've got all this useless information,' she said, throwing her arms up in false despair. 'If only I could try a case. Where did I go wrong?'

Jim stopped in front of the door and Luc helped me out of the car.

The champagne had relaxed me, and I let Luc take me by the hand and lead me into the

302

bedroom. I was relieved that no light was flashing on my answering machine, and ready to shut down the professional part of my life that so often intruded on my spirit.

We made love—Luc's tenderness and sincerity piercing the steel-like armor that I subconsciously developed to protect myself against the world in which I worked. I slept soundly until early morning, when he awakened me by making love to me again.

It was so pleasantly normal to lounge in my robe with my lover on a Saturday morning, to do the *Times* crossword puzzle, sip coffee, enjoy the omelet Luc whipped up with French cheeses he'd stocked in my refrigerator.

When eleven o'clock came and the doorman called to tell us that Luc's car service was waiting for him, he pulled me onto his lap and held me tight.

'It's only going to be a week or so, darling. I'll be back very soon,' he said.

I walked him to the door and said a cheerful good-bye, then closed it behind me, taking the paper into the bedroom so I could curl up and finish the puzzle.

He'd barely had time to get into the car when my phone rang. The caller ID showed it was Mercer.

'Good morning,' I said. 'I really admire your timing.'

'I have more respect than you think for the good things in life, Alex.'

'Where are you?'

'Closer than you'd like me to be.'

'I promise I'll call Battaglia and tell him about

Anton Griggs. I'm not going anywhere.'

'I'm in the lobby. The doorman just pointed out your friend to me. Thought the least I could do was give you the morning.'

'I'm okay, Mercer. Really.'

'It's not about you, Alex. Sergeant Pridgen's the squad commander in the sixth precinct now. Called me about a victim of his who's hospitalized in St. Vinny's. I'm going down to talk to her, and I'm sure you'll want to come along.'

'What's it about?' I asked, throwing the paper to the side.

'Her apartment was broken into a few nights back. The guy knocked her out with chloroform, just like Tina Barr.'

CHAPTER THIRTY-THREE

Pridgen was waiting for us outside the patient's room on the fourth floor of St. Vincent's Hospital, pacing the quiet hallway. We had worked with him in the SVU when we'd had our first cold hit, just after Mercer was shot by a desperate killer.

'Good to see you both,' he said. 'Wish I could sit down, but the chief of d's ripped me a new one at yesterday's COMPSTAT.'

'Been there,' Mercer said.

The brilliant Computerized Statistics program originated with the NYPD in 1994 as an aggressive approach to crime reduction and resource management. Weekly meetings of the department's seventy-six precinct commanders, on Friday mornings at headquarters' most high-tech facility, were designed to improve the flow of information between supervisors.

'The captain made me go yesterday 'cause he thought my case was so unique,' Pridgen said. 'I stood at the podium, laid out the facts, and that crew leaped on me like I was a rookie just out of the academy. "Why didn't you do this? Why didn't you think of that? Why didn't you call Special Victims?" How was I supposed to know about your case? It wasn't in the papers or anything. And mine wasn't a sex assault.'

'But one of the execs figured they might be related?' I asked. 'Is that why they made you hook up with Mercer?'

'I got a push-in with a bastard who chloroforms the vic. Those guys think I didn't question her as good as you would have about a sex crime. They think I might have missed something. Said you had a similar case a few days earlier.'

'Let's hear what you've got,' Mercer said.

Pridgen's plaid polyester jacket was so worn, it almost shined. His cheap tie wasn't knotted, just crossed—detective style—below the open collar of his shirt.

'Jane Eliot—one tough broad,' he said. 'Eighty-one years old.'

'Your witness?' Mercer asked.

'Yeah. I mean, I know we've had sex crimes with women older than that, but my guys asked her about it. She passed out and all, but her clothes were never disturbed. All we got is a push-in with a guy who ransacked the apartment.'

'Take anything?'

'Don't look like she had much of any value. Not even electronic stuff. She hasn't been back there to tell us whether anything's missing.'

'Can we talk to her?' I asked.

'Yeah. She doesn't see too good. Has real thick cataracts.'

Pridgen opened the door to the room and announced himself as we went in. 'Hey, Miss Eliot, how's it going? Pridgen here.'

'I'm doing well. Though the social worker says they won't release me until Monday,' she said. 'Observation and all that.'

The handsome woman, perfectly erect in a vinyl hospital chair with her feet on the ottoman, was dressed in a housecoat, listening to the opera on a small portable radio.

'I brought you those friends I told you about. This here is Ms. Cooper, and the big guy is Detective Wallace.'

'How do you do?' she asked, shifting her head as though trying to make us out. 'I'm Jane Eliot.'

'I'm Alex and he's Mercer. I guess you know who we are.'

'I do. And I know you're not here for my blood or my temperature, so that's just fine,' she said, smiling at us. 'Pridgen, would you bring in a few chairs?'

I explained our purpose to Jane Eliot, without mentioning Tina Barr, and told her we needed to do another interview, to probe even more thoroughly.

'It's rather odd for me, Alex. I've lived such an ordinary life for so very long that I can't understand all this interest.'

'Why don't we work backward, then?' I said, sitting on one of the chairs that the sergeant had brought into the room. 'Get the worst over with

306

first. When did this happen?'

I wanted the facts, and I also wanted to know how clear she was.

'Wednesday. It was shortly before noon,' Jane Eliot answered without any hesitation. 'I've got my favorite shows to listen to, so I know exactly what day and time it was.'

'Where do you live?'

'Greenwich Village,' she said. 'On Bedford, between Morton and Commerce streets.'

'How lovely. Such a pretty area.' The historic district of tree-lined streets and small townhouses was one of the safest parts of the city. 'That's the block where Edna St. Vincent Millay's house is, if I'm not mistaken.'

'Precisely, young lady. The narrowest house in the Village—nine and a half feet wide. Are you a poet as well as a lawyer?' Eliot asked, leaning over to pat me on the knee.

No question she was as sharp as a tack. I laughed. 'No, ma'am. All lawyer.'

'I've been there for many, many years—on the first floor, thank goodness. I don't think I could climb those steps very well anymore.'

'Do you live alone, Miss Eliot?'

'Yes, dear. Always have.'

'How large is your apartment?'

'Just a small parlor, my bedroom, the kitchen, and a little den.'

'Why don't you tell us exactly what you remember about Tuesday?'

'Certainly. I was waiting to get my local news and weather, enjoy the chatter on one of those midday shows. There was a knock on my door, which surprised me, because the buzzer hadn't

307

rung.'

'There's an outer entrance that's kept locked?'

'Always.'

'What did you do?'

'I was in the den, turning on the television, so I walked through the apartment to the living room. The knocking came again, and I asked who was there.'

'Did someone respond?'

'Oh, yes. The young man spoke to me. Told me he had a package.'

'For you?'

'That's what has me feeling foolish. I don't get many packages, other than an occasional fruitcake from my niece and nephews around the holidays. Can't give them away fast enough.' She was spunky and quick to smile. ' "Not for me, you don't." That's what I told him.'

'What did he say?'

'That it was a delivery for my neighbor. He even had the name and apartment right. Miss Ziegler in two-C. Then he told me to look through the peephole so I could see his uniform.'

While Jane Eliot was talking, I heard Mercer ask the sergeant whether there was a list of names in the building's vestibule. He nodded and mouthed the word 'yes.'

'My vision isn't too good these days,' she said, 'but I can make out shapes and colors. I can see, Mercer, that you've got a very large frame, that you're a tall man, black skinned. And you're quite tall yourself, Alex, with lovely golden hair.'

'Thank you.'

'Mine was red,' Jane Eliot said. 'Fiery red. Well, there he was in one of those brown jackets. You know that delivery service that's all done up in brown?'

Tina Barr's assailant had dressed in a fireman's uniform but lost his mask at the crime scene. Was he enough of a chameleon to change his disguise less than twenty-four hours later?

'Tell me about Miss Zeigler,' I said. 'Have you ever taken packages for her before?'

'Heavens, yes. It's hard for someone like me, without a computer, to understand how she does it, but the girl buys everything online—her books, her clothes, and sometimes even her food. She works for a travel magazine so she's on the road often, and I'm used to accepting deliveries for her.'

'Had she asked you to take anything in this week?'

Jane Eliot bit her lip. 'It's not that I like to look foolish, Alex. But she doesn't always remember to ask me.'

'There's nothing wrong with what you did, Miss Eliot. What happened isn't your fault. I don't blame you for opening the door,' I said. 'Would you tell us what happened when you did?'

She inhaled deeply and continued speaking. 'The fellow pushed his way in, and that's when I lost my balance. I didn't fall, thank the Lord, but I grabbed for the bench behind me and sat down on it. That's when he dropped the parcel—a small box—and I thought maybe he had stumbled on something.

'Then he bent over, not to get the box, but to get me,' she said, becoming a bit emotional. 'He covered my mouth with a cloth, with some kind of fabric that he'd soaked in something dreadful. I thought I was going to die, young lady. I—I couldn't breathe. I got so dizzy. I remember the room spinning, and that's all.'

'A few more things, if you don't mind,' I said, letting her recover from reliving those frightening moments. 'Can you tell us anything about the man who did this?'

'Nothing that Sergeant Pridgen found very helpful.'

'Now, Miss Eliot,' Pridgen said. 'You've been terrific.'

'You called him a young man, Miss Eliot. And I understand you have cataracts, but do you have any idea how old he was?'

'Look at me, Alex. I call everyone young.'

My turn to bite my lip.

'He was white, I know that for sure. He was an adult, not a teenager. But I couldn't see his features, if that's what you're asking.'

'No marks on his face, when he got up close to you?'

'Clean shaven is all I can say. Usually I can make out facial hair if a man's got it. Didn't see any of that.'

'Did his uniform have any markings on it? Could you see?'

'You mean like the name of the company? I'm sorry. I just couldn't tell you that.'

'We've checked those services, Alex. These days, they've got their scanners current to the second. They can account for all their drivers in the area,' Pridgen said. 'He wasn't legit.'

'Was the box still there when you came to?' Mercer asked.

'I never saw it again.'

'What's the next thing you remember?' I asked.

'My goodness, it was hours later. Almost five o'clock. There I was, right on the very same bench. Like I was Sleeping Beauty, gone for a long nap and never been missed.'

'Were you injured?'

'I—I didn't know. There's no cushion on that old bench, so I was stiff as a board. And awfully dizzy still, with a terrible headache. Must have been that stuff he had on the cloth. The doctors think it was chloroform.'

'But nothing broken?'

'How many times have they had me to X-ray, Mr. Pridgen? MRIs and all these other fancy tests.'

'I'm going to ask you something very personal, Miss Eliot. Sergeant Pridgen has explained what my job is, why Mercer and I work together,' I said. 'We need to know whether this man touched any part of your body before you lost consciousness.'

Jane Eliot sat up straighter and talked more seriously. 'Now, why would anybody want to do *that*?' she asked. 'I'm an old, old lady. Of course he didn't touch me.'

It was the specifics I had to establish, whether she wanted to hear them or not.

'What had you been wearing, Miss Eliot? Can you tell us that?'

'Pridgen knows. A housecoat, like this one, but light green. They button up the front so it's easier for my arthritic shoulders than lifting over my head.'

'And was your clothing disturbed?'

'Hard to disturb a wrinkled housecoat, isn't it?'

'Do you have any sense that this man might have touched your breasts?'

She put one arm to her chest and chuckled.

311

'They were right where I left them, Alex. He didn't have anything to do with them.'

'And your undergarments? Did you have any type of underwear on?'

'These young men probably don't remember the word "girdle." I wear a firm girdle, and support hose for the circulation in my legs. Might take a construction crew to get through all of that.'

'I'm glad to know that you weren't molested,' I said, 'and that nothing was broken. Do you have any idea why someone would want to break in to your home?'

'I've been sitting here going on four days. Plenty of time to think about it,' Jane Eliot said. 'He was either just a fool, or he broke in to the wrong apartment.'

'Do you have any valuables there?' I asked. 'Has anyone had a chance to see what was missing?'

'I taught elementary school till they put me out to pasture at sixty-five. Fourth grade mathematics. Multiplication tables and time tests—everything that became obsolete with the new math. I'm at an age at which I give my possessions away, Alex. Never had the money for fine things, and don't like the clutter. Had a sweet set of porcelain dolls people brought me from all over the world, but I gave them to my niece years ago.'

'No cash that you kept in the house? No jewelry?'

'I was wearing the only piece of gold I own. Couldn't have missed it if he was looking for something pricey to steal. It's bright and shiny, and practically the size of an alarm clock,' Jane Eliot said. 'Show her, Pridgen.'

He walked to the bedside table and picked up

the watch, noting its heft before passing it to me. 'I'll tell you what, Miss Eliot. If you had cracked the bum over the head with this, he'd have been a goner.'

'Wish I'd thought of it then,' she said. 'It's a man's watch, Alex. It was given to my father after fifty years at his job. The big size—and the large numbers—suit me well. I've worn it ever since he's been gone.'

'Fifty years,' Pridgen said to Mercer. 'Today most guys would be lucky to get a bologna sandwich and a pat on the back after working someplace half a century.'

I examined the striking face of the old timepiece. The famous French maker's name written on the dial added value to the watch, which appeared to be made of solid gold.

'He obviously missed the opportunity to take this—it's such a beautiful keepsake. I'm sure that would have been a terrible loss to you. Were there any other things like this that you had hidden away? Any reason for him to ransack your rooms?'

'Not a blessed thing for him to find, I promise you.'

I turned the watch over in my hand and read the inscription on the back of it. *To Joseph Peter Eliot with gratitude for fifty years of devoted service. September 1, 1958. Trustees of the New York Public Library.*

I had begun to think the connection to Tina Barr was a coincidence. But now my adrenaline surged.

'Miss Eliot,' I said, 'your father worked for the library?'

'Started there right out of high school, Alex, as

313

assistant to the chief engineer.'

'And you, did you have any direct association with the place yourself?'

'My dear, I was born in the New York Public Library during a snowstorm in 1928.'

'Not literally?'

'Yes, quite literally, young lady. There was an entire apartment within the library where the chief engineer and his family lived, till they threw us out. Needed the room after the Second World War. Until I went off to college, Alex, the public library was my home.'

CHAPTER THIRTY-FOUR

'Have I tired you, Miss Eliot?' I asked. 'I think you've triggered some information that can help us figure out why you were attacked.'

'I'm just getting warmed up for you. Do go on. I'd like to be helpful.'

'A girl was murdered this week. A conservator who used to work at the library but was involved with private collectors most recently.'

'I heard something about it on the radio this morning. Terribly sad.'

'Mercer and I have been all through the library. No one said anything about an actual apartment within it. Is that what you mean?'

'In 1908, even before the library opened, a man named John Fedeler was named chief engineer. There was a seven-room apartment built for him to live in with his family, and when it came time for him to retire eighteen years later, that's when my father got the job and we moved in.'

'What was it like then?' I asked.

'Quite a spectacular space, really, especially coming from a tenement in Hell's Kitchen, where my parents had lived. It was an enormous duplex, with an entrance on the mezzanine floor, facing the central courtyard of the building. All paneled in the finest walnut. Big fireplaces and leather armchairs that my mother used to sit in at night, reading to us.'

Jane Eliot seemed to delight in her reminiscences. 'It's where I was raised, Alex. We were the envy of all the children at school.'

'What's become of that apartment, do you know?' I asked, as Mercer drew his chair in as close to her as mine.

'I get invited back every few years, a bit like a dog and pony show, to some of those luncheons. The president occasionally puts me on display as the only baby ever born inside the place,' Eliot said. 'But the whole apartment is broken up now.'

'What's it used for?'

'The top floor, where we children lived, that's all become administrative offices. There was a wonderful spiral staircase, so we could go up and down without entering the library hallway. I suppose that's still in place. Our kitchen is the reproduction center—Xeroxing and that kind of thing. And the family living chambers are where some of the special collections are sorted out.'

'You're saying the apartment was self-contained, is that right?' Mercer asked. 'But were you allowed into the library itself?'

'That was the great fun of it, of course. I mean, we always had to wait until all the offices were

315

closed for the evening, but gradually, as time went by, Father let us have the run of the place. After dark, mostly, when it was quite spooky, full of great shadows that came from the streetlights outside, and an eerie quiet that settled over the enormous hallways.'

'The books, Miss Eliot,' I asked. 'Did you have access to the books?'

'Mercy, yes. We thought the whole place was just a playground for the three of us. Roller-skating down those hallways in the evening, playing hide-and-seek in that great reading room.

'Christmas Day, once, George and our cousins decided to play stickball in the corridor on the third floor,' she went on, rubbing her hands together as she pulled up images from her youth. 'He just went into one of the collections—things weren't all locked up back then—and grabbed the biggest books he could find to be the bases. Turned out they were all important double folios. Rare volumes of prints and such, worth a fortune. George got the whipping of a lifetime for that.'

'George?' Mercer said, trying to keep up with her.

'My older brother was George Eliot,' she said. 'Mind you, my mother didn't even have a high school education. When my father got the job there, she decided to name all her children after writers. She didn't know George Eliot was a woman until she began to educate herself with all the wonderful treasures under our roof.'

'For whom were you named?' I asked.

'Jane Austen. I'm Jane Austen Eliot. I had a big sister, too. Edith Wharton Eliot. Both my siblings are gone now, but my niece and nephews are very

316

good to me.'

'I can appreciate that—mine are, too,' I said. 'Tell us more about the books, if you don't mind.'

'I've always loved books, of course, and that may be because I grew up surrounded by them. They were the center of the universe in our family.'

'Did you have books of your own?'

'Our father made it very clear to us that everything in the library was very special, that none of it belonged to us. But for every holiday the trustees would present us with books. I remember our birthdays in particular. After we returned from school, if it was a birthday, we'd get called to the president's office, all dressed up in our best, and one of the board members would give us a gift, explaining the importance of the particular book and its author.'

'Sounds like a fine little ceremony.'

'Oh, it really was. I got my first *Pride and Prejudice* that way. They were always heavy on Austen for me, of course. I've had a lifetime of pleasure because of those gifts, Alex. It made the loss of my vision even more painful.'

'The books that were presented to you, Miss Eliot, were they ordinary things you could buy in a store?'

'There's no such thing as an ordinary book, is there? But these were always particularly unusual. Beautifully bound in Moroccan leather, or fixed up in those—what do you call them?—clamshell boxes, I think. I can still remember how it felt to hold and smell them for the first time.'

'Did you know the trustees?'

'Most of them knew my father well, of course. He was responsible for making sure that their

317

treasures were safe and protected, at least according to the methods available back then. He made sure their great institution ran like a smoothly sailing ship. And my mother catered some of their smaller meetings—everything homemade, right in our kitchen. She was really a saint.'

'These gifts you received,' Mercer asked, 'were they new books?'

'Some were, some weren't, as I recall it.' Jane Eliot put her elbow on the arm of the chair and closed her eyes to think. 'Later, as I learned more about these things, I'd have to assume that we got some of the castoffs, either second or third editions of books that were of no value to the great collectors, or copies that had been damaged by tears or discolorations. Still, Alex, they opened the world to me. All the classics, all the great literature you could imagine. The three of us were grateful to have them.'

I could hardly contain my excitement. The perp must have staged this burglary to get at something Jane Eliot owned, something she didn't even realize was of value.

'The books that you were presented with, Miss Eliot, are they still in your apartment?'

She stretched her right leg and groaned, bending to tug at her hose. 'I gave them away ten years ago, maybe more. What's the use, I thought? I'd read and reread them, when I had my sight. Time to let the next generation enjoy.'

'But you know where they are?' Mercer asked.

'Gone to my great-nieces and -nephews.'

'How lucky they are to have them,' I said. 'Is your family here, in the city?'

318

'Gosh, no. Some of them are upstate in Buffalo, and others are out in Santa Fe. Must be several hundred books, all split up between the relatives.'

I sat back in my chair, as deflated as the burglar must have been to come up empty after ransacking Eliot's apartment.

'Not a single one that you kept for yourself?' Mercer asked.

'Help me up, Pridgen, will you?' Jane Eliot said. 'My joints get all locked tight if I sit too long.'

The sergeant helped her get to her feet.

'Walk with me, please,' she said, linking arms with Mercer and with me as we stood up. She moved toward the door of the room. 'There was only one that I kept. Had to keep, actually. Edith's daughter would have nothing to do with it.'

'Why is that?' I asked.

She winced as she put her weight on her left leg. 'My sister, Edith, had a very special book presented to her on her twelfth birthday. I remember so well because I was terribly envious when she brought it back to the apartment.'

'What was it?'

'You may be able to make more sense of what happened than I ever did,' Eliot said. 'Because of your job, I mean. Nobody talked about things like that back then. It was a copy of *Alice in Wonderland*. Quite a dazzling one.'

Mercer and I exchanged glances over Jane Eliot's head.

'Dazzling?' he asked. 'How so? Was it old?'

'Indeed it was—old and wonderfully illustrated with those drawings by John Tenniel that became so famous. The date in it was 1866.'

I thought of the call slip that had been found in

319

Tina Barr's clothing.

'Did it ever belong to the library?' I asked.

'Not this one, I don't believe. Most of our gifts were donations from one trustee or another. From time to time, books were quietly deaccessioned from the collections of course, especially if some more desirable copy came along. But we could tell if that were the case. There were markings inside the jackets with the name of the library branch, and those were crossed through to show that the book had been discarded, so we knew we wouldn't get in any trouble.'

'Edith's gift sounds very special.'

'Oh, yes. That was obvious. It was bound in the most glorious red leather, with gold lettering on the spine and gilt designs all over the cover. And then there was its size—we'd never had books of our own quite that big.'

Jane Eliot let go of my arm and drew an outline in the air. 'You know, sort of double folio, if you're familiar with that.'

'I've seen other copies of the early editions, though, and I never knew any to be oversize,' I said.

'Well, you're right. The manuscript was of average size, for an illustrated work of that period, I'm sure. But this particular edition had been mounted on larger parchment pages and bound into this folio because it also included a rare set of prints of the photographs that Charles Dodgson—Lewis Carroll, you know—took of young Alice.'

'The photographs were inside the book?' I asked.

'There was a pocket sewn into the back of the book. That's where the photos were. We could

320

take them out and look at them, spread them out on the living room floor,' she said. 'In fact, that's what got Edith in trouble with Mother.'

Jane Eliot shuffled down the hallway of the hospital, continuing to talk to us.

'Why?' I asked.

'The book wasn't a problem. We'd all read the story dozens of times. But those photographs? My goodness. Must have been weeks after Edith's birthday, Mother happened upon the picture of that child dressed as a beggar maid, with her bare shoulders—you know the one I mean?'

'Yes, Miss Eliot. It's a very famous image.'

'Well, it convinced my mother that Dodgson was a pedophile. She wouldn't have us looking at a little girl displaying herself that way.'

'Alex was just telling me that story about him,' Mercer said. 'I'd never heard it before.'

'What did your mother do?' I asked.

'That was the last we saw of the book, until she lay on her deathbed. She forbade Edith to have it, which created its own stir at the time. Then Mother asked one of the curators in the children's collection to do some research about Dodgson. What she learned was that Alice Liddell's mother had a big falling out with him. Tore up all the correspondence that he'd had with Alice. That inflamed my mother even more.'

Mercer tried to frame a question. 'Because she thought he'd been . . . ?'

'Inappropriate, sir. That's as explicit as we got in those days,' Eliot said. 'It seems Mrs. Liddell found every letter the man sent to her daughter—mind you, she was only eleven or twelve at the time, and he was a grown man—and she ripped

321

them to shreds. That's a fact. And then, when Dodgson died, he left thirteen volumes of diaries. A record of his entire life. But someone in his family was worried enough about the contents to destroy the four years—every page of them—that detailed his friendship with Alice.'

'So your mother confiscated the book,' I said.

'First thing she did. Poor Edith—the girl had a tantrum over that. I can still hear her screams. The next thing was, my mother had it in her head to go after the trustee who'd given my sister the book. She found some letters he'd written to Edith after the day he met her, telling her how proud he was of her school grades.'

'How did he know about them?' Mercer asked.

'Some of the trustees—the nice ones—used to ask us questions like that when they came to see Father, or on the holidays. Harmless enough. What books did we like? What subjects were we studying? We were the library's little family, you see. But Edith kept the notes this man had sent her, offering to take her out in his automobile— nobody had cars in those days—show her parts of the city she hadn't seen. He didn't have a daughter, he said. Just a boy. Said he wanted to be her friend.'

'I can understand why that upset your mother,' I said. 'Edith was only twelve at the time, right?'

'Yes, ma'am. Just like Alice Liddell. So Mother went on a rampage. I was there the afternoon she came home and told Edith that she had walked all the way up Fifth Avenue to his mansion, the day after a terrible snowstorm. Knocked on the door and demanded to see the man. She wanted to give him back his book. Can you imagine her taking on such a rich and powerful person as a trustee of the New York Public Library?' Eliot asked, proud of her mother's spirit. 'She came back and told Edith there'd be no more presents from him, and no more visits.'

'Miss Eliot,' I said, trying not to get ahead of myself. 'Do you know the man's name? The trustee who gave Edith the book?'

Her slippers scuffed along the linoleum floor.

'Of course I do,' she said. 'It was Jasper Hunt. Jasper Hunt. Edith said he called himself the Mad Hatter. Oh, she was very peeved at Mother for ruining her fun.'

Jasper Hunt Jr., the eccentric owner of the rarest map in the world.

'Did Edith ever tell you what she meant by her "fun"?' I asked.

'Not what you're thinking, Alex. No, no. Mr. Hunt never did anything improper, Edith assured me of that. But Mother's concern was with his intentions. And for Edith, it seemed like she'd been deprived of a great adventure, a chance to be treated like a grown-up. In hindsight, I'd say Mother nipped something in the bud.'

'And the book—how did you come to have the book?'

'Mr. Hunt was very patient with my mother. He brought her inside, had her served tea and pastries, and removed the photographs that had offended her. He told her that she must keep the book. That one day it would be worth a lot of money and she couldn't deprive Edith of that.'

'So your mother returned home with the book?' Mercer asked.

'Yes, but she had made such a fuss about the

whole thing that she never admitted it to us. Not till just before she died. She'd kept it on a shelf in her linen closet all those years. Finally told Edith to take it and have it appraised.'

'But you said Edith didn't want it.'

'She was stubborn, my sister,' Jane Eliot said. 'She felt it had spoiled her birthday. Didn't want anything to do with it. The whole episode had embarrassed her with the staff and all that. You know how girls that age are.'

'I sure do,' I said. 'Did you ever show the book to a dealer?'

'A couple of years ago, after Edith passed on, I called someone at the library. I wouldn't know how to find a reputable dealer. The president's assistant gave me the name of a man who worked closely with them, she said. I've forgotten it at this point. Anyway,' Jane Eliot said, 'by the time I got around to contacting him, my letter was answered by the FBI. They told me the fellow was in jail. Now, that was quite a shock, since it was the library folks who had recommended him to me.'

'It must have been Eddy Forbes,' I said.

'Forbes. That could have been the name.'

'Did you describe the book to him in your letter?'

'Yes. That was the point of speaking with him, wasn't it? I had left several phone messages, too. After that,' Jane Eliot said, 'it just didn't seem worth bothering, if even the dealers turned out to be thieves. I really wasn't interested in its dollar value. I don't want for anything, and my relatives have plenty of other rare books. It wasn't mine, after all.'

'So you have it still?'

'I did, until just a few months ago,' Jane Eliot said, stopping in her tracks. 'I gave it back.'

'Back?' I asked. 'To the library?'

'No, no. I did my genealogy, dear. Easy to do with folks as well known as the Hunts. It turns out that old Mr. Hunt had one son, just as he had told my mother. Jasper Hunt the Third, who's even older than I am. I wasn't about to give anything to him.'

She squeezed my hand and smiled again.

'But I learned there's also a granddaughter. A woman named Minerva. So I wrote her a note. I told her about the book, about our family's connection to the library,' the old woman said, pointing toward the door of her room and directing us toward it. 'I left out my mother's suspicions about Minerva's grandfather, of course.'

'Did she return your correspondence?'

'She didn't seem the least bit interested at first. I didn't get a reply for several weeks. Then I wrote again. My writing isn't too neat, because of my vision. Of course, I can't see the detail on the pages of that old book very well anymore, but I tried to describe how beautiful it was. I told her about the map that the Mad Hatter had tucked in that pocket in the back, with the photographs.'

Mercer jumped in before I could open my mouth. 'There was a *map*?'

'When my mother was dying and she told Edith and me about the book, she said that Mr. Hunt had insisted she keep the map. The very first day we had opened the book, we saw the map, of course. George spread it out on the floor at once, but it wasn't nearly so interesting to us as the photographs.'

325

'But why was there a map?' he asked.

'Do you remember that Alice—the one in Wonderland—went to a tea party?'

'Sure, the Mad Hatter and the March Hare were there,' I said. 'But what did the map have to do with the tea party?'

Jane Eliot slowly started to move again. 'Let me think what Mother said. It was a big old map, folded up several times, as I recall. It was a picture of the island of Ceylon. Mr. Hunt said that's where the tea came from. The tea for the party.'

Jasper Hunt certainly lived up to his reputation for eccentricity.

'He told Mother to leave the map right where it was. That it would increase the value of the book, in the end. He said he wanted to make up for alarming her, to do right by Edith,' Jane Eliot said. 'So Mother saw no harm in keeping it. Like Jasper told her, he loved the library, too, and knew that we did. She had her piece of the Hunt legacy.'

CHAPTER THIRTY-FIVE

'Is that how your mother referred to Jasper Hunt's gift?' I asked.

'At the end of her life, when she talked about him.'

'Were those her words, or his?'

'I don't have any idea,' Jane Eliot said.

'Did you finally get Minerva Hunt's attention?' Mercer asked, helping to lower the woman into her chair.

'She couldn't have been more gracious. Came

all the way downtown to visit me. She really seemed so pleased that I had thought of her. Brought me a beautiful plant.'

'And left with the book?' Mercer asked.

As Mike liked to say, that's why the rich were rich. Minerva Hunt exchanged a potted plant for a rare book and a piece of one of the most valuable puzzles in the world.

'Oh, yes. Such a sentimental lady. She seemed almost in tears about it. Turned the pages of the book, kept stroking the map, too, though she never took it out to open it up.'

'What did Minerva talk to you about, Miss Eliot?' I asked. 'Did she speak about her grandfather?'

'I talked mostly. About the library and such. She asked some questions.'

'Like what?'

'She was very curious about the other books we'd gotten as kids. Were any of them quite as big as this one? But they weren't,' Eliot said, scratching her head as she recalled the conversation. 'She wanted to know if I'd told anyone else about Edith's gift. That's what she was most interested in.'

'And have you?' Mercer asked.

'Certainly, but years ago. No one's listened to me in ages. There was a time, after Jasper Hunt was gone, and my mother, too, that I made a few speeches at the library, to the trustees. They always seemed to enjoy stories of what we did there as kids. It kind of brought the great institution to life.'

'Did you mention the map?' he said.

'No. It never really made an impression on me as a child, Mercer. I saw it so briefly, and now I can't really see at all. At those meetings, I described how we lived, the significance of the books that were given to us, particular books—like *Alice in Wonderland*—that sort of thing.'

'Did that satisfy Minerva?' I asked.

'A touch of sibling rivalry, I guess,' Jane Eliot said with a chuckle. 'She was more concerned about whether her brother knew about the map. I can't pull up his name at the moment, but she wanted to be very sure I hadn't sent a letter to him before she'd responded to me.'

'You hadn't?'

'No, no. Young people would call it sexist, but I thought that lovely book should go to a girl. I was hoping maybe Minerva had children, but she told me she doesn't.'

'In your correspondence with Eddy Forbes, Miss Eliot,' Mercer said, 'did you mention the map that was inside your copy of *Alice in Wonderland*?'

'I certainly did. I remembered what Jasper Hunt had told Mother about its value.'

'And you've never heard from Forbes himself?'

'Thank goodness, no. And the FBI wasn't interested at all. They only wanted to know if I'd done any other business with Forbes. They didn't even come to see me.'

There was no reason for the feds, at that time, to have thought there was any significance to Jane Eliot's attempt to reach Eddy Forbes.

'Was there anything else Minerva mentioned?'

'No, Alex. Not that I can think of. She hugged me quite warmly before she left. I figured I'd made a new friend. She seemed so concerned about my health, too. Just lovely.'

'But you haven't heard from her since?'

328

'Actually, I haven't. It sounds as though you think my old copy of *Alice* had something to do with this attack on me. Am I right?'

'We'll let you know as soon as we figure it out, Miss Eliot. I promise you that,' I said. 'Can we do anything to make you more comfortable here before we leave?'

'Take me with you,' she said, chuckling again.

'You'll go home in grand style when you're released. The sergeant will get you there in a blue and white chariot. We'll have your place all straightened up.'

I knew she'd be shocked to see her home turned upside down, and to know there was fingerprint powder on most of her furniture. Someone from Witness Aid would be on top of helping with her homecoming.

Pridgen walked us to the elevator as Mercer speed-dialed Lieutenant Peterson. 'Loo? Don't worry—I've got Alex covered for the day. She's going to be with me. This Jane Eliot push-in is definitely a piece of our case—Tina Barr and Karla Vastasi. You need a uniformed cop posted at her hospital door, 24/7, in case this creep decides to come back at her.'

Mercer listened to Peterson's reply and gave me a thumbs-up.

'And I'm about to call Chapman. Seems his heartthrob, Minerva Hunt, has been keeping secrets from him. Looks like she's lied to us from the start. I think it's time to round her up and hold her fancy pedicured toes to the fire.'

CHAPTER THIRTY-SIX

'So everybody's keeping secrets from me, huh?' Mike said, combing his fingers through his hair. 'First Minerva Hunt and then you. All of a sudden I find out you're so worried about my temper, you won't even call me when one of the Griggs takes you for a ride. Do you honestly think I'd do something stupid to compromise Kayesha Avon's case after eight long years?'

The three of us were standing in front of Tina Barr's building. Mike had been on his way to the apartment when Mercer reached him as we left the hospital room.

'I apologize,' I said. 'It just seemed smarter at the time to let someone else in the squad handle last night's episode.'

'It would have seemed smarter to me at the time not to get in the frigging cab with Anton Griggs. He's got a rap sheet longer than the Holland Tunnel.'

'You didn't mention that when you testified at the hearing.'

'Don't give me attitude, Coop. Anton doesn't bother with his birth name too often. He's got a different alias for just about every arrest. Most of the collars are in Jersey, so I missed it first time around, okay?'

'What's the plan, Mike?' Mercer asked, ever the peacemaker. 'I told Alex not to call you. Let her be.'

'Falling on your sword for her again, huh? Do it too often and there'll be permanent puncture wounds in your heart,' Mike said, tapping his fingers on his chest. 'Don't say anything, Blondie. It's only a joke.'

I felt a pang of guilt and looked away.

'Bea Dutton is on the subway, on her way to meet me here. She wants to show me the historical footprint of these buildings.'

While we waited, Mercer told Mike the details of our interview with Jane Eliot.

He had barely finished the story when Mike pulled out his cell phone.

'Slow it down,' Mercer said. 'Who are you calling?'

'Carmine Rizzali. If I find that useless thug who she pays to protect her, we'll know where Minerva Hunt is.'

I could see Bea walking from Lexington Avenue, waving as she saw us standing on the steps of the brownstone.

Mike slapped the phone shut. 'Doesn't even go to voice mail. Guess he's catching on,' he said. 'Yo, Bea. What have you got for me?'

'Can we go inside, so I can spread out my maps?'

'Sure,' Mike said, leading us down to the basement apartment—the scene of Tina's assault and Karla's murder. Crime scene tape was still draped across the doorway, but Mike had brought a key with him.

When we reached the kitchen table, Bea unzipped her bag. 'What do you know about these buildings?' she asked.

'Only that there's lousy karma in this basement lately.'

'It didn't start out that way,' she said. 'You know

something about the Hunts, I take it?'

'Nothing good,' Mike said. 'Educate me.'

'Jasper Hunt and John Jacob Astor became partners in the real estate business. What Manhattan properties Astor didn't buy, Hunt did.'

Bea Dutton spread out one of her maps on the table.

'Here's where we're standing,' she said, pointing at East Ninety-third Street on a copy of a fairly primitive map of the city. 'This row of brownstones was built in 1885. Pretty swell digs at the time.'

Mike squinted and looked at the writing. 'Now, how can you tell when it was built?'

'I did the vertical search for you,' Bea said, knowing she had captured Mike's interest. 'The 1884 maps don't show any of the structures. The next year, here they are.'

'Why were these maps created annually?'

'Did you ever hear of the Great Fire of 1835?'

Mercer and I were shaking our heads, but Mike answered, 'Yes. It destroyed hundreds of buildings in lower Manhattan.'

'That's right,' Bea said. 'Everything that was in today's Wall Street area. These are called Sanborn maps, made by a company right after that fire. They were done for insurance purposes, for claims. Sanborn had the idea for these very detailed maps, showing every structure on the island. Can you see?'

Her finger pointed from building to building as she talked. 'The brick buildings, like these, were colored in pink. Things built for industrial use were green. And down the block a bit, you see the yellow ones? Those represent wood frame houses—more likely to burn, less likely to get a good insurance rate.'

'Why is this one both pink and yellow?' Mike asked.

'A brownstone, but with a wooden porch in the backyard. I want you to hold that thought, because it's going to come in handy a few maps down the road,' Bea said. 'In the meantime, I can also tell you *why* these homes were built.'

'We're all ears.'

'Jasper Hunt—the great-grandfather of Tally and Minerva—wanted a residence for his mistress. Close to Fifth Avenue, but not so close his wife would be able to smell her perfume,' Bea said.

'Now, how do you know that?' Mike asked, patting her on the back.

'I've got a library card, Mr. Chapman. It serves me well. There were tabloids even back in those days. Five buildings in this row. The one we're in was completed first, and then the one next door was built for the mother of his mistress—a deal the young lady was smart enough to insist upon. The other three weren't quite as grand, but Mr. Hunt built them for servants and staff.'

'And Minerva was still using the basement for the hired help,' Mercer said, referring to Tina Barr.

'The next structural change to note is in 1912,' Bea said, layering her maps on top of each other. 'Something very interesting has been added to the rear of this building.'

'What's that?' Mike asked. 'Can we see it?'

'Look closely. Attached to one side of the pink drawing that represents the house, there's a small black rectangle.'

'Got it,' Mike said. 'But what does it mean?'

'It's an indication that some kind of chamber was added out in the yard—something that would be impervious to fire and water. That's what the black color code tells us. It's not as deep as the basement we're in, which was really helpful for me to know.'

'Why?' I asked.

'Remember yesterday, when Mike made me cancel my meeting with the Department of Transportation about the flooding in the Empire State Building? The men were coming to study the Viele map, so that gave me the idea to search out this site on that.'

'I know you're the map maven,' Mike said. 'But I'm trying my best to follow this.'

'Let me make it easy for you,' she said. From her briefcase she removed another thick paper, which she unfolded, revealing a vividly colored reproduction of a topographical map of Manhattan. 'See there? Egbert Viele, 1865.'

This one had a street grid superimposed on the island, but no structures or buildings. Instead, it showed a city full of ponds, natural springs, and streams, from its southern to northern tips, before it was paved over and populated.

'This is Greenwich Village,' Bea said. 'You can see Minetta Stream coursing below Washington Square. And there's a creek, just underneath Broadway in the Twenties. This blue line, up in Harlem, right around One Hundred and Fortieth Street? That's also a stream.'

And then her fingertip led our eyes to First Avenue, just east of the Hunt buildings. 'And that, my friends, is an underground pond, where water pools and collects—to this very day, no doubt. The stream that leads from it comes right below our feet. You can't possibly trace them today, but every architect in the city still uses this map—like an X-ray of the island—to find out where the leaks are coming from.'

'So what's your deduction, Sherlock?' Mike asked the diminutive librarian.

'Elementary,' she said. 'Who owned the buildings by 1912?'

'You've got better sources on the Jasper Hunts than I do,' Mike said.

'Jasper Junior had just come into his own. Don't forget, he did his world tour, visiting all the European principalities, in 1905. By 1912, according to the yellow journalists of the day, Junior took over where his father left off. He moved his late father's mistress in with her mother, next door, and brought his own to live right here.'

How had Minerva first described the predilections of the Hunt men? Rare books, expensive wine, and cheap women. Jasper Hunt Jr. had a wife, a mistress, and, later in life, perhaps an inappropriate interest in young girls like Edith Wharton Eliot.

'So what is this chamber he built in the backyard made of—Kryptonite?' Mike asked.

'Not so deep as this basement, where we're standing,' Bea said. 'After all, if something was likely to flood in here, it would be ruined. Seems to me, if a man had valuables he wanted to protect—'

'And if Jasper was more than a little bit eccentric, enough so not to entrust things to a bank vault . . .'

'Maybe he built his own vault, right in his babe's backyard?' Bea said. 'Maybe that's where she kept

335

her jewels.'

Mike straightened up and smiled for the first time that afternoon. 'Or maybe that's where he kept the panels of the great map of 1507. High and dry, locked in a waterproof, fireproof chamber where nobody was likely to look. Had to get past his lady love to get to the yard. Buried his treasure under his father's favorite garden ornament.'

'Don't tell me Billy Schultz didn't know what his neighbor was digging for,' Mercer said, crossing the kitchen floor in three strides to open the back door.

Mike was on his tail just as quickly. 'That's a pretty deadly vertical search that landed Tina Barr so permanently horizontal.'

CHAPTER THIRTY-SEVEN

I had gone upstairs to knock on Billy Schultz's door before returning to the backyard, but there was no answer. Both Mike and Mercer were digging with garden spades when I joined them and said he wasn't home. Bea had pulled the collar up on her raincoat and watched them work from a bistro chair set out behind the house.

'You ever get your hands in the dirt up on the Vineyard?' Mike asked. 'You have any idea what we've got here?'

I knelt down beside him. 'The top couple of inches is mulch. These look like tulip bulbs,' I said, lifting out several plantings below the surface. 'Some people plant them in the fall.'

Mike jabbed his small shovel into the dirt again.

336

'Too bad Tina didn't stick around for the spring bloom.'

'She's still the victim,' I said. 'Is there another shovel?'

'Not until Billy Schultz gets home.'

Whoever tended the little garden kept it densely packed with perennials and small shrubs. Mercer was pulling them out to get a better angle as he dug.

Minutes later, I heard the sound of metal clanging against metal. 'I'm in,' Mercer said.

Bea jumped to her feet and both of us clustered behind him. Mike saw the hole in the ground left by Mercer's uprooting of a dwarf pine and started digging furiously. Seconds later, the tip of his shovel struck against some kind of metal vault.

'Right where it shows on the map,' Bea said.

Both men scrambled to excavate the dirt on top of the buried chamber.

Just like on the diagram Bea had shown to us, the exterior of the rectangular chest was almost ten feet long bordering the rear of the house, and only three feet wide.

'It looks like it's split into compartments,' Bea said, peering in over Mike's shoulder.

'Can you tell from your map,' Mike asked as he continued to throw dirt back onto the flagstone path adjacent to the site, 'whether there were peepers way back then in the buildings behind us?'

He raised a valid point. It wouldn't have been a very good hiding place if everyone around could see the dig.

'It appears from the maps I've examined that Hunt enclosed these first two buildings—the ones for his mistress and her mama—with a common

337

wall,' she said, pointing to the brick surround, which was about twenty feet tall. 'The family held on to the property behind us until almost 1930, when those apartments that back up on it were constructed.'

'See that stump?' Mercer said. 'Bet there was a big old shade tree right there that might have given some cover.'

'You gentlemen need to understand something about topography,' Bea said. 'The reason this chamber was displayed on the map is because at some point, the top of it must have been visible, on the surface of the ground. A hundred years later, with shifts in the land, it settled in a little deeper.'

'So what are you telling us?' Mike asked.

'That this would have been much more accessible to Jasper Hunt when he wanted to get to it,' Bea said. 'Probably only covered with a thin layer of sod.'

Mike and Mercer were both kneeling at ends of the chest. 'Doesn't seem to be any opening on my end,' Mike said. 'Totally airtight. How about you?'

'Same.'

Bea looked pensive as she walked back to the house. 'Could be another way at it, don't you think?'

I followed her into the kitchen, where she turned to study the cabinet doors high above the sink, out of reach to both of us. 'You've got me on height, Alex.'

I dragged one of the chairs over and stepped on the seat of it to climb to the lip of the old sink. I pulled at the latch, too useless a location to have ever been replaced by any of the tenants.

It stuck for my first few attempts, then opened

338

wide as I yanked again, practically dislodging me from my perch. Bea reached out to steady my legs.

The thick layer of dust that coated the interior shelf had recently been disturbed. Streaks across the width of the space suggested someone had reached inside.

'You might be right, Bea,' I said.

'Hey, Mike,' she called out. 'Come help us.'

Mercer and Mike were behind me seconds later.

'Make yourself useful, Bea,' Mike said. 'I'll hold her legs.'

He put his hands around my calves, squeezing them to reassure me that all was okay between us.

I reached back and ruffled his thick black hair.

Mercer opened several closet doors until he found a stepladder. He helped me down and, with his great height added to the three steps, was halfway inside the cabinet when he called out, 'There's a false front here.'

He leaned to the side, pulling out the piece of wood that formed the crossbar for the single shelf.

In the space behind the center cabinet—a good four feet wide—was the side of the metal chamber we had seen from above.

Directly in front of Mercer, in the seam of the concealed door, was a keyhole—an old-fashioned design, which looked like it would accommodate a notched tip turned with an ornate bow.

'Call the lab, Mike,' I said. 'Get someone up here with the key that I found in the library stacks.'

CHAPTER THIRTY-EIGHT

'It's a fake,' Bea Dutton said, her gloved hands spreading the parchment that appeared to be a panel of the 1507 world map across one end of my dining room table, after we'd made the short drive from East Ninety-third Street.

We had waited forty minutes in the basement apartment until one of the forensic biology lab techs appeared with the key that I had found along the path the killer probably took to dispose of the body of Tina Barr.

Mercer had opened the locked chamber to reveal a watertight series of metal chests within chests—like a small version of the caskets in Napoleon's tomb—and removed them from the hidden compartment.

The smallest one was fitted with a velvet lining large enough to hold double-folio-size prints. Only one thing—a piece of the map—rested within the case. Mercer removed it and Mike called the lieutenant to tell him we were on our way to my apartment to determine what it was.

'How can you tell it's a fake?' I asked.

'Remember what I said yesterday about forgeries of something as detailed as this piece? The fact that it's a made from a woodcut, not just a drawing?' Bea asked. 'It would be next to impossible to pull off.'

Bea put on her reading glasses and began to examine the paper more closely.

Mike was looking over her shoulder. 'Which of the twelve parts is it?'

'*Winturn Eurus.* The easterly skies. That's the coast of India, with Tibet above it, and the island of Java off to the side. It's one of the easier panels to try to copy because so much of it is just water rather than the finely documented landmasses, which require minuscule writing and exquisite particularity.'

Bea rubbed the edge of the parchment between her fingers. 'The texture is the first giveaway,' she said, starting to explain the flaws. 'Most experts could tell right off the bat.'

'Someone like me, Bea, who doesn't know rare maps,' I said. 'Would it fool me?'

'Stevie Wonder could tell this one's a forgery, Coop. Get with the program.' Mike pulled at a strand of hair that had fallen between my eyes. 'Make yourself comfortable, Bea. Want a soda?'

He walked into the kitchen and helped himself to a soft drink.

'Nothing, thanks. Do you have that photocopy of the entire map I made for you at the library?'

'I got it,' Mercer said. He had brought a stack of work up from the car and sorted it out from the pile he had dropped on the credenza on his way inside.

'Let's lay it out on the table. Do you mind if I move your flowers, Alex?' Bea asked.

Mike lifted the vase of white lilies. 'More where those came from, Bea. Guess this guy didn't get so lucky. The place usually looks like a funeral home when she's put out her best stuff.'

Bea ignored him. 'Grab me some tape and a few pads.'

Mike knew his way around my place. He left the room, then returned from my office with what Bea

341

requested.

'You guys keep going on your end. Let me play with the map a bit,' she said.

Mercer, Mike, and I set ourselves up around the coffee table in the living room. It was late in the afternoon, and the three of us were trying to use a quiet Saturday to regain the territory and figure out what we had to work with so far in the murders of Tina Barr and Karla Vastasi.

'You liked what the old broad had?' Mike asked.

'Jane Eliot?' I said. 'Absolutely.'

'But the guy who broke in to her place didn't bother with a mask. So why would he bother with the fireman outfit the first time he hit Tina Barr's place?'

I leaned back and put my feet up on the sofa. 'Maybe he thought she'd make him, recognize him.'

Mercer nodded. 'Possible. Didn't mean to kill her if he could find what he was looking for in the apartment.'

'Jane Eliot can't see well enough to describe her assailant,' I said. 'If he knew her vision was impaired and was confident she had no reason to identify him from any previous encounter, he didn't have to go to the trouble of hiding his face. Besides that, he'd lost the gas mask.'

'Alex has a point,' Mercer said. 'The delivery uniform he wore to break in to Eliot's was a disguise of sorts.'

Mike had found a deck of cards in the drawer of the coffee table and was playing solitaire while we talked.

'Did you ever follow up with the lab on that DNA profile in the mask?' I asked Mike.

342

'I'm on it. Partial match to Billy Schultz, but it's a combo, so they can compare it to other samples we submit.'

'So how you doing on profiles?' Mercer asked. 'Whose DNA have we got?'

'Schultz's, obviously. But his alibi works for Tina's murder,' Mike said. 'And I gave the lab the Hunts.'

'Which Hunts?' I asked.

'Let's see,' he said, folding his losing hand and shuffling again. 'Minerva's first.'

'I know they're only amendments,' I said, too tired to go at Mike full force. 'But they are still part of the Constitution. Hope the seizures were lawful, but then if they were, I probably would have known about them.'

'That cigarette butt she crushed to death in the squad room the other night? Abandoned property,' Mike said.

'I'll give you that,' I said with a smile. 'Nice work.'

'Think of it, a woman inside a fireman's uniform and mask. Who'd guess that? You automatically assume it's a guy.'

Bea Dutton looked over at us every now and then as we tried to put the clues together.

'You're right, Mike. It would never occur to me, hearing that description, to think of a Minerva Hunt—or a Jill Gibson.'

'What are you saying about Jill?' Mike asked.

'Forget I mentioned it. It's just a personal thing.'

'I'm gonna talk to you about that, Bea,' Mike said. 'You can't hold back if you think there's something that might be useful to us.'

'Sorry. I just think she plays both sides of the

street. She means well, but she's in a difficult position, as an administrator, between sucking up to the board and keeping her staff squared away.'

I made a note on the top of my pad to get back to Bea Dutton.

'So what did you get from Talbot Hunt?' I asked.

'Swiped a cocktail napkin that the butler missed in the living room yesterday. Figured the one with lipstick was Minerva's and the one without was her brother's.'

'Swiped doesn't work for me.'

'Don't get in a swivet about it, Coop. I didn't take it from *his* house. He doesn't have any standing at Papa's pad. Give me any illegal search bullshit and I'll have a seizure.'

'I'll remember to argue that when I'm taking heat in the hearing.'

'Who else should we look at for DNA?' Mercer asked. 'I'd like to go back into Forbes's apartment. See what he's got going on.'

'Ask Shalik to scoop up some Band-Aids for you while Travis is picking himself clean on the stoop,' Mike said. 'I want Alger Herrick. The man with the golden arm.'

'Because you think he's dirty?' Mercer asked.

' 'Cause he likes maps so much.'

'We have Herrick's DNA,' I said.

Mike's head snapped in my direction. 'Promise me you went back to his house and got your sample the old-fashioned way. None of this swabbing and drooling stuff.'

'Not my type, Mikey.'

'So what'd I miss?'

'Herrick told us he'd been stopped for drunk

344

driving back in England,' I said.

'And the Brits do DNA on every infraction, no matter how minor,' Mike said. 'So Scotland Yard has Herrick's DNA profile in the hopper.'

'Frankly, I don't see him playing dress-up,' I said. 'And he certainly didn't do Jane Eliot. She described a young man.'

Mercer stood by the window and dialed his phone. 'Hey, Loo. Get on the horn with that deputy inspector in London who owes you. Alger Herrick—he's got a genetic fingerprint on file there. Ask them to transmit it to the lab, stat, will you?'

Peterson must have assured him he would before Mercer thanked him and hung up.

'Jonah Krauss is another story,' Mike said. 'Walked out of his office gym all pumped and ready to fly out of town. No question he's strong enough to heave that garden ornament.'

'Kinky enough for the first night attack on Tina?' Mercer asked.

'Hey, his favorite display item is a book made out of human skin,' Mike said. 'Plus he has access to all those subterranean spaces in the library.'

'Don't forget his connection to Minerva Hunt,' I said.

'That's a pretty slimy trio—Krauss, Minerva, and Forbes the map thief, all trying to figure out how to find the panels of the great treasure.'

Bea Dutton had been assembling the pieces of the photocopied map. It covered almost the entire top of the dining table. 'Want to see what I've been up to?'

'Sure,' Mike said, throwing down the cards and walking toward her.

I stood and stretched, and we all took up positions on one side of the table, our backs to the window with the high, sweeping view over the city.

Bea stood in the center, flattening the enormous map with her small hands. 'Okay. So we've talked about the twelve panels, right?'

She reached to a chair beside her and raised the image we had found earlier in the day. 'You asked if this fake could fool anyone, Alex, and I'd have to say the answer is not anyone knowledgeable, and not for very long. The paper isn't a fit, it's probably been stained by tea—yes, just an ordinary tea bag—to discolor it a bit, age it some. The drawing itself is rather crude.'

Bea juxtaposed the parchment next to its copy on the map. It formed part of the border on the right, in the midsection.

Mike looked at the pieces side by side. 'I kept thinking of Karla Vastasi when we found this thing in the apartment today,' he said, referring to Minerva Hunt's housekeeper.

'Why Karla?' I asked.

' 'Cause she was set up, Coop. No doubt in my mind that Minerva sent her in, dressed in the madam's clothes, to meet someone who wouldn't have a clue if she was Minerva Hunt or not.'

'Rules out Alger Herrick,' Mercer said. 'And Jonah Krauss.'

'But rules in the possibility that she had brought that tote bag to carry something out—something just about the size of one of these panels,' Mike said, pointing to the map. 'And she wouldn't be expected to know if it was genuine or not.'

'She had the psalm book, too,' I said.

'Maybe she—or the killer—found it there. If

Tina Barr is the one who stole it from Talbot Hunt's apartment, she might have been hiding it on her own.'

'Waiting for the best offer,' Mercer said.

'I smell a cross,' Mike said. 'Somebody double-teaming someone else. Mild-mannered Tina Barr, the pawn in a treacherous double cross, with stakes so high she couldn't even imagine what a dangerous position she put herself in working with any of these greedy bastards.'

'So this document is a fake,' Mercer said, turning his attention back to Bea. 'Let's start with that. What else can you tell us?'

'Let's take this puzzle piece by piece. There's got to be a logic to the way Jasper Hunt broke it up and concealed the panels.'

'Like his son said, Bea, you can't assume that with a complete eccentric.'

'Nonsense, Mike. Maybe what Hunt did won't seem logical, but there had to be some kind of method to his madness, especially if he ever hoped to see these pieces reunited.'

And especially if Jasper Hunt ever hoped to leave this map as part of his legacy.

'What makes you think so?' I asked.

'So far, the two panels found weren't hidden randomly,' she said. 'What's the most important feature of the piece you found yesterday morning in the library?'

Mike was quick to answer. 'The inset about the New World as a separate continent, with the portrait of Amerigo Vespucci. Mr. America, himself.'

'And where did you find it, Mike?' Mercer said, following Bea's lead. 'Tucked inside a rare volume of Audubon's *Birds of America*. Not all that crazy, is it?'

I thought of Jane Eliot's story and looked at the photocopy of the large map, placing my finger on the lower right section that featured Ceylon and Madagascar. 'Jasper put this one in the back of his very unique edition of *Alice in Wonderland* because it made him—the Mad Hatter of the family—think of Ceylonese tea.'

'Ten to go,' Mike said. 'All we need is a list of the double-folio-size books that Jasper Hunt bequeathed to the library. Feeling lucky, Bea?'

'You get the commissioner to open the doors for us tonight, give me a handful of curators,' Bea said, 'and maybe I'll give you the world. Jasper Hunt's world.'

CHAPTER THIRTY-NINE

The combined forces of Commissioner Keith Scully and District Attorney Paul Battaglia were enough to open the great doors of the New York Public Library on Saturday evening at seven p.m.

Jill Gibson, obviously not pleased to be in the dark about what had prompted the gathering of her senior curators and her own police escort, stepped out of a patrol car as we approached the side door.

Uniformed cops had been stationed at all the entrances for almost forty-eight hours now, as investigators continued to work on processing the vast spaces within the sub-basements of the library.

'Excuse me, Alex?' Jill called out. 'May I talk

with you a minute?'

'Whatcha got, Jill?' Mike said, stepping between us.

'I'd like to ask Alex a few questions.'

Mike tapped my shoulder to keep me moving. 'She's fresh out of answers, but we're looking, Jill. We're holding court in the map division.'

The sergeant in charge moved us through the doors of the old carriage entrance and down the twisting corridors until we could see our way to Bea's department at the farthest end of the main floor.

Curators from the various private collections were seated at the trestle tables. Arents, Berg, Pforzheimer, and the rare books division were represented. A dozen young cops, at Mike's request, stood around the room, ready to help.

Mike sat on the edge of one of the tables and started to explain what he wanted the librarians to do.

'How fast can you get together a list of the volumes donated to this institution by Jasper Hunt the Second?' Mike asked.

Jill Gibson didn't wait to be acknowledged. 'If you'll allow me to go to my office, I can print that out for you immediately.'

Mike looked toward one of the rookie cops at the door and told him to take her there. Jill seemed shocked to be under guard in her professional home.

One of the men spoke up before she left. 'It's not that simple, Detective. Many of the Hunt gifts have been in and out of the library over time. I think each of us, in our own collections, could be more helpful than any master list.'

Jill's lips clamped together.

'What do you mean?' Mike asked.

'Take World War Two, for example. You know the windows in the reading room were entirely blacked out,' the man said. 'There were legitimate fears of an air raid, and decisions had to be made about the safety of the most valuable books.'

'I get it.'

'The Gutenberg Bible, Washington's Farewell Address, the Medici *Aesops*,' he went on. 'Things like these were actually carried off-site for protection.'

'And some of the books that were taken away were once the property of Jasper Hunt?' Mike asked. 'Is there some confusion about where they were housed after they were returned?'

'That, of course, Mr. Chapman. As well as the fact that some of the finest volumes simply never came back to us.'

'Because the Hunts kept them?'

The man looked to Jill Gibson before he answered, aware that he was crossing a line. 'That's my understanding. Jasper Hunt Jr., as well as several trustees, decided, rather quietly, it might be a good time to reclaim some of the things they'd given away.'

'Don't wait around, Jill,' Mike said. 'Something you already knew, apparently, and didn't feel the need to tell me. Go ahead and get me your list anyway.'

Then he turned to Dutton. 'You're up, Bea. Tell them what you need.'

She addressed her colleagues, apologized for not being able to say exactly what we were after, and asked them to brainstorm for any insights that

350

went beyond card catalogs, computer lists, and digitization.

'Let's talk about the Napoleonic *Description de l'Égypte*,' Bea said.

She was starting with the most obvious hiding place—the one in which Prince Albert of Monaco had found the copy that Jasper Hunt Jr. purchased in 1905. It was logical that Hunt might have chosen to mimic the Grimaldis. Talbot had told us the day before that his father—probably unknowingly—had given a set of the twenty-volume classic to the library just two decades ago.

'Orientalia,' one of the men said. 'I believe we have three sets of the Napoleonic expedition, all in Orientalia.'

'You know that's not politically correct,' the older woman beside him joked. 'It's the Asian and Middle East department now.'

'Yeah. Rugs are the only things left you can call Oriental,' Mike said. 'People—and I guess books—are Asian.'

I could tell he liked his new team. They were smart and sincere, and seemed to love the rare objects in their care.

'Any of you seen them, these books?'

A man in a madras plaid shirt, with a crew-neck sweater tied around his shoulders, raised his hand. 'I'm Bruce. Bruce Havens. I used to work in that department. The Napoleonic expedition volumes have been completely digitized. You can view the entire thing online, without leaving home. The originals are locked away. Only scholars with a really good reason to see them can get access under a curator's supervision.'

'Do you know the three copies, Bruce?'

351

'Let's say I've seen them, Bea. Is that what you mean?'

'Provenance, Bruce. What's their provenance?'

'Whew. It's a tough issue in that particular collection. Much of what came in was without designation.'

Bea turned to us to explain. 'Bruce means a lot of the photographs and foreign-language volumes were—what's a polite word?—pilfered by explorers during their travels.'

'Sort of like the Elgin Marbles?' Mike asked.

'You got it,' Bea said to him. 'Bruce, do you know the donors of the three Egyptian sets?'

'The prize of the three was a Lenox endowment. An absolutely pristine set of books, in a contemporary French speckled calf, board edges with gilt roll tool. Exquisite.'

'Under lock and key now?'

'Yes, it is. I know you're interested in whether any of them are Hunt acquisitions,' Bruce said, 'but I simply don't know.'

'Any of them submitted to the conservators for repair?' I asked.

'Possibly, but not on my watch. They were actually shelved in the stacks.'

Mike heard the word 'stacks' and stood up, signaling to one of the cops. 'This gentleman's going to take you downstairs to look for something. Stay with him.'

'I wouldn't have access, Detective.'

'Why not?'

'In each department, there are cages—metal cages,' Bruce said. 'Sort of wire mesh, where the rare books are locked.'

'Who's got the keys?' Mike asked.

Bea answered. 'We each have control of our own section. The front office has all the masters.'

Mercer walked to the door. 'I'll take them to Jill Gibson and make sure she gives up the key. You keep at it with Bea.'

'What's next?' Mike asked her.

The Most Noble and Famous Travels of Marco Polo,' Bea said. 'How many different versions of that would you think we have?'

'Jill will know,' one of the men said.

'Forget Jill.' Bea was on a tear.

The older woman spoke. 'We've got the Elizabethan translation by John Frampton in the Berg Collection. It was an Astor gift,' she said. 'Not the Hunts'.'

'I know,' Bea said. 'I've got a version with large folding maps, but it came to us recently out of Lord Wardington's collection.'

I recognized Wardington's name. He had been a mentor to Alger Herrick.

'There must be half a dozen of those spread around,' another man said.

'You.' Mike pointed at him as he spoke. 'Take two cops and scout them out. Any copies you find come right back to this room before anyone cracks the cover, okay?'

Bea was calling on the remaining curators. 'Think Hunt, ladies and gents. And then give me regions of the world. Japan, China, Africa, America—North and South.'

'I've got a huge box that Jasper Hunt donated,' a young woman said. 'Erotic color prints of the Ming period. Sort of Chinese sex life from Han to Ch'ing.'

'We'll take it,' Bea said.

'You got pornography here?' Mike asked.

'Art, Mr. Chapman,' Bea answered with a laugh. 'Only the French library system has the backbone to exhibit the stuff, if that isn't true to type. The rest of us just keep it hidden. Handwritten manuscripts by the Marquis de Sade, English "flagellation novels," Parisian police reports about nineteenth-century brothels, and shelves full of Japanese prints and Chinese illustrations. Some of them courtesy of Jasper Hunt.'

'Sounds like the Jasper Hunt who collected photographs of Alice Liddell,' I said.

'The Slavic and Baltic Collection has an elephant-folio chromolithographed account of the coronation ceremonies of Alexander the Second, the Tsar Liberator,' another voice chimed in, catching Bea Dutton's enthusiasm for her task.

Mike paired the young man with a cop, and they were off to search.

'We've got several editions of the Edward Curtis American Indian photographs that are in folio form in our rare-books division,' a man said, standing and ready to move.

'You want Americana, Detective, we should give those a shot.'

'Tell me more.'

'Curtis took more than two thousand photographs of native Americans between 1907 and 1930 in an effort to document their lives. Tried to sell five hundred sets but went bankrupt before he could.'

'Are they Hunt connected?'

'The set I know was donated by J. P. Morgan. That usually made Hunt try to find something as good, or more elegantly bound. I'd like to look.'

'Go for it.'

Mike, Bea, and I were now alone in the room with a few of the officers still waiting to be assigned to a task. I imagined the library coming alive at night, just like in Jane Eliot's stories, with curators and cops unlocking the cages and exploring the deep recesses of storage areas and stacks.

'I want you to see my thinking,' Bea said, unfolding and respreading the copy of the 1507 map on one of the trestle tables. 'Track these books and drawings as they report back to us.

'It's going to be a long night, guys, but maybe we can match some of these panels to the parts of the world they represent.' She cleaned the lenses of her glasses on the hem of her sweater, then took a red marker from her pocket and numbered each of the map sections from one to twelve, starting in the top left corner. 'Keep an eye on me, Mike. I've got some atlases to search, too.'

'I'd trust you with my firstborn, Bea. Need any help?'

'Come into my cage, if you don't mind.'

We walked through the room and behind the reference desk, past Bea's personal work area. She removed a key chain from her pants pocket and shuffled through the assortment until she found the one that opened the gate to a space that reminded me of safe-deposit vaults.

'These are where the oldest maps are stored,' she said, weaving between chest-high rows of long metal filing cabinets with large horizontal drawers. 'The loose ones, of course.'

Farther back, out of sight from the front desk, was shelf after shelf of old books, all oversized and many of them splendidly decorated.

'All the great cartographers are represented here,' she said. 'Mercator, Ortelius, Blaeu, Seller.'

'Are you looking for something in particular?' Mike asked.

'One of my favorite map-meisters, Detective. Claudius Ptolemaeus.'

'I know. I know all about Ptolemy,' Mike said, looking at the shelves above Bea's head. 'First guy to give us a mathematical picture of the universe. AD 150, right?'

He was quoting the information he had learned from Alger Herrick.

'You're a quick study, Mike.'

His head was moving from side to side as he scanned the shelves. 'The guy is everywhere. What do you want?'

'Once the printing press was invented, illustrated books of every kind became available. Ptolemy's work was translated from the Greek text into all the European languages. The Romans tried to outdo the Florentines, Strassburg's scholars thought they could color the maps more beautifully than in Ulm. Vicenza, Basel, Venice, Amsterdam—all over the continent printers were racing to get these maps in the hands of the rich and the royal. First, second, third editions. It may seem like a lot of them to you, but each volume in its own way is quite rare.'

'Any of these come from Jasper Hunt's collection?' I asked.

'Sore point, Alexandra,' Bea said.

'Why?'

'There it is, Mike. You mind lifting it down?' Bea had spotted the volume she wanted. 'It's a

356

Strassburg Ptolemy. 1513.'

He handed her the large book, and she caressed it as she carried it to her desktop. 'Contemporary Nuremberg binding of blind-stamped calf over wooden boards.'

The front cover was decorated in an elaborate fleur-de-lis pattern with a leafy border, gilt flowers, and gryphons adding to its striking appearance.

'Only thirty-three copies of this work survived,' Bea said. 'And before the Second World War, this library owned a pair.'

'The gift of Jasper Hunt?' I asked.

'At the time, yes, it was. He decided to take one of these atlases back. Long before my time, mind you, but no one here ever saw it again, though I'll bet Jill will still include it on the list of our acquistions she gives you tonight.'

'Sure, rather than agitate—or challenge—any of the Hunt heirs,' Mike said. 'Why are you looking for this version?'

'Because it might have been exactly the kind of idea that would have amused our eccentric friend Jasper Hunt Jr.,' Bea said. 'Remember—no use of the word "America" appeared in any cartography until the 1507 map. It certainly never entered into anything Ptolemaic. But with the development of the press and the incorporation of all the new explorations of the period, the Strassburg Ptolemy of 1513 was the first book to print a solo map of America. Only America. The first map devoted uniquely to this continent.'

Bea was turning pages in the great volume with painstaking care as she talked.

'A fitting place for Jasper to hide the panel from our map that depicts America,' Mike said.

357

'Yes, but I think I'm striking out,' she said, separating and flattening the pages as she went.

'There is a second copy of this book though,' I said. 'It never surfaced again?'

'Only in rumors,' Bea said. 'And then from the mouth of Eddy Forbes.'

'How reliable was he at gossip?'

'Almost as good as he was at stealing,' she said. 'In the 1940s, the deals between collectors were a lot different than they are today. With the Internet, we can all keep track of books and maps—who's got something to sell and who's in line to buy. Back then, there was much more discretion, many more one-on-one interactions, and lots of secrecy.'

'What did Eddy tell you?' Mike asked.

'His story was that after the war, Jasper Hunt sold the second Strassburg atlas to Lord Wardington. He was always unhappy when the library didn't treat his bequests like they were their most important gifts of the year. He represented to the buyer, of course, that he had the title free and clear.' Bea pushed the glasses to the top of her head. 'It didn't take long for Wardington, who was a real gent, to learn the truth. He returned the map to Hunt at once to let him make amends with the library.'

'But Hunt never did that,' Mike said.

'Much to my regret,' Bea said. 'Now, I had this conversation well before Eddy got in trouble.'

'You mean before he got caught for all the trouble he'd been causing.'

'Right again, Mike.' Bea closed the large book and rested her hand on its lid. 'Eddy told me that when Lord Wardington returned the book to Jasper Hunt, the old boy kept it for a while—he

358

had no intention of ever letting it collect dust in our stacks again. Eventually, he gave the book to his granddaughter, Minerva.'

'*What?*' Mike seemed stunned.

'I'm only the messenger, Detective. That's what Eddy said, and he knew Minerva Hunt—they'd had some dealings with each other. Why wouldn't I believe him? None of this had any significance until you found that panel under the water tank yesterday. Till you told me this map—which I wasn't even certain existed—might be connected to the murder of Tina Barr.'

Mike was circling the table now, punching his right fist into the palm of his left hand.

'We've got to get to Eddy Forbes, Coop. You talk to the feds on Monday,' Mike said. 'What else did he tell you, Bea?'

'Of course, my angle was selfish, too. I asked about the map because I wanted to get it back from the family. Have it here, where it belonged,' the librarian said. 'Eddy told me that for most of her life, Minerva had kept the atlas in her father's library. She had no use for it, and no real idea of its value. Then, shortly before his arrest, Eddy Forbes reintroduced her to Alger Herrick, who offered to pay her dearly for the atlas, not withstanding its clouded provenance.'

'For a reason?'

'Herrick's collection is heavy on Ptolemy,' Bea said. 'He's got the most important library of maps in private hands, now that Lord Wardington is gone.'

'Yes, he told us about his Bologna Ptolemy,' I said. 'But Herrick also said Minerva dabbled in maps. Why wouldn't she have wanted to hold on to it?'

'If you ask me, you're making too much of the fact that Alger Herrick was after that book. It's much more like the rivalry between the Red Sox and the Yankees,' Bea said. 'Herrick's a Ptolemy guy. He's been trying to corner the market on all the great editions of that work.'

'And Minerva?' I asked.

'Strictly Mercator,' Bea said, handing the book back to Mike to reshelve.

'Sorry? I don't get what you mean.'

'Mercator was one of the greatest sixteenth-century geographers, Alex. Mercator maps? Every schoolkid knows them.'

'Sure,' I said, recalling the famous images of the cylindrical projection maps, with parallels and meridians and perpendicular chartings all neatly aligned.

'Gerardus Mercator. His maps were designed for marine navigation, so that sailors could use a straight line to determine their position at sea, even without instruments.'

'What's it called when sailors do that?' I asked.

Mike brushed back his hair and answered. 'Dead reckoning.'

Bea Dutton wagged her finger at Mike. 'That's just what Eddy Forbes said about that girl. Back then, I thought he was joking. He said she was total Mercator all the way.'

'What did he mean?' I asked.

'If Minerva Hunt is doing the reckoning,' he used to say, 'anyone who gets in the way of the straight line between her and whatever she's after, the odds are they'll be dead. That's what he meant by dead reckoning.'

CHAPTER FORTY

By nine o'clock, curators and cops had been returning to the map division room in rolling waves, like eager kids gathering clues on a scavenger hunt.

Bea was in charge of examining each volume they found in hopes of coming across a panel of the missing map, but none of the rare books and atlases yielded any treasure. Jill Gibson sat glumly in a corner of the room, checking her master list against the items that had been retrieved, noting those that were reported to be missing from their proper places.

'I'm so hungry, I'm losing it,' Mike said.

'There are some places in the neighborhood,' Bea said. 'We could take a walk.'

'No time for that. Coop, you got enough cash for about eight pizzas to feed these guys?'

I dug into my pants pocket and handed him my money.

'We can't eat in here, Mike,' Bea said. 'You can lock me up before I let you get food into this room.'

'Deal.' He signaled to one of the rookies. 'Send your partner for as many pies as this will buy. Anything but anchovies. Get me some tarps from the Crime Scene wagon. Set them up on the ground at the receiving dock.'

Mike turned to Bea. 'A little brisk for an al fresco picnic, but that's what I'm offering.'

'Accepted.'

While we waited for the takeout order, Bea

continued to study the books, most of them from the Hunt collection. I caught glimpses of the Asian sex lithographs, the Curtis photos, and several versions of Marco Polo's journals. The erotic drawings were as visually stunning as the sepia prints of Native Americans and the brilliant notations made by the great Italian traveler, but nothing she searched turned up any unexpected bonus.

Twenty-five minutes later, when our dinner arrived, Mike and I—joined again by Mercer—led our bleary-eyed soldiers out to the freight entrance and tried to get our minds off work while we ate.

'I bet you're real good at trivia,' Mike said to Bea. He was sitting cross-legged on a tarp while she parked herself on one of the steps a few feet away.

'Not many topics. Why?'

'Mercer, the Coopster, and I bet on the *Final Jeopardy!* question most nights. I'm asking you to be my teammate, okay?'

'I won't be much help.'

Mike was on his second slice of pepperoni and sausage. 'You were taking your crazy cab ride last night, kid, so I know you didn't see the show. And Mercer was with me. Lucky that I've got TiVo and no life. Twenty bucks, everybody. Coop, I'm taking it out of your change.'

'Help yourself. It would have been the first time you ever gave me change.'

'The category is *Animals. Animals,* ladies and gents.'

'No fair, Chapman. You know the Q and A,' Mercer said.

'Double or nothing. I'll keep my mouth shut,

and if Bea gets it, I'm buying dessert.'

'So what's the answer?' Mercer asked.

Mike did his best Alex Trebek imitation. 'The answer is . . . Oldest living animal on the planet. Oldest living animal on the planet.'

'Wait a minute, Bea,' I said. 'I've got another idea, another possible literary hiding place for Jasper Hunt.'

'Hold that thought, Coop,' Mike said. 'I'm looking to score.'

'I give up. This is more important. Whales, elephants, rhinoceri.'

'Bad sport, Blondie. Don't spoil it for the others.'

Bea was wiping the crumbs from her veggie pizza off her sweater. 'Tell me, Alex. What are you thinking?'

'Aw, Bea. Give me an old animal,' Mike said. 'In the form of a question.'

'What's a snail?'

'Bad answer, Bea. You're letting me down. Mercer?'

'What's a . . . ?'

'I'll give you a hint. Coop's favorite restaurant in the world. Martha's Vineyard. The Bite.'

The Quinn sisters' tiny shack by the side of the road in Chilmark served the very best chowder and fried clams I'd ever tasted. But Mike revealed the question before I could shift my train of thought from rare books to shellfish.

'What's an ocean quahaug?' Mike said. 'Trebek said some researchers dredged up a four-hundred-year-old clam near Iceland this year. It's got growth rings, just like trees, so you can tell its age. Check your chowder next time. Those old

363

quahaugs could get chewy.'

He was eating his third piece of pizza, with no sign of slowing down.

I went back to the thought I had while Mike was quizzing us. 'Bea, I'm sure the library must have a good sampling of Shakespearean originals.'

'Absolutely. I'm not familiar with them, but I know we have several copies of the four folios. Someone in this group will be able to tell us,' she said. 'And we'll find out if any have to do with Jasper Hunt. What's his connection to the Bard?'

Mike wiped his mouth. 'Slip of paper on the corpse. "The evil that men do lives after them. The good is oft interred with their bones."'

Bea bent down to help me stack the empty boxes and collect the trash. 'So why are you looking for the books?'

'Because Hunt was into pranks and tricks,' I said. 'Seems like it would have appealed to that eccentric part of him to hide pieces of the map in a Shakespearean folio, if that was his favorite passage. Make it hard for his greedy heirs to put them back together.'

'Maybe that was the evil part of him,' Bea said, straightening up. 'Maybe the good—the rest of the panels to complete the map—maybe they're interred with his bones.'

Mike Chapman was on his feet faster than a bolt of lightning could strike a tree.

'You're my girl, Bea. Didn't Talbot tell us that his grandfather wanted to go out like a pharaoh, surrounded by all his worldly goods? Let's find out where Jasper Hunt was laid to rest. Let's see what's buried with his bones.'

CHAPTER FORTY-ONE

I rang Jasper Hunt the Third's apartment, and the butler answered.

'He's asleep, madam. Do you know the hour?'

'I apologize for calling so late. I'm trying to find out where his father is buried. Would you happen to know?'

'Certainly, madam. In Millbrook, on the family estate. We shall all be in Millbrook one day, God willing.'

I thanked him and hung up.

We were back in Bea's office. The helpful curators were still searching for books, with a new emphasis on volumes related to Shakespeare.

Mike was on Bea's computer. He had Googled Jasper Hunt's obituary and was reading aloud to us. 'Yeah, looks like Junior and his father were laid to rest beside their wives—no mention of mistresses—and their beloved pets. The reinterment took place in the 1980s, when Jasper Three created a plot for them on the back forty of the horse farm—immediate family, servants, and still plenty of room for Patience and Fortitude. Looks like the Dutchess County society event of the season.'

'Does it say why there was a reinterment?' I asked.

'Guess they had a layover someplace else, Coop. I see a road trip up the Hudson in your future,' Mike said. 'No mention of books, Bea.'

'Bibliomaniacs have done it forever,' she said. 'Put their favorite books in their burial chambers

365

with them. You're the military buff. You know the name Rush Hawkins?'

'Civil War general. Led a volunteer cavalry troop called Hawkins's Zouaves.'

'Well, he built himself a mausoleum in Providence so he could be surrounded by all his books after he shuffled off his mortal coil,' Bea said. 'Elizabeth Rossetti, too.'

'The writer's wife?' I asked.

'Yup. Dante Gabriel Rossetti placed his unpublished poems in his young bride's grave at Highgate Cemetery, along with a Bible. The poet had a change of heart a year later and reclaimed his work for publication—somewhat dampened by exposure. The vellum pages are at Harvard now. It's been done forever.'

'Worth considering,' I said.

'You're good at exhumations, Coop.'

My only other experience like that had been the sad task of reexamining the body of a teenage girl whose original autopsy had missed the telling signs that motivated her killer.

'How long do you want to keep the staff going at this tonight?' Bea asked.

'I think most of them are about to hit a wall,' I said. 'Maybe we should knock off and start them fresh in the morning.'

My cell phone vibrated and I reached for it to see whether it was a call I wanted to take.

'We can secure everything right here,' Mike said. 'We'll have a detail at this very door around the clock.'

Bea grimaced. It was obvious she didn't like the idea of entrusting all these treasures to outsiders who didn't respect the integrity of each book, atlas, map, and document the way these curators did.

'I promise you, they'll be fine,' I said, pressing the talk button as I recognized the number of Howard Browner, one of the senior forensic biologists at the DNA lab. 'Howard? It's Alex.'

'Am I catching you at a bad time?'

'Still working, Howard. You, too?'

'Yeah.'

Browner—whom Mike called the Brainiac—was brilliant and dedicated to his work, one of the first experts in DNA technology who had trained many of us in this evolving science since its introduction in the criminal justice system.

Mike spun his finger in a circle, telling me to hurry the call so we could help Bea close up. I rolled my eyes at him.

'You have something for me?' I asked.

'I've been in the lab all day. Got handed this assignment late afternoon. It's kind of interesting, along the lines of what Mattie's been working on with you for the Griggs case.'

'Wrap it up, Coop,' Mike said.

'Thanks for thinking of me, Howard. I'm sort of tied up with Mike right now.' Interesting was not what I needed at the moment. 'Can it wait till Monday?'

'Sure, Alex. It's just a bench hunch.'

Browner wasn't calling about a match in the databank but something his gut instinct was feeding him as he looked at profiles at his bench, as the lab workspaces were called.

'You mean a familial search?' I asked. 'Is it Wesley Griggs?

Despite Mike's prodding, I was anxious for a development that might impact Judge Moffett's decision.

'No. Nothing new on that front.'

'I'll call you first thing when I get to the office, Howard. Okay? You know how Mike is. We're trying to shut down for the night.'

'Understood. Just make a note to tell me if the father of one of your witnesses is still around. I'd like to get a swab from him.'

'A witness in which murder case?' I asked. 'Are you talking Griggs?'

Mike stood still and put his hands on his waist, staring at me as I listened to Browner.

'No, no, Alex. They've added me to the team on the Barr-Vastasi homicides. I'm working on a cigarette butt Chapman submitted.'

'That's got to be the one he picked up from the floor of the squad. The smoker is a woman named Minerva Hunt,' I said. 'What's so interesting about it?'

'I had it right on my bench when the fax came through from London a few hours ago. I'm looking through all the profiles, and I see that the smoker and this guy, the drunk driver from England—well, they've got an allele in common at each one of thirteen loci we've tested. They match perfectly,' Browner said, his normally flat delivery lifted a decibel with excitement. 'I know how you like this forensic stuff, Alex.'

My mind was racing to make the connection between the players. 'Tell me what it means, Howard.'

'I can't be certain till I get a paternal swab, but if I enjoyed betting as much as Mike does, I'd have to say I'm looking at a half brother and sister here. Same father, different mothers. Isn't that wild?'

368

Alger Herrick—the infant who'd been abandoned by his teenage mother on the steps of an orphanage in England—was in all likelihood the illegitimate child of Jasper Hunt III, the blood brother of Talbot and Minerva Hunt.

CHAPTER FORTY-TWO

'You think old Jasper ever figured that out?' Mike asked.

We had secured the map room, arranged for rides home for Bea and her colleagues, and were walking from the side door of the library to Mike's car, shortly after midnight.

'Not back in Minerva's college days, when he tried to fix her up with Herrick,' I said, recalling his story. 'And I've got no sense that any of them realize it now.'

'This might be the most unwelcome familial search since Dick Cheney found out he's related to Barack Obama.'

'The only resemblance I see is greed,' Mercer said.

'The genetic Hunt predisposition you mentioned yesterday,' Mike said. 'Meanwhile, they're ready to rip each other's throats out over old books and maps. I say Coop charms some drool out of Jasper, we firm this up, and sit them all down for a reality check.'

'Chapman!' a woman's voice called from half a block away.

We all stopped and turned, and saw Teresa Retlin, a detective from the burglary squad, jogging after us.

'Don't you answer your phone? Your voice mail box is full,' she said. 'I'm too old to be chasing you down in the middle of the night.'

'Didn't stop you ten years ago, Terry. I think the phone's out of juice,' Mike said. 'And so am I. What's up?'

He pivoted and moved forward while Retlin tried to keep pace.

'Got a baby snitch for you.'

'For me? What's he snitching about?'

'Name is Shalik Samson. Says you want what he's got.'

The three of us stopped short to listen to Terry Retlin.

'That twelve-year-old?'

'Fourteen,' she said. 'Just small for his age. Neighbor saw him breaking in to the back window of an apartment an hour ago and called 911. The kid starting throwing your name around before I could cuff him.'

'Where is he now?' Mike asked.

'In my care, Chapman. I have to take him to a juvenile facility till Monday morning,' she said, handing Mike a business card. 'Says he found this in the garbage. That you gave your card to a guy named Travis Forbes—the vic in my burglary—and Forbes threw it out.'

Mike laughed and shook his head from side to side. 'Piece of work. Where's your car?'

'My partner's over there,' she said pointing across Fortieth Street.

Mercer and I followed Mike to the parked RMP. 'Shalik, my man,' Mike said, bracing himself against the roof of the car and leaning down to talk

370

to the boy. 'What brings you to the library tonight?'

'I got locked up for helping you, Detective. You give me twenty bucks and I'll tell you.'

'You got that wrong, Shalik. I don't pay guys to break the law.'

'I got you into that building, didn't I? You paid me yesterday.'

'Tell it to the judge, Shalik. We're outta here,' Mike said, tapping the car. 'Take him away, Terry.'

'No! Mr. Mike!' Shalik shouted.

'What's on your mind? It's getting too late for nonsense.'

'I was going in there tonight for you, Mr. Mike. Tell you what he up to,' Shalik said. 'Find out why he all dressed up like a cop.'

'What? Let him out of the car, Terry,' Mike said, as Mercer stepped up to open the door and stand beside the skinny kid to make sure he didn't try to run. 'Tell me about that, Shalik.'

The boy knew he had the attention of all the grown-ups. His jeans drooped so low, they barely covered his rear end; the pant legs crumpled on top of his sneakers. He pushed them even lower when he shoved his hands in his pockets as he considered what to say to us.

'You talk to the judge for me? It's my third time.'

'I'll sing to the judge, Shalik. You tell me about Travis.'

'I seen him before in all these different clothes,' he said. 'Dressin' stupid and stuff sometimes when he go out. But he always go out alone. And I never seen him in no police officer's uniform. He ain't no cop.'

371

I thought of Tina Barr's attacker and the fireman's gear. I remembered the man in a brown uniform who had broken in to Jane Eliot's apartment.

'Travis Forbes's coatrack, Mike,' I said. 'All those jackets that were hanging in the hallway, remember? I'll get a warrant to see what kind of stuff he's got there.'

'You know real cops, Shalik,' Mercer said. 'Did his uniform look real?'

'It do. It really do. Had a hat, too, and a shiny silver badge.'

'Did he see you?' Mike asked. 'Or did he just keep on walking down the street?'

Shalik's chest puffed up. 'He didn't walk nowhere.'

'What did he do?'

'He had a chauffeur, Mr. Mike. Big fat guy gets out of a limousine and opens the door for him. Travis, he like got in the back with his date.'

'His date?' Mike said. 'You're doing real good for me, Shalik. Tell me, did you see the woman?'

'Dark-haired lady. Skinny. Skinnier than her,' he said, tipping his elbow toward me. 'Older than her, too. Long red fingernails. Smoking a cigarette.'

Travis Forbes dressed himself like an NYPD cop for a night on the town with Minerva Hunt. Now all we had to do was figure out where Carmine Rizzali had driven them.

CHAPTER FORTY-THREE

Mercer had his arm around Shalik's shoulder, trying to cut him a deal.

'We're taking him from here, Terry,' Mike said.

'I could lose my shield for this, anything happens to the kid. Rules are different for juvies.'

'I'll stay with him,' I said. 'I'll go to the judge myself.'

She walked back to her car, got inside, and slammed the door, while Mike and I followed Mercer and Shalik down the dark side street until we hit Fifth Avenue and went around the block.

'How are we going to raise the fat bastard?' Mike asked. 'Yesterday he wouldn't even take my call.'

'Let Alex do the talking. He won't blow her off so fast,' Mercer said.

'You'd better script it for me.'

'Tell him you've got something urgent to discuss with Minerva,' Mike said. 'He must have driven her to Jane Eliot's apartment. Let him know the old lady's talking about what she gave to Minerva. He'll want to collect on that tidbit. Makes him look useful. Eliot's safe, isn't she, Mercer?'

'Cops are with her in the hospital room. Not a problem.'

'If TARU can find his cell phone pings, we're in business,' Mike said, as he and I got into the front seat of the car. The Technical Assistance Response Unit had the latest gadgetry and technology to solve almost every communication and surveillance problem investigators needed.

'Who's this? Hey, Sonny—Mike Chapman here. I got two known numbers; one's going to place a call to the other. The caller's in the car with me, midtown. If I give you both, can you pinpoint the other guy's location for me?'

The answer was short and obviously positive.

'Ready for me? First one is Assistant District Attorney Alexandra Cooper,' Mike said, dictating my number. 'The receiver is Carmine Rizzali. Yeah, used to be on the job. I need to find him pronto. The nearest cell phone tower would be great. Coop'll dial him to see if he picks up. I'll stay on with you.'

I punched Carmine's number into my key pad. My caller ID would be blocked, so he'd have to answer in order to know who was calling at this late hour.

One ring and Carmine spoke into the phone. 'Hullo?'

'Carmine? It's Alex Cooper. I met you with Mike—'

'Is this more of his bullshit?'

'No, no. This is something urgent that I'm trying to speak to Ms. Hunt about, just between the two of us. I think Mike's on his way to her home now—'

'What is he, nuts? It's the middle of a Saturday night. She ain't even there.'

'Look, there's a woman who lives in the Village, on Bedford Street. She's made a complaint that Minerva Hunt stole something from her. I . . . uh . . . I—' I held my hand out, palm upward, trying to figure a direction to go.

Mike just nodded at me and mouthed the words *You're doing fine.*

'She didn't steal nothing. I drove her there myself. The lady had a present for her. All very civilized.'

'I think Mike's blowing this totally out of proportion,' I said. 'I disagree with him completely. I thought you might want to give her a heads-up, and maybe I can set up a meeting with her tomorrow.'

He wasn't ready to trust me.

'Is Minerva with you now?'

'Cute, Ms. Cooper. Real cute. Then you tell the homicide dick whatever I tell you, so I'm just the schmuck who's out of a job.'

He disconnected me the second he finished the sentence.

'Sonny? You got a location for me?' Mike asked. 'Thanks, buddy. I owe you big-time.'

He dropped the phone on the seat and started the engine, making the turn from Forty-second Street onto Fifth Avenue.

'You did good, Blondie. It seems that Carmine took the odd couple downtown—Second Avenue, between Second and Third streets. Nearest cell tower is in front of Provenzano's, a funeral home.'

'A little late for a condolence call, isn't it?' Mercer said.

Traffic moved well on the straight run south to the point at which Broadway intersected Fifth Avenue, then Mike wound his way farther east.

As we crossed Third Street, I could see the limousine parked on the west side of Second Avenue.

Mike pulled over to the curb, several cars behind Carmine, and turned off the engine and headlights. 'What do you think, Mercer? Him

375

sitting in the limo all these hours, don't you think all that weight would have flattened one of his tires by now?'

'I could do that,' our young charge said.

'You stay with me, Shalik.'

'C'mon, Coop,' Mike said. 'Let's all have a look around.'

As we got out, Mike walked ahead and peered into the window of Carmine's car. Then he kneeled down. I tried to keep Shalik occupied while Mike scored one of the tires with his Swiss Army knife.

'I don't think he should eat such heavy meals at night,' Mike said, coming back to get us. 'He's sleeping like a baby. Least they can't make such a quick getaway if Minerva and Travis aren't happy to see us.'

Mercer was on the sidewalk, checking out the block on either side of the avenue. 'There's a pizza joint, a Thai restaurant, and a neighborhood pub. We can look in each of those.'

He kept one arm on Shalik's shoulder, and I walked on the other side of the kid, closer to the buildings. We watched as Mike tried the front door of the funeral home, but it was locked and all the lights were out.

We passed an alleyway fronted by a wrought-iron gate, and kept going. The night was clear and getting cooler. Mike went into each of the open restaurants and bars on both sides of the street but didn't spot Hunt or Forbes in any of them.

'Go another block north,' Mercer said. Mike did, while I tried to find out from Shalik whether he had gotten inside Travis Forbes's apartment before getting caught.

By the time Mike doubled back, the kid had described how the cops had arrived and nabbed him just after he'd jimmied the back door and wriggled in.

'No trace of them,' Mike said. 'Time to interrupt Carmine's dream cycle and have a chat. Worst he can do is call and alert them that we're here to break up the party.'

We turned around and started walking back toward the limousine.

The light from the street lamp bounced off the gold paint on the narrow archway above the wrought-iron fence that closed off the alley to my left.

I read the words on the large sign, first to myself and then aloud: new york marble cemetery. incorporated in 1831.

Below them was a smaller tablet, also engraved. I held on to one of the bars of the fence as I read again: a place of interment for gentlemen.

'Gents like Jasper Hunt Jr. and his cronies,' Mike said. 'Get the kid in the car, Coop. I'm going in.'

CHAPTER FORTY-FOUR

'Stay here, Alex,' Mercer said. 'I don't know how Mike thinks he's going to get past this gate.'

Shalik Samson grabbed two of the vertical iron bars with his hands and tried to shake them. 'You put me on your shoulders,' he said to Mercer, 'I could be over that easy.'

'Getting you out might be the problem. Let go

of those.'

Traffic was light on this part of the avenue, and there were no pedestrians to bother us.

'You think somebody inside?' Shalik asked, craning his neck to look up at Mercer. 'It look like a little park in there.'

Mike was studying the lock, which was a single keyhole. There was no sophisticated equipment in place to protect the entrance, which seemed well groomed and tended.

'Pretty clever. If you're going to break in to someplace right on the street,' he said, 'dress Travis Forbes up like a cop to give you cover.'

Shalik was back against the bars, standing on the sharply pointed pieces that jutted up from the base of the heavy gate.

'Cut it out, Shalik. You'll hurt yourself,' Mike said. 'Coop, I told you to put him in the car.'

'Yo, look! It ain't even locked no more.'

The teenager had reached his slim arm between the bars and retrieved a metal rod that must have temporarily held the bars in place. Someone had indeed broken in to the old cemetery, and in all likelihood was still somewhere inside.

Shalik pushed on the right side of the gate, and it creaked open against his weight. Before I could stop him, he ran ahead down the alleyway, which was bordered on both sides by brick walls.

Mercer gave chase and overtook him twenty feet away, where the passage opened onto a large grassy area, almost the length of a football field but half as wide. He put his hand up to his lips and told the boy to be quiet.

I closed the gate behind me and caught up with Mike, who had stopped to read a plaque on the wall.

'What does it say?' I asked as he turned away and headed toward Mercer.

'The oldest nonsectarian cemetery in the city. A hundred and fifty solid marble vaults,' he said, breaking into a trot. 'All of them were built underground as a health precaution against nineteenth-century contagious disease.'

We were suddenly in a gardened oasis in the middle of the East Village that I had never known existed.

The tall walls around the open green space seemed to be made completely of stone, many parts obscured by the bushes and trees that had grown up around the borders.

Mercer was deputizing Shalik, trying to extract a promise from him to stay close and obey directions.

Mike jogged along the perimeter of the north wall, stopping at smooth marble tablets to note names of the occupants of the subterranean vaults. I was just a few steps behind him.

'Charles Van Zandt. Uriah Scribner. James Tallmadge,' Mike said, stopping to run his hand over the names, one above the other, as he read them from the engravings.

Ten feet farther along, another tablet, with numbers I assumed corresponded to the graves below. Some listed three or four vaults, though only one or two individuals' names had been added to the list of the dead.

There were Auchinclosses and Randolphs, Phelpses and Quackenbushes, grand names that together created a history of New York City. I paused at the marker for the infant son of

Frederick Law Olmsted, the man who had landscaped Central Park.

Mike crossed to the south wall and continued his search. Before he had moved very far along, he signaled me to join him.

'Here they are, kid. Jasper Hunt. Jasper Hunt Jr.,' he said, showing me the names of father and son, and their wives, the first dates for the family patriarch etched in the wall more than a century ago. 'Four Hunts, six burial vaults.'

Beneath the neatly carved names and dates were the numbers: 61, 62, 63, 64, 65, 66.

'They were obviously buried here originally, before the reinterment,' I said.

'And Minerva must know what's in Millbrook— and what isn't. She'd certainly have access to the family digs up on the property.'

'So maybe when they moved the bodies, nobody gave any thought to whether there was anything in these other two vaults they owned—whether any books were interred with the Hunt bones. There was certainly no record of other descendants on this plaque.'

'Wait here with Mercer,' Mike said.

'What are you going to do?'

'There's got to be a way to get below to the vaults.'

'Mike, let's get help.'

'And if something bad's going on right now? You going to live with yourself if somebody's down there, left for dead?'

Mercer was motioning to Mike. 'Check out that corner.'

The dim light filtering in from the street and wind blowing the bushes played tricks with my vision. It looked like Mercer was right—that there was a hatch open in the southwest end of the enclosed area, a wooden door of some sort, against the far wall of the garden.

Mike sprinted forward and I followed, practically slamming into him when he stopped short just ten feet from the spot.

He was fixed on something on the ground.

I knelt beside him and saw the body of a man—short, overweight, middle-aged—slumped beneath a small evergreen bush, his feet protruding into the pathway from beneath the branches.

CHAPTER FORTY-FIVE

'He's alive,' Mike said.

I looked up to see Mercer and Shalik standing over us. Mike was already dialing 911 to ask for an ambulance and backup.

'Move the kid, Mercer. Get him out of here.'

There was something white on the ground, next to the man's head. It was a handkerchief, and when I picked it up—ignoring all crime scene protocol—it reeked of sickly sweet chloroform.

I told Mike and stuffed the cloth in my pants pocket, then reached for the card in the man's outstretched hand. It identified him as a caretaker of the New York Marble Cemetery.

'Figures,' Mike said. 'They'd need a guide to find the old Hunt property. Also useful for Travis Forbes, the chloroform kid, to be in a cop's uniform to get close enough to knock the guy out, probably before Minerva stepped out of the car.'

Mercer was on the ground, trying to do CPR on the fallen man before the medics arrived. He took a pen-size LCD flashlight from his pocket and passed it to Mike, who was on his way toward the opening. I hurried after him.

'You're not gonna like this, Coop. I'll go alone.'

We had been in claustrophobic situations often enough for Mike and Mercer to know they were a problem for me. But I couldn't imagine letting Mike, who had covered my back more times than I could count, go down without a partner.

He took his blazer off and threw it on the ground, unholstering his gun as he put his hand on the top of the hatch.

Mike started down into the entrance shaft of the burial space and cleared the short staircase. I listened for voices, but heard none.

I put my foot on the top step and, afraid to lose the light that Mike was leading with, hurried down ten more until I touched the earthen floor.

I stood up straight and looked around the grim necropolis. On either side of me were narrow passageways that led between enormous stone vaults. Long slate shelves supported some of the coffins, mostly made of stone, which were stacked on top of one another.

I stayed as close to Mike as I could get while he moved the light over the dirt, then up and down among the coffins, looking for names of the dead and numbers of their vaults.

We had passed the forties, seen the markers for Deys and Cruikshanks, Wetmores and Wheelocks—adults and far too many infants, typical of the mortality rates of that century.

As we came to the intersection that marked the

divide between the vaults numbered in the fifties from those in the sixties, Mike's flashlight framed a woman's face.

Minerva Hunt was seated on the ground, her hands tied behind her with a length of rope. A silk scarf—probably her own—served as a gag between her teeth, wrapped around the back of her head.

Next to her, Travis Forbes was holding a taxidermist's skife—the sharp tool designed to skin dead animals.

'Forget it, Forbes,' Mike said.

'No, you forget it.' He pressed the edge of the blade to Minerva's slender neck and the first drops of blood spurted out. 'I can end it for her much faster than you can shoot.'

'I have no doubt you can. I've seen your work.'

I could picture the deep, gaping wound in Tina Barr's neck.

Minerva Hunt's eyes were opened wide with fear, flitting between Travis Forbes's hand and something behind me.

I turned to look but saw only the massive outlines of stone caskets and slate shelves.

Travis pulled at Minerva's arm to get her to her feet. 'Give me the gun, Detective, or I'll cut her throat.'

'Did you get what you wanted?' Mike asked. 'Can't kill her before she lays the golden egg, can you?'

Again Minerva Hunt's eyes darted from Forbes to the staircase through which we had entered. I glanced back, hoping to see Mercer and the cops he had summoned, but no one was there.

'Make yourselves comfortable, Mr. Chapman,' Forbes said, positioning the terrified woman between himself and Mike. If Mike had considered firing his gun at Forbes, he had missed his brief opportunity.

'Ms. Hunt and I have to go,' Forbes said, pushing Minerva to take baby steps forward. 'We haven't finished our conversation. Pick yourself out a slab and get some rest while we find a less crowded place to talk.'

Minerva looked to the staircase again, then jerked back her head, just as I heard the hatch crash to a close.

This time, Mike flashed his light in that direction. Against the blackness of the wall, it caught Alger Herrick's shiny chrome hook.

CHAPTER FORTY-SIX

'There's a shaft at the other end, Forbes,' Alger Herrick said, coming down the steps. 'You've got to take her that way. There's another detective outside here.'

Forbes was focused on Mike's gun. He tried to move Minerva around and drag her away from where we stood. Strapped to him was a backpack, open at the top, which appeared to have a large book—the size of a double folio—sticking out of it.

'Hurry, Forbes.'

'I want his gun.'

'We can do better than that,' Herrick said, coming up directly behind me. 'We'll take his girl.'

Mike pointed his pistol at Herrick, but it was too late. The man was upon me, the cold steel of his prosthesis gripping my forearm.

'Let go of me. I'll walk,' I said, trying to shake myself loose.

He held me tight, angling so that I was always between him and Mike, and led me around the central burial chambers to an earthen path parallel to the one on which Mike stood, inches away from Minerva Hunt and Travis Forbes.

'Shoot, Mike!' I yelled. 'Shoot Forbes.'

The stark confines of this dungeonlike underground chamber smelled of death.

Forbes responded with a laugh, a loud, guttural laugh. What was Mercer doing up above that he couldn't hear us? Probably helping to load the injured man into an ambulance.

Hunt tried to speak—or maybe she was crying. All that emerged from behind the gag was a muffled noise.

Herrick turned the corner, and for the first time I could see that the fieldstone cap had been removed from vault 65, marked with the name Jasper Hunt II. Books were strewn about, no doubt the result of this unusual break-in undertaken by Herrick and Forbes. The old eccentric had in fact gone to his grave—the first time—with some of his beloved treasures.

Minerva Hunt had played right into their hands, trusting Travis Forbes to help her search for the missing panels of the great map. She'd fallen prey to the same double cross that had proven lethal to Tina Barr.

'In fact, Detective, why don't you come over here?' Herrick said, pushing me faster, understanding the urgency with which he had to escape before more police arrived. 'There's a vacancy. Several of them, to be honest.'

Mike wasn't giving up his gun, and Herrick seemed confident he wouldn't find a way to use it, with both Minerva and me serving as human shields.

'Drag her, if you can't pick her up,' Herrick shouted to Forbes. 'If he kills her, just run. Let's get out of here with what we have.'

Herrick was ready to sacrifice Minerva Hunt, confident perhaps that she had nothing more of value to give to him.

'Minerva is your *sister*,' I screamed as loud as I could. 'Let her be, dammit. She's your blood sister.'

Alger Herrick froze at my words, reflexively tightening his grip on my arm. I winced at the pain, but knew I had shocked him.

'*Her* father is *your* father,' I said, listening as he took deep breaths, startled by the information. His chest heaved against my back. 'You're a Hunt, too. We've got the DNA to prove it.'

Mike steadied his gun with both hands, aiming at the spot where Forbes was moving with Minerva. 'You're entitled to the damn map. You didn't have to kill to get it.'

This was no time to correct Mike on the fine points of the law. I didn't think Alger Herrick would expect to go to court now to collect on the Hunt fortune.

'I never murdered anyone, you fool,' Herrick said. '*He* did. He's your killer.'

Herrick pulled at me again, moving me farther into the darkness, farther away from Mike.

Now I could hear pounding from the direction of the entrance shaft. Mercer and the backup team must be trying to get to us, but Herrick had found

386

a way to secure the hatch from within.

'I'll give you three seconds to let Minerva go,' Mike said, moving in toward Travis Forbes and his hostage. 'Kill her, and you die, too.'

Alger Herrick heard the commotion. 'Drop her, Forbes. Run as fast as you can go to the other end. There's a staircase just like the one we came in. Beat them out of here with the book—they'll think you're an officer, too. You'll walk right through them.'

Forbes's fake—or stolen—uniform might serve him well in the confusing mix of cops responding to a call for help. I didn't care if it did. I didn't care about the missing panels of the rare map and whether they were lost forever. I wanted to get out of this hellhole, with Mike, alive.

Travis Forbes was beginning to fidget like a caged animal. Herrick would give him up as Tina and Karla's killer, claiming not to have known his young accomplice was going to use violence. It would make no difference to a jury, but Herrick must have thought it would save his neck.

Mike was gaining on him. 'You wanna cut somebody? Cut yourself, Forbes. Slice your own throat.'

Over my shoulder, I thought I saw a sliver of light in the farthest remove of the room. I looked again down the dirt corridor of death, but all was darkness.

Had there been movement, or was my mind frozen with fright? It was getting harder to breathe in the dank, airless space. I knew there was a chance that none of us would make it out alive.

Suddenly, I heard a loud grunt from Travis Forbes. He lifted Minerva Hunt off the ground and threw her at Mike. She couldn't even brace herself for the fall, her hands still bound behind her.

It looked like Mike's gun—the glint of silver flashing against the black backdrop—fell to the ground as he tried unsuccessfully to catch Minerva. He was knocked backward by the impact of her body against his own.

Forbes was running in the direction Herrick had sent him, unburdened by his captive. And Alger Herrick was moving faster, too, pulling me with him, while Mike tried to extricate himself from beneath Minerva Hunt.

I was coughing now as dust particles from the ground scuffed up by the skirmish seemed to choke my airway. My own sense of panic made it harder for me to regain control.

'Forbes,' Herrick yelled out. 'Are you there?'

I could still hear his footsteps running away from us. I reached in my pocket for a handkerchief to cover my mouth.

The first thing I touched was the heavy piece of cotton cloth, the one that had been doused with chloroform to knock out the cemetery guide.

'Stop!' I said, pleading with Alger Herrick. 'I can't breathe.'

His good hand, the right one, smacked the side of my head so hard that I saw stars. 'I need you with me. Just keep moving.'

'I'll be back for you. You'll do fine,' I heard Mike say to Minerva.

He must have gotten to his feet and retrieved his gun. He'd be coming after us.

Just then I heard a thud from the direction in which Travis Forbes had run.

'Forbes?' Herrick shouted again. 'Have you

388

found the steps, man?'

There was no answer.

Herrick seemed distracted by the silence. I thought—and maybe he did, too—that Forbes had reached the exit and dropped the lid on us after he escaped.

I pulled my arm from Herrick's viselike grip, but he yanked me back, face-to-face. I swung my free hand up from my side, covering his nose with the chloroform-soaked cloth, using my height to my advantage.

The silver hook released its hold as Herrick tried to swat me away. I pressed the rag to him again, not knowing whether there was enough of the gas on it to overwhelm him.

He swiped at my neck with the hook, and I stepped back. He must have scored a cut. I felt a trickle of blood seeping behind my ear.

'Get down, Coop,' Mike said, rushing out of the dark.

Before Mike could reach me, Alger Herrick fell to his knees.

I didn't know if chloroform had done its job, or if he was brought down by Shalik Samson, who cracked him on the back of his legs with a baseball bat.

CHAPTER FORTY-SEVEN

The night watchman at the Provenzano funeral home had opened it up for the chief of detectives while he was waiting for us to be led out of the cavernous burial ground.

Mercer brought me inside the large parlor, decorated for old-fashioned comfort—sofas and armchairs of burgundy silk, with antimacassars—meant to soothe grieving relatives. It wasn't where I wanted to be right now, but I had no choice in the matter.

Detectives and uniformed cops, huddling in small groups to gossip about the case now that the emergency had passed, moved out of the way as I walked through the room.

I lowered myself onto one of the sofas and rested my head against the pillow.

The watchman was telling some of the officers about the old cemetery. 'I bet you didn't even know it was here, did you? We get asked about it all the time,' he said. 'It was because of the terrible contagion in Manhattan back then—yellow fever, tuberculosis, scarlet fever. The city banned aboveground graves, so these rich guys decided to excavate this block and build marble vaults ten feet under. Regular plague pits, they must have been.'

I shivered, wrapping a blanket around myself as I waited for Lieutenant Peterson to clear the room.

I saw a couple of the guys who were leaving make way for Shalik Samson. Mercer brought him over to me to say good night.

'You saved us, you know,' I said to him, mustering a smile.

'You gonna say that to the judge?'

'Of course I will, if you tell me how you did it.'

'Mercer was helping that sick man, you know? He made me go wake up the chauffeur 'cause the amb'lance took so long. Carmine—that guy? He had a baseball bat in the car. Guess he thought I was gonna rob him. Mercer was like gonna shoot

390

him if he didn't drop the damn thing.'

'How'd you get down into the burial vault?'

'That way you went in got locked, you know,' Shalik said. It happened when Alger Herrick dropped the lid. 'Me and Mercer, we just went around the whole garden, all along that crumbly stone wall, looking for another entrance. Had to be, he kept telling me. Couldn't have just one way in or out for all those bodies.'

'And you found it,' I said.

'Back behind a tree. Mercer didn't fit, but I did.'

I hadn't been wrong. That sliver of light I thought I saw had been Shalik opening the lid of the second hatch.

'So you tripped the guy with the backpack?'

'Dude didn't even see me. That dungeon's as black as I am.'

'What do you think, Mercer? Gold shield?' I asked.

'First, we're taking him home. I'm not ready to give Shalik any commendations yet, but we'll get those charges thrown out.'

The kid high-fived me, and Mercer handed him off to the cops who were going to drive him home.

Mike came into the room a minute later. He had cleaned himself up, and brought some hydrogen peroxide and a bandage to cover the cut on my neck.

'You know the river Styx, Loo? Greek mythology?' Mike asked as he leaned over me, dabbing the small wound before he dressed it. 'The river of hate, it was called. An old guy named Charon ferries the dead across the river to the underworld. I swear, Coop and me—we were on that ferry tonight.'

'I don't care if the whole magilla is made of marble or papier-mâché,' Peterson said. 'Couldn't get me down in there for all the money in the world. Are you telling me, Alex, that Alger Herrick is the half brother of Minerva and Talbot Hunt?'

'The lab is hot on this new familial search technology. Howard Browner says he can prove it with a sample from the father.'

'Think of it, Loo,' Mike said. 'Jasper the Third spent a lot of time in England, liked the ladies— young ones—as much as he liked his books. Herrick's mother was a single girl who deposited him in an orphanage. Alex thinks Hunt's father might even have paid to steer the infant to a good home. Placed him so well, they wound up with the same friends.'

Mercer sat down beside me and held my hand. 'You want us to put this together for you?' he asked the lieutenant.

'It's all about the map, isn't it? The rarest map in the world?'

'Seems to be.'

The backpack that Travis Forbes had been wearing when Shalik brought him down with the first blow of the bat was on a table next to me.

While Mercer talked, Mike removed the large folio from the bag. It was a volume of the Napoleonic expedition to Egypt—the atlas of the world—the same book in which the Grimaldis had concealed the panels for centuries.

All conversation ceased as Mike lifted the cover. There were four folded sheets of paper, which he slowly and carefully opened before us.

'The four corners of the earth,' he said. 'Magnificent, Coop. Aren't they?'

We all leaned in to look. The three of us had seen a fake earlier in the day, and a real one in the library, under Bea's tutelage. Experts would confirm it for us, but everything about these papers looked authentic.

The first one, the top left section of the entire map, represented the North American continent, with exquisite drawings of Zephir and Chor—the wind and the sea—surrounding the land.

The second piece, from the top right position, was Cathay and Japan, mapped with more detail than the previous segment, since they had actually been described as a result of Marco Polo's thirteenth-century journeys.

Mike opened the third of the large pages that would form the bottom right corner. Below the Spice Islands of Indonesia was the legend written by the mapmaker, attributing the name of America to Vespucci.

The bottom panel, to the west, documented the extension of the new land—the South American continent—that Vespucci had explored as far down as the River Plata. The word *America* showed up for the first time, south of what is now Brazil.

'You're looking at history, Loo. Not many people beside the Hunts even knew this baby existed, and as time went by, scholars began to think it was a myth.'

'How'd the Barr girl get mixed up in all this?' Peterson said, an unlit cigarette dangling from his mouth.

'Eddy Forbes, the map thief, he seems to have been the driving force keeping the legend of this treasure alive. First he tried to get Minerva to back him in finding the panels. You'll have to ask her, but I don't think she believed him until Jane Eliot called her a few months back to give her a gift—a book she didn't want, which happened to have a piece of the map inside,' I said. 'I'd guess it was Eddy Forbes who educated Minerva about the Strassburg Ptolemy, and the panel inside it. That's the book that Grandpa Hunt reclaimed from the library during the war.'

'Eddy had a romance with Tina Barr at one time,' Mike said. 'Once you interrogate him, check their phone records. I bet you'll find they were still in touch. He may be a convicted felon, but he's still a scholar. I'm sure he did all his research on the Hunts. He probably set Tina up with Minerva, suggested that she move into the apartment. That would have enabled him to steal the panel right out from underneath her nose.'

'Using Tina,' Peterson said, 'like Eddy Forbes seems to have used everyone else over the years— librarians, curators, trustees. So why the gas mask? Do you think that Billy Schultz had anything to do with all this?'

'Nothing at all. I'd bet it's just what he claimed,' Mercer said. 'The guy did the right thing and called the police after Tina was attacked. He probably was just stupid enough to pick up the gas mask and try it on.'

'Will you have someone call the lab in the morning?' I asked, rubbing my forehead to ease the tension headache that was building up. 'Run that mixed sample against Travis Forbes.'

Peterson stood up and rested his elbow on the mantel over the fireplace with the faux logs. 'Why'd Travis go in with a mask? Did Tina know him?'

394

'He told us she didn't,' I said. 'But Travis apparently looks so much like his brother, Eddy, he was afraid she'd make him.'

'Why was he there?' the lieutenant asked again.

The three of us—Mike, Mercer, and I—had lots of time to work through these answers. Now we were only making educated guesses.

'Because the double cross was already under way,' I said. 'Tina had quit her job with the Hunts and was working for Alger Herrick. Is he talking?'

'Not yet,' Peterson said. 'Your boss has Pat McKinney at the station house doing the questioning.'

I closed my eyes and groaned.

'Get her some pain relievers and a scotch,' Mike said.

'I hope that jackass remembers to separate Herrick and Forbes.' I was joking with Mike, trying to regain my sea legs, but it would be like McKinney to screw up the most basic rules in his rush to get back in the case.

'Don't be such a control freak,' Mike said to me, walking over to a uniformed cop and handing him some bills. 'There's a pub on the corner of Third Street. Fill a plastic cup with Dewar's and don't spill any of it running back. Coop's indicted guys for less than that.'

'This was the once-in-a-lifetime score, Loo,' Mercer said. 'Herrick wanted to put this map together to cap his collection, no matter what it cost him.'

'And Forbes?' Peterson asked.

'For him, it was his last great scam. Lead these greedy fools like the pied piper, and his endgame, with his brother's help, was to wind up with this masterpiece for himself,' Mike said. 'Sell it to the highest bidder—twenty, maybe thirty million.'

'For this, Tina Barr had to die?' the lieutenant said.

'She must have panicked when Travis showed up in the library, just a night after she'd been attacked,' Mike said.

'Tina walked away from the emergency room because she knew this was all tied into the stolen books and maps,' I said. 'She wasn't giving up a thing that would lead us in that direction, even if she didn't know exactly who Travis was the first time she encountered him.'

'But she probably recognized him when he came into the conservation lab in the library,' Mike said. 'And in her own devious little mind, began to put the pieces together. Realized she was in way over her head, playing with the bad guys.'

'Too late to help herself,' I added, thinking of what Jill Gibson had first told Battaglia. 'That's why some of the people in the library thought she was a thief. She really had been in bed with Eddy Forbes.'

'That's why Travis killed Tina with one of her own tools,' Mercer said. 'He didn't go to the library meaning to do it. He was probably looking for the key that opened the compartment in the basement. Maybe Eddy sent him to get the job done right the second time. The key might have dropped out of her clothing when he was carrying her through the stacks, after she was dead, without his knowing it. I doubt the murder was premeditated—just a flare-up about the missing goods that ended with him slitting her throat.'

'That's what Travis Forbes does,' Mercer said.

'He cuts. He mutilates. She couldn't have known that.'

'Then he dumped Barr's body the next night. Probably called Herrick when he took off for his night job at the pub,' Mike said. 'Must have been Herrick who watched us bag the body. He's the one who called Tina's cell phone—and laughed.'

That would chill the jurors as much as it had sickened me.

'It's the housekeeper who gets lost in all this,' I said. 'Karla Vastasi.'

'That has to be Minerva's doing,' Mike said. 'She in the hospital, Loo?'

'Yeah.'

'Let me at her when she's ready to squeal. Minerva had Karla dressed up as her double, carrying a forged copy of one of the panels in her tote. Travis had never met Minerva—wouldn't know her if he fell over her,' Mike said.

'My money's on Eddy Forbes,' I said.

'I read you. You think Eddy was waiting in Barr's apartment with Travis that afternoon. *He* knew the lady in black wasn't Minerva and realized the panel she was carrying was a fake. Queered the whole deal.'

'Karla saw that Tina had left behind another treasure when she moved out—the jewel-encrusted psalm book,' I said. 'The one Tina stole from Talbot's bedroom. So Karla tried to take it to her mistress, clutched on to it with what turned out to be her life. One of the Forbes boys caught her and went ballistic. Whacked her over the head with the garden ornament.'

The pieces were coming together as nicely as the panels of the great world map of 1507.

'You better get some sleep, Alex,' the lieutenant said. 'Battaglia wants all of us in his office at ten o'clock.'

'Don't stretch out here,' Mike said, sweeping his arm along the back of the old sofa. 'You stay still for very long, they'll find a box that fits.'

'Make me a better offer,' I said as Mercer helped me to my feet.

'That cemetery had me craving some fresh air. Feel like walking up the avenue to the pub? I could use a drink out of a real glass.'

I thanked the rookie who'd returned with the plastic cup of scotch. 'Give that one to the lieutenant. I've got a date.'

Out on the sidewalk in front of Provenzano's funeral home, I looped arms with Mike and Mercer. I took several deep breaths of the cool October air, steadied myself between my friends— fortitude and patience—and headed off into the night for a bracing bit of cheer as our manhunt ended.

CHAPTER FORTY-EIGHT

'That's no way to spend a Saturday night,' Luc said exactly a week later, when he returned from his trip. 'I can't let you sit in front of a television set eating popcorn with this great wine.'

'It's a whole lot better than the way I spent the last one. Besides, if you tell me you don't want to watch my Yankees play a World Series game, we've got a real deal breaker here.'

We had flown up to the Vineyard that morning,

after all the drama of the past week had played out in court.

Travis Forbes had been charged with the murders of Tina Barr and Karla Vastasi. His brother, Eddy, was indicted, too, for acting in concert with Travis on the Vastasi killing—proved by cell phone records and credit card receipts for gas and food.

Travis had rolled over on Alger Herrick and implicated him in the deadly plot to find the twelve panels of the priceless map, though Battaglia hadn't needed to promise any leniency. The detectives had continued to build a rock-solid case against the Englishman, who was indeed the illegitimate son of Jasper Hunt III.

Luc and I had walked down the path from my Chilmark home to watch the sun set, sipping a glass of chilled Corton-Charlemagne that he had brought with him. We had made love in the afternoon, slowly and without any distractions this time, and I was dressed in one of his shirts as I lay back in the sand, wiggling my toes in the cool water of Menemsha Pond.

Luc had driven to the store while I napped fitfully, still not able to get images of this case out of my head.

'Everything at Larsen's Fish Market looked *merveilleuse,* darling. I decided on those sweet little bay scallops,' he said.

'I adore them.'

'Lemon, garlic, fettucine.'

I looked at him and cocked an eye. 'How do you eat food like that at a ball game?'

I heard Mike's voice in the back of my head ordering a hot dog and a cold beer.

'Trust me. It will be better than anything you get at the stadium.'

'For starters?'

Luc stood up and dug his toes into the sand as the gentle waves receded. 'Clams. Fresh ones.'

'Let me help.'

I sat up and we scratched below the surface until we filled a towel with a dozen quahaugs.

'That lady at the library, the one you really liked,' Luc said, sitting beside me as a bright red ball of sunlight started to slip down behind the hills of Aquinnah.

'Bea?'

'So she was right about the places that the eccentric Mr. Hunt hid the panels of the map.'

'She was dead on,' I said.

'You think they will ever find the entire thing?' Luc asked.

'So far we're more than halfway there. Four that Hunt tried to take to the great hereafter with him, the one that Jane Eliot gave to Minerva, the other that Minerva had all along—in the Strassburg Ptolemy—and the one that Mike found inside the library, under the water tank.'

'You said Bea found others?'

'Yes, during the week, when the search continued, two of the curators discovered pieces tucked inside books from the Hunt Collection, just as Bea had predicted,' I said. 'And Talbot Hunt is cooperating now.'

The Friday morning we first met Talbot at the library, he had hinted at the fact that he was in the race to find the entire map. He had unearthed one not long ago in an atlas he inherited from his grandfather, which he'd ignored until Tina Barr

400

began to work with him.

'So that accounts for ten of the twelve,' Luc said. 'What will become of the map, if it is ever put together?'

I sipped at the wine, then stretched out again in the sand, watching the crown of the sun disappear.

'The Hunts have finally agreed on something, after a lifetime of acrimony and unpleasantness. A substantial piece of damage control,' I said. 'They've made a gift of the map to the New York Public Library, along with a sizable contribution for the restoration of the Hunt Collection. The money will also help the library try to find the last two pieces.'

'Are you getting cold, darling?'

'No, I'm fine. I don't want to go in yet.'

The involuntary chill that swept over me had nothing to do with the weather. There would be hearings and trials to follow, a system trying to make sense of the senseless deaths of two young women.

'You can get this off your mind now, can't you?'

Judge Moffett had approved my application for the familial DNA search of Wesley the Weasel Griggs. A homicide case that had languished for eight years might now be solved by science, and I would have a new challenge to fill the fall days.

'Tonight, yes,' I said, as Luc swept back my hair and put his lips against my forehead.

'And tomorrow?'

'Yes.' I laughed as he moved his lips to the tip of my nose.

Months earlier, after Joan and Jim's wedding, Luc had embraced me for the first time in this secluded cove. All the best memories of my life were connected to this peaceful, glorious island.

'And Monday, after I've flown home to France?'

'Hard to predict,' I said. *'Au revoir, mon amour.'*

'Tuesday?' he asked, entwining his legs with mine in the shallow water that lapped at our feet.

'Maybe.'

'Only maybe? I've got some serious work to do before I leave,' Luc said.

I put my arms around his neck and we kissed each other, over and over again. Then I pulled him to his feet and led him up the hill to the outdoor shower. I wanted to wash off the sand from the beach—and some of the grit I carried with me, always, from my job.

'C'mon, Luc,' I said. 'Time to play ball.'

ACKNOWLEDGMENTS

My earliest childhood memories of books are of those from which my mother read to me every night before I went to sleep. I still have the frayed volumes of poems by Robert Louis Stevenson and A. A. Milne, and the stories of Beatrix Potter and E. B. White. I remember the first time she took me to the public library in our small city, and with what delight I left that day carrying the three books the librarian entrusted to me. Our favorite weekly excursion—an hour of pure happiness with my mother—was the trip downtown to return the small stack I had selected and replace it with another.

Most bibliophiles love reading *about* books, too, and for me, the opportunity to do some of my research with literary treasures was a thrilling experience. One foundation for my exploration was a 1923 tome I picked up at an antiquarian book fair—Harry Miller Lydenberg's *History of the New York Public Library*. I studied Phyllis Dain's *A Universe of Knowledge*, Nicholas Basbanes's *A Gentle Madness*, Ingrid Steffensen's *The New York Public Library: A Beaux Arts Landmark*, and a slim little book published by Educare Press, *The Waldseemüller World Map* (1507).

One of the most riveting articles I relied on for an understanding of the world of rare map collectors appeared in *The New Yorker*'s Annals of Crime, called 'A Theft in the Library' by William Finnegan. As always, my research notebooks were teeming with clippings from the *New York Times*, whether about the structural bones of Manhattan buildings or transparency in the boardroom's of libraries and museums, or even the obituaries of long-forgotten individuals.

Perhaps the most extensive private collection devoted to cartography was in the unique library of England's Christopher Henry Beaumont Pease, the second Baron Wardington. The essay written by Lord Wardington for Sotheby's 2006 sale of Important Atlases from his library captured the passion these treasures inspired, and the elegant descriptions in that catalog helped me design the volumes that line the bookshelves of my fictional characters.

My dear friends Cynthia and Dan Lufkin invited me to their spectacular apartment when they moved to a landmarked building on Central Park West several years ago. It's still a mystery to me how elements of their stunning home took such a sinister turn in my imagination, but I am grateful for that introduction to the chapel over cocktails.

Dr. Cecilia Crouse, chief of the Palm Beach Sheriff's Office forensic science laboratory, is a woman I admire enormously. She solves crimes, saves lives, does justice every day, and trains scores of young scientists to do the same. Cece is a great force for good against evil in this world, and she remains my DNA guru.

Paul LeClerc, President of the New York Public Library, has the most splendid professional home in America. He has called libraries 'the memory of humankind, irreplacable repositories of documents of human thought and action,' and I agree with him that the NYPL is such an institution, par excellence.

David Ferriero, Andrew W. Mellon Director of the New York Public Libraries, was my brilliant personal guide through all the amazing wonders of the great library. The NYPL was founded in 1895, he said, with the mission of making the accumulated knowledge of the world freely accessible to all, without distinction as to income, religion, nationality, or other human condition. David knew that I was likely to invent murder and mayhem within the historic walls of the central library as a result of the time he spent with me, but still he led me from the rooftop to the basement stacks and through every secret passageway in between, and put me in the hands of each scholarly curator and conservator along the way.

My lifelong love affair with librarians reached a fever pitch while working on this book. David's enthusiasm for the world he inhabits is impressive and infectious. He and Zelman Kisilyuk led me from the rooftop through the treacherous stacks with great care. Isaac Gewirtz educated me about the Berg collection; John Lundquist let me explore the Asian and Middle Eastern works; Shelly Smith and her colleagues in the Barbara Goldsmith Preservation Division helped me understand the critical nature of their work—and the incomparable gift bestowed on the NYPL by Barbara; and Alice Hudson, and her assistant chief Matthew Knutzen, thrilled me with their displays of the breathtaking and vulnerable riches of the Lionel Pincus and Princess Firyal Map Division. I borrowed a bit of Alice's wisdom and spirit to enliven the plot.

Everyone should have a friend like Louise Grunwald. She's smart, beautiful, funny, wise, and fiercely loyal to her many, many friends. Her quiet generosity never ceases to amaze me, and she exercised it this time to open the massive doors of the NYPL and place me into the hands of David Ferriero.

My team at Doubleday—led by Steve Rubin and Phyllis Grann—is the class of the field in the publishing world and includes Alison Rich, John Pitts, John Fontana, and Jackie Montalvo. To Esther Newberg and everyone at ICM—especially Kari Stuart—goes my gratitude for helping make my dream of a writer's life come true.

Wherever you are, use your libraries and support them. And when you are in New York City, come visit the great New York Public Library and behold its treasures.

My mother was the kindest person I have ever known, with the most enormous heart and a dazzling smile that invited all comers to share in her happiness. Among the very best things she ever did for me—and there are many—was to nurture my love of books and reading. She is forever, as I said in the dedication of my second novel, simply the best. Dearest Bobbie, rest in peace.

And like all the books before it, this one is for Justin, always—my first reader, my great warrior.